I0670357

Under the Moon: The Dark War

A Paranormal Shifter Romance
Vera Foxx

Foxx Fantasy Publishing

First paperback edition: April 2022

Publisher: **Foxx Fantasy Publishing LLC**

Thanks and Dedication

To the women that believe in fairy tales, happily ever afters, and the special someone that is destined to be their soul mate.

Contents

Dear Reader

It would be advised to read, Under the Moon, The Alpha's Kitten, The Fae King's Darling and The Exiled Dragon to fully understand every couple's role in this book.

There will be werewolves, fae, vampires, fairies, fighting, love, and sex with kink.

If you aren't into the Mr. Grumpy and Miss Sunshine couples, dominate and a bit crazy obsessive men, cheesy lines, and happily ever afters, I would avoid reading.

Because there is a lot of... all of that.

Chapter One

Clara

"Harder!" I grunted, holding my back. "Harder, come on, put your back into it!" Moans and groans left the other side of the room with one final push of the large elaborate crib that now sat at the base of a beautifully painted woodland scene. "Perfect!" I squealed with glee, rubbing my overly enormous belly.

"I hope you realize how much we love you." Raine and Leia sighed as they leaned on the mahogany crib. Both panting from their exertion, they looked at each other, tired. "Carrying that up the stairs was brutal." Raine straightened herself, coming over and sitting on the floor next to my feet.

"You're a werewolf. Is it really that heavy?" I snickered. Leia rolled her eyes with her hands on her hips. Raine had been my right-hand woman when my mother wasn't around. Technically, she was taking the role of the beta's wife with how she helped me make schedules of renovations, new pup playgrounds, hosting luna seminars, planning parties for the unmated wolves, mating ceremonies for pack members, or even visiting with my new royal friend, King Osirus.

You name it, and Raine was by my side, especially when my mother came by every few days to help me learn my new role of queen in a few years' time. I was barely hanging on as luna; I wasn't sure how I would make it if Raine stayed in the pack.

"We haven't been training like we should. I've been busy, mind you." Leia and Raine had become my new interior decorators. We had slowly redecorated the alpha and luna's bedroom, along with the new nursery that sat just beside our room. The inner connecting doors were the most helpful, so I didn't have to walk my way down the hallway in the middle of the night and stare at some random wolf guarding our door. Kane had put guards on either side of our quarters' doorway. He would have no one get in without us knowing.

After Darius came in through the large balcony window at the Ever Green pack on Earth, he also had our beautiful balcony with a hot tub boarded up. At first, I was angry he had taken away the beautiful view, but Kane had to be sated in some ways, and there were new dangers I wasn't aware of.

Many kinds of shifters—not all friendly—lived around the territory. The first few nights we spent living here, a panther shifter had climbed up the trees just outside our window and peered in with their bright yellow eyes while I was sleeping. Torin ripped through Kane's body so fast that he himself didn't realize what he had done until the panther's guts lay on the ground.

I had never screamed so loud in all my life hearing a panther's cries. I think anyone would have. Luckily, I could heal them, but not as much as I wanted. Their innards were put back inside safely, but Kane made me stop so they could heal themselves. Kane was too worried about our little pup inside still growing, afraid if I used too much of my energy that the poor little thing wouldn't grow properly.

"And why did you choose a large mahogany crib?" Leia scoffed. "It's almost too gaudy looking and takes away from the beautiful mural I had painted." Leia's hand traced the animals in the wistful willow trees that came over the crib. She even made small pieces of fabric for the baby to grab once it got a little older.

"Kane was a teether and went through five cribs before he was four months old," Raine replied, twisting her hair. "If this little alpha inside Clara is anything like Kane, this baby is going to grow fast, and teeth will sprout within a month or so. Might as well get a strong crib that will last at least six months before he or she crawls out." I choked on my own spit, sitting up in the padded rocking chair.

"Six months? Aren't babies supposed to crawl around at six months?" Raine laughed while Leia put the finishing touches to the ruffles on the bottom of the crib.

"That's a human baby. This is a pup born of two very strong lineages. Werewolves alone start crawling at two to three months and walking by four or five. Climbing out of this thing"—she slapped the crib—"will be nothing for the little alpha." I sat back in my chair, rubbing my forehead. This whole pup baby thing I was not prepared for.

I had done too much the previous three days, helping Osirus get his mate, Melina. She was a poor human girl that came to watch her best friend—almost sister—Tulip have their mating ceremony. They had just left the previous day, and I had to make sure Melina didn't run off like a frightened lamb with the ever cryptic fae king.

"Calm down. Everything will be all right," Raine rubbed my hand. "I'm here for you through it all. Dean too. He says he loves babies," she cooed. "I wouldn't be surprised if he would want to practice making babies after seeing your little one born." I smiled, rubbing my belly. The little pup kicked and poked Raine as she poked my belly back.

"A little fighter, aren't you, little alpha?" Both of Raine's hands held my stomach, kissing it gently.

"That's just weird." Leia turned her nose up. "What would you do if I came up and rubbed my nose all over your belly?"

"First, I'd punch you because talking to my food baby isn't cute." Leia snorted back a laugh. Raine stuck out her stomach, trying to push out as much as she could on her washboard abs. She was built athletically, matching the alpha physique of her father.

"I'm just saying, people have bubbles, and I'm sure Clara doesn't appreciate you rubbing your cold, wet, dog nose all over it," Leia snapped. Raine sat back against the wall.

"But I'm the favorite aunt," Raine whined. "I have every right to shower the baby with love," she cooed right into my belly.

"Let me remind you, you are the only blood-related aunt. I, on the other hand, am the favorite friend-aunt." Leia laid the final blanket in the crib, studying her work.

"That's not even a thing!" Raine retorted. They both argued, giving reasons for who would be the better aunt to the little one inside. Excited about the ruckus, the pup rolled inside me, causing me to wince at the kick in my ribs.

The pregnancy, overall, had been smooth sailing. Once Kane announced that I was pregnant at his alpha takeover ceremony, it was like clockwork that I felt sick the next day. Kane coddled me like a tiny baby, making sure any food I craved was brought up and rubbed my feet every night. The best part was when he would rub my feet. My poor feet were swollen every day, and my fast-growing belly made it that much worse.

Kane wouldn't leave my side once he found out, neglecting his alpha duties, and his father had to step in, explaining that every woman would go through this, and his mother was just the same. Any groan I made, every trip to the toilet, Kane hovered over me like I would break. Thankfully, his mother came to help me during my sickness period that lasted only a week, and she had me back up and running with all the ginger-ale she had me drinking.

Kane reluctantly went back to his duties, taking the warriors out for random drills of fighting, running, cardio, weightlifting, and the sort. Even with his constantly busy schedule, he managed to link me once an hour, making sure I was doing all right. *Five months*—Five months for a werewolf pregnancy, and I was so over it. How humans make it to nine months, I'd never know. I was glad I won't ever endure that pain.

I stood up, holding my back as I rose from the chair. I was missing the barely-there abs I had before the baby. Now, I had to roll across the room to get anywhere.

Raine and Leia continued their banter, not even bothering to look up at me as I waddled out of the room.

"What is that screeching?" Marcus walked into the main living area of the alpha-luna suite. Raine and Leia still squealed in laughter, with a few playful slaps echoing in the room on their skin.

At least I hope they were playful.

"Just Raine and Leia having an argument." I picked up an apple from the table, wincing as I lowered myself into the closest chair.

"Here, let me help you, Luna." Marcus's sweaty body glistened as he pulled the chair out, lowering me onto it.

"Thanks, Marcus, but please, call me Clara. I don't need all that title stuff, all right? If it bothers you that much, do what you do with Kane." Marcus's pearly white teeth made a show as he sat on the other side of the table. Marcus always called Kane by his first name when they were alone, but in public, he referred to him as Alpha. It shows a sign of respect, the same way that when my parents come on their frequent visits, even Kane calls them 'Your Majesty' in public.

"I can remember the day you didn't even know what a luna was, and here you are, one of the most famous lunas in all the kingdom and future queen. The little waitress has grown up in just six months." I sighed heavily, no longer hungry after the one bite of the apple. I placed it on the table, pushing it away.

"Yeah, I sure have," I said with a hint of sarcasm. Marcus's smile faded, his hand reaching out to grab mine as it retreated from the tasteless food.

"Hey now, what's going on, Little Fox?" Pursing my lips, I glanced at Marcus. I envied him as a wolf some days. Sure, he was a beta and had some responsibility, but now I had the weight of the world on my shoulders, it seemed.

I really went from a small quiet life as a waitress to a big new world as a princess. How was I going to bear the weight of it all along with a baby?

A luna, a future queen, a mother, a mate, a healer. I didn't know how to be any of those things, and I had to be all of them. Where did I draw the line? How would I separate the four? I wanted adventure not so long ago, and I got it all right—along with a whole other set of responsibilities.

"Just a little stressed, is all." A small smile replaced my pursed, thin-lined lips. Marcus opened his mouth to speak until heavy footsteps led into the room. Kane's heavy musky scent filled the area before his powerful stance stood at the double-widened doors. The lighted hallway was so bright I could only see the outline of his sweaty body heaving his heavy breaths.

"Hi, Alpha." I grinned widely as his bare feet hit the granite floor. "How was training?" Kane stepped in, his muscles swollen from working every part of his body, and the dripping of sweat rolling down his sculpted ab muscles had me squeezing my swollen legs.

Come on, baby, get out of me.

"Hello, my love." Kane bent forward, holding his chest to keep the salty drops from ruining my thin dress. The salt that tainted his lips made me laugh.

"You both are disgusting to watch. Too much love in this room, I'm out." Marcus chuckled, patting Kane on the shoulder. "I've got a date with some twins. Don't wait up, Kane." Kane rolled his eyes, pushing my long hair behind my ear. "Luna, try not to stress. Everything will work out." Marcus walked down the hallway to his quarters.

"He doesn't listen to me about his private life, but he does a wicked job listening as my beta." Kane sighed, rubbing his fingers through his wet hair.

"That he does. He'll be great at running things around here while our pup grows up and when you need some time off." Kane's lip curled, kissing my cheek again.

"As long as he protects the pack, I won't push it, but he of all people should realize, especially after Jasper, he should keep his dick in his pants," he grumbled.

Taliyah and Jasper had swiftly gone to the Vermillion Kingdom shortly after we arrived in Bergarian. Vermillion as a whole was in shambles, and Taliyah did what she could to reestablish any sort of Court that was left. Mother and Father sent many trained soldiers from their own lot of warriors to help Taliyah as much as they could. A lot of pushback came from the residents that were happy that Darius was gone but were wary of the wolves. We quickly receded as soon as we could so the trust of the Vermillion nation could fall back on Taliyah.

Most of the Court was taken to the dungeons, where they sat awaiting trial. Taliyah wanted to make everything as legal as possible to show that she would have full evidence of anyone that was to be put to death. The steep incline of learning the ways to rule a nation and becoming queen so quickly was one that I did not envy. I couldn't imagine having to take over from being a slave to being a queen.

Darius didn't make it easy for her. The treasury was empty; soldiers were few, and the people who obeyed Taliyah's new laws were starving. The surrounding territories of gnomes and the occasional ogre didn't help, and her first plan of action was to get proper food brought in. Even if that meant having to breed their own animals for slaughter.

"I couldn't agree more, but let's not worry about Marcus." My eyes turned away from Kane, tired of worrying for everyone else. A sharp pain ran across my abdomen, causing me to grip the table.

"Baby, what's wrong?!" Kane spoke louder than I was expecting. I rubbed my stomach, sitting back up in the chair.

"Just Braxton Hicks. My body prepping for the baby." Kane grabbed hold of my hand, kissing my fingers.

"Please tell me, what's going on?" Kane kneeled on the carpet before me. I smiled, my eyes softening at Kane's concern.

"Just overwhelmed. I didn't realize how quickly werewolf pups grow, and I think that has thrown me through a loop." I fake giggled. Kane's hand went to my stomach.

"You are not alone in this. Your mother and mine will be here to help. They'll show us both how to be parents. I know this happened fast, but I believe the gods wanted it this way. Even with your heat, it doesn't necessarily mean you will become pregnant. We live for so long, but only the gods know the right time for a pup. They know our hearts and if we truly desire and deserve a child at the time of conception. This pup" —Kane's other hand went to the other side of my belly—"is here for a reason."

Kissing my stomach, his sweaty hair fell into his face. "I promise, Clara, everything is going to work out." Kane pulled me from my seat, leading me into the bathroom. Raine and Leia came out laughing hysterically, waving us off, knowing where we were going.

Kane had wanted me to take a bath for the past several months to ease the pains in my muscles, but I remember working in the diner just a year ago, a human woman complaining about not being able to take a bath. "It could cook the baby!" her own mother yelled. Human pregnancies and werewolf pregnancies were different, sure, but that put enough fear in me not to want to even try.

Kane had his own routine with me, and that was to literally shower me with love and affection. At first, I hated it. I hated him seeing my changing body, but Kane continued to amaze me with his words and his hands as he washed every part of me, even the parts I could no longer see.

Kane turned on the shower, as hot as I would allow so I didn't 'cook' my pup, and washed his own body quickly. I stood under the heated waterfall and waited for the steam to take over the shower and hopefully cover up my large rear in the process.

Kane's gentle hands took the washing primrose oil and rubbed my shoulders down to my lower back. His large hands pushed and kneaded all the sore parts, causing me to groan with relief. "You know where all my aches are." I hummed while I leaned on the shower wall.

"What kind of mate would I be if I didn't?" Kane continued, squeezing my hips, rubbing down my legs, and finally washing my hair. His thick fingers rubbed my scalp, which had me rolling my eyes.

"I can't wait until the pup is here." I grabbed hold of my stomach again, feeling the pulling sensation in my lower abdomen. "I'm not a very graceful pregnant lady." I chuckled. Kane hummed, turning me around.

"You are a beautiful pregnant lady, and you are mine." His lips grazed my cheek, finally reaching lower to my lips. He kissed me sensually as he dug his fingers through my hair. "With that being said, you have a clinic appointment in the next hour," Kane brushed his nose with mine.

⚜

Kane laced our fingers together, helping me down the stairs. He insisted on carrying me, but I refused because my pride was too important. Secretly, I didn't want to hear a small grunt from him when he picked me up, but as strong as Kane was, that could have been an irrational fear.

The pack house had been cleaned from top to bottom; beautiful granite polished floors in the more formal rooms of the house, such as the guest living room and dining room. The rest of the pack house was decorated modestly with a homely feel, something I wanted from the very beginning when I first walked into the pack house. I wanted kids to run in and out, screaming with laughter, not fearing their alpha and luna as they ran to the enormous entertainment room and now new playroom and daycare area.

That's right, a daycare area. Seeing so many of the tiny ones relying on the older pups had me scared to death. Now, unmated females and males who loved children got to hold babies all day and care for little ones in one area of the pack house. It was the best idea ever, and the female warriors were ever grateful for it so they could pursue their dreams and have a family.

"Oh, lookie there, they emerged from the shower at a decent time." Raine flipped a pancake. I glared at her playfully. She knew good and well I was not about to be doing any lovemaking this big.

"Good morning, Raine," Kane grumbled as he sat down on the large kitchen island that held an assortment of food. The big buffet breakfast happened at six a.m., and leftovers were set in the kitchen area for those who would like to sleep in if they had a late night.

I found myself down here in the early morning while Kane got up early to train, helping with breakfast and eating before the warriors came in, hoarding food and taking it to their room. Raine slapped another pancake on the plate, pushing it toward me.

"You're gonna need the carbs if you push that baby out soon," she warned. "Once you go into labor, they don't let you eat a thing, fearing you will throw up all over the baby." My face paled while Kane picked me up, setting me in his lap like I was light as a feather.

"She's teasing," he cooed, kissing my ear. "Aren't you, Raine?" Raine bit her lip, shrugging her shoulders, walking away to clean up her mess. Another pain went across my stomach, causing me to grip Kane's leg too harshly. He took it like a champ and rubbed the back of my head with his large hand.

"Eat some fruit, then I'll take you to the clinic. Maybe today is the day." I shuffled in my seat, trying to get comfortable. Even with a padded butt, I had to distribute the fat properly, or the pup would protest.

"Luna!" A tiny voice from the living room ran into the kitchen. Kit had been with us since we had moved into the pack house. His parents were still preparing to move all their things from the Ever Green pack to stay in Bergarian so they could at least be in the same realm as their son before he went off to private training.

Kit ran into the kitchen, huffing and puffing with his hands on his knees. "I didn't miss it yet?" He marched up to me, putting his hand on my belly. Kane let out a soft growl, his hand now being slowly removed as he looked into his alpha's eyes.

"Sorry, Luna." His head bowed.

"Kane, gosh, leave the boy alone. Kit is my protector, remember?" I winked at Kit, who only shyly smiled. "But no, the pup hasn't come yet. Any day now." Another pain rippled; this time harder than the ones before. A cry spilled out louder than I expected; Kane was too worried to move me in case it hurt worse. The pain subsided, but my bladder didn't like the pain, and I leaked all over myself.

"Oh, goddess." I almost sobbed. "I peed on you!" Kit's eyes widened, but Kane's did not, holding me tight.

"That's not urine, love." His lips kissed my forehead. "It means our pup is coming. I can even smell their scent now." Kane's voice was strained. I knew that voice. He was worried sick, and I felt it through the bond.

How could I not realize my water just broke?!

"Raine, mind-link the pack doctor!" Kane called out. Leia, not far behind us, grabbed cleaning supplies to clean up. My face reddened in embarrassment. How could this happen to me?

"Love, I feel your worry. I am not angry, and there is nothing to be ashamed of," his statement cut short as I gritted my teeth, trying not to scream. Groaning painfully, Kane's pace quickened, but the bouncing only made it worse.

"Walk." I gritted. "Don't run, *hurts*!"

Kane was now swiftly walking down the hallway, and quickly, a crowd came behind us. Mostly doctors and nurses and a few wandering eyes of other pregnant women who had check-ups today.

"So, we think your water broke?" the nurse chirped as she put on gloves.

"It *did* break," I said, my teeth still baring while we walked. My fangs even pulled out, Giana feeling the tension in our body. She was ready to let this baby out so she could run. Giana had only been let out a few times before I had heat, and she had been a hot mess ever since then.

"We will check just in case, all right?" she said. I growled, my head turning to the nurse. "It *did* break. Now get me in a room!" My luna voice sounded in the hallway. The entire ward stood still, watching the scene unfold. Kane's patience, wearing thin, gripped me tighter around my legs and back.

"I can smell it on her. It is amniotic fluid," Kane's voice clipped, trying to remain calm. "Is your wolf's nose defective?" Another nurse ran up to us, pushing the questioning nurse away.

"Alpha, Luna, I'm so sorry. She's training." She glared at the young nurse. "I agree. She's in labor. Let's get her into the room." A cry left me again until Kane finally set me on the hospital bed, curling up behind me. As new contractions filled my belly, the soft rubbing of Kane's hand on my stomach kept me calm and even took some of the pain away.

Chapter Two

Kane

Holy fuck, how is she standing this? Another pain ripped through my own stomach. I had felt different kinds of pain throughout my training, but this was something unworldly. The tightness in your stomach leaves you breathless, and then the sudden urge to push the most giant shit out of your body left me weak in the knees.

"Hurts like fuck, doesn't it?" my father's mocking voice came through the link. I growled, only making Clara jump with surprise while she rested between contractions. The nurses had left the room. I had barked at anyone that dared to enter. An alpha with his luna giving birth to a pup is a dangerous thing. Our wolves are protective of not just their mate but their family.

Another pain had me gripping the bed. Knowing that the pain was only a quarter of what my mate felt broke my heart for her. Clara's hand gripped mine as I tried to calm her, my hand sitting on top of her swollen belly to give some comfort through our bond. Breathing out heavily, her tired eyes looked up at me, only to smile.

"It will be worth it." She sighed. My nose went to her neck, kissing my mark. The taste of salt on her neck made me frown. Even for werewolves, there was no escaping the pains of childbirth.

"Of course, but I don't like you in this much pain. Torin has been whimpering for ages." The hours had ticked by. Being the first pup to grace her womb, it could take many more, but it wasn't until her sharp cry that put me at attention.

"Doctor Talbert!" I roared loud enough to be heard throughout the pack house. A frantic doctor came rushing in, his hair disheveled, his heart racing from the alpha command I had been sending him every five minutes to check on my mate.

"I... I think it's coming." Clara groaned, rolling to her side while she gripped the bed. The side rails cracked, her wails now dull whimpers. Her mother's head peaked through the door, frowning as her only daughter winced. Her eyes met mine, only nodding to leave the room.

It was a tradition that werewolves only gave birth in the presence of a physician, nurse, and their mate. Being surrounded by too many wolves could put the father and mother's animals on edge. Hell, Torin didn't like the doctor checking on her now, and I cursed the day I told him he could deliver my pup.

Dr. Talbert's hands shook as he spoke. "Alpha, I need to check..." His shaky hand pointed to the sheet near Clara's feet. Torin snarled, pushing forward. The nurse that had accompanied him whimpered, scurrying out of the room.

"Baby, it's all right." Clara's hand reached for mine. I laced them with hers. "He's a doctor. He'll know what to do." Torin held back, settling back in my mind, but I kept my eyes on Dr. Talbert.

"Luna, I'll need you to lie on your back." Clara groaned, rolling over and spreading her legs under the sheet. Torin did not like that one damn bit. I didn't care if our pup came out of her and needed help. Someone was looking at what was mine. My mate!

Torin ripped through me, pushing the wolf to the ground with a crash. All of his instruments fell to the floor, cursing, while he crawled out of the room.

"Kane!" Clara whined. "Get someone, or you are catching this pup!" Clara's yell was laced with her luna and royal aura and even had me cowering. "Shiiiitaki..." Her head flew back into the pillow, causing me to run up to her. Sweat poured from her face until, finally, Raine bolted into the room.

"I'm here! I'm here!" Raine came to the bed. "Kane, you are in some deep shit," she muttered as she looked under the sheet. My wolf, still pacing, held onto Clara. Running my hands through my fucked up hair. *Somehow, I make everything worse.*

I couldn't help it. My mate was hurting, and some other damn wolf was going to touch her. *I don't let anyone touch her but me.*

Clara pulled my hand and laid it on her stomach. "It's all right, Alpha." She panted. "I'm scared too." Fuck, I didn't want to damn cry, but I was close. I didn't enjoy seeing her like this, not on a bed with pain racking through her body and nothing I could do. Beating the shit out of something wouldn't help me with this situation. I had to be soft, and it was so damn hard.

"Breathe, baby, just breathe." My voice was much softer now that I could feel her relaxing into me. Her breath was now slow and steady. Raine coached her to push. Leia stood at the door with blankets, keeping her distance since we didn't share a close bond like Raine and me.

Thank goddess she was my sister. "Tell Torin he owes me big time." Raine winked. "You're lucky I read all those baby books to Clara when she was puking in the toilet," she said, chuckling. "Now, Clara, the little pup is right there. I need one big push." Clara nodded her sweaty face.

"You are doing so good," I cooed in her ear. "It's almost over, and you never have to do this again." Clara let out one more push as cries entered the room. Leia ran over with a towel, rubbing the debris away. Clara and I both let out a sob, Raine handing us a swaddled baby into my mate's arms. A fucking baby. We made a fucking baby, and my mate glowed brightly at me like I gave her the world.

"Boy or girl?" Clara sniffed as she pulled back the towels. "Thought you might want to figure that out." Raine winked, pulling Leia away. "We will send some female nurses in to help clean up." Raine twirled her finger around the bed. Clara and I didn't watch her leave. I climbed into the bed, holding my mate and the beautiful pup we now had.

"We're parents," Clara cried again, wiping away the pup's wet hair. "Can you believe that?" My lips kissed Clara's forehead, who was still pulling the wrappings away.

"A girl." She laughed. "Queens all over the place, huh?" I hugged her tightly, finally putting my large hand over our new little girl's head. She was so small compared to me. I could hold her in the palm of my hand.

"Queens are stronger," I muttered. "They don't rule with a beastly wolf and desire for blood. They rule with their heart, just like you will." Clara's lip wobbled, trying to hold back her tears. There weren't many times I had seen my mate cry, but when she did, it was with her entire heart.

"I'm so proud of you, My Luna." Her green eyes watered as she looked up at me until her forehead was buried into my chest. "Thank you for a wonderful gift, Alpha."

"*I love you,*" I mind-linked, keeping our precious moment to ourselves as nurses came in to help.

"*And I love you.*"

Once Clara was cleaned, both sets of parents came into the room to greet our new little girl. Gifts were being piled up in the next room from our pack and the surrounding ones. The next generation of royalty had been born, and it was spreading like wildfire.

"I can't believe you kicked out the doctor," my mother scolded. "Even your father held it together. Why can't you?" I rolled my eyes, sitting back down in the bed with Clara. My father didn't have Torin, his wolf was strong, sure, but Torin I swore had a demon inside him. We were like a damn wolf demon human sandwich. Mom continued to glare at me, but I paid no mind. Torin and I were enjoying our new pup.

Clara was peacefully sleeping, curled up with the baby in her arms in the bed, just like an actual wolf would curl around their own pups. She unconsciously rubbed her thumb along the baby's back, which nuzzled toward Clara's neck.

"Have you named her?" my father asked, sitting on the far side of the room. "People are asking so they can make special blankets and wreaths for the new little royal." Clara's father was proud. Not only did he get his daughter back just six months ago, but he now gained a granddaughter and a new pup of his own on the way.

King Elijah took no time knocking up his wife once Clara was safely back in Bergarian. Just like she promised, she would give him four more children after this.

"We have, but it's best if we announce it together." My fingers brushed Clara's hair away from her face. Color had returned to her cheeks, and her freckles stood out more clearly.

Mother nodded. The room continued to filter in with people, with Clara's parents sitting on a comfortable couch. They cleared out their entire schedule for the next three days so her mother could help Clara learn how to feed Evelyn. Despite breastfeeding being short for pups, Clara was still adamant about doing it.

"It isn't that hard. Pups are easier to nurse than human children. She read so much about human pregnancies I don't think she realizes how quickly pups grow," Eden mentioned.

"I told her that," Raine said, leaning up against the wall. "I think I really freaked her out. I didn't mean to. Hope that isn't why she went into labor."

Queen Eden waved her hand. "Oh no, she was due any day. In fact, I saw a vision not but a day ago that it would be very soon."

"That doesn't count," King Elijah spoke. "We all knew it would have been soon. She was as big as a her belly was as big as a dragon's egg." His hand waved to Clara. Eden slapped Elijah in the stomach, who only laughed.

"It's a hard gift to decipher." Eden snorted. I'm just glad it gave me some idea when the baby was coming. She could have gone another two weeks, according to the doctor!"

Clara stirred as our daughter wiggled in the blankets. Picking up my tiny daughter, I bounced her to keep her sated just for a few more minutes until Clara woke up. Her enormous eyes looked up at me, blinking several times to focus on my face. "Hi, little one," I cooed, sitting in the rocking chair. Holding her close, she yawned and fell asleep right in the crook of my arm.

"Wow, what is this? Another lady that has the terrible Alpha Kane wrapped around her finger?" Raine nudged Dad, who only laughed. Throwing the middle finger toward her, Clara woke up and saw exactly what I had done.

"Not around the baby," she hissed.

"Sorry, baby." I stood up, kissing her forehead. She gave a hazy smile, then blushed those rosy cheeks around the room.

"You should have woken me up." The back of her hand rubbed her eyes. Clara's wolf had already healed her from birth. Her body was almost back to normal except for her breasts to help feed the baby. Torin purred at that, the horny bastard.

"So," her mother prodded, "do you have a name?" Clara looked at me as if asking me if it was all right to say. I nudged her, giving her a smirk and the little one a smile.

"We did. Evelyn Margret." Clara's mother grabbed her chest, rubbing it longingly, remembering her sister Margret and her mate saving Clara all those years ago from Darius.

"Thank you, Clara." Everyone in the room cooed at the baby, finally passing the pup around. I sat on the bed, watching my daughter get passed from parent to parent and even Marcus, who had been standing watch by the door. His nose went to smell her, imprinting the smell in his mind so if he ever needed to find her, he could. His beta nose could find her anywhere in the pack house or territory now.

Small repetitions at the door had Clara's head perk up. Her smile widened, leaning over the bed. "Kit," she whispered, motioning for him to come forward. I waited for Torin to growl at Kit, but it never came. Evelyn was now tucked in her arms as Kit crawled into the bed.

"You dressed up," Clara cooed at him. His eyes were sparkling, hair parted to the side. He looked like a damn mini warrior in his dress uniform. This was the same white uniform with the red sash specially made for our mating ceremony. He was the littlest future warrior the pack had ever seen.

"You only get one chance to make a first impression, right, alpha?" Kit's begging eyes of approval had me nod my head. Chest puffing out with pride, he stared down at little Evelyn, whose eyes were trained on him. Clara gently put Evelyn in his arms. He held her with such care and devotion.

"I'll protect you," he whispered in her ear. "From all the bad stuff, you and your family." The room stood silent, watching the two.

"*I have a feeling,*" Clara mind-linked me, "*that little Kit might be closer to our family than just a guard.*" Queen Eden's eyes were distant. A smile was painted on her lips. "*Mother sees it as so too.*" She giggled internally.

My face frowned, but Clara's glowed. I didn't want to think that my daughter had already found her mate. She was still mine to take care of.

"Your Highness and Luna." A special forces warrior came into the room, matching Kit's uniform. "We have come to gather Kit for his training." Clara cleaned off a wisp of hair from Kit's forehead, looking at him and Evelyn adoringly.

Kit would travel to the Blue Waters pack, a special school, Alabaster Shifter Academy, which resided there for gifted shifters with warrior high warrior ranking intentions. They stayed and lived in dormitories to train for many years. It was a rigorous training process, and few strong shifters were taken in. Most of the pack at Blue Waters were held by former alphas, retired but willing to help train those with no alpha blood. The training was so difficult many dropped out, but those who graduated became just as strong as their alphas.

Kit looked to Clara, who only nodded for him to go.

"I hope to see you real soon, Luna." Kit's cheeks blushed red.

"Oh, you will. I'll come to visit you. That's a promise," she whispered.

Chapter Three

Jasper

The Vermillion Kingdom was dark, desolate, and nothing good.

When we first arrived in Bergarian, Taliyah wanted to immediately head to the Vermillion castle to figure out what kind of shambles her half brother had left it in. Taliyah did a lot for Darius, from calculating taxes to taking from the people down to spells to make his compulsion stronger.

Taliyah knew the nation was already in shambles, and digging deeper into the archives of the treasury, the Parliament, and the welfare of the people only made her mood more somber. There was much to be done, and not many willing vampires and witches left to help.

Upon arrival, there was nothing but dead trees, crumbled leaves on the ground, and decaying corpses of animals laid barely intact. The homes on the outskirts of the main square were broken down, shutters crumbling to pieces. Several vampire children were running and playing with sticks while their parents hung up clothes on the line riddled with holes.

Many of the small towns we passed by were ancient and burned to the ground; not a single life was left.

The carriage trudged along. Taliyah looked out the window sadly. Her white hair was pulled back into a braid, her red eyes tearing up from the lack of shelter for the vampires and witches that dared to live their lives in this land. "I don't know where to start." Taliyah sighed. I jumped up from the other side of the carriage, putting my arm around her. Her head went straight to my chest, my fingers tickling down the side of her cheek. The wetness of her bloody tears pooled on my thumb.

"You can't blame yourself, Taliyah." I pulled her up to look at me. "Darius did this, not you. He left the country in shambles, let the rogues take over, and now the innocent suffer. We can ask for help. We are friends with the Cerulean Moon Kingdom, remember?" I smiled, pulling her chin toward my lips.

Her cold lips met my warm ones, sparks flying across them. How I almost gave this up, I'd never know. Taliyah sighed, her fingers entangled with mine. "Are you sure you want to do this, to help me?"

"I couldn't think of a better way to spend my time." I chuckled.

The months flew by. Kane and Clara had become Alpha and Luna of the Warrior pack and welcomed a new alpha and future queen of the throne, Evelyn. We missed it all, too busy working with various members of the Parliament, weeding out who needed to be thrown into the dungeon and who we should keep. There weren't many options for vampires with enough education to help us through anything. Taliyah was literally running everything herself.

She poured herself into books night after night, learning how to rule a nation. She was at a loss. Her frustration pulled at my heart, knowing how compassionately she put the desire to return Vermillion to its former glory. She was so poorly treated for so many years she didn't owe the country anything. But here she was, being my selfless little witch.

The first area of the castle we worked on was the study. It was dark, dreary, and held many years of Darius's morbid paintings of vampires feasting on humans. The Cerulean Moon Kingdom sent a large sum of money that helped us get started, most of it going to the people, but some we left to clean up the dank office.

Her office was now the brightest room in the entire castle. Fresh green plants lined the windows, and a small bird flew around in the corner of the room. Filled with creams, tans, and whites, it brightened my mate's mood considerably, that is until she dove deeper into her studies.

"Taliyah, please, let's go to bed." Taliyah's crimson eyes didn't leave the paper, her hands in her disheveled hair. Shaking her head, her finger slapped the book where she lost her place.

"I can't. I have so much to do." She sighed, sitting back in the chair. "I don't know what to do. I can't fill the Parliament chairs. Education, the welfare of the people, and distribution to the poor are empty. The only seats filled are for the General of the Guard and Land Operations. Nothing I can use right now! There are barely any soldiers, and there is no life left. The animals have fled, and now we have to rely on the gnomes' deer population, and they are strapped. The deer population has plummeted immensely." She threw her hands up in the air, rubbing her eyes.

"There isn't anything you can do now." I came around the desk, rubbing her shoulders. She groaned, feeling my fingers kneading into the knots of her back. "How about you come upstairs? I've drawn you a bath, and you can relax for a bit. I've already taken care of a few dark fairies that are helping out at the blood bank in the middle of town. The children have been fed, and an old industrial garment building has been cleared out. Cots have been set up for them to have a roof over their head."

With Kane and Clara's gracious help, they asked wolves to donate blood. Each wolf could produce a bag a day, enough to help the starving families in the city who stood by the standards of not force-feeding on other supernaturals. The past month had been a success. We received enough blood from several packs alone to stabilize those who sought nourishment. Luckily, we didn't have to feed fated mate couples since they could feed on each other, but the children suffered.

Taliyah's red eyes glistened. Red tears dripped down her cheeks. "Don't cry, my little witch." Her vampire blood was equally strong as her witch genes. It would either help this nation or destroy it.

I had heard the whispers of the few that supported Taliyah. They worried no one would accept her because she was a hybrid. First of her kind, the people were scared of her. Taliyah refused to have a crowning ceremony to save money and distributed it among the poor to show her compassion and willingness to help. Those hungry were grateful, but the dukes and duchesses that still held most of the money—Darius's most significant supporters—did not find that amusing. Unfortunately, that was who we needed to gain favor from if we would make this country work again.

"Come, My Queen." I lifted her out of the chair, one arm under her knees, another behind her back. Her head leaned into me. Kissing her forehead, I took her up the winding stairs. The very few servants that still worked in the castle had done a fantastic job helping with cleaning up in exchange for food, shelter, and hope for a new nation. Many were grateful that their families could move into the castle as well.

The dark hallway containing the few candelabras on the walls led us to our room. The first was at the top of the stairs. It wasn't the royal suite; it was a simple bedroom with just a king-sized bed, a few pieces of furniture, and enough clothes to get us by.

It was comfortable, just enough for both of us.

Carrying Taliyah to the bathroom, I set her down gently. We had not taken our relationship further, just a few stolen kisses and sleeping in the same bed. I wasn't pushing, she wasn't asking, and I was happy with the arrangement. Proving myself was my goal; even if I had raging blue balls for the rest of my life, I would be satisfied as long as she was.

"Thank you, Jasper." Her eyes blinked up at me. Stepping up on her toes, Taliyah gave a quick peck on my lips. She lingered longer than usual, my wolf reveling in her touch. "I don't know what I would do without you. You've done so much…" She sniffed.

"No, no, I haven't done enough," I whispered to her lips. "I owe you the world, Taliyah. I owe you everything for giving me a second chance, and I will prove my undying love to you." Taliyah smiled, her lips brushing mine again until her tongue reached into my mouth. I groaned, pulling her close to me, but respecting her boundaries. I wouldn't push anything on her. I was at her mercy.

Unfortunately, she pulled away, her white fangs shining against the candlelight. I had spread rose petals in her bath along with hibiscus oil. "I hope it's all right, but I put your night clothes on the counter. Once you are done, I can feed you."

Taliyah, being half-vampire and witch, could eat regular food, but blood gave her more strength. She didn't like to feed on me, thinking she was using me. Anything to get her to touch me was a reward, and I didn't mind the euphoric feeling it gave me after using her venom. "Jasper, I'm all right." She sighed, wrapping her arms around me.

"You need your strength, and I'm happy to do it. That's what mates are for, right?" I used to think vampires sucking blood was disgusting and an abomination at one point in time, but one little vampire caught my heart, and now it wasn't as bad. Just as Clara said, one lousy vampire didn't mess up all of them. Kane had to learn the same thing, even with the majority of Vermillion up in arms and still wanting to carry out Darius's previous scrutiny.

"Take your time." I kissed her forehead. "I'm going to clean your office."

Heading down the stairs, maids walked by, asking if we needed anything. It was already late into the night, so I urged them to sleep. Even the omegas didn't stay up that late, but more work needed to be done to the castle to get it into running order.

Taliyah had shown paintings of Vermillion's lands before Darius was crowned. The images were different from what I had pictured Vermillion to be. Vermillion had always been a darker nation, but the deep colors did make it captivating. Deep navy blues with hints of white flowers hung in the trees. The grass was lush and rich, dark green with red tips. Plants that didn't need the sun thrived well here, but the bright blue moon shone most brilliant on this side of the world. It was beautiful in its own right, just like all the other regions of Bergarian. If we could help the land and people recover, it would be beautiful once again.

Large animals of deer, moose, and even species I had never seen that were large enough to feed an entire vampire family for days roamed the lands. Taliyah said they died quickly once Darius took over. There were once regulations to ration the blood since it did not give them the 'full' feeling like human or supernatural blood. Taliyah had passed a law that no animal could be fed upon until numbers came back up while they were bred and brought back into the kingdom.

After cleaning up Taliyah's desk and putting the final book away, I headed back upstairs to see Taliyah in her robe, reading on the bed.

"My little witch, you need to be resting." I kissed her cheek. She hummed, thumbing through the pages as I changed into joggers and just a tight muscle tee. She didn't want the bond to take over and have us go too far physically before we mended our relationship, so the more clothes, the better. That was the rule.

Her little stomach growled, her hand pushing it down to hide it. "I think you forget I can hear so well." Taliyah's breath hitched, feeling my hand grab hers, kissing it gently. "Come on, you need your strength. I even donated some blood today, and my wolf regenerated quickly after I ate lunch." Taliyah bit her lip, looking from the book to me.

"Shy, are we?" I smirked. Huffing, she crawled into my lap. This was my favorite part at the end of every day, sitting here with her while she bit into my neck. There were other places she could bite. It was an intimate spot for vampires to feed on, and it made me feel closer to her. On top of it all, it is said to taste better because it is closer to the heart.

"You promise it doesn't hurt?" she questioned. I shook my head.

"You know it doesn't. If it makes you uncomfortable to drink there, you can—"

"No, no, I like it there." Her cold finger ran down my neck. "And, I like it here." Her fingernail trailed across my collar bone, reaching the other side. Gods, she was going to kill me. Her fanged smile widened, that smile that could have me fall on my knees to worship her. "You've been really patient with all the craziness, my big bad wolf." She giggled. *Fuck.* It had been so long since I heard her laugh.

"How about after I meet with Duke Mortus tomorrow, we go on a real date?" Her lips kissed my cheeks, now trailing down my neck. My cock was straining against her thigh. I knew she could feel it, and she only laughed. Her teeth grazed my neck, sinking into it. I groaned, feeling the venom numb the area, causing a euphoric feeling to bolt straight to my dick.

Her fingers dug into my shoulders, pulling me closer. I didn't deny her. I felt her throat gulping down my blood, my eyes rolling back into my head as she finished. I swear I could almost come with her just sucking.

To my surprise, she straddled me, taking her fangs from my neck, now kissing me. It was weird, still tasting a bit of metallic on her tongue, but still damn hot. "I want you to know how hard it's been for me, too." Her finger circled my pec muscles. "I care about you a lot, Jasper, and you have been nothing short of an angel to me. You've pampered me, took care of me, heck, you even baby me, making sure I'm fed and clothed."

"Only the best for my mate," I purred. "Anything you ask me, I'll do it." Taliyah giggled, pecking at my lips again, rubbing her core against me. My hands went to her ass, gripping her between the satin shorts and robe. *I don't know how to resist her.*

The dark purple robe fell off her shoulder, showing her skin brightly in the dark. My hands traced up her hip, and finally, her neck, having the fire touches run up and down her body. Taliyah leaned forward, her breasts now pushing up against my chest. I growled heavily into her mouth.

Her head leaned back, baring her chest to me. *Damn. Do I go for it?*

Kissing down her neck to the top of her chest, my hand went up to her camisole top, rubbing the hardened nipple under her nightgown. She hummed, putting her hands in my hair, and meeting my lips again. Pulling her bottom lip, my tongue slipped into her mouth.

"Jasper," she spoke between breaths. My cock was painfully hard. She rocked into me, causing delightful friction. "Is this okay?" Her sweet voice crossed my ears.

"More than okay." I heaved heavily. Continuing to rock, I pushed her faster on my cock, feeling her heat. "Does it feel good?" Taliyah was comfortable enough to let her arousal seep through my nostrils for the first time.

"Yes," she muttered under her breath. Pulling her close, pulling down on her top, I sucked on her pink, hardened nipple. Gasping, whispering my name, her claws tightened on my shoulders, feeling her wetness pooling around my thin linen pants. Roaring, I finally released my pent-up sexual tension and then sucked on her neck repeatedly until my mate caught her breath.

If I can't sink my teeth into her yet, I can leave a mark, right?

Taliyah sat up; her lips were pouty and red from the stubble on my face. It was the 'just fucked' look without the fucking. "Woah." She laughed out loud.

"Yeah, woah." I grinned wickedly.

Chapter Four

Jasper

Taliyah had been in a meeting with vampires from the small group of Parliament, along with Duke Mortus, our only duke who was the kingdom's lifeline. Everything rode on his support, and luckily, we had the strongest of the dukes wanting to fight for Taliyah's crown and a new nation.

I stood outside, standing guard while they spoke. They didn't trust me to be inside. I heard every word anyway, but from the sounds of it, the duke was more than willing to help. I wondered if he had ulterior motives.

The duke humored the rogues, let them come inside his home, gave them something to eat, and let them go on their way. He said he was playing both sides and would help the outcome in the end. It meant that the uprising didn't happen any sooner. Gaining a stronger military force would be wise. I understood the logic, but something was off.

His right hand, Enoch, has been spotted going into the dead forest many times, but I never saw him come back out. I spent the entire night waiting, only for him to come out of the mansion the next morning refreshed. Enoch was sneaking back into the duke's mansion, and I didn't know why. Magic must have been involved.

Being in constant contact with Kane was crucial. Several attacks around the surrounding territories were of vampires. Vampires never came in large numbers. They were small militias of maybe ten to twenty, but their speed was incredible. The rogues went after the weaker wolves, despite wolves supplying blood to those who listened to our laws. The rogues received no fresh blood unless they pledged allegiance to us and spent time in the new army to build protection. None of them wanted that, so fighting was their only way to eat, and that was attacking smaller packs surrounding the Cerulean Moon Kingdom.

Duke Mortus, putting on his long trench coat, flipped the collar and grabbed his decorative cane from the servant helping. He eyed me suspiciously, only to nod and head out the door. The other vampires, still speaking with my mate, walked out with her, speaking quickly about their opinions of the new members. They weren't so sure of the names gifted by Mortus to help with the rebuilding. These recommended vampires had been with Darius's father before the fall of Vermillion, but now the rumors of them drinking human blood were rising.

"Thank you, I'll keep that in mind." Taliyah rubbed her hands together, her eyes tired from debating with the vampires she could trust. "You are aware Duke Mortus is our lifeline? If there are only rumors about him being with the rogues and drinking human blood, then that isn't enough evidence to disbar him. I need proof, or we all suffer." I smiled at her, watching her delegate and speak to these vampires with such diplomacy.

My Taliyah had to serve under Darius for so long. She had to keep her head low, doing his bidding until now. Now, her back was straight, her head held tall like the real queen she was meant to be. The noble vampires bowed to her, muttering their agreements to turn to me. Several eyed me from head to toe, giving darkening glances.

There was no secret. The Parliament knew that I almost gave up Taliyah for another. Those in her inner circle found it repulsive, which is why we had not solidified our bond yet, along with the never-ending lists that Taliyah had made to help repair a broken country.

"Jasper," she said breathlessly, ignoring the vampires now walking to the door. "I'm so glad you are here." Taliyah's arms held open wide, and she wrapped her arms around my back.

"I'm never far." I pecked her cheek. "Are you ready for our date? Or would you rather rest?" Taliyah shook her head excitedly.

"No, I'm ready. Our first proper date, huh?" She ran up the stairs halfway before turning around to meet my eyes in the foyer. "How should I dress?" I wiggled my eyebrows as she began to laugh.

"No, seriously! Are we going to a pub in the forest? Heading to the Cerulean Moon Kingdom?" she continued to ramble. I leaned my arm on the banister with a large lion opening its mouth. My mate looked adorable when she was excited. Her eyebrow would cock to the side when she thought about something difficult, yet the other would remain impassive. When she was excited, hopeful or maybe shaking in pleasure I would give her, they would both raise, giving me the perfect look inside her beautiful red eyes.

"Outside, my sweet," I joked. "We will be outside. Now hurry." Squealing, she ran up the stairs to change while I arranged the carriage.

I had the drapes closed. I didn't want her to see where we were going. We wouldn't be leaving Vermillion, just staying right on the outskirts near the fields of dried wheat and grass. It wasn't much to look at. Just a few months ago, it was nothing but black dirt and tan stalks of dead vegetation. The carriage went slow, going around the palace perimeter a few times before it actually reached our destination. The area I had prepared would surprise her for sure, especially since she thought that the soil was no longer useful.

Taliyah continued to pour out her ideas of what it could be. I only laughed, licking my bottom lip and biting it slightly as her own mouth moved. I thought she would be at least tired from her long meeting this morning, but she was anything but.

My wolf pranced in my head, excited we would spend the entire afternoon and evening with her, the first time since I pleaded for her to keep me as her mate. Taliyah had given me a second chance, and I would not waste it. After four months of proving myself, I was close, if the previous night was any sign. Soon my mate would bear my mark, and all would be right with the world from my view.

"Are we there yet?" her voice squeaked. Small bits of electricity tingled her fingers, lighting up the dark carriage. Chucking, I pulled her close, her head already nuzzling into my neck.

"Yes, we are close. Here." I pulled out a black silk blindfold. Her eyes widened as I wrapped it around her head. "Don't get any crazy ideas," I whispered huskily in her ear. Feeling her body shudder had my cock springing to life.

Down, boy.

Her rear moved, causing fantastic friction in my pants. Holding her waist down, her hands gripped my shirt. "None of that, not unless you want to get marked right now, in the open." She bit her lip, her red lipstick staining her teeth. Shaking her head, I laughed, kissing her until her stains were gone.

Once the carriage stopped, the driver took extra precautions to let her out. "You can head back. She'll ride on my wolf when we return." The driver graciously bowed, thanking both of us. Watching as the driver whipped the horses, I found Taliyah wiggling her fingers.

Taliyah had her hands out, adorably trying to reach or touch something that would give her a clue. "Taliyah, what are you doing?" I pulled on her hand, pulling her into my embrace. "You won't figure it out like that." She pouted, my lips tasting hers again.

"Can I see now?" she whispered. I bit my own lip, rolling my tongue across the bottom.

"I guess so." I sighed. I kind of liked her blindfolded, with me to take care of her. She could perfectly take care of herself, but it would be nice if she would finally let go of the leadership pressure and let me do the work.

On her, that is.

We stood outside the large circle of trees, hiding the real present. It was a small forest inside the large, dead field. It was its own little oasis inside the darkened world of the Vermillion nation. Without the glamour spell to hide it, it stuck out like a sore thumb. Right now, we could only see the sway of the trees that held the small garden inside. Taliyah gasped, her hands covering her mouth.

"You got trees to grow here?" Lacing my fingers into hers, I kissed the back of her hand. "They are transplants from other territories, and the soil is rich, so the trees took to it well. This is only the beginning, though." Taliyah's eyes widened, touching the bark of the healthy tree.

It took many months to plan this. The ashes of burned homes, dead carcasses of animals, and the bloody tears of vampires all dissolved in the soil, ground together so new life would emerge. If the people worked together, the entire nation would hold the beautiful, darkened trees and exotic flowers it once had. With past death, new life would arise.

Pulling her through the thickness of the rows of trees, we walked into a paradise. A small pond lay in the middle, and rows of Blue Moon flowers, similar to tulips of Earth, lined the path to a small table in the middle. Deep red bushes, budding with abundant white flowers called to the whisps that drank their nectar. The dark crows that ran the land of Vermillion, scouting for scraps of food witches left behind, were now pecking the rich soil for worms.

Black rabbits nibbled at the growing garden in one area of the oasis. It was a testing spot for me, trying to understand what vegetables and fruits could grow here the best. I laughed, watching several rabbits nipping at each other's heels while trying to grab a carrot from another.

Taliyah touched each bush and small tree while walking on each stepping-stone, afraid to step in the meticulously trimmed grasses. Pixies from the north had noticed the new small paradise in a land in which it should be dead. Their laughter rang through the wind, walking into a new home they made in a nearby tree, slamming it shut, making Taliyah laugh. "Jasper, how?"

"I had help." I dared not take the credit. Hoping she wouldn't have asked who had helped me, but of course, she did. I bit my cheek, saying the name I didn't want to bring up.

"Clara did," I whispered. Taliyah only nodded, bending down to pick one lone deep red rose, accidentally pricking her finger.

"She will make a wonderful queen," she whispered to herself. The back of my index finger brushed her pale cheek, her long lashes looking through to meet mine.

"You already make a wonderful queen." Before Taliyah could argue with me, my fingers slipped around her waist, playing with the light blue cardigan that complimented her skin. My head tilted, meeting her lips, her gasping at the sudden forcefulness of my embrace.

Taliyah

Heaven.

Was this what heaven was like on the other side of the veil? For so long, I had been alone, doing the bidding of someone else, a mere servant having no hope of finding someone to love me. Now here he was, taking his time, showing me how a mate should be loved despite his many mistakes. The last mistake almost cost us our entire future.

I wanted to forget all our worries. My fingers tangled in his dirty blonde hair that had grown just to his ears. My fingernails scratched his scalp, causing him to moan into his kiss. His warm tongue slid into my mouth. I giggled, feeling how needy Jasper and his wolf were. His wolf's voice was just as loud as his.

"Easy there, Xander," I cooed at him. Jasper's eyebrow raised, intrigued I had learned to talk to his wolf all without a mind-link. I could link my mind to shifters well, but talking to their animals was a different story. Now, I could play with Jasper's wolf more.

I had not only been studying ways to build a nation from the ground up but enhancing some of my powers. It would have been a shame to have them and not use them when the time came.

Placing my hands on either side of his face, I gently pulled away. He whined, and I couldn't help but feel terrible. He had waited so long for us, and here I was worrying about a country that didn't care that I was the personal slave of my half brother for so many years. I had been selfish, and it was time to rectify that.

I didn't hold any resentment toward Clara. In fact, I was thankful for her. Without her, I think Jasper would have fallen apart. I would have rejected him if I hadn't seen such a new, wonderful side to him back on Earth. He had proven to me he was patient and willing for his mate. He would make the perfect king.

My only problem was that Parliament didn't like the idea. They wanted a vampire to even out the genes of the new heir that was to take over the throne. Of course they would think about a new heir now, even with the problems we had. There would be no heir, no babies, no happy times unless we continued to take back control of the nation.

They would have to deal with my decision because Jasper was my mate. The goddess deemed it so, and I was never letting my wonderful mate go.

"We should eat." I caught my breath. My heart beating rapidly only had me thinking of last night, the first time we had made each other feel pleasure I had never really known.

"Right." He grabbed my hand. "Can we do more of that later, though?" I laughed out loud, trying to hide my fangs. "Don't you hide." He growled playfully. "I enjoy seeing that smile. I haven't seen it enough." His wink had me weak at the knees while he led me down a stony path.

The flora and fauna were beautiful. It was brighter than the vegetation before Darius took over. I'm not sure if we even had seeds from hundreds of years ago for the plants that had taken root here. I'm sure Jasper had already done his research, finding vegetation that would still grow under the clouded and darkened sky of the day and the brightness of the moon.

"Don't worry," Jasper said as he pulled out of my seat. "The plants grow well here. I think the gods want Vermillion's land to flourish again." Jasper sat, his hand reaching across the small table set up in the middle of the oasis. "This is just the first step, and from the pictures you showed me the other day, I'm sure we could find similar plants in all the territories. There are so many places still left unexplored." I nodded gratefully, blushing at how Jasper had taken another project in his hands without telling me, trying to help.

Jasper pulled a basket from under the table. It held cheeses, wine, and a few bags of blood. Jasper didn't like the idea of me drinking other were-wolves' blood that had been graciously donated, so he often gave blood twice a day to make sure I would stay full.

Smiling, I watch him pour it into a glass. He tended to every need I had, never letting me lift a finger to help. "Jasper?" I questioned. He hummed, finishing setting the neat spread. Brushing his hair back with the palm of his hand, I pulled his hand away, interlacing it with mine. His eyes softened, his lips coming to a curl of a smile.

"Are you ready?" His head cocked to the side, blinking a few times, opening and closing his mouth.

"For what, little witch?"

"To be king?" Jasper immediately shook his head.

"I don't want to be king, Taliyah." His hand didn't let go; he only squeezed it tighter. "This is your land, your people, your home. I am but a werewolf." He placed his free hand on his chest. "Your people won't accept me. They are having a hard time with just you. I would only cause problems. I am happy to be your mate, and support you where you need it. Hell, I'll be your concubine if you want me to have a status." He reared his head back in laughter. "I'll do my job well, too." He grinned wickedly.

"All I ask is that I am your mate, and I am the only one to touch you because Xander wouldn't be able to stand it." I giggled, watching his face turn red. Clearing his throat, he took a piece of cheese on a steel fork to put in my mouth.

"I just want you, Taliyah. I will follow you to the ends of the world. Do as you ask and help when you need it. But that"—Jasper pointed behind us, the dark castle seen from above the trees—"that is your destiny, to bring the country back together. Bringing me into it, making me king as an equal to you, won't help." Placing the cheese in my mouth, I chewed, pondering his words.

As much as I wanted him to rule beside me, the rogues would only stir more. How Jasper grew up in just a few months of meeting me, I'm not sure how he managed. He was so much more handsome as the days grew. The bond was utterly strong, his wolf patiently waiting for me.

"How about a prince?" I muttered, taking a sip of blood.

"If you have your heart dead set on it, I'll do as you ask." He shook his head, sipping his wine.

Whisps buzzed around us, coming from nowhere. They kissed my cheek but pulled on Jasper's hair. "Stupid fuckers." He waved them away. "Never did like those things."

As the afternoon progressed, we lay on a blanket where the grass grew abundantly. It was a dark green, not the grass that used to grow in this land, but it was too close to tell. Once the entire land was covered in vegetation, I could see the animals returning. Catch and release for their blood if we needed it, and even plowing the land and trading food for blood could come to fruition.

Things were looking up. Time was speeding by more quickly than in previous months now that Jasper had calmed me. His head lay on my chest while I played with his hair. His fingers played with a nearby deep purple leaf.

"How did I not notice this little oasis? Surely I would have seen this looking out my office window." Jasper chuckled, the vibrations pulling into my beating heart.

"The kitchen chef is a witch. Her powers aren't that strong, so she would come out every day and cast an enchantment on her way to work in the castle. I gave her an extra day off a week to do that."

"So that is why my toast was burned some mornings." I snorted. Jasper's arms wrapped around my waist.

"Don't know what you are talking about, little witch."

Clara

"Come on, little one," I said quietly as I tried to breastfeed Evelyn. It wasn't as easy as mother made it out to be. Evelyn was having a terrible time, and finding out she was tongue-tied didn't help either. Kane almost snapped at the doctor when they clipped the extra skin under her tongue to allow her to suckle properly.

It was taking all my strength to keep Kane calm. It wasn't a joke when he said an alpha fiercely protects his family. It was for the best having Evelyn have the procedure done, the numbing medicine wouldn't have worked on a werewolf, and she was one-hundred percent werewolf. Tiny little teeth buds were already sprouting in her mouth, like you would see with most tiny little puppy newborns. She was strong and fierce just like her father, a perfect ruler to inherit the throne one day. She was everything I wasn't, and I was happy with that.

Ten pounds, ten whole pounds of baby, came out of my five-foot-four frame. Dr. Talbert said if I was a human, I would have ripped from top to bottom, causing me to be on bed rest for weeks. Luckily, Giana had a paw in this because otherwise, I would have been a mess of trouble.

Kane sat in the rocking chair beside me, watching me try to get the baby to latch. I swear I could see the lust in his eyes when I peeked at him, but he only would clear his throat to look over his laptop filled with endless emails and budgets.

Evelyn cried because she couldn't draw my milk out quickly enough. It had been two days of her crying, driving me up the wall. I couldn't understand why my milk wouldn't come down fast enough until Naomi, Kane's mother, began to help me.

"I had trouble with Kane too." Naomi pulled the baby from me so I could adjust myself. There was no shame in the room. My breasts were exposed to the air, feeling the cool breeze to help ease the pain of Evelyn's vacuum of a mouth. "I was so stressed—Kane being the firstborn, plus luna duties—that I couldn't relax enough to let the milk flow. That tingling feeling in your breast should follow quickly after she begins eating, have you felt that?" I shook my hand shamefully, only to feel her hand grip mine.

"This is your first baby. It takes time for milk to come in. The first couple of days, the baby is small, and her tummy doesn't need much. She's just extra fussy because she is impatient like her father." Glancing over to Kane, he pretended he didn't hear, mumbling a curse under his breath. Chuckling, Naomi went to a food cart brought in.

"Drink this, it has fenugreek and blessed thistle. It will help your lactation. I can grab a small bottle for her if you wish to get her tummy full so you can sleep."

"Will that disrupt me feeding her?" My voice trembled. I wanted nursing to work. I wanted to feed her like nature had intended. Stroking her overly long locks for a baby, Naomi sat back on the bed. Her warm hand felt my forehead. "You need sleep. You won't make milk unless you sleep." Kane crawled into the bed, now taking Evelyn.

"My mother is right, I'll feed her, and you sleep. Maybe your milk will be here when you wake up." I sighed sadly again, only nodding. I would feel like a complete failure as a mother if I couldn't nurse Evelyn. It was what I had dreamed of since I had found out I was pregnant. Nursing was the way to achieve the close bond I desired with the baby.

"Listen here," Naomi's words became stern. "You are not a failure if you do not nurse your baby," she scolded. "I couldn't nurse Kane, and he turned out"—she eyed him up and down—"okay." I laughed, covering my mouth. Kane gave a menacing glare as he bounced a screaming Evelyn.

Kane propped the bottle up for Evelyn to take. She guzzled the bottle down quickly, her screams silenced. She was hungry—too hungry. Biting my cheek, I nuzzled my head onto Kane's lap, staying close to Evelyn and to Kane.

"Sleep, my love. You did so good." Kane's big hand pushed my sweaty hair away from my face until I finally fell asleep with the warmth of the tingles soothing me.

⁂

As I woke up, heavy rocks sat on my chest. I groaned, feeling painfully sore. My mother gently rubbed my shoulder, asking me to wake up. "I smell your milk has come in, darling," her voice said sweetly. Evelyn was stirring, trying to reach for me. Smiling, I took her quickly, feeling the heaviness in my chest, wanting to explode.

"I told Kane to go to the office and that I'd watch you."

"I don't need a babysitter," I grumbled as Evelyn latched on perfectly. I wanted to cry tears of joy seeing the long sucks and the little gulps that let me know she was drinking.

"See, I knew it would happen." My mother pushed my hair away. I still sniffed, unable to control these weepy hormones.

"This is a lot," I whispered, still feeding Evelyn.

"It is, for the first time anyway. At least they weren't twins, huh?" My eyes widened, leaning my head back on the headboard.

"That would be so hard," I whimpered.

"Hey, love, are you hungry?" Kane walked in, setting down a tray of food. I hummed, Kane now hovering over me. "You did it, love. I'm so proud of you." He nuzzled my cheek, kissing my mark. "You know you don't have to do it though, right?" I nodded. Still, being stubborn, I wanted to do it, even if wolves only nursed their babies for a few months.

I had all these goals and duties since becoming luna to help better the pack. Mother had so many tutors from the palace come in, teaching me the history of this world, bits and pieces of other kingdoms and territories. Everything was complicated. Ruling with just knowledge wasn't enough. You had to have a kind heart, but at some point, you had to draw a line. Wolves to this day think I was too lenient on both Jasper and Sebastian. I didn't regret my decision one bit. Deep within me, I felt that they should have been let go, given another chance. Now Darius, he was a different story. I felt nothing for him. He was beyond redemption the first day.

Of course, I was overwhelming myself. I begged for more information on how to learn to make the best decisions, but the things I wanted to know how to do didn't come from a book. It came from within. On a smaller scale, as luna, I felt like I could maybe do it, but as a queen, could I ever?

Even raising my family seemed like a daunting task. To raise my children to not be selfish, humble, and caring, how was I to do it all?

"I need to talk to the both of you." Mother got up from the bed to sit down in the rocking chair. Kane had a plate of fruit, feeding me as I fed our daughter. His gentle fingers traced my jaw, leading me to look at him.

"You know the vision I had about the upcoming war back when you first had your mating ceremony, correct?" Elijah, my father, walked in with a large turkey leg, taking large bites. Mother just shook her head, rubbing her temples.

"I thought—Owe thought"—Mother stared at Father, gripping his hand—"that the battle with Marcellus and his rogues was the war or battle I had envisioned, but this does not seem to be the case."

"What do you mean?" Evelyn cried, releasing herself from my breast. Pulling her away and switching to the other breast, mother cleared her throat.

"There have been small groups of vampires attacking smaller prides and packs that prefer the more traditional lifestyle of living. You know, without electricity or what not, living more like their ancestors. This means they are late to be warned of any potential attacks. Your father and I are going to meet with some of the alphas, the Thorn Paw tribe, a panther shifter tribe was almost wiped clean. Vampires drained them completely, and some just left to die for no reason. Those that survived said the vampires had incredible speed. Only five took out a pack of sixty."

Kane growled, pulling me close to him. "Is it just those five? Or are there more?" Mother looked at Elijah; sadness in his eyes glanced to the ground before us.

"More," he grumbled. "We have contacted Taliyah. Vermillion is in complete disarray. No fields and crops to barter for blood, three-quarters of the nation has gone rogue. Those that are pledging their allegiance with Taliyah are still skeptical because of her mixed genealogy."

"That's right, she's half-witch and vampire." Father nodded. "And we have a theory for why that is." Father walked to the large bay windows. "Darius's father, Hugo, was originally mated to someone that was not his true mate, Nicholette. She was chosen. Once she died, he met his true mate, Simone, a powerful sorceress that hid in the shadows. She got pregnant. Darius was furious, believing his mother was his father's true mate."

"This is so complicated," I whispered.

"It is, but the gods allowed their genes to mix. It's never happened before. This means Taliyah is destined to do something, something powerful," Father spoke quietly.

"So, we have some work to do." My head automatically leaned into Kane, no longer hungry for the food he tried to feed me. Kissing my forehead, he nuzzled contentedly, feeling Torin growl within.

"Yes, we do, and that means, my lovely daughter, the past months of your training to be a queen will be put to the test, especially since..." Mother trailed off, rubbing her belly. "If you can heal the sick and afflicted, it would better our chances, give hope to the warriors because even numbers aren't going to help with this. Proper planning, strategic training and the right defenses will help us battle this new evil."

"Our peace will come." Kane growled in my ear. I shivered. It had only been a few days since we made love last. I could feel his desire through our bond. My body was physically ready, but my mind sure wasn't right now. Now I had to worry about not just my newborn daughter, but a nation going down a dark path and fast.

"I'll speak with Jasper. We will have donations of werewolf blood sent to Taliyah and Jasper. Having their soldiers prepped to help defend what is left." Kane's eyes glazed over as we waited.

"We leave in the morning, asking the smaller tribes to set up a basic camp around the Cerulean Moon Kingdom. Don't be surprised if some decide to gather around the Crimson Shadows pack. They are eager to meet you, as well as Evelyn." Mother kissed Evelyn's forehead.

"I'll be back in time to have your brother or sister, Clara." Mother smiled. My heart flipped in my chest. I was excited to have a sibling, even if we were twenty-some-odd years apart. I'd love them with all my heart.

Once Mother and Father left, I sighed in relief how the room was now holding just our little family. We had visitor after visitor the past few days, and now we could rest comfortably.

"Would a walk or run do you some good, love?" my wolf, Giana, yipped in my head. Naomi had become the unofficial nanny since being luna was going to take a lot of my time. I was going to be there for each feed, however. That was something I was not going to give up.

"Yes, that would be great." I giggled at Kane, who jumped excitedly off the bed. "I'll get mom!" He ran out the door like an overly excited puppy. Snorting, I swung my legs off the bed, placing Evelyn in the cot next to the bed.

"That won't be necessary." Naomi picked her up gently. "I'll rock this precious little thing." Her nose rubbed on Evelyn's. "She and I will become such wonderful friends, huh? Yes, we will!" As she cooed at my daughter, Kane pulled me down the stairs.

"A run will take the stress away, love." I was hoping so, because the weight of the news that my mother dropped before me was now tenfold.

"Torin hears Giana howling. How can you stand it?" He laughed at me.

"Oh, I've just learned to block out the annoying things." I pushed him playfully. Growling, he tried to throw his arms around me until I took off into a sprint. Kane was fast, but he was bulky. He had almost doubled in size since we had mated, constantly lifting when he was upset instead of taking his emotions out on a poor unknowing warrior.

Not that they would spar with him willingly, anyway.

I ducked into the trees, flinging my bare feet across the dirt. The tiny shorts I wore fit just like I had never been pregnant. Thank the gods for that. As I ran, I stripped my clothes, not wanting to ruin them, but Kane had already shifted, his large paws almost touching my heels.

Jumping over a large log, Giana sprung forth, our red fur covering our body and the white underbody now looking like lightning.

"*It's on now.*" I laughed through the mind-link to my mate.

"I'll catch you, Little Fox." His voice sounded sultry, even while chasing me.

Chapter Five

Clara

The red fibers of my fur bristled on my back, Giana feeling the soft touches of Kane trying to grip onto our footing, only to have me laugh. Giana shook her head, springing forth new life into her step. Jumping over the pack's nearby stream, we headed south, jumping through overgrown trees and trampling the beautiful purple moss I had fallen in love with. The white lights that hid inside the moss bounced around us.

Whisps flew through our fur, howling as we jumped in several puddles along the way. My wolf did not know where we were going, just that staying away from Kane and Torin was our goal. Springing through several heaps of leaves, the rabbits and deer that lay close in the underbrush of purple bushes lifted their heads in amusement.

Roars from Kane's beast had me smiling inside. His frustration with being the largest beast meant he could not run as quickly as my small foxlike body. Zooming past the largest tree, I turned to face the wind and sat directly behind it. The bark, smooth and cool to the touch, had me leaning against the welcoming branches. The branches stood out far and wide; the entire diameter of the tree was massive in the middle of this wooded area. Thick vines trickled down that I could only describe as that of a willow tree. Small flowers, white with hints of yellow, glowed. Petals from the flowers would easily fall to the ground if disturbed.

Kane stood tall in his form, standing on the other side of the vines that circled the trunk that I had used to hide. Kane had certainly bulked up since the last time I saw him in his form. Being pregnant had me holding my animalistic form and not enough time to frolic with Torin. My nose rose into the air, sniffing for his scent. The warm woodsy pine had me licking my teeth.

Biting had become our new way to play. Biting our marks had me shiver each time we found our release. He made us stop once I had a Braxton Hicks contraction that lasted for far too long for his liking. "Come out, Little Fox," Torin's voice taunted. I could hear his tongue brushing across his maw as the pads of his feet stumbled closer.

Wolves loved the chase, and Torin more so. I had always felt disappointed in myself that I wasn't able to give him the proper chase once he found me, his mate, but here we were, me giving him his just reward. This time, I wasn't running up a tree and giving him a fair run on the ground.

My wolf laid her paws on the ground, lifting her rear in a playful stance. Torin could smell us. We knew he could, but this was so much more fun to play. Torin's paw hit the tree, and Giana lunged forward, nipping at his hindquarters.

Torin roared playfully as I pranced around his feet. His large hands swiped, his claws cutting bits and pieces of my fur. I had become too fast for the overgrown beast, or he was being too playful to catch me. Giana pranced continually until she went right through his legs and bit him in the butt. We yelped playfully until Torin could take no more.

Flying backward, his body landed on the ground, and his arms engaged us. Giana and I relaxed, putting our nose up to his shoulder. The warmth of his smell had us sighing blissfully. "I got my prey." He growled, licking our ears.

Kane shifted. His shift was flawless now that he had practiced his half-shifted form so frequently. It took several seconds instead of an entire minute of breaking bones and elongating them to fit Torin's large stature. Shifting back took me more time, not being used to shifting for over five months during the pregnancy, but it was a great back-cracking experience.

Kane and I both laid naked, our bodies lying underneath the massive tree, small white petals falling around us from the wind knocking the vines together. The vines were certainly welcomed; the wall kept any prying eyes away from us. We hadn't been the exhibitionist type, not since I was pregnant, anyway. I was too worried about someone catching a pregnant woman with a heavily tattooed alpha breaking his mate in the middle of the woods.

Kane's lips grazed my shoulder, kissing it up the column of my neck and to my lips. His usually rough kisses, his passion, and the fury he liked to help take out on my small body had me questioning what was going on with my possessive mate. As much as I liked this newfound attention, my soul searched for his answers.

Love was all I found, burning love and tenderness.

"I love you, Clara, my mate." Kane's words melted into my ears while I hummed into his mouthwatering kisses. His gentle, now pierced tongue rolled over my parted lips, giving shivers up and down my naked back. Before I could reply, his hand encompassed my back, roaming from the top of my shoulders down to the small of my back.

Humming, content with the extra care my mate was giving me, my hands massaged his chest, feeling his taunt muscles that he worked on every day, not just to please me but our pack. His biceps were larger than my torso. I gripped him tightly as his hand traveled south.

"Are you healed?" he whispered into my ear, his fang scraping my lobe, causing an unbearable shutter, having me throw my leg over his. My arousal was swept by the gentle breeze of the vines, Kane taking large breaths through the nostrils of his nose.

"You know the answer to that." I giggled under the dark gaze as he appreciated my body. We enjoyed every moment of having Evelyn in our lives, but it gave us very little time to enjoy, well, each other.

Kane's erection was now close to my entrance, his hand holding the small of my back now trailed my behind as he squeezed it gently. A gentle moan left my lips and became Kane's undoing. "Goddess, you are beautiful," Kane rasped, his soft kissing now becoming erratic, dominant. His fingers found the opening where my leg covered his, now tracing the small bundle of nerves between my thighs.

My body gave a jolt, feeling it down to my toes as they pointed. The scruff of Kane's afternoon stubble brushed down the column of my neck, sucking harshly against the white of my skin. Hands running through his hair, I tugged harshly, feeling his canines brush my mark.

Whining, wanting him to sink those white teeth into me, he mumbled an incoherent, "Not yet," and rolled me to my back. "Do you know how long it's been?" Being a blubbering mess, my head rolled back and forth on the forest floor to give an answer. The thick green mosses caressed the backside of my body.

"Too long." His wet finger slid into my body, tickling every inch. He put such force into the thrust of his finger it had my breasts bouncing freely. Growling obsessively, he latched himself to me, pulling and nipping at the tender skin. The nerve endings in my breasts were heightened, not sure if it was from breastfeeding or my hormones in complete overdrive, but I wasn't complaining.

"Our daughter needs to share." The hotness of his breath fanned over my chest. "It isn't fair." Sucking on the underside, I felt his teeth nipping, leaving love marks.

"Our mothers will see those when I feed her," I whimpered, feeling his thumb continuously rubbing my clit.

"Let them." He growled. "They can see how much I pleasure you." I wanted to laugh. That is the last thing I wanted them to know. My claws extended, my first rush of pleasure hit me, my back arched, and my breasts felt the cool breeze. Kane groaned appreciatively, running his claws down my skin.

"I need you, baby." He growled. "I need you so badly." Kane spread my legs. It had been quite some time since we had used this position. My legs were wrapped around his waist. He didn't wait for me to be ready until his mighty beast thrust into my body.

Goddess, it felt like I was a virgin all over again. The pinching, how my skin healed so quickly, made everything so tight. I was a moaning mess. Kane didn't stop, his brows set in a firm set of determination that he was going to rail me into the ground.

"Oh, Alpha," I egged him on. His cock swelled. I could feel the tension in his body. His soul was calling out to me to sate his beast.

Kane had undergone so much, almost as much as I had carrying Evelyn. His constant worry over my health, leading a pack to continue making it the strongest of the entire kingdom, the impending war that was now coming. Who knew what else he would have to face along with the doubt that I felt within myself?

His emotions were climbing. The tension he wanted to release so badly was going to go straight into my core. Kane's pelvic bone pushed into me, giving me the extra sensation of being too full. "Alpha," I groaned again. His hand pushed my chest down as his teeth lengthened, biting straight into my shoulder. Screaming, he growled a vicious, "Mine," making the petals of the gorgeous tree fall around us, giving us the impression of white snow.

Kane's body fell on me. The heaviness of his body and the sweat we both expelled mixed together, giving us the scent that truly made us. Every werewolf around could smell what we had just done, but I had to learn not to care. Kane's heavy breathing slowed. My fingers scratched his muscular back.

"I needed that," he whispered, already kissing me up and down my neck. I knew he did. The burden he carried was significantly lightened. Out of the books I had read about strong alphas, everything ran true. Strong alphas needed their mates not just to calm their beasts, but for them to release tension.

And oh boy, I wasn't complaining. He made sure I got my pleasure before completing his.

I couldn't imagine not having the extra boost of Charis' gift of calming and healing. There would have been a good chance we would never leave the bedroom.

"*Alpha, Luna.*" Marcus's voice resonated through our mind-link. Kane sighed heavily, now pinching his nose. The warmth and heaviness of his body had me pulling him back down on me. Chuckling, he continued to kiss my neck. "We have a situation. I wouldn't disturb you unless it was extremely important, but I think the Fae Kingdom Treaty has been implemented." My head rose just enough for Kane to take a hint to remove his body. We had already sent warriors to help him with some unruly Court members, but more?

"What kind of situation, Marcus?" my voice rang out. *We literally signed the treaty a few weeks ago, and now they already need more help?*

"King Osirus's Parliament, as well as his Court, has been compromised. He wants to do a full takeover by chasing out his Court and Parliament and starting anew. His small band of supporters wants our help, reinforcements if you will."

"Dumb bastard fae planned this," Kane grumbled, helping me get up from the ground. "He signed that treaty knowing damn good and well this was going to happen. He could have had the decency to warn us. We've got enough problems."

Aaaaand here comes Kane's tension back again.

"*Did you hear that, Marcus?*" I linked.

"*Yup, loud and clear. I'll prepare the meeting room.*"

Our romp through the forest started out to be playful and fun, but now that it had quickly gone sour, my terrible attitude was back. Having a beautiful baby just upstairs and now a mate that was both frustrated with the new treaty already having to come into play within just a few short weeks had him stewing.

Anytime a treaty of this magnitude was signed, there was always a chance we would have to answer its calling. As much as Kane believed Osirus had this planned all along, I couldn't say for sure. On several occasions, Osirus has written there were problems with his Court, but never stated he would need our help so desperately.

Since my parents were off talking to outlying tribes, I was the person to speak to in their absence. I didn't want that to happen, but I didn't have much choice. Mother frequently told me that this time would come. I just wished it wasn't so soon after my daughter was born.

Marcus sat next to Kane on the right side of the large conference room table. August, our gamma, held many piles of papers containing maps, trails, and recent budget inquiries from the Cerulean Moon Kingdom castle. "For you." August held out the papers. I blew my breath out through my nose harshly, not excited to be dealing with accounting.

The top warriors, Sean and Carson, sat at the end of the table. I remembered them because they protected Melina from that awful werewolf, Esteban. But where was Rex?

Sitting on Kane's lap, he pulled me closer to his body, his head resting on my chest. I only patted his head.

My poor alpha.

Marcus stood up, dusting off his chest, holding a clipboard, and clicking a pen over and over. "First item of business is... where the fuck is Rex?"

Nudging Kane, I whispered, "I didn't put the 'f' word on the agenda. He added that." I pointed to Marcus.

Kane only chuckled, patting my back with his enormous hands.

"He's missing," August spoke up. "Rex asked to leave three days ago. Alpha approved, but he was supposed to return today. He hasn't shown up yet." Kane growled angrily, running his hands through his hair.

"He has until sundown, then we will send out the trackers." Sean and Carson looked at each other. Their eyes showed concern as they realized their friend, the leader of the group, was now in trouble.

Marcus cleared his throat, interrupting the worried staring contest between the two friends. Sean shook his head, looking into his lap. "Now for the real reason we are here. We have received word that King Osirus has requested our help. The fae Parliament and Court have been trying to raise a coup. Osirus has known this for some time but has waited for his mate to give him the extra motivation. They have yet to mate, but she has been sent to the Isle of Dragons for her safety. Now he needs us to help overthrow the Court speaker, Cosmo."

A young female omega rushed into the room, looking up and down at the table. Once she spotted me sitting on Kane's lap, she raced to me, her hands trembling. "Luna." I grabbed her hands. The omegas and I had gained a wonderful friendship, seeing each other as equals with work around the pack house. Anytime I had a free moment, I was in the kitchen helping them prepare meals and showing them minor tricks on how to make a dish more flavorful. Now that Evelyn was here, I barely had time to visit.

"Luna, I'm sorry to interrupt. There was a message from the speaking mirror from Alaneo." The entire table sat up straight, listening to her. Her eyes were petrified at all the high-ranking werewolves staring. Pulling on her hand, I had her eyes look into mine.

"Just look at me and breathe." Her heavy breathing subsided.

"Alaneo gave more reasons for why they need the extra forces. Cosmo has his own soldiers, and magic is involved. Rex tried to kidnap the future queen, Melina!" the omega word vomited all over me. Sean and Carson slammed their hands on the table.

"Lies!" they screamed. "There is no way he would do that!" The table erupted into arguments, yelling across the table and more growls. Concentrating, I tried to emit calm from my body, using the techniques my mother and the sorceress tutor had taught me. Kane's body relaxed first. Watching the table, Marcus, along with August, sat back in their seats, and other high-ranking warriors sat down as well until Sean and Carson stood, stunned.

"It's Luna's aura. She emits calming and healing properties in the air. Now, sit." Marcus ordered Carson's friends. I hadn't used my power much because of my pregnancy, but I was definitely going to use it now.

"Now, let's talk about this calmly," I spoke. "What do you mean Rex tried to kidnap Melina? He's shown only friendly protectiveness over her."

The omega continued to hold my hand, her hair swaying down her back. "Alaneo said there was an enchantment, and now he fears witches might be involved!"

Chapter Six

Kane

"Witches?" I questioned. Bergarian had a low number of witches since the War of the Shifters. They were considered a dying breed. Now they huddled in small covens all throughout Bergarian, not hailing to any kingdom but lived as small individual covens that protected each other. They never dared hail allegiance to one kingdom or another to give the upper hand.

If the witches had formed an alliance with the rogue vampires, we were going to be in trouble. Clara, who had been training in both history, war techniques, luna duties, and her future role as queen, leaned back in the chair with me. Her back filled my torso with warmth. Giana purred in her body, giving me pleasant vibrations straight to my dick.

Concentrate. Not now.

"If this is true, then we are in for a fight." Rubbing my chin with my tattooed fingers, Clara sighed quietly. If in any way she could avoid a war, she would jump at the chance. She wanted to preserve all life no matter mated, unmated, or even if they were deemed too evil for redemption. Her heart was full of compassion and light, the perfect balance to the darkness and thirst for justice.

Marcus cleared his throat, obviously getting impatient while Clara and I pondered our next moves. There was no brilliant answer on how to handle the situation, just that we would be in for a fight. "What next, Alpha? Should we prepare the squadrons? Alert the Cerulean Moon Kingdom warriors?"

Clara remained silent. Her finger traced her name along my ring finger. She laughed when I came home and presented it to her as a human symbol of our love as a tattoo on my finger.

"What say you, love?" My nose went to her shoulder, kissing it lightly between the covering of her shirt and her shoulder. Wanting nothing more than to rip it to the side and suck the ever-living shit out of it, she wiggled her ass causing me to groan.

"I know what you are thinking without linking my mind to yours," she whispered. Her body sat up straight, presenting herself as the regal queen she would be. Her hours of preparations, studying throughout the night, certainly showed. She was everything her mother was, but I could feel the lack of confidence in her heart.

"Ready the Crimson Shadows pack's squadrons one through three. The remaining two will stay here to protect the pack. If we need assistance, we will call for them. The Cerulean Moon Kingdom palace warriors will remain, making sure this isn't some sort of ploy to take the throne while my parents are away."

August's head ticked my way, giving a curt nod and heading out of the room to prepare the warriors. "We leave in the next hour." At Clara's command, they bowed their head. Then, they stood, mind-linking while walking out the door.

"What of us?" Carson chimed in. "We are your highest skilled trackers. Do you want us to hunt out the magical deities?" Clara's nose scrunched, wiggling it from side to side. Her body shifted, eyes pleading for what to say.

"How about they fight with us? They can determine unfamiliar smells or magical properties that keep us from spelling anything." My mate smiled at me, pecking at my lips.

"You're pretty smart, Alpha." Her head rested on my shoulder, body relaxing into mine.

"Out then." I grunted, ready for the rest of the room to clear, except my beta, who was grinning like a damn idiot.

"Even in acts of battle, you are both lovesick puppies," he cooed until his smile faltered. "I'll meet you out back behind the pack house. We will depart when you arrive." Marcus stepped out of the room, only looking back one more time in longing.

He didn't long for my mate. I understood my best friend's look. He longed for his own mate, but his mind was made up. She would never come. Why he would give up that thought, I'd never know, but soon he would have her and I'd make sure he loved and respected her. First thing my dumb ass would do is make him put his dick away or cut it off.

"I will go feed Evelyn before we leave." Clara's bright smile became forced. "We will be gone for a few days, won't we?" Kissing her lips gently, I hummed in agreement.

"I expect a week." Her head fell to her hands. Roughly grabbing her chin, I growled.

"None of that. She will be fine." My rough lips slammed against her, dominating her mouth. My lips were the Sahara desert, and she was my oasis. Forcing my tongue into her mouth, she gripped my hair, breathing slightly through her nose since I would not let her come up for air. Clara's lips, now red from my fangs pulling on her tender skin, pulled away. Half-hooded eyes stared back at me.

Her frown now turned, smiled, held so much love. "I know. I feel bad leaving her. She is just so young."

"She will grow quickly," I mumbled into her lips. My nose trailed her cheek. "A luna and being a princess will be a lot of work, but I know you can do it. I will ask you one thing, though." Clara's lips tried to capture mine, but I pulled away.

"Stay here," I pleaded. Clara giggled, pulling the hair band from my hair. I didn't want her to fight. I never would want to, and my reasons were just. My mate is a strong one. I just didn't want to put her in danger.

"You know I can't. Not when our pack fights for our safety as well." A grumble rattled through me. It was true. If there was no treaty in place, we would still fight. Having Osirus as a ruler would be far better than a wicked Parliament and Court trying to overthrow the sneaky fae. I didn't need things to get any worse.

Clara stood up, slapping her ass hard. She yelped in surprise, sashaying her body out the door. If we weren't leaving in an hour, I'd take her to the nearest closet and fuck her there. Our daughter would soon crawl, and hiding our romps in the sheets would be limited to the pattering feet in the middle of the night. Finding new ways to take my mate in the most unexpected places was now my new goal, and closets were on the list.

Clara

My legs grew heavy walking up the stairs to the fourth floor. It wasn't because I was weak or my body was exhausted, but that my daughter would have to be left alone for days, and the sadness radiated through my body. The few weeks of breastfeeding were wonderful. I felt like a real mother, and now she, as well as the rest of my children, would have to be raised by a nanny or by their grandmothers in my absence.

To have a 'normal' life as a human and raise a child as 'average' looked wonderful at times. Spending every waking moment with your child, loving them, caring for them, and wiping away every tear. I craved that, spending every moment with them, but that was not my life and never would be.

The loneliness some mothers felt as their mates or husbands worked through the day, to be left alone with just children would be difficult. Being a mother in general was hard, each of us facing our internal and physical battles. The grass was always greener on the other side until you found the random piece of cow poop in the middle of the lawn.

Grinning ear to ear, I had thought of all the wonderful times my children and I would spend together once this battle was over, once all battles were over. My gut told me things were coming, evil was coming rather. We were far from over from fighting just Osirus's war to win back his crown and right to rule over his new nation. There would be others, and that brought dark, ominous clouds over my always cheery attitude around others.

Opening the nursery door, Naomi had Evelyn on the floor. My sweet pup was swatting at the beautiful playmat with hanging toys above her head. Her eyes concentrated, using her tiny hands to grab a hanging moon above her.

"There's Mommy," Naomi cooed, picking up Evelyn. Could it be possible that my daughter could have grown a few centimeters while I was gone? It had to be possible because she was holding her head up as strong as a human three-month-old. Her tiny fingers widened and closed to a fist as she saw me reaching.

"Hi, my little Evelyn." My eyes watered as I grabbed her. Pulling at my shirt, her tummy growled, causing her to grunt. Lifting my shirt to feed her, Naomi laughed silently to herself as she stood cleaning up the mess of toys.

"I see my son had a good time." Blushing, I tried to pull my shirt lower only to have Evelyn pull it up and away from my body, showing more of Kane's love bites. "It's all right. His father is the same." She chuckled.

"I need to ask a favor." My eyes steamed with warmth. The tears were coming, but I promised myself I would not cry, not in front of my pup. I had to be the good, strong mother for her.

"Anything." Naomi came to sit beside me, watching Evelyn guzzle down the last of her meal.

"King Osirus is at war with his Court and Parliament, trying to take over his throne." Naomi gasped, gripping my arm. "I need to leave for a while, hopefully no longer than a week." Her eyes softened, understanding the conflict I felt in my heart.

Leaving my daughter, my pup, my little girl, would be devastating, but I knew I had to go to protect her future. There would be more firsts for me to watch, her first tooth, her first bike ride; I hoped to be there for it all, but until then, I had to keep her safe, and that was to help Kane lead a pack of wolves into my first battle in over six months.

"She will be fine." Naomi rubbed my back.

"It's hard." My voice cracked. A traitorous tear fell down my cheek, landing on Evelyn's bare leg. "I don't want to leave her, but I must protect her." Naomi petted my hair, pulling it behind my ear. Her soft touches comforted me of the family bond we shared.

As much as I craved my mother, this woman has been strong and kept me held together. I saw her as my beautiful mother-in-law turned best friend when my mother wasn't around. She had seen me at my worst and at my best, coming home from dealing with the old rogue Marcellus.

"She will be fine," she cooed. "She won't remember much of her first years of life. You will be with her in spirit and the bond you share with her. I don't know if you realize, but a child being born of a bond is special. You can feel their pain, their fear, and their happiness if you concentrate hard enough. Radiating your love to her from afar, she will never forget you. No matter how quickly she grows physically." Naomi tickled Evelyn's feet as she finished. "Isn't that right?" she cooed at the little squeal she let out.

"You are right." Squeezing her tightly, she cooed while I held her out to see her beautiful face. She had her father's eyes, electric blue, and the dark hair we both shared. Her little toes took after me and her strong fingers, of course, after her dad. The perfect combination of the both of us.

Her personality worried me. I wanted my daughter to be fierce, but calm enough to make the right decisions.

"And so you know," Naomi added, "I know you read human books about breastfeeding, but werewolves can go long periods without breast-feeding their children. Until Evelyn flat out refuses you, which will be around three months of the average wolf, you will feed her when you are around her. The gods understood the importance of wolves and fighting for territory. You won't dry until Evelyn deems it so."

These stupid hormones raging through me! My eyes dropped more tears, no matter how much I tried to pull them back. "Thank you, Naomi. I don't know what I would do without you." My forehead landed on her shoulder while Evelyn pulled my hair.

"I worried the same. My mother taught me everything. You have been dealt a tough hand being born a princess, but the gods have blessed you as well. Every step of the way, I'll be there, hmm?"

Kane's heated body alerted me he was standing in the doorway. Turning to see my mate, his normal scowl lifted to a smile as his eyes locked with me. "There are my three favorite girls." His deep voice reverberated in the room. "It's time to go, my mate, defend our pack."

"And our future," I muttered, tracing my finger across Evelyn's cheek.

Chapter Seven

Clara

Half the warriors stood shifted into their wolves, while the other half strapped packs of supplies to the wolves' backs. Wolves pranced around the area, yipping and nipping at each other's heels with excitement. Drills were standard, not taking the command that Kane implemented earlier seriously. Being prepared was Kane's motto, and the extra supposed drill this week didn't disappoint anyone.

I, on the other hand, was sweating with uneasiness. Giana was circling in my mind, mumbling and grumbling. She could have been praying to the goddess or just preparing herself for our first battle, but I was too distracted to ask her. Kane strode up to the front of the lines. The final wolves were being strapped with large packs of supplies for tents from the ever-helpful omegas with food and spare clothes.

Kane stood in front of the awaiting crowd, bare-chested, in just a pair of black shorts. Wolves continued to mind-link each other, ready for the drill to be over with and get back to regular activities. I stood to the side of it all, watching the platoons of wolves lined up in perfect rows. Colors of black, gray, tan, and whites filled the area. Marcus and his sandy wolf approached, sitting on his haunches as Kane waited for the growls and howls to settle.

"This is not a drill," Kane spoke powerfully. The wolves stilled, listening to the authority of Kane's power. Heads perked up in question. "This is real. Lives could be lost if you don't remember your training. I advise you to look out for one another. Remember, we hunt and fight in packs. We are not the singleton hunter in times of battle. Your pack is your lifeline. Remember to rely on each other."

After watching Kane for so many months on the sidelines, showing me how he and Marcus strategically assigned smaller packs within our larger one, it helped take down stronger enemies more quickly instead of fighting alone. It saved their energy so warriors could fight for more extended periods.

"Your luna will be with us." The entire Crimson Shadows pack's eyes went to me. I stood still, head held high like mother had taught me, even though I swore Giana was peeing herself on the inside. "Please be aware this is her first full-frontal battle. She may have beaten the best of you, such as Baslik." Kane's head nodded to his strongest warrior. Baslik only grinned, bowing before me. "But she has yet to face more than one enemy at a time. Clara is more than capable of taking care of herself." Kane smiled at me. "She is your luna, the heart of the pack. If her heart stops, so does mine." Letting out a shaky breath, I joined Kane at the front line.

"We travel today, meeting just north of the Golden Light Kingdom in the province of Sallee. There, we will give further orders." Howls erupted, the grass being entirely ruined by the claws pulling at the soil.

At least it wasn't my flower bed.

Torin flashed his eyes toward me, his shorts falling to a heap on the ground. His tall half-beast form standing in front as I pulled the enlarged shirt over my head. Shifting, my bones cracked, and fur sprouted on my body instantly. Giana stretched her body, shaking our tail playfully, letting her front paws wiggle in anticipation. "Are you ready, My Luna?" Kane's voice sounded in my head.

"Ready when you are."

The Bergarian continent was large. It stretched as far as the United States on Earth, but it could take us hours rather than take days to cross the land by running. The speed at which wolves could run was astounding, but the paths were not wide and not well-traveled. It would still take us a good portion of the day to arrive at our final destination.

Giana yipped, waiting for Torin to lead the way. The warriors behind us loomed closely, especially behind me. Marcus was to stay close, along with Baslik, the poor warrior I defeated when I had my hissy fit when Kane kept information from me all those months ago.

"No racing today," Kane mentioned in my head. "We have to keep everyone safe, travel as a unit." Torin's body knelt down before me, putting his enormous claws next to my cheek.

"I would never." I giggled. "But maybe you all should work on your conditioning." Torin stood up, howling for the warriors to follow as we began our long journey to the northern area of the Golden Light Kingdom.

With the impending battle pushed back into my mind, I enjoyed the scenery while it was to last. Many did the same.

The pounding of paws against the dirt, and the clouds rushing by as the wind parted our fur, brought all of our animals to the surface. There were yips of joy at feeling the soil between the pads of our paws, the leaves touching our fur, keeping us close to the ground instead of flying toward the sky with our speed. The entire pack's hearts beat as one, one unit, one pack.

When going from one region to the next, the terrain shifted quickly. The pride lands reminded me of the African plains, brown grasses, sparse trees, and the few lakes and ponds where many colorful and different animals not familiar to Earth gathered. The prides of shifter felines had taken root back closer to their homes, no longer wandering about as they usually do. Mother and Father had planned to visit each one and invite them to stay at the palace. My worry was that many would try to fend off rogues themselves.

Once we left the pride lands, we stayed north, avoiding any areas that could lurk with vampire rogues. Further south held dense trees, perfect places for vampires to hide and slink in the dark. The mountains to the north kept the cool wind blowing in our fur, keeping us from getting too hot with the constant running.

Passing by the divide of the kingdoms, the elven colonies sat at the mountain's base. Reading about their culture intrigued me by how they kept the area of their tribes safe from enemies and the weather. Taking the leaves of the forests above them, they etched them together using a string of magic-like thread, sewing them together, turning the leaves into a giant glass piece that would bring in the sun but keep out the rain and snow. Each day, they took the time to water all the plants that surrounded them in their hive-like living area, homing in on their passion for nature.

Further up the mountains, dragon tribes settled. They liked their privacy; few records in the palace or our pack house had information regarding their history. Most of my information came from Kane, who has befriended the current alpha of the largest dragon shifter tribe. Adam met us the first day I walked through the portal and had visited us several times over the past months.

Moving forward, we entered the Golden Light Kingdom territory. The suns—or 'light sources'—here shone brighter than that of the Cerulean Moon Kingdom. My eyes took minutes to adjust, only for Giana to groan in my head, trying to filter the rays.

"This is terrible." Kane blinked his eyes. "Why is it so fucking bright?"

"Duh, because it is the 'Golden Light Kingdom,'" Marcus replied sarcastically. "I brought some shades with me just in case. You guys want a pair?" Giana laughed, her yip sounding like a howl.

"I just didn't expect it to be this bright," I replied. "I just thought it was sunny all the time."

"Think of Vermillion. The light sources are weak there to help house the vampires. The Cerulean Moon Kingdom has light, sure, but it is comparable to Earth. That is why the shifters tend to stay closer to our side of the continent. The light isn't as bright. Our eyes are sensitive, so we may see in the dark. Our bodies have to accommodate the light, but it takes time for our wolves to adjust." Marcus's feet pounded the dirt as we ran. The heavy pack on his back did not cause him any difficulty as he ran beside us.

"Look at you being all smart and shit," Kane replied through the link. "Maybe you will make a strong alpha once it's handed over to you." Marcus snorted, shaking his head.

"Well, I had to make sure I upped my game since there are some horny fairies over here. I would not be blinded by their beauty and make my wolf use all concentration to adjust to light when we could adjust something else." Marcus howled as Kane shook his head in annoyance.

We trotted toward Sallee. It was a tiny encampment of fae families that preferred the quiet life away from its capital. The hordes of wolves approaching startled children playing on the dirt path and ran back toward their homes. Kane and the rest of the warriors took this time for us to shift and be able to speak with our fae comrades.

Once the last bit of clothing was put on my body, a fae with a long red beard approached. He looked much older than a fae should look with his bushy eyebrows and unruly hair. "I am Everett, Your Highness and Alpha." Everett bowed with one arm across his chest. "I will take you to King Osirus's tent. He should arrive within the hour. He had to get the future-queen Melina away for her safety."

I smiled outwardly at Kane. It had only been a few weeks since introducing Melina and Osirus, and I was happy to see that progress was being made. Osirus had waited for his mate for so long, and once I saw her, my mind went straight to him. My gifts had helped me place the two together because that night when I slept, I saw them together again, this time both bearing each other's marks.

"Where will she be going?" I asked as we walked inside the enormous leather tent. It had been set up with a rudimentary table, a map of the entire palace grounds, with pins sticking in various places. My hand brushed over it, feeling the cool, smooth texture of the parchment.

"Land of Dragons." Everett adjusted his sword on his belt. "Horus took her. The seas are too rough for any boat, and the wind is too harsh for any fae or fairy." I hummed, agreeing with Osirus's plan. Osirus had told me of Horus, the mighty dragon still living on the mainland. Osirus had protected him when he was just a hatchling, and now the dragon sees him as his master or parental figure, no matter how many times Osirus told him to leave and be with his own kind.

"When do we fight?" Kane grunted. His hands sprouted claws, scratching the worn table. Ribbons of wood fell to the floor as his eyes glared at Everett.

Giana soothed Torin for the entire run. Thoughts of blood spraying from enemies made his heart pound faster, the excitement of how his claws would pull the skin of those who dare try to hurt this pack or me. This was his first battle involving me by his side, and along with Torin's rage to protect, I could feel Kane's inner turmoil. He was worried I would look at him differently and not the big puppy I saw in our bedroom.

Everett chuckled but dared not pat Kane on the back. "Soon, Alpha. There is a small militia of fae enemy soldiers under the power of the Court Speaker Cosmo just south of here, but His Majesty has a request before we take the charge."

Kane lifted a brow, waiting for an answer. Everett stood back, holding his hands out in front of him. "I am but a messenger. Please understand." Kane growled in irritation, shaking the posts of the tent. He wasn't in the mood to prance off into another land, risking our warriors after just signing a treaty several weeks ago.

"His Majesty wants the least amount of casualties possible. In fact, not killing any of the opposing soldiers would be preferable."

Chapter Eight

Kane

My fist came down brutally on the wooden table in front of me, ripping the map and splitting the wood into tiny splinters. Those stupid little pins scattered to the floor. Clara jumped back, putting both hands to her mouth to hold in a squeak. My head darted to her, hoping the pieces of wood didn't hurt her perfect skin. Her eyes glanced at the table and back at me. This was the most anger she had seen come from Torin and me. Anytime she was around, she made me melt, but the request sent by King Osirus was ludicrous.

Clara's eyes softened, her tiny steps coming up closer to me by putting her arms around my bicep. The shirt I was previously wearing was now ripped to shreds by the hair trying to sprout on my back as Torin tried to force a shift. "Are you fucking kidding me!?" I roared, the tent flapping because of my monstrous voice rather than the swift winds of the Golden Light Kingdom.

My mate lovingly tugged at my arm, not harsh like some dick would do to get my attention during a rage. No, she gently tapped it, causing my pussy self to look down at her lovingly. She blinked those lashes at me, giving me the sweetest look of adoration. "Baby." I growled, my other hand flying out to look at the monstrosity of King Osirus's bodyguard. Why the fuck did he need a bodyguard anyway? He was a fucking fae king. Didn't he have some deep powers or some shit?

"But, baby," I whined again, glaring at the red-headed fool. I wondered if his carpet were the same colors as his drapes.

"He said I can't kill anyone!" Torin growled inside my chest while Giana was chastising him. Giana had more of a mouth than Clara. She wasn't afraid to nip at Torin in the ass from time to time. My Clara knew how to handle me. She had me melting just by giving me my pet name.

"Babe," she cooed, trailing her finger around the small wolf tattoo with her foxlike markings I recently had placed on my arm. "Let's hear Osirus out." Her voice was barely a whisper, making me listen to the soft pants of her breath. Her eyes glanced toward Everett, who was slowly backing away, and Finley, who had barged in at my outburst.

"Don't you go anywhere." I growled, pulling Clara into my arms. Turning around so I didn't have to see the nasty pre-pubescent beard he was trying to grow, I nuzzled into my mate's neck. Her legs went around my waist as I felt her hand leave my neck, waving at the fae to leave.

This was bloody insane. How could you have a damn battle—actually, a fucking war—for the crown if I couldn't kill anybody?! What was the point? Might as well let those stupid fae soldiers just walk into the tent and ask for a fucking tea party. My breathing picked up, thinking of what type of mess we had gotten into. We could have been walking into a bloody trap.

"My big Alpha," Clara cooed, wrapping her fingers around my unkempt hair. It had grown the past few months. Clara had really enjoyed pulling on it in the bedroom, and hell, I'd grow it out as long as she continued to yank on it when I ate her pussy raw. "Let's hear him out. I'm sure there is a reason. If you are a good alpha, we can play a game." My head perked up at 'game'. Fuck, even Torin was rolling around on his back, wagging his tail like an idiot.

Clara had become more adventurous, even while pregnant. Now that she was without pup, the possibilities were endless.

"What kind of game?" I grumbled, trying not to show how excited I really was. I didn't want to look too desperate. Shit, I was. I liked her games. Like the one where she dressed up as some dominatrix in that leather skirt and pleasured herself in front of me, tying me to the bed and making me watch. I wanted that again. Torin purred too loudly, making Clara giggle.

"A racing game," she purred into my ear. "With obstacles." Clara got my attention at obstacles. I loved a challenge; Torin demanded it. "What do I have to do?" My hand trailed down to her ass, squeezing the plumpness from the curve of her back.

"Well" —she sat up in my arms—"it's a race to capture as many fae soldiers as you can, without killing them." I groaned, putting my forehead to hers. This was gonna be fucking hard. "You are to capture as many fae soldiers without mortally wounding them, either. Don't be tricky." She kissed the shell of my ear. Leaning to her lips, she pulled away. "But you have to capture more than any other werewolf from our pack." My claws lengthened, pulling her skin with the bluntness I willed. Clara gave me a heavy challenge, but I could do it. I would show her I was the best mate for her.

"And the prize?" I growled. Clara giggled like it was the funniest thing in the world, her finger tracing the steel crescent moon necklace around my neck. Rolling her bottom lip into her mouth, biting it with the fangs that were slowly growing, her green eyes impaled my blue ones.

"Uninterrupted playtime, no baby, no alpha or luna duties, and an un-limited amount of whipped cream, some ropes, feathers, and play outfits of your choice." Her eyes fluttered innocently. My mate was doing this for the sake of both of the kingdoms, to save us from having to go to war later with the Golden Light Kingdom under the wrong rule, but I couldn't help but be intrigued at the idea that my mate thought she was in control.

Who was I kidding? She was in control.

"And something else to consider," she whispered seductively. "Mother says my heat is approaching." *Fuck.*

My Clara in heat was a fun Clara. Damn, she could go almost a week straight. My grip tightened around her ass. "Does that mean I can put another pup in you?" I growled lowly. Pushing her up against the post of the tent, my cock ground into her core, having her moan my name as I continued to assault her.

"If you think I'm an okay mother," she whispered more seriously. "I'm already away from her now, and she is only weeks old." One hand went to cup her cheek. "Baby"—I kissed her lips—"there is never the 'right time' to have a pup. Just like you will never be prepared to be queen, a werewolf, a mate," I whispered. "You could wait your whole life for the 'right moment' for something, and it will never come," I cooed, pushing her hair behind her ear. "You are an amazing mother. I couldn't ask for anything better." My mate smiled, still hesitant to believe me. "We don't have to have another pup right now. Having your heat arrive is enough of a prize." Clara laughed, her beautiful smile flooding her cheeks.

"Can I get a preview of the prize? You know, to make sure the goods check out?" My hand lowered, cupping her pussy, palming it so the friction would drive her wild. Her arousal went deep into my lungs until Marcus cleared his throat.

Fucking shit, just three minutes, and I would have had her creaming in my hand.

"What?" I barked, gently putting my mate down. She pulled her hair back into the ponytail that had ripped out of her hair. "Even on a battle-field, huh?" Marcus smirked as he walked in. "King Osirus requests you in the new royal tent since you destroyed this one." We all scanned the splintered wood on the floor. Shrugging my shoulders, I grabbed Clara's hand and walked to the new tent.

King Osirus' followers were nothing but farmers with pitchforks and fairies that wouldn't be able to stay in full human form for more than a few hours. Osirus's army, which was now under the complete control of

Cosmo, was going to crush us. I ran my fingers through my hair, Clara took several steps to my one until I pulled her up.

"Stop!" she whined. "I'm a warrior right now, not some dainty thing," she grumbled. Chuckling in her ear, I kissed her cheek. "You will always be my dainty little mate. Besides, the fighting hasn't begun yet."

Entering the tent, Osirus was wearing different battling attire. None of the fancy metals adorned him the last time I saw him fight, helping Clara with Marcellus. The cape was gone, no gold cuffs around his hair and wrists. He was down to the bare minimum, his chest open like the rest of the fae eating the light of the light sources.

"Now that the information has sunk in, are you ready to do this, Alpha Kane?" Osirus's tone was clipped as he flipped through the pages of maps, most likely of the underground tunnels of the castle. Clara stepped forward, being the more diplomatic of our pairing. She stood at the table, her back straight and her hands ready to write notes on the parchment that was handed to her.

"As mentioned before, the least amount of casualties possible. In fact, I don't want any," he repeated the phrase. Marcus shook his head, crossing his arms in disbelief. Hell, I was too. What was he trying to accomplish?

"There is something wrong." Osirus's voice strained. "I don't know what it is, but they all so willingly took to Cosmo without hesitation, many of the soldiers who have followed me for years under a haze or fog. The only soldiers that have remained dedicated are the ones I see daily. Such as Everett, Finley, and Braxton, and my close attendants, Peoni and Primrose."

"You think that there could be a spell they are under, then? Fighting against their will?" Clara asked. Osirus's lips were now in a pursed line. He nodded. He waved for one of his untrained soldiers, dressed in nothing but linen pants and a worn tunic. Setting a small darkened glass vile, he bowed. "Thank you, Drew. You may ready yourself. We attack as soon as the first light source hits the trees to the west." Drew bowed again, leaving the tent.

"What's that?" I stepped up to pick it up. To any ordinary wolf, this would look like a werewine flask that could be easily concealed in a coat pocket or dress pants. The intricate design of the glass was purposeful, even though there was no set pattern. "That"—Osirus pointed—"is something I haven't seen before. I was hoping you two would know. As I sent Melina away, I found it on the outskirts of the palace grounds. I sent it to a small coven who gratefully decided to join the cause. The only thing they could find that would be of use was a drop of vampire blood on the inside."

"It's a pretty bottle," Clara mused, looking through the small-rimmed glass. "Was it entirely filled with blood at one time?" Osirus shook his head, taking the bottle back. "No, they mentioned other dried herbs and spices, maybe a fingernail or fang of some animals. It may be nothing at all. I just found it interesting it was near the palace walls."

Clara scribbled on the parchment in front of her, drawing the glass vile along with notes of Osirus's words. Clara had grown her knowledge in just a few short months. Her mother had tutored her well, learning to seek out information that she may or may not need in the future and filing it away in her own library she had created herself.

"If you find more, let us know," Clara mused, shoving the parchment in her pocket. "If you find it strange, it must mean something." Osirus hummed as two more farm soldiers approached. "The first platoon is ready for you, Your Majesty." Primrose, a fairy with bright pink hair pulled back into a neat bun, held a sword at her side. "Peoni is still on patrol. Last word twenty minutes ago. The first wave of Cosmo's soldiers are coming, making their way here by sunset."

"Excellent." Osirus rolled up the map, handing it to Everett. "I hope this doesn't put a damper on your fun, Alpha Kane." Osirus held out his hand for me to shake. Taking him by the forearm, we shook with all our strength. How could I kill an innocent soldier? If magic was involved, my duty to my luna, my king and my queen was to bring justice to those who could not speak for themselves.

That was what my mate wanted from the beginning: to help, give second chances. This fight would be for her, for those innocent being played as pawns in the battle of a power struggle. "If they are innocent"—I stared at Osirus in the eyes—"they will live. If not, give me what you will, and Torin and I will take care of it."

Chapter Nine

Under the Moon

Osirus stared over at the map of his kingdom. It was vast, and the very few warriors who agreed to help him would hardly make a dent in the soldiers he had trained. Osirus's nails gripped the table, ripping the corner of the map. He had nothing but farmers with pitchforks, but it was more than he thought that would come to his aid. They had been ready for a revolution for some time. Little did they know it would be him revolting against his own kingdom. Osirus would take any help he could get. He was at a significant disadvantage and was desperate to take back the crown. He could not fathom how his entire army would turn against him in such a short amount of time.

Clara sighed, putting her hand over his, patting it lightly.

"We will get through this." Her power had made him succumb to her calmness. Osirus sighed heavily, now thinking of his mate that had safely landed on the Isle of Dragons. He had only had her for such a short time, and she had broken down her walls to let him in. If he had just a few more days, he could have marked her if he didn't have to deal with this mess.

Pulling out his sword, causing the room to stand back, he held his back rigid as his head, General Finley, stood close. "Awaiting your orders, Your

Majesty." Holding the handle to his sword, Finley bowed with his arm across his chest.

Osirus fumbled with the parchment before him, circling areas with a red root that bled on the map in just the right areas. Clara and Kane looked on, watching where they were to 'dispose' of the soldiers once they were knocked out or had surrendered.

Kane was more than ready for the challenge, not that he was ready to take orders from a fae, but that of his mate. His mate concentrated heavily on the red marks scattered across the map, taking her time to memorize the entire area. Kane's hand wrapped around her waist, feeling her heart beat heavily in her chest. His mate was more than ready for this, all the preparing and learning strategic planning from Kane on nights when their daughter could not sleep. He could feel her unease through their bond while he tried to concentrate on her.

Torin growled lowly in his mind, upset that he would not see blood today from that of the enemy. Kane continued to calm him using his mate's calming aura, which seemed to sate him just a little.

"Remember, enough to maim, but not kill," Osirus reiterated. The fae in the tent looked at Kane, who only nodded his head in recognition. Kane's knuckles cracked, fisting one at his side. Kane was never one with words, but when he spoke, everyone listened. Everett and Braxton looked on in worry, wondering if the blood-thirsty alpha would even heed the king's words, but with one quick kiss to his mate, they all let out a breath they didn't know they were holding.

The future royals of the Cerulean Moon Kingdom left the tent, hand in hand. Kane's mind-link was going a mile a minute. Taking the two platoons he had brought would not be enough, but during the journey, he and Clara had requested any shifters in the pride lands to come to help. They were a few hours behind them to pack and ready themselves for war. Slowly, they came into the camp, panthers, lions, and cheetahs. Clara gripped Kane's hand tighter, watching them shift and enter the camp.

All the shifters gathered the enormous crowd now at the beckoning call of Alpha Kane and his luna. Standing on the small platform, Clara stood by her mate's side, looking at him with such warmth and love. Would she still feel the same once he sees him in his beastly form fighting against an enemy? Even if it was just to maim them?

"Listen up!" Kane growled out to the crowd. The once murmuring shifters silenced, no longer speaking of the excitement. Kane gripped his hands again, causing them to crack, holding Torin at bay just a few minutes longer. "There will be no killing today," his voice spoke deeply with conviction. His luna had agreed to Osirus, and Kane would follow her every word. "You are to maim and capture. These soldiers will be put back into the fae society. There is something amiss, and we will not harm the innocent."

Shifters from the pride lands whispered to each other, their shoulders slumping and pointing their hands accusingly to Kane. Kane's watchful eye had Torin growling out. His fangs lengthened to an abnormal length from just an ordinary wolf. "My words stand!" He roared. Kane's warriors only bowed their heads at the sheer power that radiated over the crowd. The pride land shifters knelt, feeling the overwhelming feeling that befell them. They had witnessed nothing of this magnitude, but they had felt it today.

"My command stands. Fail to obey, and you will be taken care of. Personally. By me." Torin's eyes flashed yellow, even Marcus feeling the heat of his half-beast. Marcus's worry went to that of his alpha. He knew it had been a long while since Torin had had a good fight. Since Clara came into his life, he had a different wolf, but could a mate completely sate the warrior?

Clara stood holding Kane's hand like nothing had happened at all. Her mind was reeling at how her daughter was doing, if she was safe, and if her parents had made their rounds to the Cerulean Moon Kingdom's small territories. Once she came to, she realized all the warriors were either on their knees or shaking in fear.

"Babe." She nudged him. Kane shook his head, his yellow eyes retreating. "We need to get going." Clara pointed to Osirus, mounted on his horse, gripping the reins tightly. Montu pranced unsettled. The heat of his nostrils flaring had Osirus gripping the reins higher to control his battle horse.

"The first wave approaches!" Osirus shouted. The first platoon had shifted in a blink while the others were mind-linked by Marcus to their respective positions. Clara stripped the light dress over her head, only for Kane to stand before her until she completed her transformation.

Kane didn't bother to take off his shorts. He ripped them in an instant as his beast fully transformed. The blackened hair, deep golden eyes, and muscles doubled in size since his mating with his Clara had wolves taking long walks around him. His breath was heated and heavy as the steam came from his maw. "Everyone out!" His roar could be heard down the foothills. The pounding of paws hitting the bright grasses is now being scuffed and ripped by the passing claws.

The opposing fae heard the mighty roar down the foothills, the rumbling of paws hitting the ground. Many shook in fear, but they were trained soldiers of the crown. They woke up in the morning not knowing they would be in battle. Cosmo, the speaker of the Court, had said their king had lost his mind, trying to bring in a human girl to be their queen and ruining the ways of the fae. Many protested, believing that their king would never do such a thing.

Osirus trained with these same soldiers every day. He stood quiet and listened to generals, taking part as a regular soldier. All looked on with him in pride that their own king would go to war alongside them. He wasn't what the rumors had said. He wasn't the womanizer, the cold-hearted king. He cared, even for them.

As the fae argued in protest, their vision had hazed. They shook their heads, watching the smoke clear until they saw King Osirus in Cosmo's place. "We must fight until the end!" The fae didn't question. They raised their swords in honor of their king.

As they approached the small valley between the two hills, they saw King Osirus on the opposing side. "A trick!" their king spoke as he rode upon a black stallion, not that of his usual mode of transportation. His normal horse was a beautiful gold hue, hair braided down the sides of his mane. The fae looked at each other in question until a horn sounded. "Into formation!"

The fae scattered, pulling swords and bows ready to fight the animals that rushed the hill. Not once did any of them falter. Cosmo sat upon his horse, watching the rabid animals make crude noises. He snorted. "Stupid animals, not that of a fae at all." He scratched his nose as his horse backed away. Cosmo would not fight this, just command the army that Osirus so gracefully trained himself. Snickering to himself, he watched as the front line readied themselves to charge at the unruly animals while he stood in the background.

Kane was ahead of the charge, Clara running alongside. Their paws were in sync as Kane took the first fae down. His teeth ground into the leg of one, and his claws ripped the back tendons of another. Clara growled not to the opposing enemy but at Kane. "Easy!" She growled in his mind. Kane only whimpered, trying his best to calm Torin.

Fae, one by one, fell. The fae were the ones with the numbers, but the numbers dwindled quickly, with Kane taking out ten at a time by nipping their ankles. The rest of the wolves followed, nipping at their ankles to render them helpless and low to the ground. Finally, Osirus's unskilled fae rushed in, helping the fallen on wagons and securing them tightly to be taken to the encampment.

Cosmo faded into the background as he left the head general in charge of the battle. This was supposed to be quick, a battle that lasted only a day, but with Kane and King Osirus running in on his prized horse, Montu, Cosmo wasn't so sure. Gritting his teeth, he pulled his horse back, traveling back to the safe walls of the palace while the battle continued.

Meanwhile, Kane and his warriors began herding groups of fae like sheep. Kane had headed the charge, running the terrified fae near a rock wall. The soldiers had no commander with the general maimed, all done by Kane. Kane sneered, growling, his back paws scraping at the dirt until more wolves surrounded the captured fae to complete the large herd. Clara howled, running after the ones getting away. Using her sharp teeth, she took one down by the ankle. The female fae rolled on her back, looking back in fear. Not seeing the beautiful colors that the eyes of fae held, she saw a murky mist over them.

"Their eyes, Kane." Clara continued to pull the woman into the center of one circle. Dropping her ankle, she bolted out of the circle letting the warriors guide them to the proper holding space. "They are clouded. They look glazed." Clara perked her head up to her overly massive mate, who stared on, watching the now large army succumb to that of the shifters and farmers.

"Are you hungry, mate?" Torin rasped, still watching the wolves herd the fae. "I can fetch you a deer." Clara huffed her nose, shaking her tiny head. "No, I mean... there is something wrong." Clara ran to Osirus but could not communicate. She barked at him like she was speaking, ripping the ground up with her claws to get his attention. Montu huffed in annoyance, trying to step away. Osirus dismounted, pulling his cape from his body and laying it on Clara until she shifted back into human form. Torin watched from afar, angry that his mate would shift in front of another man.

Stomping toward them, Clara wrapped the surrounding cloak, explaining the situation with the warrior's eyes. Her voice was frantic, voice raising in high octaves, making Torin wince at the crackling of her voice. "There is something wrong, like a spell or curse! That bottle, the bottle from earlier!" Clara continued speaking, only to have Osirus's neck gripped by Torin's large clawed hands.

Clara screamed for Kane to stop, but Torin was in control. He pulled Osirus up by his neck, bringing him close to his face. "I come to help you, and you dare look at what is mine?" He salivated until the drool touched the bottom of Osirus's boots. Osirus only smirked, enjoying the altercation. Something about messing with the tremendous alpha had him reeling with laughter.

Torin went to crack his neck, but Clara was faster. She climbed up the back of her mate's tall body, completely naked and having her teeth elongate and pierce his marked shoulder. Torin's eyes rolled in the back of his head, letting go of Osirus, feeling the intense pleasure his mate had put into his body.

Clara didn't let go, her legs wrapped around his back. Torin slowly fell to his knees, succumbing to his mate. "Now that's enough!" Clara yipped at him, wiping the blood from her mouth. Torin pulled her around, holding her small, fragile body to his hairy one. His arms were so large they covered her entire body. No one could look at what was his. "Mine." He growled so all the surrounding shifters and fae could hear.

Torin purred, rubbing his scent onto his mate. She had forgotten who she belonged to. Only he could be around when she was naked. Torin growled, linking Marcus to take care of the soldier captives. He would teach his mate a lesson, make sure that she would never get naked in front of another male ever again.

Chapter Ten

Kane

T orin had taken over. I couldn't control him. I could only hold him back for so long as we gnawed at their ankles, rendering them immobile. Pulling him back from killing the fae, especially when they tasted like chicken on our tongue, had us shaking with rage. Once our warriors had bitten them, the haze in their eyes lessened. Not sure if it was the venom from our wolves or the sheer amount of pain that shook them from their stupor, they looked confused as they were led away.

Torin had mind-linked Marcus, ensuring Osirus's opposing army led to their proper quarters. They were already healing, but more questions spouted out from them as their weapons were seized. Torin growled as anyone got near, acting like a savage beast. My sweet mate only calmed us slightly as the frustration boiled in our blood.

Our warriors barred their necks, watching Torin holding our mate tightly in our arms. Her fingers tangled in the fur hanging from our jaw. "Torin, it's all right," she cooed at him. My mate was the only one that will calm him, but he radiated much resentment as he looked on the bloodless battlefield. Blood. He wanted more.

Huffing loudly, we turned, carrying our mate off into the nearby woods. The forest was dense and dark as the light sources set. Perfect for keeping prying eyes away from our mate. As much as Clara had become more comfortable shifting around our warriors, I hated it, and Torin loathed it.

It was natural to walk naked in Bergarian if you were a shifter. Many thought none of it, but not with us. Clara was ours, and we wanted no one to look at what was ours. Clara continued playing with the fur on our chest, twirling it into small loops of curl. She laughed, rubbing her head on our chest, Giana seeping her scent into our fur. This calmed Torin, only slightly.

Once we arrived in a small clearing, away from any shifter, fae, or fairy, we laid her down in the deep purple moss. Her eyes looked up at me, not taking her hand away, petting our cheek. "Now I know you are upset, Alpha," she tried to reason. "But that was uncalled for." Torin huffed in irritation, both claws pinning beside her shoulders as our body leaned over to pin her to the ground. This alone would bring any wolf to their feet, burying their nose into the sand to get away from such power. Not our mate. Our mate didn't fear us, even in her human form. At least when we weren't killing something.

Torin's nose trailed up her neck, breathing heavily, taking in her scent. "We are in the middle of a war, Torin." She pushed our chest. "I have to tell Osirus what is going on. They are under a spell. They aren't willingly fighting against him."

Torin growled, hearing the name. He didn't like Osirus one bit. He had seen her near-naked once before, and it was all we could do to keep it together. Torin growled, pulling his head back from Clara's neck. Not once did she flinch as she stared back into our eyes. "I know you are frustrated," she hummed, tickling our nose.

"You didn't get to release your frustration. You thought you were going to be killing some creatures, huh?" she cooed. "You know what else you haven't gotten a release from?" Clara chuckled as Torin shifted back into our human form. Bones cracked, and the fur sucked into our body until the tattoos beneath the fur formed. The piercings I refused to remove had Clara lick her lips. Her fingers pulled gently on our nipple piercing.

"Maybe you need to ravage something else?" She winked. Torin picked her up, having her straddle our waist. Clara's eyes flickered to show Giana on the other side. "Is my Alpha feeling frisky?" The growl in her chest tickled my piercings once I pinned her to the smooth bark of the tree. Torin's mouth descended on hers, sucking her tongue into our mouth. Moaning, her hips pushed forward, straight into his erection. The piercing in my mouth tinkled against her teeth.

"Torin." Her fingers went into his hair. There wasn't time to get our mate ready. Our cock was painfully hard while we lined up our leaking tip. "I don't think you have won the bet yet." She bit into our lip with her fangs. We groaned, not caring about the damn bet. We wanted her body now.

"Fuck the bet. Better yet, let me fuck you." Pushing into her deeply, her back arched, and her ample breasts leaked with milk for our child. Latching onto one nipple, she pulled my hair as I pulled at it harshly. "Torin!" she yelled out while we fucked her against the tree.

"You are our mate." Torin forced himself inside. "My mate," he mumbled into her tits. "Mine to fuck, mine to hold, mine to bare our pups." Giana couldn't reply, each thrust leaving her speechless as she held onto our shoulders. "*Mine.*" He growled again. Feeling our balls tighten, Giana rolled her eyes in the back of her head as we came into her womb, wrapping her in ropes of our seed.

"I'm not done." Torin growled in her ear, pushing her to the ground on all fours. He wanted to dominate all of her, each and every part, as her ass laid plump in the air. The yellow lights escaped the moss as we again lined up into her core. Rolling the ball of our piercing between her lips, we slipped back inside, only for Giana to wiggle her ass.

Fuck, she felt so good.

Torin was relentless, not able to release his blood thirst. He took it out on Giana, and she reveled in it. Mind-linking Clara to make sure she was all right, she only hummed in desire. "More," she whispered to me, as I could take back control over Torin. "Kane, more!" My claws gripped her hips, leaving bruises. She met me thrust for thrust so I could earn my pleasure from her, mark her as mine over and over. No other cock would descend into her, my cock alone, to travel into her cunt.

When this battle was over, and we won back Osirus's crown, I would have her for days. All mine, this pussy was mine. "Come, mate." I growled, watching my tattooed fingers grip her tighter. A silent scream left her lips. Turning her head to the side to watch the perfect sight, I placed my thumb into her mouth. As she left her high, she pressed her lips around it. Growling, I thrust two more times before spilling into her again.

Panting, I leaned over her back, pulling her to the side as my cock twitched inside her. "Kane." She panted. Pulling her wet hair away from her face, I hovered over her, watching the now rising blue moon sheen over the sweat on her brow. "I need to put you on a schedule." Her finger touched my nose as she panted.

"You and Torin get cranky when we don't get alone time." She giggled. Smiling down at her, I planted a kiss on her lips. "You're right, and I do feel better." I sighed. "I didn't hurt you, did I? I... couldn't control him." I looked away and checked our surroundings for any noises, but my internal battle with Torin still raged.

He couldn't do this, he couldn't hurt the innocent lives on that battle-field, but it was so damn hard not to keep him sated. He fucking lost it when she saw her shift. It was too much after fighting him to kill anyone. I couldn't fail her. I couldn't fail my mate and go against her order. I loved her too much to do that.

"Kane." She pulled my face back to her. "You are conflicted. Talk to me." I couldn't hide things from her. She paid way too much attention to the bond we shared.

"I don't want you to see the beast in me. It was hard today." I nuzzled my nose into her neck. "It was so damn hard not to kill them all," I whispered. Clara kissed my cheek, playing with my shaggy hair.

"I know it was, and you did so good." I snapped my head back up to see her beautiful green eyes.

"But I wasn't. I about killed Osirus!"

Clara scoffed. "He deserved it." She laughed. "He knew what he was doing. You didn't kill him once I got to you. You just needed some play time to release the pent-up frustration with Torin. I am totally okay with that, by the way." Clara winked. My little minx. My shy little fox had turned into a sex addict since being my mate. She loved it as much as I did.

"You are okay with"—I cleared my throat—"me letting my... pent-up feelings out on you? To relieve the stress?" I raised a brow.

"I am your mate, made for you, snookums. I think I can take a pounding or two." She giggled. Laughing with her, I rolled her into the moss, letting the light escape into the night as I peppered her with endless kisses.

⚜

Taking Clara back to camp, both in our animal form, I took her to our tent, making sure she wasn't seen. My heart had lightened, now knowing my mate understood the turmoil that stirred with Torin. If I couldn't kill, I'd fuck my mate until I felt better. And that was a damn good feeling.

I smiled, almost with a skip in my step, as I headed to the royal tent. Marcus ran up beside me in some short, flowered swim trunks. "The fuck are you wearing?" I eyed him suspiciously as I sauntered to the bonfire.

"Showing off my powerful legs, some lady fae said they loved my quads. They are used to seeing some dainty stick legs of the male fae. Thought I might get laid." I rolled my eyes. Marcus had to get his head out of his ass before he met his mate.

Pushing the flap open, I stared at a seething Osirus. The last time I had seen his complexion this dark was with the battle with the rogue King Marcellus, when Clara was taken. It wasn't a good look for him, I'll tell you that.

Finley waved two fingers to meet me outside as Osirus stared at the two women sitting in the chairs. One named Peoni, a fairy that was his right-hand attendant, and the bitch fae we were fighting against, Daphne. "Daphne gave us information about where to find Cosmo." Marcus's face lit up, smacking me on the back.

"Ah, we will get this battle over with soon then." The blue moon was high in the sky, and no battles were to be held at night. Fae could hardly stand the darkness and could barely heal without the light sources. Another reason shifters were better. We thrived in the night. My best warriors were out pulling the enemy fae out of their tents while they were sleeping. Best damn idea I ever had.

"That's not all." Finley sighed. "Peoni has been playing both sides." Marcus gasped loudly like a schoolgirl learning the latest gossip. "Fuck, no!" he hissed, wiping his mouth.

"Aye, and the worst part is she did it because of her mate. Carson, your best tracker, has been cursed by Cosmo in some way. We have yet to find him. Magic is now a part of this war. It only confirms Clara's findings earlier this evening."

That's because my mate was damn fucking smart.

"When you find Carson, keep him here. He is in your land and mated with Peoni. I'll let Osirus deal with what he wants to do." I growled. His friends will be disappointed, but there is nothing I can do. Sean and Carson were ordered to head back to the Cerulean Moon Kingdom and help sniff out some sneaky vampire rogues that keep disappearing and reappearing around the smaller packs surrounding the kingdom. Many hid in the shadows while we traveled here and it was best for my most competent trackers to find the hive of rogues.

Running my hands through my hair, Alaneo stomped out of the tent, watching a bound and tied Daphne and Peoni. Alaneo looked longingly at Peoni as she was led to the camp imprisonment. "What's wrong with Alaneo?" I asked.

"Peoni and Alaneo had been a fling the past couple of years. Alaneo was in love with her, but recently she was only using him to keep her mate safe. That's why she betrayed us all." I hummed. That was a fucking awful predicament.

Glancing at Marcus, he somehow got a leg of meat he was gnawing on ravenously. "Did you hear that?" I snapped at him. Wiping his mouth with the back of his forearm, he muttered, "What?"

"About Alaneo and Peoni?"

"Yeah, real shame." He chomped again on the meat, not caring. I rolled my eyes, watching him stare at some poor fairy woman's ass. He was a damn idiot.

Chapter Eleven

Kane

Tracing my finger across my mate's body, her skin rippled with the tingles I could feel with my fingertips. Her sleeping face was in the crook of my neck and the soft pants of her breath had me gripping her tightly. We should have both been back at the pack house with our daughter, not on a battlefield fighting a war with the fae.

The blue moon on the outside of the tent was setting, now waiting for the light sources to appear. Clara was usually up at his time, ready to start the day even before our daughter was born. Was our daughter all right? My mother was excited to take care of her. She enjoyed having Raine as a child. I gave her way too much trouble as a kid. If we had a son she would have been more reluctant.

Gently putting my mate back on the pillow, she stirred as I placed my pillow next to her. Sniffing deeply into my pillow, I chuckled at her while I put on my shorts. How did I get so damn lucky?

"Kane?" She rubbed her eyes cutely, her dark hair covering part of her face. "Is it time to get up?" Her head dropped back into the pillow, groaning. "I feel like we just went to bed." We sort of did, but I wouldn't tell her that. I was making sure the night shift dragged fae from their sleeping quarters in the night that had to be dealt with promptly. My mate wanted to be present as they woke up from their fog as we poured tainted water over their heads, so she refused to sleep. The witches working with Osirus had some use, I suppose using their magic to help them wake.

I didn't mind chomping on their ankles to wake them to save time because that seemed to wake them up from their stupor too but, of course, my mate said that was too mean. So the slow route we used, using the enchanted water and dumping it on their heads.

"Baby, stay and sleep. The panthers are outside guarding the royal tents." Clara ignored me, shaking her head. "No, no, I'm up." Standing up in nothing but a t-shirt, she sauntered to me and had me lean down to give her a kiss.

"What's the plan, Alpha?" She grinned, rubbing her cheek to my chest. I chuckled. My little luna was the one that gave orders. Now she was willing for me to take over? I rubbed my stubbled chin, trying to think of something thought-provoking to say to her, but fell short. I was a man of action, not of planning.

Gripping her ass, I lifted her, so her head hung over mine. As she looked into my eyes, I could see the fatigue that circled her. My little queen didn't sleep well last night. "I was wondering if you could question the fae soldiers." Clara cocked her head to the side, giving me the perfect view of my mark on her shoulder. Pulling myself together, I heaved out a breath. "It would be helpful to find out what they remember before they attacked us, don't you think?" Clara's heavy eyes lit up, nodding her head frantically.

"That's a great idea!" Kissing her roughly, I put her down, gently nuzzling into her neck. "I want at least three warriors around you at all times. Panthers and lions are in charge of the encampment today. I'll gather them so they will watch you." Clara hummed as she reached for her pack to put on leather pants and a corset top. My mouth watered as she tightened up the front. Her breasts still looked damn delicious, and I couldn't wait for more that was promised me.

"Remember Kane, I've got a tally going on how many soldiers you can bring back alive. Beat the pack, and you get your special surprises." She giggled, wiggling her chest.

I was going to win that damn prize.

Flipping the flap over, hearing it smack against the leather of the tent, three lions stood at the watering hole, filling their canteens. "You have guard duty at the camp?" They grunted in acknowledgment, slinging the packs over their bare chests. "See that tent over there? That's the future queen's tent."

They stiffened their backs and crossed their right arm over the chest. "Your duty is to guard her for the day, the three of you. If I come back finding one hair missing from her pretty little head, I'll let my wolf rip your dicks off and shove them up each other's asses, you hear?" Nodding frantically, they ran to the tent to wait for my mate to appear.

Proud of myself, I stomped over to Osirus. He was already in his battle armor, adjusting his gloves, getting ready to mount his horse. "Plans?" I eyed him while Marcus strutted up with his hair a mess and pulling up his shorts. He reeked of fairy fae cotton candy shit that I couldn't stand.

"Ready!" Marcus gave a mock salute as Osirus walked us over to the small group of generals. Generals Storm, Alaneo, and Major General Finley stood around the table lit with lanterns as we waited for the light sources to rise over the horizon.

"Daphne said there is a bunker, just to the east of the castle grounds near the sea. It's located here and has been sprayed with scenting sprays. There is no magic or wards, so they could not be detected by the few witches that are willing to help us. Should be a clean sweep." Alaneo huffed, pulling at his sword's handle from the sheath. "War should be over with by dusk." He pushed it harshly into his hip.

"Excellent work, Alaneo." Osirus grabbed his shoulder, giving him a squeeze. This was why you shouldn't fall in love or have relationships before finding your mate, because when you lose that someone because of their mate coming around, it hits twice as hard when you are stuck alone.

"Wolves and bears come around from the south, cheetahs and fae from the north?" Grumbling in agreement, I gathered the shifters accompanying my command and walked to the edge of the encampment. The shifters not a part of my pack stood tall, trying to show their willingness to help our new allies, but I couldn't care less if they wanted to impress me. *Just don't die, and don't freaking get in my way.*

"Same as yesterday!" I yelled. "Retrieve, no kill, maim only if needed. Leave the fae to deal with the nobles. If we fight right, we will be finished by dusk." Growls and roars filled the encampment as shifting ensued. Torin howled with fury, bursting right out of our shorts.

The land to the south was a smooth run. The pounding of hundreds of shifters with their paws on the grasses as we traveled the long way around kept my heart light. Our speed was fast enough that we would meet the target at almost the same time the fae would meet the enemy's hiding spot.

Growling, keeping our vocal cues to a minimum, we arrived at our destination ahead of schedule. We all sat in the shadows of the Fairy Forest until we were to be given word to attack. Marcus licked his teeth as he watched for the flicker of blue light we were seeking. My gaze goes back to the wolves, lions, and cheetahs that accompanied. Some were very young and shivered with fear. Those who shivered were the bravest among us or were just plain stupid.

The light flickered in the distance. Marcus headed the charge as I stayed in the middle of the pack. I kept my body crouched low until the hiding fae soldiers rushed from the other side of the cave-like bunker. Their eyes fogged over, just as Clara had seen yesterday. They kept their swords outward, ready to slash into the surrounding shifters. Many fell, feeling the blood pour from their wounds.

Fur flew into the air. The ripping of flesh beside me had me swipe the fae attacking a fellow wolf. I roared into the fae's face, causing spit to paint his pointed facial features. Blood poured from the wound by gripping his arm and breaking it in half. Torin pushed for me to break his neck, but our loyalty was to our luna, our mate. We would not kill this day.

One fae dared to blow his sword into my hind leg. Dropping the screaming fae in front of me, my claws reared back, swiping the sword from his hands. His head pulled back in fear, falling to the sand.

Howling, I had the front line of warriors retreat far enough so they could heal. My claws ripped through flesh on the back of the fae in front of me. The fae couldn't heal as quickly, leaving them stranded in the sand. They shrieked in pain, but as soon as enough blood pooled beneath them, the fog retreated from their eyes. Standing by one that shook their head in confusion, my half-beast form hovered over them.

"Please! I don't know what's going on!" The blood from my maw dripped on their leg. Trying to scoot away from the sandy area, I held out my claw for them to cease. "I mean no harm." I panted. "Now that you are lifted from your magic." Shifters dragged fae by the collars of their uniform with their teeth to the one I stood over, now protecting the small group of wounded fae that now lay in the sand. Many gripped their wounds, huddling together.

More and more fae were knocked out of the fog, questioning why they were on the beach in the first place. "Where is Osirus?" I mind-linked Marcus, who was in the middle of his own fight. His face was covered with blood, and his head jerked to the cave just beyond him.

Taking mighty strides to the cave, my paws sank into the hot sand as the sun had risen halfway above the water. My colossal form bent over to walk further into the cave. Lanterns hung in the dark, and yells and screams echoed in my ears until I reached a door at the end. The few fae farm folk stood at the door, holding their dull swords, eyeing inside.

"Alpha." One bowed in the sign of the shifter. "His Majesty is inside, taking care of... them." His eyes squinted shut, hearing a rip and an ear-piercing scream that made my own body shutter. Pushing the door wider, I saw Osirus and Alaneo hovering over eight members of the fae Court lying in pools of blood. Wings laying on the floor, throats gutted, and clothes hanging off bodies. Only one soul remained.

Cosmo.

Osirus's heavy breaths could be seen in the firelight, the light in front of him casting an evil shadow on the walls. His body stiffened hearing my claws scrape the cave floor. "You missed the show." Osirus chuckled. For the usual playful and damn right annoying fairy, he seemed creepy as shit. His head turned, slowly turning his body toward me. Blood splattered across his perfectly silver face.

"I left one." His fangs glistened in the firelight. I hadn't even known they had fangs. "I told him I'd feed him to the dogs, but I guess you will have to do."

There he was, that cocky little piece of shit.

Growling, I stepped forward, gripping Cosmo's throat. The fae pissed himself, screaming for his mommy like a little shit. My maw came close to his face, opening my mouth to let his eyes feast on the rows of sharpened teeth. Pulling my head back, I chuckled, dropping him to the ground.

"How about you do your little trial you fae like to do. Public humiliation?" Osirus grinned maliciously.

"Ah yes, delayed gratification." He hummed as Alaneo wiped off his blade. Sheathing his sword, I nodded to the both of them, seeing they had things under control and left.

The battle outside was already over. The magical haze wiped away from the once enemy's eyes. "More troops near the palace," Marcus barked out, getting my attention. I howled, getting the shifters' attention.

"The lot of you." I growled, pointing to the large group of fae soldiers shaking in fear. "You bears, stay with them. The rest move on to the palace." The bears roared back, standing on their feet in agreement as I mind-linked the pack to follow.

Taking the shortcut through the forest, wolves jumped over streams, logs, and the underbrush. More bottles we found just two days before littered the ground. "You see that?" Marcus linked, nearly tripping over the bottles. I grunted, continuing to run.

"I'm starting to think Cosmo was on the tip of the iceberg on this. He was getting help elsewhere. What do you think?" I grunted again, not in the mood to talk. Torin was screaming for more blood as we approached the palace walls. Sets of red eyes and a male with a black cloak jumped over the wall before I could catch a good look.

"There." I pointed to them. "I smell them." Marcus took half the warriors, almost questioning my hand movements for him to take the shifters around with him to find the gate while I scaled the wall. My claws were so sharp that they seeped into the brick, leaving white marks on the pristine white granite. I'd leave my mark all over Bergarian, and Osirus wouldn't have any say over it.

Once I reached the top of the courtyard, I stood and held the pointed spire, leaning over the grounds. The courtyard was bare. No sign or smell of any vampire or witches. There was no way that I imagined it. Torin sniffed as well, not doubting what we saw. But there was no smell, not even a shred of hair on top of the wall.

"See anything?" Marcus called out. I grunted, piercing my palm with my claws.

"No." I huffed, jumping from the wall. Landing in front of him, I eyed the bloody mess of warriors. "Check the palace. Bring all servants and anyone wandering the castle for questioning by their true king." The shifters behind Marcus stormed the steps while I continued to scout the courtyard.

Marcus shifted, walking in the buff. "Great job, done by lunchtime. I guess we really got them all. Maybe one of the scouts was mistaken when they linked me." Torin's claws lengthened more, hair standing on the back of our neck. "Uh, not done?" Marcus looked up at me as we climbed up the stairs. Howls inside the palace doors had me run halfway up the stairs. Shifting behind me, Marcus hurled in front, sliding to burst through the decorative palace doors as we watched the shifters continue to pull on the legs of the fae.

"Can none of my warriors mind-link and let me know what the fuck is going on!?" I howled, scratching the perfectly polished floors. Marcus whined, pawing my leg. His eyes flashed with his wolf and back to his blue-colored eyes. *Holy shit, they really can't mind-link.*

Chapter Twelve

Clara

The lions behind me had been stalking me all morning. Their movements were fluid, very much catlike and their quick reactions to things falling beside me, such as leaves, a canteen or any sudden movements by others, never went unnoticed. The glares they sent to other shifters daring to speak with me left them cowering.

Lions, if they were anything like the animals of Earth, were dominant creatures, very alpha-male and very territorial. I wondered how these three male lions could stand to be around each other. In my time here in Bergarian, I had not spoken to many shifters other than wolves.

"If you don't mind me asking," I questioned while we went to the next group of captured fae soldiers, "I was wondering, with such powerful auras you have"—they puffed up their chests as I turned around to stop them in their tracks—"how do males get along since you are lions? With wolves, they just accept the head alpha and live among the pack, the same as a full animal. How does it work for lions?" One lion scratched the blonde scruff on his chin, thinking how to word his answer.

"Well, you see," he muttered, "we don't have large packs like wolves do. We can inflict enough damage with just a few lions. Wolves like to hunt in packs, while male lions do not." I hummed, begging him to continue.

"We have a head alpha lion that is in control of the pride land territory, but there are several other sub-communities within the said territory. We can usually handle each other in small groups, but too many male lions cause trouble." I hummed in agreement.

"And all the males get along with the head lion?" The one lion with white hair and red eyes that I had seen in his shifted form of a beautiful albino lion stepped back. "The head alpha lion earns the title. He is not born into it. He fights for the right. Every five years, we hold a ceremony, and lions fight for the head position. The strongest male gets to rule over us all, and we do not question unless ethical issues arise."

"Ethical issues?" I questioned, having them follow me to the fifth group of fae to question.

"Yes, ethical. Such as taking on a mate that is not your destined, fighting for rutting rights if a female is in heat and refuses you. Most males cannot control themselves, especially the head alpha. It is required to gain permission from the female for the male to tend to her during her heat. The head alpha has a strong desire to want to plant his seed to continue his line, true mate or not. If the alpha cannot control it, he is deemed unworthy and has to be fought with the rest of the males." My face formed into disgust. I was glad wolves didn't act like that.

"It's a very thought-out process, not as barbaric as it may seem. Lions are strong, and the animal can overpower the human form rather quickly. Females and males both drink a special tea to ward off pregnancy, so our animals do not bear young of those we are not destined to. Wolves have done a better job when working with their animals. That is why wolves are the royals." The albino shifter shifted into his lion. He let out a fierce human scream turned roar while the fuzzy mane fluffed on his head. I paid no attention to him, continuing on my walk until I felt him rubbing his fluffy head on my hip.

It was so fluffy!

I restrained myself, gripping my fingers into a fist so I wouldn't dare touch him. "Better watch out, or Kane will be after you," I warned. The shifters behind me chuckled.

"He is scenting you as his queen. His animal wants to show his support." I stiffened until he was finished, unsure if I should keep walking while he assaulted my leg with his excessive purring. The blonde chuckled. I trudged on seeing the last group of fae in the tent.

Lifting the flap, the three lions stood behind me as I walked in. Fifty fae stared back at me with wide eyes. The tent was not only filled with worried looks but those of anger with the panther warriors staring down at them. "That's enough." I waved for the panthers to leave. "I think they are out of their trance now. Go help the other tents and get those fae fed and suited up. They all want to help if it is called for."

The panthers left the tent, but the lions stayed by my side. "I know you all are scared right now, not understanding what's going on. I'm here to help."

One fae shouted in anger. "How do we know that? I woke up with a wolf gnawing on my ankle!" His fist raised, and the albino lion lashed out and pinned him to the ground with a heavy pounce. The lion's breath was so heavy that it had the fae rearing its head deeper into the dirt.

"That's enough!" I yelled as he let the fae sit back up. He turned, bowing his head to return to his place by my side. This was going to get annoying so fast. At least Kane knew when to calm down. Rubbing my eyebrow, I looked at the shaken fae in the room.

"Look, you all have just healed and are confused, but this happened," I began explaining. I told them about the heavy fog that was over their eyes and their disregard for King Osirus as they tried to shoot arrows into his heart. Their faces of confusion went to horror, all the same looks that had appeared in the other tents. None of them had any idea what they were doing, and they were all ashamed.

"Listen, it isn't your fault. There has to be something that connects the dots here of why you can't remember." I pulled out the decorative vial that I had kept in my pocket. The witches found a few more scattered around the battlefield where the generals had sat on their horses. Still, they could not find what ingredients sat inside. The vials were small enough for anyone to contain in a pocket and contained a highly concentrated dose to work on so many.

"Does anyone recognize this?" I wasn't expecting an answer. The other fae did not know, but I saw one lonely hand raised at the far back of the tent. This fae woman was smaller than the rest. Her darkened skin and deep purple hair had me picking her out instantly. "I... I recognize it." Her voice shook.

Rushing to her, I had her stand up, only a head taller than me but shorter than the average fae. I begged her for answers. Some fae scoffed when she stood, sending unapproved glances. My face contorted in confusion as I held out the vial to her. "Don't mind them," she whispered. "I'm a bit of a klutz and not the most graceful." Her hand traced the vial, and I growled warningly at the fae that dared look at her. Giana didn't like the idea of these fae disrespecting her.

Her movements were graceful to me. She studied the glass and let out a sigh. "What's your name?" I whispered. She smiled. "Skye." She bit her lip and handed the vial back.

"I was late to the emergency gathering..." Another fae let out a laugh. "She's always late."

I growled, baring my fangs. "You dare disrespect me and my time?" The fae cowered back in fear. The aura I shared with Kane oozed from my voice. Skye flinched, but my hand caressed her arm.

"Continue, Skye, it's all right." Skye wouldn't look me in the eye, too afraid from my lash of anger. That was something I could thank Kane for. I'd become a little hellion if I didn't have my cuddles in the morning.

To smile at her, I lifted her chin. "I'm serious. It's all right." I needed answers, and I needed them now. If there was anything she could give me, we could use this to prevent anything like this rising in our kingdom. Brushing her purple lock behind her ear, her uneasiness lifted.

Skye bit her lip, handing back the vial. "Someone in a cloak was there. It was pulled over their head, and they chanted as the vial had this smoke come from it."

"Male or female?" I pushed, but she only shook her head. Gripping the vial in my hand, I heard it crack. "I'm sorry, your highness." Shaking my head, I urged her to continue.

"A male vampire stood beside them once I came into the room. He whispered in the hooded figure's ear and nodded his head in my direction. Cosmo then told the first platoon to take the palace, and they were to protect it with their lives until they returned. Then the chanting from the magical entity intensified, and it was like I fell asleep." Skye gulped. "Then I woke up on the battlefield with a bleeding leg." Skye sighed, and I patted her shoulder.

Stepping away from her, the fae in the room watched Skye sit back down on the floor. I stood speechless before them all as I pondered Skye's words. This was not a war of just the Fae Kingdom fighting over a throne. It was much deeper than I realized. We had two races helping a dirty fae, and for what reason?

Witches and vampires were working with Cosmo. Were they all working together to take control of just the Golden Light Kingdom? Was that vampire part of the rogue vampires we had heard of going from tribes, packs, and prides around my kingdom? Feeling the heat of my face, I gripped my fists together. This was going to be much larger, much deeper than I realized. Once the battle was over today, if it was truly to be over, it was just a battle. Something much larger was coming, and this was only the beginning.

Turning to see the albino lion standing in the doorway, his tail swayed while my other two bodyguards waited for orders. I hadn't even had to chance to know their names with all the thoughts running through my head.

"I'm sorry," I whispered. "What are your names?" The blonde put his hand on his chest, eyebrows raising in confusion as I stepped forward. "I am Naheim. This is Tyndall, and our friend here"—Naheim patted the albino lion—"is Snowflake." I snorted, trying to hold in a laugh.

'Snowflake' roared out a growl, snapping his massive jaws toward Naheim, who only shoved him back. "Kidding, this is KaRon. He would be the equivalent of a beta to your alpha." I smiled, greeting them all by name before stepping out of the tent.

Spouting orders to the cheetah shifters outside to get food and warm blankets, I stopped speaking mid-sentence. My heart pounded in my chest with worry. "The first platoon," I whispered. Tyndall grabbed my arm in question. "The first platoon is in the palace," I muttered. The lion shifters looked at one another. "Meaning they will be on the inside waiting for King Osirus and Kane after they capture Cosmo!" My voice squeaked. Surely they would know that there would be some other army inside. Cupping my hand to my mouth, I opened the mind-link. It was going to be iffy if I could reach his connection this far, but I had to try.

Trying for several minutes, hordes of shifters stood in a circle, waiting for an answer. Letting my hand leave my face, hundreds of shifters looked at me as I circled around to see every single soul that waited. I had hoped we didn't have to use shifters other than the wolves we brought. They were not trained to fight as an army. Instead, they lived their lives quietly just with one-on-one combat training.

Skye pushed through the crowd, her dark purple hair slinging in her face as she reached me. "I would like to travel back with you." She panted. "I know the palace. I can take you or any of your army through a secret door inside." Growling, I nodded, confirming what we should do. As much as

I hated battling the first day, it caused me so much anguish to nip at the heels of those who were tainted with magic.

The light sources towered over the sky, leaving us with just a half day left. "Gather all willing to fight. We are headed to the palace," I ordered. Shifters ripped through clothes, not even sparing a minute to take them off. The fae soldiers that stood so strongly for Osirus left the water holes and gathered their confiscated swords from the warrior tents. I had hundreds, maybe a thousand, warriors at my beckoning call.

I was out of my element. I was for sure going to screw this up. "You've got this, Your Highness." Skye laced her fingers between mine.

"Are you sure? Because I don't think I do." I choked, trying to hold back a tear. I had grown up at a diner, served hot plates of food, I had only known this world a little less than six months, and here I was about to lead an army onto the Golden Light Kingdom palace. This is never where I saw myself, not in my wildest dreams. I barely could grasp what it was like to be a mother and be thrown into a whole other world of trouble.

Where was Kane? Where were my parents?

"You got this." Skye shook my hand again. "Tell us what to do." What was left of the Crimson Shadows pack growled, bowing their heads to me for orders. The other shifters, whom I could not even mind-link, did the same. Rows and rows of animals turned into small waves of bows and growls.

Biting my lip until it bled, I stood up straight. Kane would want me to be strong, but most of all, I had to be strong for my daughter. "Skye will lead the way!" I shouted. "Half will go through the hidden entrance." I pointed to one section of the crowd. "The other half will follow me, straight through the front doors."

Chapter Thirteen

Clara

My bright red fur was a dazzling contrast among the grays, browns, and blacks that covered the sea of fur. I jumped in front of my lion protectors, unable to keep up with my speed. I had become exceedingly fast since being mated, and this was putting the rest of the army to the test.

Deafening roars and growls grew rowdy in protest as my white padded feet hit the long grasses. The Golden Light palace stood tall and bright through the mid-afternoon light sources. I wish I had time to admire its beauty, the beautiful colorful windows, and the way the light shone at the top of its bright pointed towers, but it would be for another time.

Pouncing through a small puddle, I slowed, knowing going in headfirst alone would not be wise. KaRon somehow caught up, his big bulky form not used to the long run. His tongue lagged to the side to cool his heavily furred body. I yipped at him for encouragement, which did the trick, his enormous paws now nipping at my own.

This could all have just been a misunderstanding, there could be no troves of soldiers, but without a mind-link to be sure, I was going to protect my mate and the fellow wolves and shifters that could be on the other side. Giana was still trying to push through the invisible barrier that halted our communication. That minor detail was now shoved to the side when growls and howls filtered through the opened double doors of the Golden Light palace.

As if inviting us in, we leaped up the stairs, my lion companions not heeding the howls for me to stop. These lions knew I would not stop. They went in stride with me. Pushing through the doors, my mate stood on his hind legs, his teeth gnashing at the ankle of another wolf.

The wolf was not of our own; the smell wasn't right, and the stench filtered through the tip of my nose of nothing but rogue. Could he not smell the stench? "Kane!" I yelled again through the link, but nothing could be heard. Getting a look into his enemy's eyes, his eyes were not clouded like that of the fae. They were in control of their own bodies.

Wolves, vampires, and witches were now fighting against my mate and the rest of our team. Blood scattered the floor. No shifter was healing, and these rogue beings were winning. The fae still fought, the fog in their eyes worked with the rogues, but once the pain shattered through their bodies, they lay helpless on the floor.

Kane's side was torn, blood pooling beneath his thigh. I barked, leaping before thinking. My paws slipped into the blood but quickly gained my composure enough to land my small mouth on the underside of the rogue's throat.

Kane growled, looking down at me, seeing I was covered in the blood of his attacker. Head cocking to the side as to why I would do such a thing. I pawed the rogue wolf's eyes. Nothing was clouded. Kane shook his head, not understanding, and it was too dangerous to shift into human form.

Shifters behind me watched the scene unfold. They took the hint that both their alpha and comrades could not understand that these animals were not under a spell and needed to be taken care of. My team charged the room in at full force, now doubling and tripling the numbers fighting against the enemy. They still fought on, bolts of lightning coming from witches and warlocks who filtered into the middle of the room.

Cheetahs snarled, gripping opposing shifters that fought back. There weren't many rogues, and the smell that lingered on their dirtied bodies had us gagging. Pulling a half-alive witch before me from the corner of the room, I pushed her eyes to Kane. She shook in fear, trying to bring up her fingers to set another spell before us. Hissing in her ear, she screamed, letting go of whatever beacon she was creating. Kane's head shook. He howled as his claws raked at his ears. Silencing the witch with one swipe to her chest, I pushed the limp body.

Kane's eyes blinked, watching the chaos surrounding him. Our pack all shook their heads, now darting their heads back to the opposing enemy. Their eyes widened, realizing who they were fighting. They were no longer trying to maim these rogues, thinking they were just under a spell. They were now ready for the blood of those with unfogged eyes.

The hair stood up on Marcus's back, deep golden fur spiking from all sides of his spine. Grinding his teeth into the gums of his mouth, he lashed out at the witch coming toward me. My body sprang into action, taking the attacker of a bear coming for Marcus. Kane roared; his mind-link was now wide open as the witch beacon's lifeless body was now being trampled by the stampede of shifters.

"Get the rogues, protect the fallen!" Torin's voice echoed through the magnificent entrance of the palace. Shifter after shifter tried to attack the witches and warlocks coming down the stairs.

Skin tearing, blood spilling, my razor-sharp fangs finally ripped the throat of the opposing rogue bear, causing it to fall on top of me. Not being the strongest, it took several moments for me to wiggle free until my mate pulled up the dead beast from my back.

"Stay close." Torin's voice was ragged as he continued to bleed from his side. Another witch or warlock was keeping us from healing. One by one, I watched our numbers dwindle. The felines that were not used to fighting in packs were collapsing, not able to understand our formations of protecting each other's backs.

Naheim was struggling in the corner, the large lion trying to take on two bears. Roaring at the swipe the one bear made across his hind leg, the other stomped on his mane, unable to lift his head. Kane came running behind me, seeing my bodyguard gasping for breath.

The bear stepping on his mane came to swipe his throat dramatically. I swear I saw the evil grin his animal made. Taking the time to strike, I rounded him, jumping high enough to catch him in the weakest point, the throat. He wasn't the biggest bear I had ever seen, but he still fell with a large slam to the ground while Kane ripped the head off another.

Kane was still not healing. I growled to figure out another point of attack until Skye whistled for me through her fingers. She stood at the base of the stairs, her sword pointing to the top. Two figures, one in a black cloak and the other a pasty vampire, grinning ear to ear.

Not looking back to get Kane's attention, I bolted for Skye as she ran up the stairs. I barked at her, trying to gain her recognition, but her sword held out in front of her. She was on a mission of her own. Hearing Kane's mighty roar below the steps, he took a step forward, letting the meat of his wound dangle from his body as he watched me top the stairs.

A deep chuckle came from a darkened figure in the cloak, possibly male. The loud noises kept our pounding feet and paws to a minimum. It was then the vampire snickered and pointed to Skye, running toward them both. Swinging her sword, she slit right through the blackened cape, hearing a rip not even touching the magical figure before her. Before I could pull her away, the vampire pulled out an iron dagger, lunged forward, and struck it straight through Skye's heart.

An evil chortle came from his throat. His darkened hair and the tattoos that peeked out from underneath his black dress shirt held nothing but skulls and blood. The silver rings on his fingers, filled with jewels, glistened in the light that was trying to evade the sky. His fanged smile showed no remorse while he twisted it in her chest.

I howled a cry, Kane grabbing me as I slowed down as I watched Skye's body drop to the floor. It was straight through her heart. The small glow in her chest that was made for the light source rays to help heal her dimmed. Her body turned to an ashen color in an instant.

Howling again, Torin held onto Giana and my body tightly, his blood staining our fur. Skye was too good for this. What was she trying to prove? She should have waited; she should have stopped to let me help her! I wasn't fast enough. I didn't catch her in time. I was supposed to be a leader. I was supposed to keep as many people from leaving the soil as I could.

"Let me save her!" I cried to Kane. Torin's body wrestled with us.

"She's gone, baby, she's gone." I knew I could save her. I had to save her. "If you try to save her, it will kill you. She is dead!" Torin's deep voice snapped.

The cloaked figure waved their hand across the battle below. The room stilled, causing not just our own shifters and fae but the rogue's to freeze in place. The foyer, once bustling with noise, was now silent, all frozen in time. My mate and I stood in awe of how defeating the silence was. It hovered over us like black clouds while the cloaked figure turned to us. Were we next? The deep vibrations from their chest had Torin grip hold of us tightly, backing away from the evil magic that oozed from their body.

It was thick, hard to breathe at the magnitude of this power. The vampire, who only gave a leer in return, licked the blade and then his black fingernails that had grazed Skye's chest. Whimpering for justice, I squirmed, wanting to rip the throat out of this beast, this monster that took away my new friend that had given me enough courage to carry on. I had to do it for her, in remembrance of her.

Fingers letting go of a white cloud of dust brushed forward and seeped within the room. Covering our eyes, we coughed violently. Torin only held me tighter as the still room now slowly came back into motion. Blinking several times, we looked in front of us, only to see nothing was before us. Torin's grip loosened, having my four paws reach the ground.

Why were we up here? Padding across the floor, I sniffed the pool of blood. It smelled of fae, a familiar smell that I could not place.

"What happened?" I linked Kane, who stood over me with his broad shadow.

"I don't know." He ran his claws through the top of his hair. Rubbing his leg absentmindedly, blood coated his fur heavily, but there was no cut, no wound.

"When did I even get here?" I muttered to him. "Last thing I remember was being at the camp. Why am I here in the foyer of the Golden Light palace?" Taking my paws and putting them on the railing, looking below, large pools of blood lay on the floor. Shifters and fae walked about the room in confusion, looking to us for answers. I had none to give. I don't even remember why I was here.

My mind returned to the large pool of blood on the floor. It smelled so familiar to me, yet not. It was a horrible feeling I had, something that I should have remembered. Giana whimpered inside me, our heads ticking in confusion.

"Baby, what's wrong?" Torin's enormous body hovered over me as I stared into the pool of blood to see my reflection.

"Everything," I replied. "Everything."

Chapter Fourteen

Clara

Hot breaths left my maw as I climbed the endless stairs. The blackness that donned the never-ending staircase had me running faster. "Help me!" a woman screamed from the blackness of the shadows. Deep chuckles reverberated between the walls. Giana's nails continued to click, our tongue lolling out of our maw. "I'm coming!" I kept yelling inside my head. Giana continued to whimper and growl at the stressing calls for help.

The stairs circled, coming to a platform that held a dark figure hovering over a body. The dark cloak swam in dark pools around a helpless woman who lay on the floor. Scooting to a halt, my paws slid across the slick marble floor covered in crimson blood.

My eyes widened; my fur coat was coated in the sticky residue. The dark figure backed away, chuckling deeply inside his chest, watching as I fell on top of the body. The woman's eyes opened from shock, and her mouth hung open. Wings laid broken and torn, a dagger buried in her chest.

Whining, I stumbled backward, looking at the lifeless eyes. It was like I was supposed to remember her. Her hand was reaching toward me, begging me to come to her aide. Giana whined again, wanting me to go forward, try to heal her, until I felt powerful arms pulling me back. I yipped in surprise, trying to squirm out of the hold.

The fire touched across my fur to let me know it was my mate, but why was I being dragged away? The manic laughter grew louder. He reached inside a satchel that stretched across his shoulder, and my eyes widened as white dust flew into the air.

I moaned, watching the dust fly not just to my mate and me, but down below to the darkness on the platform. My eyes closed, and the white dust invaded my lungs until I cried out, trying to reach the fae woman's body.

"She's gone, baby," Kane's voice rasped until my eyes closed. Opening them, the dark figure was now gone, the body that once lay on the floor along with it. Giana howled in anger, the retreating cloaked figure flashing in my mind's eye.

Thrashing once again, trying to sniff where the body once lay, Kane's arms gripped me from the scene, carrying me back down the stairs, leaving the darkness.

No!

I bolted straight up in bed; Kane's arm lay on top of my body, but the sheer shock had me moving his arm. He jolted in surprise, seeing the sweat beaded on my forehead. "Love, what's wrong?" Kane pulled me to his lap, heaving. His hair was messy, and his back tensed while he looked around the room.

Evelyn stirred. Her gentle cry made me forget the horrible dream and climb from Kane's arms. "Love," he cooed, but I reached for my baby, who lay in the cot beside my bed. Her eyes opened, staring at me with the beautiful blue eyes of her father.

"Hi, baby girl." I pulled her to me. Her hair and her body had grown so much for the six days we left her to help Osirus and travel across Bergarian. I was missing out on everything, her first babbles and smiles, her sweet little swats at the baby toys.

It wouldn't be long until she crawled, and would I be here for that, or would I miss that too? My heart clenched, clasping her. Kane's enormous arms came around us, picking up the both of us and settling us in his lap.

His lips brushed my forehead, wincing at the wet hair that gathered around my face.

"Love." He rocked us both. Evelyn's heavy eyelids fell back down to her chubby cheeks. Her hand rested on mine as I held my fingers close to her heart. "Another bad dream?" Kane's consistent purring in his chest calmed me, Torin pushing Giana to speak of our dream to them both.

"Yes." I choked, feeling the threatening tears hiding behind my eyes. I wouldn't cry. It wasn't the queenly thing to do. I was to be strong for my mate and the rest of the kingdom I was to inherit. I couldn't let the feelings inside me stir me, deter me from the mission that I now fought within my own head.

Something was wrong, utterly wrong, and no one seemed to notice it but me.

After Kane and I were left standing at the top of the stairs in Osirus's palace, the entire area took minutes until we all began moving again. We couldn't remember anything; we couldn't decide why we were even in the place to begin with.

Blood pooled on the floors, blood that wasn't our own. Much of the blood was foul and smelled nothing but rogue. The few spots of blood we found were that of our pack and shifters from the pride lands weren't that many. We did a head count, trying to find out who was missing.

Most of them were unmated, but a few did have mates. It meant mates on the other side of Bergarian could be dead as well with their bond being broken. "Why can't we remember?" I leaned into Kane's body. Kane had gathered a large tunic from one of the guest bedrooms as we came down the stairs. My body was covered, just the way he expected it to be.

"I'm not sure." Kane glanced around the room. His shifting eyes to the corners of the room only led me to believe he wasn't sure what he wanted to do or say. Even Marcus, who was constantly coming back with something to retort, only went through the motions to help clean up the palace.

Osirus seemed undisturbed by the whole thing. He was happy the battle was over, and his kingdom had won. He thought maybe we all had a lapse of judgment and blocked out the bloody scene. But all of us? We all blocked that from our memory?

Osirus continued to stare down at me as if looking for something. His eyes softened, his hand patting my shoulder. Kane, of course, pushed his hand away, making Osirus smile. "I see no evil, no darkness in you or your mate." Osirus glanced to the top of the stairs. "I see no dark magic at all." He hummed. "We will figure this out. For now, let's celebrate."

Osirus held a large party for the warriors, but Kane and I decided to go home. Our Evelyn was being watched, and I was not in the mood for partying. The run home was much needed and greatly appreciated by both Torin and Giana. The first platoon of warriors came home with us, their concentration on fighting off the vampire rogues more important to them.

August, who we left behind to oversee the pack along with Kane's father, Liam, had nothing new to report. Falcons had brought in word from my parents, who had continued to travel to the northern part of the kingdom and were on their way back. Mom's pregnancy caused them to slow down in their return, but the danger was now too great to continue their deeper travels into Bergarian.

Rogue vampires and wolves that were siding with the enemy had them take back roads with the carriage. My worry for my mother only grew by the day. I wasn't sure how I was supposed to take charge of it all once my next sibling was born. Mother had mentioned giving more power to me, but I was barely hanging on as things stood.

"Love, come back to me." Kane's chapped lips kissed my ear. My worry over everything and everyone only grew by the day, and now Kane was feeling the brunt of it. Our bond was so intertwined with each other it was hard to hide anything from him.

"Is it the same dream?" he muttered. We had been back for three days, and the dream was always the same. The dark-haired fae woman screaming for help, but by the time I arrived, she was already dead. I wanted to say I had seen her before, maybe in real life, but I couldn't be sure.

Dreams in the supernatural world meant something. They told you a story, a part of you that you may have not seen or remembered, or something you were supposed to know as the gods willed it. This dark-skinned, purple-haired fae woman, I couldn't put my finger on how or if I was supposed to know her.

"Yeah," I whispered, gently putting Evelyn back in her basket. She had been a wonderful baby when I was around. Naomi was the perfect nanny for her, along with Raine. They spoiled her rotten, but they both told me she began to cry out in the night, even daring to say, "Mama."

My heart was crushed hearing that.

"I still think it is strange how we don't remember," I muttered, curling back around Kane. He pulled me to his chest, having my head rest on his bulging muscles.

"Osirus said he didn't see any dark magic," Kane's graveled voice rumbled through his chest. His finger rubbed my back, causing me to melt into him. "Osirus can detect those sorts of things, right?" I hummed in agreement, too busy trying to concentrate on the fae woman's face.

She haunted me, those eyes. I would play with Evelyn on the floor, and she would flash into my mind. Other fae laughing at her, the tight shoulders. Small little pieces of her appeared in my head in scenes I didn't remember.

That was the other strange part. We couldn't recall most of the morning. I couldn't even remember how we got to the palace. Asking around the different warriors and soldiers, they were the same. Could there be magic that no one could detect?

"You have to stop stressing." Kane tilted my chin up so I looked at him in his electric blue eyes. "You got this, baby, you got it." I bit my lip until Kane's head drew closer, pulling the lip out with his teeth. "Or I'll fuck you until you aren't stressed anymore."

I giggled, trying to be quiet. I didn't need to wake Evelyn up again. "That sounds nice, actually," I purred back to him. "It's been about four hours." I pretended to look at the invisible watch on my wrist. "That's a long time without having you up in my business."

"What?" he whispered.

"Yeah, you need sexy time about every four hours, so you don't get grumpy. Just like Evelyn when she gets too hungry." Kane rolled his eyes playfully, pushing my back into the mattress.

"If you say so," he mumbled before his warm lips touched me. It wasn't rushed; it wasn't forced; it was the sweet side of Kane. As much as I loved taking him hard, fast, and possessive, this was a side I rarely saw.

Kane knew I was hurting; he knew I was worried. There was so much more than battle with Osirus and his previous Court members. Kane's lips gently kissed my cheek, tracing my neck. The harsh sucking on my breast caused me to moan, running my fingers through his hair.

"Shhh," he whispered quietly. "Let's not wake the little warrior." Kane leaned over the bed, pulling up the canopy over the tiny cot near our bed. Evelyn was tucked away from sight, so if she did wake, she wouldn't see something vulgar.

Kane loved taking the sheets off the bed, having me bare underneath him, but this time the sheets kept us covered, his body hovering over me. "You are so beautiful, you know that?" My lip wobbled, feeling the soft side of my mate. "And strong, so strong." He kissed my ear. "We are going to figure this out, I promise you."

My body already seeping the sheets with my arousal, he pulled down my terry cloth booty shorts and my tank top pushed up so he could get an ample view of my breasts. "I'm going to take care of your burdens. That's why I'm here." His lips kissed me again, and my thighs rubbed together, feeling Kane's already naked body brushing against my core.

"I'm going to protect you, our baby, our pack. Leave your worries to me." The tip of Kane's cock pried my lips open. I kept my hitching breath silent as my cavern clenched around him.

"Fuck," he whispered into my ear. "Going slow is going to be so hard." He pushed his body into me as I swallowed him whole. His slow movements were full of love while he kissed me. His arms came under and around my shoulders, making sure he didn't leave any part of my pussy untouched. He had so much control; it had my worries drip away.

"Kane." I moaned quietly, wrapping my legs around him. "I'm going to—"

"Yes, come on me, My Queen. Let me feel your warmth." Giana growled inside my chest as I exploded around him. It urged Kane to pick up his gentle pace, his eyes never leaving me. "I love you. Let me take care of you." I smiled, cupping my mate's face.

"And I love you too, Kane." His hip thrusts went faster until he spilled inside me; his heat filled me, giving me a satisfying sigh. Why it felt so good feeling his come inside me, I'd never know. Kissing my cheek, he leaned his body on top of me, trapping me in his embrace.

So comfy.

"I still haven't forgotten about my reward," Kane whispered playfully. "I captured all those fae unharmed just for you." I bit my lip, laughing as his body relaxed into me.

"Oh, I've got great things for you, Alpha." Kane kissed my cheek, rolling me back on top of his body, keeping his thingy firmly planted inside.

"Sleep, mate," Kane grumbled, and with that order, I did.

Chapter Fifteen

Clara

I wish I could have told Kane that I slept much better last night, but the horrible feeling in the pit of my stomach wouldn't go away. That beautiful tanned fae's eyes continued to haunt my nightmares, glaring at me like she was searching. Kane grumbled. He didn't even have to ask what I had dreamed about.

"I'm just scouting the southeast area." Kane leaned in and pecked my lips. The big, tall alpha had a whole squadron of wolves behind him. Some snickered, albeit quietly, and he growled, having his hair stand up on the back of his neck. The warriors stiffened, backing away slowly while Kane bent over to kiss the shell of my ear. "Osirus sent a falcon about his intentions of meeting up with Cosmo's daughter to retrieve Melina's friend, Tulip."

I bit my lip, holding Evelyn tight to my body. She cooed, waving her hands around my back and watching Raine make funny faces. Tulip was a werewolf from the Earth realm who met her mate that was in our pack during a mixer on Earth. Tulip had grown up with Melina. They were basically sisters and brought to Bergarian for Tulip's mating ceremony.

I had dreams about Melina before she came here. The goddess even whispered in my ear that this girl was special. Me, trying to be rational, thought it was because she was mated to my good friend, Osirus, only to find out she was indeed half-siren. Talk about a major plot twist.

Now Tulip was captured by Daphne, who was holding her hostage in a rogue witch coven holding vampires as guards, and my mate was going to just 'scout' the area. "Are you worried?" I looked up into his eyes. His jaw tightened, his hand reaching for my shoulder to squeeze.

"Of course not," Torin purred in his chest. He was trying to make me feel better, but the hesitation in his voice didn't leave. "If he needs help, I'll be around."

"Yeah, or make sure that Osirus cleans up his mess." Marcus sauntered up, smacking the ass of some she-wolf. I glared at her, her eyes now darting to the dirt. She had a mate somewhere, and she was playing with this big player.

"Marcus," I barked out, causing Evelyn to turn her head. Her wide eyes saw the man she saw as an uncle reach out to him. Marcus took her in his arms, rocking her back and forth until she slapped him in the face.

Ha, good one.

"You need to keep it in your pants." I shook my finger. "What are you going to do when you have to tell your mate you had your willy in different she-wolves?" Marcus held back a laugh until his wide grin overtook his face.

"Willy? Is that what you call Kane's dick?" Kane rubbed his face, groaning.

"No, I call it the Kraken," I snipped. Marcus raised a brow, Raine roaring with laughter behind me. "Because it rises from the depths and gets things wet!" I bit my lip, trying to be serious.

Forgetting the wolves behind us, many thundered in laughter at my joke. Kane's body flinched, slowly turning to see everyone backing away. His nasty glare even had Marcus pull back. Evelyn giggled, watching her daddy's hair stand up again.

Feeling the rage in Kane, I put my hand in his while he put Evelyn back in his arms. The scowl on his face was going to get stuck like that if he didn't stop. "Alpha," I cooed, pulling him back to me. "I was trying to lighten the mood. I'm sorry." Kane's face instantly softened. He pulled me up in his arm while holding his daughter and me.

"I know." He chuckled, only speaking to me. I thought some of my personality would rub off on him and be more sociable with people, but that was still not the case. Evelyn and I would be the only ones meant for him to show his soft side. His nose trailed up my neck, kissing me under my ear. "I have to show them who's boss." Rolling my eyes, he pinched my butt, causing me to cry out.

Kane's body turned. "Shift!" He growled out. Dozens of wolves now shook their fur. Evelyn watched in awe, clapping her hands in delight.

"I'll be back by nightfall." With a kiss on Evelyn's cheek, he shifted into Torin's half form. They all ran into the forest that held our large pack house in nature's protection.

"He'll be all right." Raine rubbed my back. She had known about the nightmares I was having. Kane had briefed almost all of our family of the worries that fell on my shoulders. As much as I didn't want others to think I was weak, Kane made it very clear I wasn't to do this on my own. We were a team, just as much as his family was.

"Would you like me to take Evelyn?" Evelyn's face buried into my shoulder, her fists holding onto my now waist-long hair. My baby needed me.

"No, I think I'll put her down for her nap," I whispered. "You should spend some time with Dean. Isn't he working the blood donations?" Raine bit her lip. Her fangs that could once be controlled by her wolf now always sat short in her mouth. Her transformation of taking some of Dean's genetics was difficult for her. She had a hard time stomaching the idea of drinking blood. Luckily, it was only his she would drink.

Raine held off as long as she could before she had her first feed. Once the thirst fever hit, it hit her hard, and now she makes sure she will never become that hungry again.

"You're right. I'll go see if I can round up some more 'volunteers'." She snickered. It was part of the pack's obligation to donate blood now, only for non-rogue vampires, of course. Taliyah and Jasper had been very thankful for that. Once they begin rebuilding the kingdom, there are plans to bring human blood through the portal. A small coven that Sebastian had arrived at months ago proved that their methods could work on a larger scale.

Sharp pain in my shoulder had me rotating it. Evelyn had just finished her dinner, and I placed her on the floor. An area of the kitchen was closed off. It was a smaller kitchen within the larger pack kitchen used by the alpha and luna. A small fridge, stove, dishwasher, and kitchen table sat. It made the pack house feel more like a human home having this small kitchen to my specifications.

I liked to come here when Kane wasn't eating with us. It gave me time to spend with just Evelyn and not have numerous wolves interrupting our dinner. I guess I was pretty popular when Kane wasn't scowling at everyone to leave us alone.

We kept a highchair, a small two-person table, and a small fridge filled with the few chocolate silk pies only meant for Kane. Putting some measuring cups on the floor so Evelyn could bang them together, I turned to finish washing the small number of dishes that were left. She squealed happily as I watched her from the corner of my eye. Accidentally dropping a plate, my hand went to my shoulder, and I saw sharp claw marks appear.

"Raine!" I yelled, feeling the tearing of the skin. Kane was in trouble; he had to be. Using the mind-link, I couldn't hear anything but the static. The static felt so familiar, like I had heard it before. "Raine!" Raine came running into the room, her lips stained with blood. Dean wasn't far behind. He gasped, pushing Raine aside and helping me sit down. Blood dripped down his lips, and I couldn't help but shiver.

Ew, they were eating.

"I'm sorry." I whimpered, feeling the sting. The pain wasn't going away. He wasn't healing. Rubbing it, Evelyn whimpered until Raine pulled her up into her arms. "I think there is something wrong with Kane!" I blurted. With concern in his eyes, Dean looked to Raine but shook her head.

"You know something?" I growled out. Giana was getting pissed, and I was too! "What is it? Are you keeping things from me?" Raine stuttered while Evelyn looked on at my state of distress. I had to calm down. I couldn't break out in anger with her in the room.

Putting his hand on my back, Dean whispered, "Kane told us not to say anything." I growled lowly. Dean squatted down, his knees on the floor. My eyes flashed, Giana pulling to the surface.

"I am the luna. I should know what's going on!" I snapped.

"He's trying to keep you safe," Raine pleaded, her back to the wall. "He doesn't want you to worry. You have too much on your plate right now."

"As sweet as that is," I said, "we promised each other we wouldn't keep secrets. Now spit it out." Raine's mouth hung open, looking at Dean who was sitting with Evelyn. "I am the luna, future queen of the Cerulean Moon Kingdom. My order trumps Kane's!" I gritted my teeth. Stomping over to Raine, I grabbed Evelyn, her body instantly relaxing as I held her head to my shoulder.

Sighing, trying to bring reign in my anger, Dean reached for my hand. "He's down at the southeast border. Osirus used the shifter horn for backup. He told us they were fine, just a bunch of ordinary witches." I let out a sigh. Fighting was Kane's thing, I shouldn't be mad about that, but the nagging in the back of my head still festered. The static that still strung over the mind-link had me clench my fist.

"I can't link him," I muttered. Raine stood in the corner, holding her hand to her mouth. Her eyes glazed over, trying to reach him. "I can't either." Her eyes held worry. "He just linked us fifteen minutes ago." Kissing Evelyn's cheek, I handed her back to Raine.

"I'm going after him." Arguments ensued behind me, but it was already too late. I had made my decision.

Stomping through the kitchen and into the dining room. The entire room went silent. I must have been leaking some sort of powerful aura because not one breath could be heard. "I need ten of the fastest wolves. We leave now." The growling through my chest reverberated against the doorway as I pushed the swinging door out of the pack house.

Not caring if I ripped through my pale blue dress, I shifted. Yells from Raine, Dean, and even Naomi, who was coming out of her cabin, could not stop me. My mate was hurting, and there was no other place I could be right now. Evelyn was safe. The pack had our strongest warriors keeping our fortress hidden.

"Wait!" Liam, Kane's father, tried to link me, but my mind was too busy thinking about my mate. The static continued to shift through my head, burning holes in the far corners of my mind. Giana howled at the annoyance, but we followed the pull.

I jumped over streams, bushes, and thickets of thorns. Pulling hunks of fur from my body, they regrew in an instant, but as I traveled, feeling Kane's pull becoming stronger, my body began to weaken.

I grew tired, something that shouldn't be happening. Wolves behind me caught up; their whimpers as they ran with me had me blink several times. I blinked too hard for too long, and my paws tripped in the mud below me.

We ran so far in such a short amount of time, the fastest I had ever tried. Surely I couldn't be tired. Giana was to regenerate me. One of the warriors nudged my side. My eyes blinked in surprise, jumping back up on all fours.

Trying to link them, I realized the static became louder. We all shook our heads.

Whimpers held one concerned wolf; he nudged my hip where my body met the mud. A long scrape, nothing that would inhibit my ability to run, but blood tricked down the fur. I wasn't healing.

Checking the other warriors, they had cuts and scrapes too. Their bodies could no longer heal either.

What is happening?

Trying the mind-link one more time, the static roared in my ear. I howled a whimper and buried my ear into the mud. It was so strong it had me clawing my head until the warriors tried to make me stop. One shifted, screaming in pain as he did so. He jumped over my body, holding my paws away.

His torso was riddled with scrapes, his face contorted with pain as I saw one last bone pop into place. Howling one more time, a large roar made the trees around us shake. Thick leaves of green fell to the ground around us until the pounding of paws vibrated through our bodies.

My wolves whimpered, backing away from my body. That mind-link that held static became stronger until I heard the voice that I needed to hear. "Love, what are you doing?" His voice was soft, trying to calm me.

It was a reset. Kane's voice flipped a switch in my head that caused me to close my eyes to watch the movie scenes before me. Those eyes, the dark wings, and the skin. She screamed out my name as I watched a knife plummet into her heart. The deep chuckles of darkness, the twisted grin of a vampire, and the clinking of his overly large rings on fingers as Skye fell to the ground.

Skye.

The fae woman in my dreams that called for me every night, it was her. Instead of my mind remembering each scene individually, it hit me like a freight train that never planned on stopping. Memories, sickening memories of bloodshed in the palace. The vials of potions, the white dust floating into my eyes, it was all there.

Giana shifted our body back into our human form, the memories proving to hit my mind so hard, her healing abilities stuck in my head. I screamed out in pain, seeing the wolves surrounding me, their backs to me to cover my naked form.

Kane hovered over me, still in his beastly body. His arms came around me, cuddling me into his chest. "I've got you." His wet nose pushed into my neck. My body hung in his arms like a rag doll. "Skye," I whispered. "Dust, the powder," I mumbled. Giana pushed into my head further, the ripped memories that flashed in my mind slowly being sewn together by Giana's paw.

"Rest," Torin's rumbled voice filled my ears. My head turned, checking for wounds on his shoulder. "Rest," he urged me again. Once my fingers rubbed the once damaged area of dried blood, my eyes closed of their own accord.

Chapter Sixteen

Kane

The cleansing flame pushed my fur behind me. The heat of the blaze, the ash floating around the dead bodies of rogue witches and vampires, burned my nose. Torin purred in my head, happy that at least some of these mother fuckers were dead.

Osirus had blown the shifter horn, immediately calling us to his aide. I knew the fae would need some help, some damn muscle to push through the enemy lines. I couldn't believe he actually thought his small platoon of fae soldiers would be enough to rescue his mate's friend. If I had learned anything in all my dealings with bloodsuckers, it was that they couldn't be trusted, and now they were working with magical beings to make it all the worse.

We were losing. A dark force had penetrated the walls of the old, ruined compound used hundreds of years ago. The magic around me had my fur stiffen, knowing that the leaking aura of darkness was seeping into our blood.

It was so difficult holding this higher power Torin and I had. We could sense things others couldn't, and oftentimes, it could be too late. Once we entered the glamour spell that hid them inside their hide-out, our healing abilities were severed from our wolves. My warriors were hurt, blood spilling to the ground faster than I ever intended.

The smell and sight of my warrior's cries felt familiar as they tried to dodge fire, electricity, and frozen streams of magic impaling their bodies.

Too familiar.

The worst part was that I couldn't put my finger on where this smell was, this power I had felt before.

Melina, striding in on Osirus's pet dragon, saved us all. She blew the whole shit up in no time. No doubt Osirus was going to be pissed she put herself in danger, but her blue and green wings, the paleness of her hair, and the determination in her eyes let me know she wasn't just a human anymore. She had mated with the fae becoming something entirely different.

"Alpha Kane," Alaneo's voice broke my thoughts as he strode toward me. Osirus had taken Melina out of the burned ruins, along with his dragon. They spoke quickly to each other, mounting the dragon and taking off into the air. "I wanted to give you this." Alaneo pulled out a parchment stamped with the royal seal of the fae.

Grunting and trying to be gentle with my claws, I opened the parchment. It was the coronation of Melina, the lost princess of Atlantis and King Osirus.

Well, I'll be damned.

"Two days," Alaneo spoke loudly as if I wouldn't listen. I probably wouldn't have anyway. Clara was more the diplomatic one. I was a man of simple taste and would give my left nut not to attend this petty coronation.

I take that back. I need it.

Rumbling, I handed it to Marcus, shoving it in his pouch. "Why the fuck are you carrying invitations around during a battle?" I spoke harshly.

"Osirus wanted me to thank you for your appearance today. It was most appreciated," Alaneo said, completely ignoring my question. My warriors brought out other wolves that were burned in the fire. Some groaning, some not moving at all. Gripping my fist, my eyes didn't leave them. They were all good wolves, and I didn't want them to perish over poor planning on Osirus' part.

"We lost many of our soldiers before you arrived. The magic they held was powerful," Alaneo mused, watching the rest of the warriors leaning hurt wolves against trees. "After storming in the ruins, I realized that the entire area was subdued of all of our healing abilities as I saw your wolves not regenerating. It seems they are healing themselves now, however. It's like a ripple. Now that Sorceress Prinna is no longer alive, the magic will fade."

"Fucking hell," an all too familiar voice came up behind us. Jasper, bare to the world, joined us, watching the flames.

"I thought it was surely some joke, but a Dark Fairy passing by told me the whole thing. A sorceress? A rogue sorceress?" I grunted in agreement while Jasper shook his head. He rubbed the stubble on his face, his hair a mess.

"Where are your soldiers from? Do you not have any scouts?" My voice rumbled through my chest. The sharp stings of the wounds that I had sustained now healed.

Thank the gods.

"We're short," Jasper murmured. "We don't have the manpower. I run along the southern border between the territories during the day while Taliyah works with the Parliament to figure things out." I rolled my eyes. Fuck, they were in deeper shit than I thought. If they didn't have any soldiers just to scout the area of their kingdom, their nation was nothing but skin and bones.

"Prince Jasper." Alaneo pulled out another parchment and handed it to him, no doubt another invitation. "For the coronation." Jasper's eyes widened, taking the parchment and holding it to his chest. "Queen Taliyah has already claimed you as a prince. It looks like you didn't know." Alaneo smirked, fixing his armor on his chest.

"Uh, she hadn't told me she had announced it." He scratched his head. "I'm a little shocked." I hummed, now feeling static in my head. Someone was trying to mind-link me and was having trouble hearing the voice.

"Ka—" my mate's voice crackled.

"Could the magic ruin the mind-link?" I growled out. Alaneo stood back, watching Torin flicker his eyes.

"Quite possible," Alaneo mused. "This is a deeper, stronger magic. I wouldn't be surprised if Prinna cast something to block out communications." Growling, the warriors that were once hurt shifted and gathered around me.

While in beast form, I had the ability to speak. I hardly ever used the mind-link, just shouting out orders to those who needed it. What if a warrior needed me? I would have never received the message! Fuck!

"That is something I need to talk to you about, how their magic is stronger—" I cut off Alaneo, now concentrating on my mate.

"We're leaving!" I yelled out. Wolves gathered, watching me approach the woods. "I'll be in contact, Jasper, Alaneo." The long list of questions continued to grow longer. The sorceresses—and possibly sorcerers—that were now helping the rogue vampires were a problem. A big one.

My paws were buried in the stained soil of blood. My maw breathing heavily, letting the soft wisps of steam flow over my face. Clara's call continued to weaken the further away we traveled from the center of the battle.

The magic was still strong here, waiting for the ripples of magic ceasing the outermost parts of the region. The bond still held true, not able to break by some deep magic. Clara and I were too strong to have that break us. No magic ever would.

A howl ripped through me, letting her know we were coming. I felt her pain, her worry. Did she know that I was in trouble from so far away? Sure, bonds were powerful, and maybe the lack of healing of my shoulder proved to worry her more.

Fuck, she ran all the way from the Crimson Shadows pack just to find me? Growling, we pushed forward, almost meeting halfway home. The magic extended far and wide, much farther than any magic should. Nature trembled in fear, Torin radiating the power we held until we stepped into a small clearing of mud and debris.

Warriors, the fastest of our pack, stood by. Their build was not as large, but their swiftness catered just to the luna herself. One hung over her, naked, pulling my mate's claws away from her face. Giana's body shook, clawing at her ears.

Static infiltrated my own ears, trying to hear her call. My voice sunk out of Torin's maw, which ceased Clara's rapid movements. Kneeling before her, I pulled her into my arms. Her warriors stood back, kneeling, baring their necks. I hummed into her ear, her body covered in dirt.

"I've got you." I pushed away the mud from her face. "Everything is all right." She clung to me, only to open her eyes, feeling over my shoulder. So she did feel it, every bit of my pain.

"Rest," I urged her. She rested her head next to my shoulder, my arms so large it covered her tiny body. "Skye," she murmured. "Dust. The powder." Clara's hand touched my chest, her cold body a stark difference from the warm glow that invaded my heart.

She was using her healing powers unknowingly, but why she would try and use them then, I wouldn't understand. "Rest," I urged her again until she fell asleep.

Not saying a word, I ticked my head in the direction of home. The magic fading quickly, enveloping us all as the warrior that tried to help my mate shifted again. The scratches from their run, the exhaustion that loomed over them now lifted, ready for us to return home.

Clara lay in our bed. Her deep breathing had me at ease. She wasn't thrashing, trying to grip onto me as I sat beside her. Our daughter watched her intently, holding onto her arm as she lay with her. Evelyn's eyes drifted, watching her sleep until she too succumbed to her mother's calm aura.

When I entered the pack grounds, the warriors were frantic. My father went into alpha mode, trying to get a handle on things. When word got out that the luna ran off the pack territory, it made them fear I would come after all of them, seek my wrath on them all if anything happened to my luna.

I probably would have.

But I was a different wolf now. After bathing and setting her in bed, Raine and Leia stood at the door of our room. "Watch over them." I growled, heading to the doorway. "I'm sorry," Raine muttered. Her eyes didn't meet mine as I continued to walk down the stairs.

It wasn't her fault; none of it was. I tried to save my mate from the worry. There were no plans to battle this day, but the nagging feeling in the back of my head told me something was amiss. As much as Clara had confided in me about her strange dreams, I had them also.

Running up the stairs, finding darkness and blood, yet no recollection of anything else. As she held her hand next to my beating heart as we traveled home, more scenes pulled together inside. Being the unemotional piece of shit, Torin pushed them away and concentrated on our mate.

"Powder, the white powder," Clara was mumbling into the mind-link. Giana must have kept it open, so if Clara had another nightmare, I could run and find her.

"I'm so sorry." August ran through the foyer of the pack house. His heavy pants and waving his hand in front of his face didn't have me forgiving him so easily. "What happened?" I gritted my teeth. I wouldn't let my father elaborate on how Clara was able to run past all the warriors and get free of the protection of the pack. I had to keep her safe now since I failed to do so earlier.

"I wasn't with her when it happened. I was told she panicked and ran after you when she couldn't mind-link you. I was in the office." He puffed out his chest, trying to gain his confidence. "I was in a meeting with a sorceress."

My head perked up in surprise. Sorceresses don't just talk to anyone. They stick to their own kind, their covens. You would have a better time talking to a witch rather than a sorceress. "Who contacted who?"

Children ran by, giggling, breaking the tension between us until he stiffened again. "She contacted me; she was specifically looking for Clara's parents, but they are not near any reflecting mirrors for communication. She found me when I sat in your office going over financials."

Shit, shit, shit.

"Office." I growled. Opening the door to my office, papers spread across the desk. August was an effective gamma; his organizational skills were lacking, but he knew where everything was. My desk, on the other hand, I hated that it was a fucking mess.

"Sorry, I'll clean it." He cowered back. Torin was soothing Giana inside my mind, causing me to be distracted. "Just spit it out." I huffed, sitting on one of the black leather couches, pouring myself some scotch.

"Anyway, this sorceress, she had a vision. I am surprised Queen Eden hasn't had one yet," August mused.

"Clara's mom can't pick what to see in the future. She sees what is granted. Sorceresses can pull strings, dance with the devil, and prance around a field of dead cats, shit that Queen Eden doesn't do," I said sarcastically. Taking the drink down in one go, I poured another. "What did she say?" Gulping the rest of my second glass, I set it on the glass table. August jumped at the sharp sound, and my head turned to meet him.

Why the hell is he so nervous?

"It was Sorceress Cyrene, from the Earth realm."

Shit.

Chapter Seventeen

Taliyah

I pulled the magnifying spectacles off my face, rubbing my painful eyes. Even the whites around my irises were red. Papers sat scattered across my desk, the computer I had used taking some of the mess with it, but even then, I had windows open with budgets, laws, past laws, and the sort.

After going through an extensive library day in and day out, there was nothing I could find. Nothing in the history of the Vermillion Kingdom to give me some sort of hope for the future. Not only had most vampires turned on the kingdom, but now witches and warlocks had too. I prayed to the gods that no sorcerers or sorceresses were being pulled into the dark; otherwise, we would really be in some trouble.

The magical beings usually had covens scattered across the land of Bergarian, but many took residence in Vermillion over the years. Covens were small, nomadic, much like the gypsies I had read about on Earth. Wadding up another piece of worthless parchment, I threw it in the nearby trash. Its contents were already running forth with nothing but dead ends and disappointment.

This kingdom used to be such a lovely place. Within the last thousand years, it had become desolate as the centuries went on. The pictures that hung on the walls showed life filled with animals in the darkened forests.

It reminded me of the Brothers Grimm stories and the artists who would paint their tales.

Bare feet hitting the cold stone floor stood outside the office door. The candles blew toward me as the air shifted. Jasper, my constant rock the past few months, came in bearing nothing but black slacks and a bare chest. His feet were bare yet clean of dirt. His eyes softened once he met mine. His heavy footsteps carried him around the desk only to pick me up and put me in his arms.

"My mate." His nose went into my neck. "You've been working too hard. It's late." I smiled softly at him, tracing his sandy beard with my finger. His hair had grown just to his cheekbones. He wished to cut it, but I wouldn't let him.

"I was just waiting up for you." I kissed his cheek. Jasper frowned, narrowing his eyes at me.

"That's a lie. You've been working," he whispered accusingly.

"Well, I worked while you were away," I corrected myself. "Now tell me, what did you find?" Jasper growled in his chest as he pulled away from my neck. The scruff left chills down my body.

Our passionate kisses, feeding on his neck and rubbing in places, had me begging for more. My body was ready anyway, but my mind was still apprehensive. He was so much more experienced.

Experienced in a way I really hated.

"By the time I got to the ruins, it was up in flames. Melina brought Horus, Osirus's dragon, and torched the place of all the rogue vampires." Jasper rounded the desk, tapping his middle finger on the hardwood surface. "A sorceress was there, Prinna. Blood Coven leader." Jasper rambled off. "She's dead. We don't have to worry about her," he said without emotion.

I let out a sigh, pulling my hair around my shoulders, braiding it as I leaned back in the chair. Jasper came behind me, putting his hands on my shoulders. "Are you sure she's dead? She may have done something to..."

"She's dead," Jasper snapped, running his hands through his hair. "Horus swallowed her whole." I gulped, not liking his tone. Xander was growling obscenities at him. I'm not sure if Jasper was aware, but Xander was becoming louder every day. Shooting off comments in his head about how we haven't mated. It only made me more agitated and more stressed.

"Maybe that is the only one." Jasper cleared his throat. "I'm hoping so anyway." Xander crawled up in Jasper's mind. I swear I thought I saw him looking straight at me. His once angry eyes softened, his eyebrows raised, whining at me as his jaw sat on his paws.

He didn't feel wanted.

"Osirus and Melina's mating ceremony and coronation are in a few days." Jasper pulled an envelope from his pocket. "They understand if we can't come. They know we are trying our best." I hummed, taking the envelope and putting it on the table. There was no way I was leaving the broken kingdom in this state.

I had dived into the world laid out in front of me, trying to rebuild a dying kingdom. Rogue witches, vampires, and who knows what else was building. It was getting stronger by the day, and there was nothing I could do. Jasper leaned against the desk, his muscles stiff with worry, and I wasn't sure if it was for the kingdom, me, or the both of us.

I had put mating off for the longest time and always remained busy. The sparks were hard to ignore, and they were both suffering. It had been long enough, long enough for him to show me he was more than willing to wait.

My soul couldn't stand it, he couldn't stand it, and Xander had already voiced his opinion. Walking my body around where Jasper had leaned up against the desk, his rippling muscles still gleaming with sweat. His downward glance at the cream-colored carpet became but a memory as he looked at my face.

"I'm sorry." I bit my cheek. Jasper's knuckles brushed the cheek I was biting, shaking his head.

"Don't be," he whispered. "I sure made a mess of things in the past. Maybe I haven't made up enough for it. I shouldn't be upset." He chuckled, dropping his hand. I grabbed it, putting it back on my cheek.

"But you have," I pushed. "I'm... I'm just inexperienced, and I worry—" Jasper pinched my chin, tilting it upward. His teeth caught my lips, sucking them into his mouth. Arms wrapping around my waist, he pulled me into his warm embrace. Hands digging into my hair, he growled, his shaft pushing right into my stomach. I moaned, scratching my nails down his back.

"Taliyah." His lips left me briefly to whisper a silent prayer of my name. "Taliyah, I don't fucking care about experience. You are perfect for me." His tongue invaded my mouth. The warmth of his tongue and his fingers digging into my hips had me melting.

Holding me up as my weak knees trembled, he broke away, panting. "Anything important on this desk?" I tilted my head in confusion until his arm swiped the entire desk. Papers, pens, and the cursed computer dropped to the floor.

Jasper picked me up, having me straddle his waist as he roughly sat me on the desk. "Now tell me"—his eyes flashed to Xander—"what have you been hiding from me, little witch?" I hummed, looking down at my hands only to have that damn finger lift my chin up. "Answer me." He growled. As angry as Jasper was getting right now, I was utterly turned on. My inner thighs were shaking with anticipation. His nostrils flared, his eyes rolling back in his head.

"I worry that I will not know what to do." I panted. "That I won't be good enough." Jasper shook his head, both hands sitting beside my hips.

"Oh, Taliyah." He chuckled. "Don't you know it is I who is nervous?" My mouth hung open, shaking my head. "Oh yes. What you fail to realize is I didn't care for any of those other women. I got what I wanted and left; I was a dick." Shutting my mouth, I stared at him. "Now that I have my mate," his finger trailed down my neck. "I want nothing more than to fucking please her, and I have been dying to try one thing I have never done on any woman."

I visibly gulped, watching Jasper and that devilish smirk slide across his face. "And I want to do it right now." My mind went a mile a minute, trying to think what he had never done to a woman. I ended up blank as he parted my legs. The dress I wore inched up my thighs, his eyes never leaving me while biting his lower lip.

"May I?" Xander flashed before Jasper's eyes. "We won't go all the way," he whispered in my ear. Hands ran up my thighs until one hand had a claw scratched the desk.

"Gracious," I whispered, feeling the heat of Jasper's breath. "Okay." My voice shook. Jasper breathed deeply, his fingers trailing near my inner thighs. My hands went to grip his shoulders. He licked his lips as his fingers inched forward.

"How do you feel about..." He growled, taking a claw and pulling down one side of my dress. The fabric grazed my shoulder, falling down my arm. My body was so turned on that there wasn't a way I was saying no. Not under this gaze of lust he held in his eyes. I felt wanted and adored, and all the things he had done for me in the past few months came to the forefront of my mind.

He wanted me; he had pursued me, and now he asked if he could do wicked things to my body. "Yes." I breathed heavily into his mouth. Jasper pulled down my dress harshly, the silk-like fabric falling just above my breasts. His groan of impatience had him curse between his teeth as he pulled the fabric just below my nipples, pushing my breasts upward.

"Oh fuck." He pushed me down on the desk, hovering over me, pawing at every inch of my skin. One hand pinched my nipple while the other was being sucked on by his mouth. His tongue circled my nipple, pulling it with his lips. My knees rose, and my legs rubbed his torso as he stood over me with a heated breath.

"You are so fucking gorgeous." His teeth bit into my skin. "And mine." My hands pulled on his hair, only for his head to slip away. The golden eyes of Xander stared back at me, my elbows lifting from the table to hold the upper part of my body steady while he inched down. The cool air caused my nipples to harden from Jasper's absence.

"Ready?" Jasper's lips kissed my hip bone, my dress now bunched around my torso. My poor panties didn't know what was coming as Jasper ripped both sides with his claws, throwing them to the floor. My body was completely open to him, my hands balled up into fists, staring at his hungry eyes.

"W-what are you doing?" If it were possible, Jasper pushed my legs wider, his nose going straight for my pussy. *Oh, gods, he wouldn't!*

His nose grazed my clit, and my body shook with pleasure. My head leaned back; my breasts were exposed so openly as his warm tongue flicked my clit. "Jasper!" I yelled, only for him to hum in response. His tongue licked every lip, dipping his tongue deeper into my pussy. Hips gyrating on their own. He tasted me, loved me, and poured every bit of himself into my pleasure.

Legs shaking without control, my thighs gripped around his head. Jasper's chuckles only vibrated his assault until he sucked my clit with all his might. "Gods!" My back arched, slamming into the desk. My hands pushed into his hair, making sure he didn't leave that sweet spot he was hitting.

His hands gripped my ass, pushing his face impossibly deeper inside. Screaming his name, I felt utterly damp while he sucked me dry. My breath came down in heaving pants until my mate hovered over my body.

Hand caressing my breast, his mouth descended to me, now able to taste not just him but me as well. "So damn delicious!" Jasper nipped at my neck. The fabric of his tight pants pushed against my bare pussy. My hips moved on their own accord. My desirous mind had me thinking of doing things to him and no longer worrying if I was a clumsy fool.

"C-can I?" I muttered. My finger and thumb rubbed against each other, slowly unbuckling his pants. His eyes widened as he groaned, pushing his cock between the apex of my thighs. His belt dropped to the floor with a clang. I tried to use my power to unbutton his pants. To my surprise, Jasper stopped me with a tender kiss. "It's all about you, Taliyah. Tonight is all about you." His fingers ran back down my leg, his mouth sucking my neck as I felt his fingers wiggle between my lips.

"Let's see how tight you are."

Chapter Eighteen

Jasper

I would not mess this up. None of this was going to be ruined. I had this planned down to the very last pucker of my lips to her clit.

I wasn't lying when I said I was a dick when I was younger. I concentrated on myself. My other partners' pleasure was definitely not on the top of my to-do list. If they came, great, the more, the merrier, but this—*this*—I wanted to make sure it was perfect just for her.

I hoped to make her come, and come often. I couldn't stomach it if she didn't, and with it being her first time receiving and my first time really giving, I was a nervous piece of shit. How would I live with myself if I did something wrong? Hell, I had never concentrated so hard in my life as I made out with her pussy. Each breath hitched, the trembling of her legs. I watched it all, trying to find hints I was doing the right things to her body.

Xander wasn't any help either. The damn mutt had gotten me into trouble before. I thought your wolf was supposed to be some sort of guide in your life, but damn it, I got stuck with a faulty one. He could only concentrate on watching her glorious pussy drip with her arousal and having a brain fart, not giving me any guidance whatsoever.

Great job, Xander.

Xander howled for joy as Taliyah's fingers rubbed together, causing her magic to pull at the top buttons of my jeans. The gentle pop on my abdomen had me groaning with desire as my belt hit the floor with a clang. The sound woke Xander from his stupor, his body pacing in the back of my mind, growling, waiting for me to stick my dick in what was ours and claim her. Xander was blatantly clear he wanted to mark our mate. He had no fucking patience, and he was playing the devil's advocate, trying to get me to fuck up. He was all damn wolf and had no feelings toward making our mate comfortable during this rough transition of being queen and our mate.

So damn close to having her sweet lips wrapped around my cock. It was all that I had ever dreamed of since I met her.

"Tonight is all about you," I muttered, trying to restrain myself. Even though my dick was waving in front of her glorious pussy, I would not let it sink deep into her. Gods, it was so hard. She was damn pulling off my jeans with her magic, but I had to keep my cool. I wanted her to want me not just in body but in soul as well. We had come so far; I had worked so hard for her to see the real me and push Xander back into my mind. The damn devil couldn't keep me away from her, and I was going to do whatever I could to let her know she was mine, and all I wanted was to make her happy.

My other hand trailed her wide hips, pulling in the claws that I had used to rip off her clothes. She was bloody amazing, laying out, sprawled on her desk as before I violated her pussy. Her back arched, and the sweetest whimper left her lips. Her desk was now damp with her juices, her glorious white thighs still shaking with anticipation.

My lips hovered over her mouth, her eyes swimming with pools of desire as I inched my finger inside, spreading her lips wide. Her eyebrows raised, feeling the intrusion of my fingers. Taliyah's eyes closed, and for a moment, I closed mine as well, thinking that my fingers were about to finger fuck the ever-living shit out of my mate.

If only it could be my cock.

Using just one finger, I curled it inside her body. A sweet gasp left her until I pulled it out and pushed it back in, ever so slowly. Taunting her, touching her, my fangs pulled at her mouth. "Tell me what you like," I whispered into her mouth, hovering over her, leaning over the desk.

"Faster." Her heart picked up, her hair no longer spreading across the desk but floating around her. Her mind had been closed off. She was living in the now, not thinking of all the troubles that surrounded her.

Make her forget her problems was now my mantra. Her pussy walls clenched my one finger. She was so damn tight it would take time to stretch her to fill my raging erection. Slow and steady, that's what we would do, so I wouldn't hurt her when I finally marked her as mine.

"Another," she rasped. My finger had been pushing deep into her body, curling at one particular spot she loved. Her lower back was fully off the desk, giving her body that sweet curl of the spine. I couldn't wait to see it when I plummeted her from behind one day.

"You want to feel an orgasm?" I chuckled. "I'm working on it." Biting my lip, trying not to come like a pubescent teen, my body fucking humped her leg like a damn monkey. "More... fingers." She barely rasped the words until surprise sprung on my face. Her eyes were still closed. I dare not question her, not wanting to pull her out of the trance she had put herself in.

Her hair was lifted from the desk, her back now hovering an inch above the wood. Holy fuck, making love to her was going to be interesting. Readying my thick middle finger to insert into her dripping pussy, her body lifted completely off the table as I stood. Her arms wrapping around my neck, I stared at her in awe while her eyes bore into me.

Fucking angel.

"Jasper," she begged. I wouldn't have that, not one bit. Legs wrapping around me, I stood there, barely holding her up because whatever magic shit this was, gave me plenty of strength to push my digits deep inside.

Sliding in the next finger, her head threw back as she groaned. Holy fuck, so damn tight. Pushing into her, her walls fluttered. My head went straight into her neck, sucking her tender skin as I pushed in and out of her body. Her hovering body moved with the rhythm of my fingers. "Jasper!" she cried out, her fingers pulling my hair.

Groaning, I continued to finger fuck her as her body tensed. "That's it, come on my fingers, little witch." She groaned again, pulling my head into her breasts as I bit into her nipple. "Jasper!"

"You like it when I talk dirty?" Moaning, scratching down my back, she came around me. So damn tight, even with the come dripping out of her body. "That's my sweet little witch," I cooed in her ear. Her body relaxed, her hair no longer floating in the air, until her body sweetly rested in my arms.

Feeling the full weight of her body now leaning into me, I wrapped my arms around her, licking my fingers while her head lulled into my neck.

I could see wonderful dark hickies strung all over her neck in my peripheral. No one would touch her. She was mine; she bared my temporary mark, my scent. Nipping her shoulder, she shivered, humming in contentment.

"Did I satisfy my mate?" Xander came to the surface, pushing me to the side. "Did Jasper and I provide for you?" Xander isn't one to please other people, the selfish prick. This time, he really wanted the approval of Taliyah, the only one that was made for us.

"Yes, Xander," Taliyah whispered, her heated breath tickling my now sweaty back. "I'm very pleased." She softened her laugh and had Xander purring. "I'm sorry I've been staying away from you."

Xander growled, his disapproval of our mate's words getting under his fur. "We deserved it." He hummed. "I don't want anyone to steal you from us." The whine had Taliyah's body stiffen. I placed her delicately on the desk, Xander still wanting to speak to her.

Cupping our face, she rubbed her nose against ours, her tits trickling down my chest. "I won't go anywhere; just stop giving Jasper a hard time." Her eyes narrowed into Xander's. "I mean it." Fuck, she was hot when she was bossy.

"I... I haven't..." He trailed. Taliyah only squinted her eyes, raising a finger to tap our nose. "Xander," she scolded. He retreated back into my mind, and my body fully returned to me. Pecking her lips, she hummed playfully, pressing her tits to my chest.

Fuuuuuuck.

"Let me run you a bath." I grabbed a decorative blanket that hung over her white couch and pulled it around her shoulders. I didn't need any of the help seeing a naked queen being carried around. Wrapping her up in a soft burrito, she giggled, trying to get out of my hold.

"Nope, I'm carrying you." Kissing her forehead, I walked up the stairs, albeit a bit weirdly since my belt was gone and my jeans now sat very loosely around my hips. Trying to keep my pants up was difficult, but luckily my muscular thighs wouldn't allow them to go much lower.

After getting my mate ready for bed, I tucked her inside the covers, pulling her toward me. My raging blue balls would have to wait until she fell asleep so I could take care of that problem. The soft silk of her nightgown rubbed against my body, causing me to shiver when her nipples strained against it.

"How is Clara?" Taliyah had already closed her eyes, her nose into my neck. I try not to bring up Clara since it was such a sore spot for her, yet she surprises me with this question.

"She's fine." I tightened my hold on Taliyah. "She's been trying to balance her luna, future queen duties, and dealing with Evelyn." When I found Kane staring at the burning ruins of the rogue witch coven, his face was worse for wear. His eyes were sunken in, and his heart's heaviness wore him down.

Clara was having difficulty balancing it all, and who could blame her? She was a fucking waitress a little over seven months ago. Now she was a werewolf, princess, luna, mother, and now dealing with a damn uprising of rogues, mostly from Vermillion. She had a lot of shit going on. I guess you could also include trying to keep Kane calm as one of her jobs too.

That was a full-time job right there.

Clara was thrown into a messy world, and she wanted to help everyone. Her decision to stay back and take care of Evelyn instead of accompanying Kane with a lead on who might be in charge of the black magic broke her. Kane ended up fighting in an enormous battle with Osirus over some rogues, and Clara felt every hit, cut, and tear of his skin. It worried her to death because she couldn't mind-link, and she ended up running halfway to the battle until the spells had broken for her to speak with him.

Kane mind-linked me later, telling me she had broken down crying in the middle of the forest. The magic had been too much, the bond was stretched thin, but they made it. They made it back to the pack house to have her recover.

"She's having trouble, but she will be fine," I explained to my mate. She obviously was not. "I have hope for her. Goddess Charis gave her many gifts to help her. She'll do great things," I mumbled. Taliyah's eyelashes fluttered on my chest. Rubbing her arm tenderly, her head looked up at me.

"She and Kane have done a lot for us. I don't know how to ever repay them." She hummed. "Maybe we should have them come visit, see what we have done so far with the help they have sent us with the blood bags and the funds." Petting Taliyah's head, I purred, causing her body to completely go limp. My mate was tired.

"We made her tired." Xander growled playfully.

"As much as I would love for them to see what we have done so far, they must go to Osirus and Melina's coronation. It is expected of them to go since Clara's parents are busy visiting the outlying territories of the shifter kingdom."

"Hmm, another time then?" She yawned until I felt her breathing go even, falling into a deep sleep.

Chapter Nineteen

Kane

Cyrene was powerful; there was no doubt about that. She kept hidden in the Earth realm, helping a small coven grow to its full potential. She liked the quiet life, especially since her power grew. Cyrene was no fool. She knew that people would try to extort her power, try to use her, and hurt her friends or family to do it.

"She resides in the Black Claws pack with Alpha Wesley and Luna Charlotte," August mentioned. I rubbed my face with my palm.

"He found his mate," I muttered, crossing my arms. Wesley was the most powerful werewolf in the Earth realm. He kept things quiet, and kept the other packs in line. If there was to be a king of shifters in the Earth realm, it would be him, but that wasn't how things worked over there. They were all very territorial.

"Yes, Cyrene said she defeated a demon." My eyes twitched, turning to August. He stepped back, Torin growling in the back of my throat. "A demon?" I questioned.

"Something about Hades losing control on one of his demons, or demoness, I should say." August sat on the opposite couch, taking a glass of ice and pouring himself a drink. August wasn't a drinker, so this must be some interesting news.

"A demoness called Trixten. Hades was involved and even showed himself to the entire pack of wolves, including Cyrene's coven. He gave them the job of finding the demoness since he couldn't find her himself." Leaning back into the couch, I scratched my head. My body was still riddled with dried blood, leaves, and dirt. I should have taken the time to bathe myself, but I was too worried about Clara.

"And why is she divulging us this information? This seems like an isolated incident?"

"Is it, though?" August raised a brow. His body hung over his now spread legs, his elbows resting on the upper part of his body. "Think about it. Hades lost control of one of his demons. Do you think there are more?" I shook my head. Surely not. He was a damn god. He would have more sense than that.

"Why couldn't he control Trixten? Why her?" August's eyes dropped to the floor. "Something about not putting a drop of blood in her system when she was created, so he is able to track his creation. This makes me ask myself, did he forget? Are there more demons like this? Could this be filtering over to Bergarian?" August's voice raced, his heart pounding in his chest.

"Well, if a luna could beat the demon, that means there is hope then. We can easily destroy the rest." I waved my hand absentmindedly. My eyes trailed out to the window, pups ran across the yard, and the playground Clara had installed was filled with little warriors swinging from the bars. I smirked, thinking how I couldn't wait for Evelyn to begin her training.

"Trixten may have been easily beaten," August mentioned, following my gaze. "Trixten possessed a weakened witch's body. She used it for her own desires and stayed hidden from Hades for years. Trixten was ultimately defeated because the body she inhabited was mortal." Growling, I slammed my fist to the coffee table, causing the glasses to click together.

"Spit it out, August. I don't have all damn day!" My fucking mate was upstairs, sleeping, and Giana was chanting in my head for Torin to listen to her and let her heal him. Torin being a dick was blocking her because he didn't think he needed to be fixed.

The dumb fuck.

August flinched. "Trixten possessed this witch's body and was able to use her powers to walk about the soil of both realms. Rogue witches and sorcerers have now realized they can pull down their barriers and let demons possess their bodies, combining their powers." August licked his lips, shaking his head. "If a demon moved their spirit into a magical entity such as a witch and used their body, you could kill the supernatural's body, but not the demon's. That demon could jump from body to body that harbors ill-will until the deed they want to be accomplished is done." August's face went pale, his body cowering at my heated gaze.

"And this is what Cyrene has told you?" August nodded, gulping down another shot of scotch.

"And what of this Trixen? Has she inhabited another body yet?" I rubbed my brow. My stomach was going to end up with an ulcer by the time this was done.

August shook his head. "No, Trixten has been destroyed by Hades himself. She purposefully pissed him off before she left the Underworld. These demons that are possessing magical entities are going under the radar since their bodies aren't leaving the Underworld, just their spirits."

Well, shit.

"Cyrene's had a premonition." I heaved a heavy breath. August was on my shit list now, even if he was the messenger. The room fell more silent if ever possible, a passing cloud hiding the blue moon outside the window.

"Cyrene has seen three demons with dark intentions. She doesn't know their names, but these demons are trying to break free from the bonds they are being held from deep within the Underworld. Cyrene has limited contact with Hades as it is, and her power is weak when she tries to summon him. Cyrene is no longer trying to use her power to summon him for questioning to save her power. She says it is time to prepare for the worst."

I returned upstairs, treading lightly. Three demon spirits we now had to worry about. Was it all connected, or was it a strange coincidence that we were having problems during the same time the Black Claws pack had their trouble?

At least Trixen was dead, but now having to worry about killing the spirits would be another problem. Peeking my head in the doorway, Raine and Dean sat on the nearby sofa, holding onto each other. They watched Clara's steady breaths as they whispered to themselves.

Quietly, I came across the room, their eyes holding nothing but worry. "I'm sorry," I muttered. Dean's eyes widened, his body coming up from the couch, pushing down his black dress pants. "Clara has been having trouble adjusting to her new role as luna. I'm trying to give her less to worry about her because we all know when my mate is upset, I can lose my head." My sister smiled, pulling me into a hug.

"Thank the gods you found her," she whispered. "She's too good for you," she chided.

"Believe me, I know," I kissed her cheek as they left the room.

Crawling into bed after a scalding shower, the mind-link was still left wide open for me to listen to Clara's thoughts. She was rambling in her head, unaware anyone was listening.

"The white powder?" she thought in her dream. Giana was curled up around Clara's mind, comforting her with whines and licks. My grip on my family grew tighter with Evelyn smashed between us. Kissing her forehead, purring in my chest, Clara's ramblings fell silent as we all fell asleep.

The next morning, to my surprise, Clara was already dressed. Evelyn was sitting on the bed, pounding on my chest, looking at my piercings.

"Morning, Alpha." Clara's words were quiet as she buttoned up the front part of her dress. The tea-length dresses she liked to wear were sweet and flowed with the wind. It gave her the young look she loved so much. A bright pink ribbon tied around her French braid held her hair away from her face.

"Love, come here," my voice came out more harshly than it should, but my mate only smiled at me, crawling into the bed. Her head landed right on my chest as I stroked her cheek with my thumb. Evelyn cooed, now trying to pull my damn piercing out of my nipple.

"No, no," I whined. Evelyn, finding it funny, continued to try and pull it more.

"You need to tell me when you are going to fight, Kane." Clara's eyes narrowed. "I know you are trying to help me, but keeping things from me won't work. I thought you learned this when you tried to hide the whole rogue king fiasco." My head hit the back of the pillow. Closing my eyes, I let out a slow breath.

"I know, and for that, I'm sorry." Clara's head perked up, her body leaning over to meet me square in the eye. "The big alpha is sorry? What world have we been transported to?" She giggled, kissing my cheek.

"I've been apologizing a lot lately. It seems you are rubbing off on me." Her face visibly softened, kissing my lips. "Good, I've been worried about how you have treated some of those warriors."

"Hey, I didn't kill that one warrior that had his paws all over you yesterday," I defended.

"Really? Good. Otherwise, I'd have to punish you." She winked. "He was trying to save me from myself. The static was deafening." She rubbed her ears again.

"That was because of a spell Sorceress Prinna had cast. It kept us from healing, blocked the mind-link too." Torin rumbled in my chest, causing Clara to grip hold of my leg with hers. I smiled, biting my lip so hard not to say anything.

So damn responsive.

"So that is why I couldn't reach you." Her finger trailed my stomach. Evelyn found toys on the bed, playing as she rolled to the other pillow. "That doesn't explain how I am piecing back together memories."

"Are you sure they are memories?" I questioned. "They could very well be some sort of spell." Clara shook her head, touching her heart. "No, Skye is real," she said determinedly.

"I remember it much more clearly. She was helping me." Clara paused, sitting up in the bed. "We all were, the entire encampment. We couldn't hear you through the link then either." Her head darted to me. "That was why we went to the palace."

"You mean, you think this same spell we just experienced was used on us just a week ago?" Clara hummed in agreement. "I just need to know how the powder fits into this. I wish Torin would stop being a dick and let Giana heal her so I wasn't the only one seeing these scenes be put together." Her eyes narrowed, Torin taking control of my body.

"I need you safe. My mate needs to be safe." He growled in her ear. She shivered and laid back down.

"Well, if you keep Giana from healing you, then you won't get the special prize I owe you and Kane." Clara stuck out her lip. "Like, it's a good one too, and my heat is almost here." She snickered.

"Is it now?" Torin purred, pulling on her earlobe. Evelyn sat up in the bed, looking at us, questioning. "As long as it involves me fucking you to oblivion, I don't think I really care what it is." Clara gasped, slapping our chest.

"No cursing in front of the baby!" she hissed. Evelyn crawled over, pointing to my eyes. The dark eyes of Torin stared right back at her. "Pa." She pointed.

"Oh my goddess! She said, 'pa'!" Clara cried. "Torin, you are now known as 'pa,' and Kane is now daddy!" Evelyn clapped her hands repeatedly until

I came back to the surface. Picking up my little daughter, I rubbed my nose with hers.

"Is that right? Who am I now?" Evelyn turned her head. "Da!" she squealed in delight.

"That is so precious," Clara cooed, laying back down with all of us. Evelyn continued to pick at the barbell on my chest as Clara sighed.

"You are doing better, right, love?" Clara hummed, pushing back a dark curl from Evelyn's hair. "Right now, yes. I'm always going to worry until we figure everything out." I smiled, pulling her closer to me.

⁓⋆⁓

After asking her countless times if she was safe to travel, we headed to the Golden Light Kingdom. Instead of running, we had an entire caravan behind us as we traveled. It was easier to travel with a baby in a carriage than try and strap her to our backs. We ran straight toward the light sources until we arrived at the Golden Light Kingdom.

Clara's eyes widened as we approached, the Golden Light Kingdom much brighter than what we had experienced when we last battled. There were no pools of blood, not a single tree branch misplaced. Just over a week or so ago, you would have never thought there was a battle for the crown.

"It looks like nothing has changed." She hummed. "Like nothing ever happened. I just hope those who lost their lives are never forgotten." I put my arm around my mate. Her delicate heart wept for those that we lost.

August again stayed behind, taking care of those who had lost their mates. We had at least twenty of our men gone, no bodies accounted for. Some that were mated with children. Their mates, who were devastated, still held onto small children who would continue to live on until the child could take care of themselves. A small memorial service was held in the short time we had been at home, but with more impending battles with rogue vampires, wolves, and magical beings, it was back to business as usual.

"They won't be forgotten." I kissed her forehead. "Once we figure things out, maybe we should do a larger memorial." Clara instantly agreed, her hand wrapping around my thigh.

It had been almost a full day, and I hadn't gotten much time alone with my mate. Once she realized we were invited to Osirus's coronation and bonding ceremony, she made us hop in the carriage at once, barely packing anything.

Adjusting my pants, Clara threw me a wide grin. "Are you all right, Alpha?" she purred.

Fuck no, I wasn't all right. I had a raging boner. I was trying to be a good mate, she fucking passed out yesterday, and I was trying to make her rest as best as I can.

The carriage came to a stop, and confusion covered my face. Raine poked her head in, looking around. "Where's Evie?" Clara handed our daughter to my sister. "What are you doing?" I growled out, ready to take our daughter back. My mate put her hand on my arm, only whispering it was all right. Instantly calming, Raine threw a wink my way and headed back to her own carriage with Dean.

"What are you doing?" Before the carriage could begin again, Clara was straddled in my lap, her lips reaching me and pushing my head back into the soft cushion of the seat.

"You've been so good taking care of me," she purred. "Thought I should take care of you before we arrive."

"You have a hidden motive," I snapped. Clara rolled her eyes, her finger trailing down my open tunic. "Maybe, but at least we both get something out of it."

She had a point.

Chapter Twenty

Clara

Yup, I knew what I was doing.

Before we came up to the palace, I knew I had to relieve some of Kane's tension. He had been stiff as a board the entire morning before we left and while we traveled. Torin's eyes flickered between me and the scene outside. Even Evelyn was watching him intently.

I apologized profusely to Raine and Dean through the link for how sorry I was. I lost myself, upset that my mate was in danger, but they denied my apology, saying it was perfectly reasonable. At least they knew not to hide things from me because of what Kane said.

I was the future queen. I snickered to myself.

"What are you smiling about?" Kane's husky voice whined, leaning his head back while my lips grazed his neck.

Pancakes, he can read me so well.

"Just thinking how I should relieve some of this tension you are having." My breath tickled across his neck. Nipping it with my fangs, he growled, pushing his claws into my butt. "You have been stiff all morning." My pussy rubbed against the soft, tanned leather he was wearing.

He was, indeed, stiff.

"You passed out yesterday, and here we are traveling to the Golden Light Kingdom. Of course I'm going to be tense. You should be resting." His actions didn't match his words, his hands pushing me harder into his erection. A giggle slipped my lips, and his eyes darted to me.

Hard and rough, his lips pushed into me. He ravaged my mouth, tongue sweeping into my own. I panted, rubbing my panties on the bulge in his pants. "Well, right now," I managed to mumble, "I want to take care of you." Groaning, he let go of my hips as my mouth kissed down his chest, sucking on the barbell that pierced his nipple. He gasped, making my thighs rub together at the thought my body could do this to my mate.

"Baby." He groaned, trying to pull me up, but I wasn't going to listen. I trailed down further, untying his tunic until my knees hit the bottom of the carriage floor. Hands rubbing up and down his inner thighs, my lashes fluttered while my hands tugged at the tie of his pants.

"These are amazing," I mused, tilting my head as I thoughtfully pulled the string. "So much better than jeans. I'm sure your dick appreciates it." Kane groaned again, sitting up as I pulled down his pants to his muscular thighs. The tattoos running across them had me running my finger through the thick tribal bands. One tattoo, in particular, stuck out. It was new.

"Oh, Kane." I wanted to pull him into a kiss, but instead, my finger trailed across my name that was embedded in his innermost thigh. It was so close to his manhood; I knew it had to hurt. For any human, this would have been something cheesy, but this was my alpha that had his soul sewn into mine.

"I wanted to do 'property of Clara,' but the tattoo artist in the pack said that would be too much." I burst out laughing, trying to hold my hand over my mouth. Nodding frantically, I leaned forward, kissing him on the lips. "It would have been too much." I kissed his lips again.

As I leaned forward, his raging erection poked my still-covered breasts. "Pull them out for me." Kane's finger pushed down on the elastic that held my breasts in my dress. It was the perfect nursing dress for Evelyn, and apparently, Kane wanted me to continue to wear them long after Evelyn was done nursing. Pulling down my top, his cock brushed over my breasts. The pearl of come on his tip wiped down the front.

"Fucking beautiful." My own desire had me rubbing my thighs again, and my head dipped lower to lick his cock from base to tip. "Shit, shit." He pushed my head lower as soon as my mouth opened, pulling him in. "Fuck. Clara, damn."

One hand trailed down to his balls, cupping them both, massaging as Kane pushed my head further down. Choking, Kane pushed his cock further into my mouth. Something about him taking over the control had my heart flipping in my chest.

"Play with it," he commanded me. "Play with your clit while you suck me off." Giana purred in my head, obliging. Lifting my dress, my breasts feeling the cool air from the outside of the carriage, Kane's warm hand wrapped around my breast.

Rubbing my clit as Kane's cock dominated my mouth, I felt myself falling apart way too fast. As much as I wanted to be in control of everything now that I had all these titles hanging above my head, I loved it when Kane took me in the bedroom. I forgot who I was, forgot all the troubles, and just fell into a space I could call my own.

"I'm so fucking jealous of your fingers." Kane strained. "It should be my mouth." I hummed, pushing my fingers deeper into my pussy. Falling over into oblivion, I hummed into Kane as he spilled inside my mouth. Gulping him down, my hair now a mess from the pulling and pushing from his large hands, he pulled me to his lap, not before he pulled down my hot pink thong panties away and stuck them in his pocket. "For later," he mumbled more to himself, then licked my fingers clean.

He's so kinky.

My breasts still hung out in the open, and he massaged each one, his cock becoming hard again. My mouth started sucking on his neck. "Fuck,

I need another round." He growled. There were no breaks when it came to my big scary alpha. Giggling, he pulled up my dress to cover my breasts, brushing my hair out of my face.

"So damn lucky," he purred, kissing the shell of my ear. "I love you, baby." I hummed, pulling at his sharp jaw with my lips. "I love you too, Kane. Let's try and be on our best behavior, huh?"

Kane was not on his best behavior. He scared the bejesus out of everyone that came near us. Now that Giana was streaming pieces of scenes back into my head, knowing they were memories, Kane wasn't sure of anyone.

He eventually let Giana work on his head the next day, which I wasn't sure what all that entailed. Whatever power or magic that fell on us was fading, albeit slowly, but it was. Kane now harbored hard feelings toward Osirus, not even sure if he was being truthful to us at all.

If we couldn't trust Osirus, who could we trust? As far as I could tell, he was so happy to have his mate. Sure, he might have concentrated on his mate more than the bigger picture, but he waited longer than Kane to have Melina. Osirus would never betray us, and Giana agreed.

While Evelyn and I traveled to Atlantis for Melina's pampering party, Kane was left with the men of the group. Osirus's three bodyguards, Alaneo, and Osirus's father, accompanied them. They smoked something that made Kane have a raging hissy fit and threatened to kill everyone in the room.

Not knowing how far mind-links could go, my dumb self forgot to tell Kane where I was going and caused a heap of trouble for Osirus. My panties were involved and were stuck on a crystal ball for a witch to find me. Everyone saw my underwear as my face came into view in the crystal ball, calming Kane somewhat.

My face flamed red when Raine retold the story that the witch had seen. Her brother was grumpy the entire time and went to sit on the beach until I arrived for the evening. Could my brooding alpha not have any fun? I shook my head at how horrible it all sounded. Part of me felt pride in how much Kane cared about Evelyn and me. But still, he was to be king one day, and he had to control that raging temper when I wasn't around.

"Never again." Kane growled in my ear. We both sat in the overly large bedroom. It overlooked the ocean that was falling into darkness. The blue moon was rising over the calm waters. It never ceased to amaze me how this moon was always full, so unlike Earth. It never waxed nor waned as I remembered Kane and I's close first kiss on the balcony overlooking the wolves that partied in the Ever Green pack.

No, this moon was large and alien to me. I didn't think I would ever get used to its glow. Kane hugged me tightly, listening to the soft snores of Evelyn in the crib on the other side of the wall. Osirus gave us a room with a nursery. Filled with toys, a crib, and a door to give us our own privacy. It was a room that very much reminded me of our bedroom back at the pack house.

"Never again will you be allowed to go that far away from me. I can't fucking swim that well, Clara, you know that." I snorted a laugh, patting his chest.

"I guess you're right. I should have known better." Watching my beast alpha swimming in the lake, trying to chase after me almost seven months ago, had me laughing. Muscles certainly did not float. "No, you don't understand." Kane hovered over my body, pushing my chest into the mattress. "I almost fucking lost it, Clara. With whatever strange stuff is going on, I need you with me. This magic, this darkness." Kane shook his head, then planted his forehead into the crook of my neck.

"If we can forget the bloodshed of a battle right in Osirus's palace, forget how we even got there, what makes you think that if they use enough of this magic, we would forget each other?" Terror ran through Kane. He gripped me tighter until my arms squeezed his neck.

"Kane." I sighed, playing with his hair. Kane didn't worry. Kane was my action alpha, he took things as they came, but something else was swirling in his mind. Giana purred, causing Torin to follow while my fingers ran down his muscular back. "Talk to me. We promised each other." He grunted, kissing my forehead until he had me straddle him with his back to the headboard.

"Do you know of Sorceress Cyrene?" Tilting my head to the side, I tapped my lips with my finger. "Yes, something about her being the most powerful sorceress in the Earth realm. Not a lot of info about her." Kane hummed, pulling me to his chest. The heat of my breath on his skin caused him to calm, wrapping his arms around me.

"August spoke to her." He tightened his hold. "She said something dark is coming." Kane began telling me the story of Charlotte and Wesley, luna and alpha of the Black Claws of Earth. My body shook, thinking how scary a demoness would be to face, and the poor luna had to deal with it on her own. Literally dealing with her own demons.

"What happens now?" Kane pulled me up by my chin, pecking my lips. His fingertips continued to roll up and down my sides. "August said she is traveling here and bringing reinforcements."

"Huh? We have all of Bergarian, even Osirus's army if we need it." I flopped my hands to my side. Kane ran his fingers through his hair, tugging it. Pulling his hand to my chest, I kissed his knuckles.

"Whatever this is, if it has Cyrene thinking we need more wolves, then we need them." My mouth hung open, now wringing my night dress. "Do you think it's connected? These rogue witches, vampires, demons, this strong magic?"

"I do, mate, and Alaneo spoke with me privately before you came back." Leaning closer, almost nose to nose with Kane, he pulled me in, smashing his lips to mine. The hungry desperation fueled my fire to help calm his worries. It would calm mine too. For a moment, we would be in our own heaven.

Kane pulled me away, his breath heaving, and both of his large hands engulfed my face. "The witches have been experimenting with blood," Kane's voice rose. "Virgin vampires, wolves, and each other to put a boost into their magic. Now they are hunting, trying to get to the dragon tribes, thinking their blood will be the strongest to use in their dark magic." I gasped. They were in the Cerulean Moon territory, and no scout had come to warn us.

"How did we not know?" I stuttered. "How did we not know this with all the patrols that Alpha Adam makes his dragon take to take care of the tribes? The Toboki tribe is the strongest of them all!" Panicking, I tried to leave Kane's lap. I had to tell my parents. I had to let them know what was going on.

"Adam was warned. He seems like he has it under control," Kane urged.

"Apparently, he doesn't," I snapped. "This should have been reported to us straight away! Not just by Osirus, but straight from Adam. Osirus has his own kingdom to run!" Kane put both hands around my arms. Shushing me, he petted my head and put me right back on his chest.

So warm.

"I know, I know," Kane murmured. I grumbled a few obscenities, and Kane chuckled. "I just found out about it while you were gone today. We will deal with it." Kane's grip tightened, not sure if it was for his comfort or mine.

"This just isn't adding up at all," I whispered. "Especially since—" A loud crash came from the outside. Sitting up from Kane's lap, we both darted to the open window. The spiraled tower next to ours had Osirus and guards trying to break the outside door open. "Melina," I whispered.

"Open the damn door!" Osirus yelled, his wings turning dark gray and his bright complexion dimmed. Raine and Dean didn't knock; they ran into the room. "Go. The guards are asking for both of you." Kane and I wasted no time. We ran out the door to the open walkway outside leading to Melina's private room.

"She's gone!" Osirus's breath panted; his usual straight white hair was now full of tangles. His ears elongated, and large fangs sunk further from his mouth.

"We'll find her. I'll take the perimeter." Kane growled. He jumped from the sixth floor of the palace, shifting into Torin in mid-air. Ripping through my night dress, Giana already had a trail for us to find. Looking over my shoulder, Osirus gave a stiff nod as I raced toward his mate's aroma.

Chapter Twenty-one

Clara

Melina's scent was faint, almost nonexistent, as I followed the tainted path. The smell intertwined with it reminded me of bleach. It was so faint; I was afraid it was an old path that Melina had taken to her bridal chambers earlier in the evening, but the entanglement of darkness I felt with each paw hitting the cold floor of the palace had me hopeful.

Osirus's wings were hot on my tail as I rounded the corner at the top of the magnificent entrance to the palace. The clicking of my claws across the upper floor of the main foyer had me skid to a halt as I looked over the marvelous landing. A flash of strobe light memories filled my vision. Blood, wolves, bears, and witches lay on the dirtied floor.

Shaking my fur, the vision ceased; the haunting visions shaken away. "What's wrong? Did you lose the scent?" Osirus's frantic plea had me leaping down the stairs, jumping, soaring ten steps at a time until I reached the far corner of a hidden passageway on the opposing wall. My paws scratched the door until a nearby servant opened it as Osirus watched me run down the foul-smelling dungeons.

The cries of prisoners didn't deter me the further I went. One fae, in particular, chuckled, his ammonia-reeking cell leaving me gagging. We reached the lowest part of the palace. Cries and tears of ripping flesh stayed muffled on the other side of the door. I howled, letting them know this was the door.

Osirus ordered the soldiers to pull me away from the rusted doors. With one gigantic kick from Osirus like a freaking SWAT team, the door was pushed inward, now seeing Melina lying on the floor in a pool of blood. Whatever spell that had been used almost completely deteriorated. Most of the blood I smelled was that of a familiar wolf.

Esteban.

The stupid wolf that tried to claim on Melina just a month and a half ago.

He laid in on the stone floor, his heart no longer beating, his claws wrapped in Melina's blood. Shifting now would cause me to be stark naked, but luckily my mate wasn't far behind. "Get the medical chambers ready," Kane barked out an order, repeating what Osirus had just spoken. The guards had stood still in bewilderment how Melina was taken down to the lowest part of the palace undetected.

"It's that magic, that dark magic," I linked Kane. "It has to be." Kane only mumbled under his breath, picking me up like a puppy and pulling me up the stairs behind Melina, who was being held by a frantic Osirus.

The palace was in an uproar when we reached the top of the stairs. Marcus was ordering wolves to check our bed chambers and extra guards in front of Raine and Dean's room that now held our daughter. My body stiffened, watching everything in front of me flash back and forth between the seams of dreams and reality.

Blood dripped from the steps of a fallen warrior was one of those bodies we could not find. Its head lay at the bottom of the steps, eyes staring at me. A lion was calling my name as he was pushed back into a corner with three bears. Kane, ripping one of the bear's throats as I ran to help.

"Goddess," I whispered.

"Luna!" The cry was distinct and familiar, the beautiful dark fae that laid lifeless before me in my dreams now full of life.

Jumping from Kane's arms, he growled behind me, bellowing me to stop. I couldn't stop now, not when I was almost there, returning the memories from which we had all lost. The heat of Kane's breath had my scruff stand on end as I tried to follow the darkness.

Once swallowed whole by darkness, Skye reappeared, her sword taken from her sheath as the vampire leaped in front of the cloaked figure. His fangs sparkled against the setting sun, pushing it into her chest.

"Clara!" Kane roared behind me, gripping me, and feeling the strange repeating scene all over again had me whimper. The dream sequence faded, the darkness falling around me until my green eyes met back with my mate. "Fucking hell, baby, what are you doing?! We don't know if the palace is secure!" His half form hovering over me, something about the strength in his arms had me melting away Giana's wolf. My body shifted so quickly that I barely felt a crack in my bones.

"Fuck." Kane gripped me tightly, the warmth of his fur enveloping me again. How many times had he saved me in the last few weeks? Far too many. I seemed to keep putting my nose where it shouldn't belong, trying to put things together all on my own.

"I'm sorry." I pulled on the thickness of his fur. His piercings also shifted with his beast, rubbing against my cheek.

"We are going back to the room." He growled at not only me, but soldiers standing by, watching in curiosity.

"Alpha." One fae soldier dared approach. Kane's eyes glared at him in a warning.

"Osirus has another room for the both of you. Your room was too close to Princess Melina. It has been compromised. Please, follow me." Kane growled, his fangs dripping with his saliva. If I wasn't in so much trouble, I'm sure I would have a snarky comment to go with that.

I whimpered, feeling Kane's anger. I couldn't recall him ever being this mad, and this time I was sure it was directed toward me. His furred eyes softened as my heart raced deeper in my chest. My body tensed up as his large, padded feet and claws clicked against the surface of the floor.

"His Majesty gives his thanks. Melina will take a few days to heal, but overall, she's in good health." The soldier bowed, opening the door for Kane. Kane's tall stature warranted him to bend over to get in the room.

"I should go check on Evelyn." I tried to wiggle free, but Kane's grip tightened.

"Raine just linked me. She's fine, sleeping in their room." My body slacked as Kane leaned over the bed and placed me delicately on the fluffy white comforter. Kane's body cracked. I looked away, knowing I would see the disappointment in his eyes.

I didn't usually run when he called for me; I stopped and listened to what he had to say because it was important. But this memory, the one that could link me back to all the other memories of the days battling against Osirus's rogue soldiers, could have been a key to something greater. I couldn't let it slip away. Giana was so close to sewing in that last piece.

Kane's body, now completely in his skin, let out a breath. He walked over to the only small window in the room. It was less luxurious than the previous room, but it was homey and made me feel safer than having a massive suite. The room was dark, having to use my enhanced vision to see Kane's face.

It was contemplative, not the normal face my mate would have. His mouth would open and close to say something, but he immediately rubbed his face with his calloused hand.

"Clara, I—" His once prideful stature faltered, and his shoulders slumped. "I don't know how to fix it." His hand ran through his hair. "I know you are going through a lot, and I can't fucking fix it!" His eyes glowed bright gold, Torin seeping forward until his fist went right through the wall beside the window. I gasped, scrambling off the bed to run to him.

His hand flew out, having me pause until he took another swing, this time ruining the lamp beside him. I didn't wait anymore. My arms were slung around his waist in an instant.

"I'm sorry you are mad at me. I'm sorry I ran!" Kane winced when I began to plead for forgiveness. It was all me; I was screwing things up. Trying to be a princess, a luna, a mate, a mother—it was all so much. On top of it all, this magic made me forget. I was losing it. I couldn't be all these things.

"Mate." Kane pulled me up, making me wrap my legs around his body. "I am not mad at you." His nose trailed my mark, automatically licking it. Thrumming in my clit was felt, but I tried to concentrate on him. He needed me. He needed me to sate him. "I'm mad I can't make things better, easier," he grumbled. Rubbing my nose on his shoulder, I sniffed.

"Did you just... wipe your nose on me?" I snorted, shaking my head. "No," I mumbled. Pulling me back, his fingers gripped my chin. Kane was too darn handsome for his own good. Any woman would be happy to do whatever this wolf said to please him, and here I was running off.

"I know you are strong." Kane gulped. "You are strong here." He pointed to my heart. "Here." He pointed to my head. "Here." He pulled up my arm, making me flex my bicep. "And most of all, here." He pulled me forward, having me kiss his lips. His lips were soft as he massaged them. The heat of his breath fanning my neck.

"And I know you follow through when you have a mission." I hummed, putting my head back on his shoulder. Leading me to the bed, he sat at the headboard, making me straddle him. "I want to protect you, keep you safe. You want to protect everyone else and bear the weight on you."

"You are getting awfully philosophical on me," I muttered. He chuckled, rubbing my back. We were both completely naked, but the gentle hums in his chest had me feeling more at ease. "It isn't like you."

"Maybe you are just rubbing off on me," he defended. I felt the smile on his lips as he grazed his mark. "Now tell me, what did you see, not unless you were just wanting me to spank the shit out of your ass for running away from me."

"I might like that," I whispered. His deep chuckle went straight to my lady parts, but I had to tell him.

⚜

"Two figures? One covered with a cloak and the other a vampire with crazy ass rings?" Nodding my head frantically, I played with my own fingers. One finger in particular held a ring that Kane gave me. It had magical properties to change sizes when I shifted. It was one of a kind, passed down from his mother.

"Yeah, I want to say they are important. It keeps sticking out in my mind. I do think there is some dark magic, and you said that rogues are experimenting with different types of supernatural blood." Kane nodded again.

"They are trying to get dragon's blood, or Sorceress Prinna was anyway. Alaneo said it would hold a lot of power since the blood has magical properties in it and being a shifter."

"Do you think the magic used on us had the blood of a dragon?" Kane shook his head, scratching his neck.

"I don't think so. Alaneo said that this dragon's blood would be extremely potent. If the spell is breaking after just a week from you, then they couldn't have possibly used it." Biting my lip, my body shifted. Even if we were completely naked, we were so deep in conversation that Kane hadn't once tried to use it to his advantage.

Poor baby is stressed.

"Maybe my healing power is doing it?" I questioned myself. My healing abilities had been mainly for outward wounds. I could heal the flesh, but anything else had been too difficult, and I wasn't sure how well I could heal magic that harmed the body.

"No, it's strong magic that was used, definitely dark. Prinna was adamant about getting dragon shifter blood. She knew it would make the dark magic more powerful."

"You don't think someone else already has the dragon's blood, do you? And that is why she is trying to get some?" Kane's eyes widened, taking a heavy breath.

"That's something to think about." I groaned; my stomach was becoming uncomfortable. Did I forget to eat? I winced a little, rubbing it as the heat fluttered further down my body.

This feels familiar.

Shifting from side to side, Kane's claws gripped into my hips. "Love." His nose flared. "Are you?" The heat between my thighs heightened, and I felt wetness now on Kane's thighs.

Uh-oh.

"You're in heat." Kane grinned wickedly.

Chapter Twenty-two

Clara

*O*h *dear.*

Kane's eyes flashed bright gold, the wolfish grin playing on his face. His grin was so vast that tiny wrinkles appeared around his eyes. Claws lengthening, I felt the small scrapes behind my back. Taking a large breath, his eyes rolled in his head.

"Kane, we aren't at home," I said nervously. It had been months since my last heat, and we were at the cottage by the ocean. Warriors had to stay at least a mile away, or Kane would have a hissy fit.

"Marcus." Kane kept the link open so I could hear him. "My mate is in heat. Take the unmated wolves out of the palace and make camp elsewhere." Marcus grumbled through the link, swearing.

"Oh, come on, I just got everyone calmed down. The perimeter is clear and..."

"*Now*! Post two mated warriors outside our door." Kane's loud growl through the link echoed through our room. I could almost see Marcus rolling his eyes as he cut off the link before Kane could pounce on me.

Did Marcus have a death wish?

Crawling backward on the bed, he let me go. My naked body fell back, and my legs spread faster than I could close them as Kane darted straight to my lady parts. He bit his lip, his fang just barely hanging over his mouth. "Where are you going?" he huskily whispered.

I squealed, pushing him away, but he was too far gone. His tongue swiped my clit, and my legs fell back to the mattress. "Oh goddess, Kane!" The burning in my stomach, the heat of his breath moving into my core, was so tantalizingly good I couldn't make him stop.

This was my heat, for goddess' sake, and we had no protection. "Kane." I panted. "Wait!" There was no conviction in my voice as I told him to wait, but because his beast's tongue lengthened, I felt the rough feel on my clit as it dove deeper into my pussy.

"Goddess!" I squealed again, falling over into oblivion. Kane growled, his stubbly beard rubbing against my mound. "Say my name; the goddess can do nothing for you now." Shivers ran through me while he hummed between the apex of my thighs. He was eating me like I was his last meal until he stuck his fingers inside me.

"I need your smell on me." His eyes flashed red, a color never before seen in his eyes.

"Kane, your eyes!" I squealed. Chuckling darkly, Torin came forward, crawling up my body to lick up my neck. Pulling on my ear with his fang, my body convulsed, feeling the rush of another orgasm trying to peak. My clit was on fire, swollen from the tugging, but I wanted more. I craved more.

"Kane," I whined, forgetting his bright red eyes that bore into me. My daze post-orgasm had me pushing my breasts up into his face. My whole body was hot, and I needed him now. Screw the protection. I needed this sated.

"You're mine." His thick shaft pushed into me. Letting out a yelp, my legs wrapped around his torso. There were no small movements of lovemaking; he was an animal. Those red eyes planted on me caused me to blush and look away. It was so dark, but Kane was there. I felt him on the other side of his wave of desire.

"Look at me while I fuck you." He growled. The bed shook under his weight, causing the lamp on the nightstand to fall over. As it fell, the light flipped on, causing the light from the floor to push forth into the room.

This was no ordinary room that Osirus put us in. I was covered wall to wall with mirrors.

"Kinky-ass fae." Kane grunted, changing the angle of his thrusts. "I think I'll enjoy it anyhow." Watching Kane plummet me from the side mirror, he roared out for me to look at him. His demanding tone had me whimpering. I was helpless beneath him, and it made me feel not vulnerable as one would think. It made me feel powerful.

"Fuck, Clara. You are always so damn tight." Slapping my thigh, he pulled out of me, causing me to groan in protest. "I'm not done," Torin's haggard voice rang through the room. Pulling my ass up, he inserted his cock into me without warning. The sweet intrusion had me pulling him deeper, not wanting to let him go.

"Look up." Kane growled. My hanging head was heavy, filled with bricks, while the haze of pleasure weighed me down. His shaft grew impossibly more brutal inside me. "Now, or I stop." He pushed forward again, almost having me lose my balance on my arms.

"Yes, watch me while I conquer you."

I whined, falling repeatedly. He wasn't going to stop, was he?

After each orgasm, I watched his determination in the mirror as he pulled on one shoulder and held one hip to get a better grip. His red eyes went brighter as I felt his cock begin to twitch. My nipples felt the soft comforter below me as they swayed to the now sporadic rhythm he played.

"I'm going to come, fuck." His hair flew from his face, roaring so loudly that I knew the entire palace had to have shaken. His muscles tightened on his chest, his ab muscles glistening with sweat until he put it straight on my back. Rolling me to my side, he kept himself buried deep inside me.

My heat subsided, but we both knew it would only be a matter of an hour until it heated up again. My eyes were forced to close with exhaustion.

The fleeting thought of trying to prevent a pregnancy left my mind while Kane began to pump his cock into me again.

His hand came around my side, pulling at my nipple. Grinding my ass back onto him, he growled again. "Kane?" I whispered. His head came around, pulling my chin to look at his handsome face. "Your eyes?" The bright red that shone earlier had now faded, and the coolness of his electric blue shined down on me.

"Your eyes were red," I whispered as he patted my stomach. "I've never seen that before." Petting his cheek, my hand dropped from the exhaustion. Picking my hand back up, he put it next to his cheek.

"You're like a drug," Kane mumbled. "Your smell is intoxicating. I can't stand it. I need more." His lips smashed into me. Shrugging my shoulders, my fingers pulled at his hair while he groaned in enjoyment.

It took Melina three days to recover from her wounds. She was lucky that Osirus had such skilled healers in the castle. She was dressed in her perfect gown and walked down the aisle with her father, who I only got to see the back of. I had only helped decorate mating ceremonies in our pack. This ceremony was beyond beautiful and seriously fit for a king and queen.

"That will be you one day," Kane mentioned as we sat in the very back. We had mated warriors sitting around us as I was in between my heat cycles. I was almost finished. I didn't feel the roaring heat like I did into the night after Kane took me so quickly.

"And you too, Kane." I laced my fingers between his. He shook his head and kissed me on the cheek. As we watched, I couldn't concentrate. The only time I was free of worry was when Kane was taking me over and over in the bedroom.

Raine and Dean were over the moon watching Evelyn. Raine would suit well to be a mother, she had that fun aunt personality, and I'm sure her children would be just as wild and crazy as her.

As the ceremony concluded, the outside reception was bright. Atlanteans came from the sea, riding in large bubble-like carriages to the surface. Blue and green jeweled necklaces allowed them to stay out of the water longer than just twenty-four hours. Sorceress Calista of Atlantis made them just in time for the occasion. She was a powerful undersea sorceress that swore she would never surface again. Her place was down, deep below the waters.

As sirens approached the beach, fae and wolves gathered around the fire away from the party. Mates were made, perfect matches for each other as they ran off into the woods to seal their bonds. It was interesting to see the different species combinations. I laughed, watching two completely different species come together. It was considered unheard of not long ago for it to be very rare to be mated to one of your own kind. Since I arrived in Bergarian, it seemed to be the norm.

"Princess Clara!" Kane had Evelyn in his arms, we were still surrounded by warriors, and they were given explicit instructions for others not to come too close. The man that stood before me wore a deep navy-blue suit; his dark hair had streaks of blue and green. The side of his face held small splotches looking like scales that decorated his eyes. Pearls and shells adorned his neck over the vastly different attire he wore.

"Hello." I curtsied like my mom taught me. I could feel Kane's warmth flood through me as I nervously came forward. Our warriors growled in protest as this siren approached. "It's all right." I waved them down, but they stood their ground.

"He isn't mated." One graciously bowed. "We are sorry; we are trying to stick to Alpha Kane's orders." Another woman strolled beside him. A fae with soft, delicate features, a vast difference from the standard sharp features of the fae. "He is my mate. We haven't solidified the bond yet. I've been weak."

"Oh!" I gasped in surprise. Kane stood beside me, holding me close to his waist. "King Girard and soon-to-be-queen Elaine! I'm so sorry I didn't recognize you." Girard waved his hand, the warriors stepping away as Kane nodded to them.

"No worries, it's been a long time since I've been to the surface, let alone let my portrait be taken to the kingdoms. I've come to speak with you about urgent matters, nonetheless." Looking at Kane, I pulled on his arm as Girard led us to a secluded table next to the ocean.

Girard's feet stayed bare, his feet dipping in the ocean. He let out an audible sigh as he held his soon-to-be mate. "There is disturbance here on the surface." His voice became hard. "That boy, Esteban, was using deep, dark magic." I hummed in agreement as Evelyn crawled into my lap. "I've seen dark magic, but this magic is different."

"It's laced with blood, supernatural blood," Kane said sternly. "They are experimenting on different blood types to strengthen the dark magic." Kane growled.

"They are after the dragon shifters' blood," I interrupted. "We think they may have already obtained it," I said. Girard's fist gently hit the table, his mate rubbing his chest.

"What do we do?" Elaine asked. "How do you know they have it?"

"We were exposed to dark magic recently. I believe it messed with our memories." I huffed. "My wolf continues to tell me it was white powder thrown at us and an entire battlefield. Whatever it was, it didn't last long because my memory is slowly coming back. They haven't found the right concoction of the strongest supernatural's blood."

"Has anyone else regained these memories?" Girard asked, leaning over the table. "Or just you?" Kane squeezed my thigh.

"Just me." I gulped. "My wolf is trying to heal Kane. He's beginning to see the scenes unfold as well. I think that is because he is my mate." I smiled softly back to Girard.

"Right, the bond," Girard mused. "Do you think the magic used on you was the dark magic laced with dragon's blood I keep hearing about being used?" I bit my lower lip, drawing blood.

"I'm not sure. I can heal mortal wounds, but I haven't been able to reverse magical ones—"

"That's in other supernaturals, though," Girard interrupted. "Have you ever tried to heal yourself of the dark magic with the healing abilities bestowed upon you?" Leaning back in my chair, I shuffled my feet in the sand. Giana was trying to fix my memories, but not necessarily the magic that was put on me.

"You think I could be healing myself then?" I asked. Kane grunted in agreement.

"I believe it to be true. No one else has awakened from this memory you say is missing. Osirus told me you swear there was a battle that no one remembers. The blood that lay on the palace floors is enough proof there was obviously something. As to why you were made to forget that battle is troubling." He tapped his finger harshly on the table.

"Those two people at the top of the landing. The vampire and the cloaked figure. I can never see their faces. I just remember the evil smile as he killed—" I sniffed, Kane, pulling me to him. "Before that vampire took Skye's life."

Chapter Twenty-three

Clara

As the sun set, that was when the party really began. The giant leaves that had hovered over the reception area during the day to keep most of the sunlight away lifted, opening it up for supernaturals that weren't invited initially. Melina and Osirus had taken off on the massive dragon they called Horus for their month-long honeymoon at the Winter Fae palace.

Evelyn stared longingly as the enormous golden dragon flew off into the distance. "She isn't afraid of anything, is she?" Kane mused as he helped put the last of our belongings into the carriage. Evelyn had been awake for most of the day, too excited about the events around us. Her little eyes were wide with wonder as she watched whisps fly around us.

After reading books upon books about the fae and the meaning behind the whisps, it only brought me comfort. Whisps were nothing but great omens of the future and could lead you to your destiny. Unfortunately, one got too close to Evelyn, and her quick reflexes had her pull one to her chest to hold it tight. The shrill from the tiny blue light caught my attention and made her let go. In protest, Evelyn grunted, only for the whisp to come back and twirl her hair into one giant curl and leave abruptly.

"Don't want to get those mad, Evie," I cooed at her. "Then they won't lead you to your mate." Evelyn grunted. Her attention went back to the golden dragon fleeting into the retreating light sources.

"Like I said, not afraid of anything, is she?" Kane closed the carriage door, the caravan behind us now loaded and ready to depart home. As much as we should wait until morning, my parents would be arriving back at the pack house, and I wanted to make sure their quarters were ready.

"She has more of you in her than me," I chided, putting her in her traveling bassinet. As much as she wanted to look out the window, once I swaddled her in her blanket that she was now almost too big for, she sighed contentedly, fluttering her lashes.

"She's a much better baby than me." Kane's deep lulling voice soothed Evelyn. "I think it is because of your calming effects." He winked at me. His large hand settled over her stomach as she fell asleep.

"Oh, so when she isn't around me, she's a little fighter then?" Kane leaned back to the seat, pulling me into his lap. Nuzzling into his chest, my droopy eyes touched my cheeks.

"I'm saying just that." Kane's finger brushed my hair away. "Raine says she's been a feisty little thing, nothing that she and Dean can't handle." I hummed, wrapping my arm around Kane's neck.

"I think they are just making that up. Evelyn is too sweet for that." Watching Evelyn sleep, the carriages began our long journey home. Warriors that had not found mates traveled back with us, their wolves growling at the sight of anything that moved in the forest.

King Girard had expressed his concern repeatedly about the dark magic, and now we believe that dragon's blood is being used. This dark magic was used to block out mind-links and heeded the healing abilities, and it didn't sound like Sorceress Prinna had full access to the dragon's blood just yet. She had just learned to wield the dark magic, and its properties made the typical magical spells obscenely stronger. She was hunting for the dragon's blood like she knew that it was the strongest blood to use. It only brought more questions about who was actually using the dragon's blood and where it was coming from.

"You're thinking too loud." Kane's back was lying on the cushion of the bench. Laying on top of him, I watched Evelyn sleep and thought of things I couldn't change right now. It had me awake the entire trip home.

The blue moon showed so bright outside, which was perfect for the warriors to see even further into the deep woods, giving me some sense of comfort. Kane's hand resting on my butt squeezed, letting me know I needed to answer.

"Sorry," I murmured. "Just thinking."

"You've been doing a lot of that. You need to stop." How could I stop thinking? What kind of statement was that? Not when the entire Bergarian world was under threat, hiding under our noses. Who knows how much of that magic had been used to make people forget? How long had this been going on?

"Clara." Kane growled, his chest tickling my breasts. Squeezing my legs tighter around his body, he squeezed my butt harder. "You need to rest, or do I need to make you tired?" Biting on my lip, I tried not to laugh.

"You can't, not with Evelyn in here," I protested.

"Oh, I can." He massaged my butt. Shaking my head, I traced his shirt with my finger.

"She's growing up so fast," I muttered. "She doesn't even want to nurse anymore." Kane's rough demeanor had him let out a breath, wrapping his arms around my body.

"Baby, pups grow fast. It's just how it is. I know you feel like you are missing out on a lot. But, the way wolves live, they have to in such a dangerous world." My shaky breath had him hugging me tightly.

"We will have more pups to get your baby fix." Breathing out a quiet laugh, Evelyn's face popped out of the basket. "Oops," Kane muttered.

"Da!" Evelyn spoke happily, trying to climb up from the whickered basket. She held out her hand, waving it frantically until we sat up. Picking her up, Kane cradled her into his chest.

Smiling at my little girl, I wiggled her toes. She was so tiny, so vulnerable, but even at the young age she was, she was strong. She could sit independently and play with toys, and her cognitive development was just the same as a ten-month-old.

"Little warrior," Kane mumbled. "You are supposed to be sleeping." His head tilted, squinting his eyes in warning. Evelyn smiled, two tiny teeth popping up through the gums.

"Kane!" I whined, putting my fingers into her mouth. "She's got teeth now!" I sniffed. "My baby isn't going to be a baby much longer." Kane laughed, pulling me back into his lap, his two favorite girls now resting in his large body.

"Like I said, I'll be happy to give you more pups." He wiggled his eyebrows. "As many as you want to satisfy that baby hunger you have." Slapping his chest playfully, Evelyn did the same, smiling back at me.

"Is Daddy being a stinker?" I playfully spoke to Evelyn. She babbled back her partial gummy smile and tapped his broad chest again.

"More like daddy is being a dick," he whispered, raising his brows and kissing her cheek.

"Language," I muttered while nudging him. Then my little Evelyn said her third word.

"Dick!" she squealed.

Please, gods no.

"Oh, shit," Kane said under his breath, but those dang wolf ears on our daughter picked it right up.

"Oh, shit!" She waved her hands in happiness. Glaring at Kane, his face went from shocked to pure horror as my mouth opened to chastise him. Pulling my finger out to wave it in his face for teaching our daughter dirty words, a blunt bang came to the side of the carriage.

Rocking the carriage back and forth, Kane set Evelyn in my lap, pulling the drapes back. Marcus banged on the side of the carriage with his fists, blood dripping down his face. "Alpha." Marcus frantically hit on the carriage again.

Why isn't he mind-linking?

"Stay here, lock the door," Kane's commanding voice left no room to argue as he opened the door and stepped out. Pulling Evelyn to my chest, I sat by the window, peeking outside. The dark curtains that hid the blue moon so we could sleep were the worst decision.

Wolves rushed out of the nearby forest, covered in blood, panting. As much protection as we brought for our caravan, it wouldn't be enough if we were dealing with the enhanced dark magic.

The horses came to a halt, causing my body to jerk forward from the movement. The howls streamed through the trees as more and more of our warriors came closer to the carriage for protection.

Raine and Dean, both of their fingers intertwined with one another, stood beside the carriage that kept my daughter safe.

Was my daughter safe?

It was nothing but a carriage made of wood and metal that could be easily torn apart by any supernatural. Whatever they were fighting in the woods could easily break in if they wanted.

Raine let go of Dean, coming up to me. Unlocking the door to hear Raine, her heavy pants and beating heart let me know there was more trouble.

"There's a small rural pack a half a mile from here. The pack is being attacked by three rogue vampires and a witch. They are almost completely slaughtered," Raine rushed. "Our warriors went in to help, but they can't heal. The rogue vampires' ability to fight and withstand the blows is unbelievable."

More wolves came limping from the woods carrying precious cargo on their backs. Children gripped the furs tightly as they trotted closer to us. "Get the pups in the carriage," I barked out.

As the small children were led to the carriage, I made room for them all. Many had cuts and bruises, one with white powder all over their tiny body.

"Don't touch it." Giana growled in my head.

"Fudge." I growled out loud. Reaching behind one of the seats, I pulled out water and a cloth, wiping away the powder, making sure not to get it on my skin. Each child had some sort of dust on them. I wiped them all clean while Evelyn sat in her basket in wonder. Her eyes took in the scene, and I swear I saw her fingernails growing.

"Shit," she muttered.

Oh my gods. I'm going to kill Kane.

Kane's enormous howl burst through the trees. Another howl from Marcus, one of heartbreak, filled my ears. The children cried out as I tried to hush them, throwing the cloth outside the carriage.

"Shhh," I cooed. "It's all right." Grabbing two little girls and watching the four boys who sat on the opposite side still shook.

"Can you tell me what happened?" One of the boys' eyes continued to look out the window, watching three dark figures ascend from the forest. They all shook their head, except for one boy, maybe eight years old.

"Them," he spoke utterly quiet as the children sobbed. "They killed my family, my pack." Not one tear fell from the little boy's cheeks. His brows furrowed, fists tightening. "That witch." His mouth ticked. "I'm going to kill her."

My mouth hung open, and my hand went to lock the carriage door to make sure he didn't flee, but he was too fast with the girls in my arms. He pushed the carriage door open, falling into the dirt.

"Wait!" I cried, causing Raine to turn around. "Get him! He's going to the witch!" The witch heard her species being called. The dark smile strewn across her face had her huff with laughter. The boy grunted, his fingernails lengthening into claws. A growl left the boy's lips only for Raine to grab him, wrestling him to the ground.

Shit. Is he shifting!?

Raine cried out, the claws in her forearm causing her to bleed. Wincing, she looked down at the boy. Pushing his hands back, the blood continued to drip down her arms. "Stop this." She growled, showing her fangs. "You're going to get yourself killed!" The boy didn't listen, his back coming up off the ground, face contorting with hair.

"He's shifting!" I cried. Dean, who was making sure the vampires and witch didn't come closer to us, looked back, allowing a vampire to strike him. Dean took a hit to his jaw, his neck contorting backward. The crack was heard by Raine. Smelling the blood of her mate, her grip loosened. The boy growled, pushing her back onto the ground, and took a running start to the witch.

Giana howled inside me. She was shifting us faster than I could think. Putting the girls down, Giana's voice used our luna command, telling them to stay. The opened door of the carriage had me leaping outside. Trying to mind-link Raine, static hummed in my mind.

Right, no mind-link.

Giana pounced three times, pushing the boy into the dirt. He groaned, feeling the abrupt impact. With the witch's loose long, blue hair, the witch swayed in the calm wind. "Silly wolf." Her hand reached into her pocket, and a white substance decorated her fingers. Using our swift speed, Giana pounced on her before she could blink. My jaws clamped down on her neck, twisting as her screams filled with blood gurgled until her breathing stopped.

I just killed her.

I stepped back, blood dripping down my maw. The little boy looked up in horror as he watched me approach him. He fumbled back, staring at me. His body shook, continuing to fall as he crawled away from me.

My heart fell into my stomach as I watched this terrified boy be afraid...
of me.

Dean rushed over, his neck cracking back into place as he ran. "Thanks,
Luna, you just saved my neck." He chuckled, pulling the boy up to standing. "If you didn't kill her when you did, I don't think I would have made
it." Raine stood by the carriage, watching Dean and the little boy. The boy
continued to stare at me and back at Dean, who he then realized was a
vampire.

He screamed, pushing away from him and falling back to the ground.
Shifting into my human form, I went toward him with my bloodied body.
"It's all right. He's with us. He won't hurt you." The once stoic boy that
stared out the window, the courage deep inside him broke. He began to
cry, putting his arms around my neck.

"It's all right." I rocked him. "Everything is going to be fine."

Kane's shoulders slumped, anger in his eyes, and the horrible feeling in
my chest let me know. Everything was not fine. This little pup had no
family, no home to go back to, and the way Kane and the warriors just
walked out of the forest, I would have to say his entire pack had been
slaughtered.

"What's your name, honey?" I petted his hair.

"Roland." He sniffed. "Alpha of the Gold Paw pack."

Chapter Twenty-four

Under the Moon

The carriage continued to roll along with a smooth dirt path. No voices could be heard inside, and there were little pants from the tiny, sleeping princess. Marcus's wolf stayed glued to the side of the carriage caravan that went through the countryside of Bergarian.

They had just crossed over into the Cerulean Moon Kingdom territory, the sky now darkening as opposed to the Golden Light Kingdom that had the constant glow of flora and fauna. Warriors continued to walk in their wolf forms, keeping quiet and listening to the small breeze that blew their way.

The wind shifted, causing Marcus's fur to stiffen. Wolves continued their trotting, staying true to the path. Unfortunately, Marcus's curiosity made him wander off the path. His wolf urged him to go just beyond the trees, to search deeper within the forest. No sounds could be heard, and the thick darkness inside that held only small creatures that slept in their burrows.

Marcus paused, looking back at the carriage and back into the wood. Something was calling to him; his wolf pushed him further into the blackness as he traveled half a mile. He could still hear the carriage on the other side of the thickness of the trees, making sure to pay attention to how far away he was.

"Round them up," a cold voice snapped. Marcus's fur stood up on end, crouching into the thickness of a deep purple bush. Peering over the large vegetation, he saw a fire that had been put out, the smoke still rising from the water covering the ashes. "Hurry up, don't have all day." The lack of a heartbeat in the person's chest had him growling.

Vampire.

Why couldn't he smell them? His nose went straight in the air, and not one bit of their scent was pulled into his lungs. "I've got the ward up, should be an in and out job," a woman's voice came from a small rudimentary building.

It was one of the outlying packs, one that stuck more closely to nature. They had their small cabins, washing hung on the line, furs and skins stretched across easels for the light sources to dry. A small group of wolves, mostly women and children, were all huddled together, maybe twenty to thirty of them. They did not fight back.

Where are the men?

Just on the other side, where the fire once was aflame lay a pile, which he thought was dirt at first, but it certainly wasn't. It was a pile of bodies. His stomach churned. All the men were gone.

Marcus tried using the mind-link, calling out to his alpha, who was asleep in the carriage, but all he heard was static.

Fuck.

Backing away slowly, he raced to the other side of the forest. He couldn't do this alone, not if that witch was using the dark magic laced with something powerful. In his brief encounters with dark magic, he knew that it would be suicide for his wolf and himself if he tried to do this alone. Especially if they took an entire pack's men out so quietly and quickly.

As he exited the forest, he snagged his brow on a thorned bush, breaking the thick hide. Blood trickled down his face as he pounced on the carriage.

Kane, taking charge, left the carriage while he yipped for others to follow. The magic was so strong it radiated a half mile causing the mind-link to fail.

His wolf howled inside him; he was being pulled back to that group of women. It wasn't just to save them, but something else that had his soul reaching out. Hope sparked in his chest. Could it be?

Three-quarters of the warriors followed him. With no mind-link, Kane roared out through his maw to attack and be wary of the magic. Wolves surrounded the clearing perimeter. The vampires only smiled, their fangs dripping with their venom.

Four more vampires jumped from the trees, landing on warriors, clawing at their hide. The surprise on his alpha's face was not one to want to witness. He roared out a cry so loud that the ground shook. Vampires trembled with fright stopping their assault. It gave the wolves just enough time for an upper hand.

Marcus looked for the witch. She was stalking the women who held children in their arms. Her hands weaving electrical currents, purple and black in color. Before Marcus could pounce on her, the ball of light went toward one woman who tried to flee. Falling dead with her eyes open, the women and children screamed.

Lunging forward, he pushed the witch to the ground. His mouth salivated, trying to rip out the witch's throat. Her forearms were bloody from breaking her skin, but they healed at an alarming rate.

Witches aren't supposed to heal this quickly.

He continued to scratch, paw at her skin. Marcus heard Kane order the warriors to grab the children. Wolves ran past him, kids pulling on the tough hides as they bolted through the forest.

A long scratch to the face, he howled at the tenderness under his eye. Pushing his paw to the rogue witch's forehead, her necked lay exposed. During the brief moment that the witch lost her concentration, he picked on a scent that had his mouth watering for another reason.

His head turned to see a woman with long, chestnut brown hair. Her hands trembled as she stood behind a tree. A vampire stalked closer to her, his nails lengthening, hissing at her while he approached. The overwhelming feeling to protect this woman caused his grip to falter on the witch. He fell over with a thump, only for the witch to scatter away from him and transport somewhere else.

Now that the witch was gone, he concentrated on the brown-eyed beauty that hadn't noticed him. His growl caught the attention of the vampire, and he grinned wickedly. Using the black magic, he shifted forward, his speed almost unable to be seen as he gripped the woman's arm. Pulling it behind her body, his nail caught her throat, having her look straight into the eyes of Marcus.

"Mate." She breathed. Her eyes watered, trying to struggle free. Marcus's eyes went soft, only to become fierce again as the vampire cut her tender neck. Before he could form a plan in his mind, the vampire pierced his nail straight across her throat.

The vampire's head reared back in laughter, giving Marcus the opportunity to pounce. The head was ripped off in an instant as his mate fell. He shifted so quickly, feeling the burns and crack of his bones, he was able to catch her before her body fell to the ground.

Marcus's eyes watered. The pain was like the rushing waves of the ocean into his heart. The pressure, the constant beating of his heart, had him hover over her as he cried.

Putting his hand over her neck, hoping to stop the bleeding, he howled out in anger, pain, and loss. Her throat gurgled. He screamed for anyone to help him, anyone to save his mate. But the dark magic still hovered in the air, her wolf unable to come to the surface to heal her.

"Gods, don't leave me. Not when I just found you," he pleaded with her. His hand stayed firmly at her neck, blood still spilling. Her glassy eyes looked up at him, and a brief smile came to her face. Her hand tried to lift, but her body became weaker by the second. He took her shaky hand, putting it to his face.

Cradling her like a child, his tears flowed endlessly, studying what little bit of life was left on her face. Her lips moved, her body's heat leaving her. "It's okay." She barely got the words out. The pressure on his hand slowed the bleeding.

Maybe Clara could help? He could run with her, take her to the carriage, and she would be healed. Marcus shook his head, standing up with her. The entire pack clearing was empty, void of any life. Kane had already returned, the wolves carrying the helpless children to safety.

"No," he muttered. "I'll save you, just wait..." She groaned, forcing her hand to touch his chest. "It's okay," she whispered again.

Setting her back down, he held her to his chest to rock her. He didn't want her to leave. He just found her. He had been a complete dick, running around with all those women, trying to sate some of the jealousy he had for his best friend and alpha.

Kane was ruthless, but he got his mate. Marcus, for a long time, had been good until Kane got his mate. He was tired of being alone and going to bed each night with his nightmares. Sure, sex was good and all, but damn, he was a cuddler. He wanted to feel the warmth of someone else's body and get rid of the nagging depression that hung in his heart.

He was foolish. He should have waited. Gotten rid of the silliness in his mind that he would never have a mate or wasn't granted one. Now fate had other plans in store. Marcus was to be given a mate, then brutally taken away from him because of his transgressions. It wasn't fair. It wasn't right.

He was just a person, not perfect, but did that warrant him not to ever have a mate? Because now, the match to his soul was dying in his arms, and it was all his fault. He should have been faster, stronger, and forced himself to be a better person to hold out.

Because this feeling in his arms, even though the warmth of her body fading, was the best damn thing he ever felt. He yelled out a cry, a cry so loud he hoped the goddess heard him. The regret, the soulful sorrow in his body, caused him to be limp. He pulled her to his chest, her body unable to move. Her breaths had slowed long ago, her eyes now laying wide open, unable to blink.

"Second chance," she whispered as the last bit of breath left her.

Chapter Twenty-five

Kane

Dried blood covered my chest. Clara's arms were full of children of various ages clinging to her as if their life depended on it. Tiny tears streamed down their dirty faces, leaving small paths of sorrow in their wake. They were no longer crying, their eyes filled with darkness, void of anything that they once were. As Clara questioned them about what happened, they weren't able to answer. They just knew they were no longer with their parents and were completely broken from their families.

The ages ranged from four to ten. We couldn't save any of the younger ones. They all died when their little hands clung to their mothers' chests as the witch sent the electrical currents their way.

I couldn't look at Clara, not when she asked if there were any babies that had survived. I wasn't sure if we would have been able to save them if we wanted to. The shifting alone was painful as I half-shifted to Torin's form. The area was riddled with dark magic. Not being able to sense it when we entered the territory was disturbing.

I would have been the only one able to carry the babies, but the vampires attacked me two and three at a time. I was just too late, and that would haunt me for the rest of my days. Clara stayed quiet, hushing the children and letting them cry into her chest. They trusted her more than I. I let them get their peace, let her healing aura protect them as I held Evelyn.

Evie looked on in wonder as her mother held the others. I wouldn't be surprised if Clara wanted to adopt them all and the funny part was, I think I'd let her.

My mate would be the one to heal them, and I couldn't deny that.

Roland sat staring out the window into the darkness. The young alpha pup had seen more than any child should, but his wolf that lay dormant in his body knew it had to do something. Protect the children that were left and gain revenge for the death of his parents. My fists tightened, and Evie's squeak had me loosening the hold.

Marcus had stayed behind. He and three other warriors stayed to help burn the bodies of the vampires we had been able to slaughter. The wolves, the whole innocent pack that was slaughtered, would be given proper burials, but the ceremony to watch their spirits ascend into the stars would have to be put on hold.

One massive ceremony at the end of this war would be for the best. We couldn't take the risk of having wolves travel to the dark wood to wish them well on their journey to the afterlife.

At least they had their mates.

At sunrise, we reached the pack borders. The link had been restored after the witch's body was killed by Clara. It didn't settle well with her, not in the slightest. The dried blood that coated her skin made her body itchy. The way she tried to scratch it away with her claws had me grabbing her hand constantly to steady her.

Warriors, briefed on the ordeal, came forward. Men and women who held extra rooms in their homes came to the children. None of them cried or complained as they were taken into their temporary homes. Their bodies clung to whatever adult they could, daring not to let go.

"Thank you," Clara said softly, taking the youngest out of her hold. "Sweet one, Leia is going to take care of you until we figure out what to do." The little pup sniffed and gave one more hug before going to Leia. "I don't know if she remembers if her family was attacked by vampires," Clara said through the mind-link. Torin purred, pleased that Clara would leave her link open for us to hear.

"Don't worry, we will take it slow. Kyler is helping the warriors with patrolling right now," Leia replied as she held out a wolf stuffed animal. "We are going to be great friends, huh?" The little girl nodded, smiling, taking the stuffed wolf.

Clara breathed heavily as we took our daughter into the pack house. Keeping my hand placed on her lower back, she carried Evelyn, who had dozed off in her arms. Placing her in the bassinet, Clara stared longing at her. Her mind twisted into darkness, spiraling down faster than I could pick her up and put her in my arms.

"Love." I growled in her ear. "Let's get you cleaned up."

Clara didn't move, still staring down at our daughter. "I'm scared to leave her; I have to protect her." Growling, I picked my mate up, taking her to the bathroom. She whimpered, but she didn't protest as I led her to the hot shower I already had running. The warriors stationed outside our room would alert us.

Holding her under the shower, I let the steam fill the room. Her head lay on my shoulder, her exhausted body letting me work those tired muscles as I sat down in the shower. We let the water blast over our bodies. I reached for the soap, slowly washing her, taking care of my mate as she silently cried.

I could tell her to stop, tell her to dry her tears and I would take care of everything, but there was fucking shit I could do. There wasn't an impending war; the war was upon us. The battles around the Cerulean Moon Kingdom were becoming too frequent.

On top of it all, my mate felt obligated to fix it. She was a fixer. She fixed me, she fixed the rage in my heart, but hell, she didn't have to do anything. Just having her was what I needed. She sated me, Torin, and the rage that boiled inside me.

The worst part was I knew it was her mother that was pushing her. Clara had lived so carefreely, the sunshine to my darkness, until she began her lessons. She felt like she should please her parents—her mother, most of all—because she was the one to take control of the kingdom. Too much pressure, too much shit my mate had to deal with.

It was going to stop.

Rocking her back and forth, her cries stopped. My lips grazed her forehead as she settled. The dried blood washed away, bringing new life to the darkness that tried to hover over her. "I'm sorry," she whispered as the heat rained down. "I'm overwhelmed."

"Anyone would be," I muttered. "You were thrown into all this shit, and now your mom is giving you too much responsibility too soon." Chuckling, emerald eyes gazed into mine.

"She feels like she has to shove it all in my head quickly, huh? Like I'm supposed to take over soon." Torin growled, my chest vibrating. Biting her lip, her head laid back on my chest. The blood had completely washed down the drain, and her wet hair stuck to my skin.

"You don't think she's planning on doing it soon, do you?" she muttered. The back of my head tapped the wall.

Fuck, I sure as hell hope not.

"Alpha," August interrupted our conversation. Clara's head tried to leave my chest, but I put it back to feel her warmth. Sighing, she listened through our link. "The king and queen have been attacked while their carriage was just over the ridge. Her majesty is healing, but they fear the life of the baby."

"Goddess, no!" Clara jumped up, but I held her in place. "Get her to the infirmary. We are on our way," I ordered. Clara began to shift her body out of my arms, and the panic crashed down on her in waves. My hands reached to keep her face trained on me.

"It's going to be fine," I told her sternly. "She's healing. We are going to go check on them, all right?" Nodding her head frantically, we exited the bathroom, and she threw on one of my shirts I forced her to wear. My scent would calm her just enough to get her through.

My mother stood in the doorway, watching us intently. "August told me." Mom put her hand on my forearm. "I'll watch Evelyn." Clara ran up to her, wrapping her arms around her body. "It's all right, Clara, go." She hummed, kissing her head.

It was all I could do to hold my mate back. She was tripping over her own feet. Her heart raced in her chest so quickly I worried it would stop from exhaustion. Once we arrived at the infirmary, I finally let my hand go watching her bare feet slap the floor.

"Mother?" she cried in panic, pushing the drapes away. The doctors hovered over the queen, pulling blood from her body. Clara's hand went out to touch her mother's head, her head bowed, letting the light pass through her hand.

"Baby, hang on," I muttered. Clara mumbled to herself, letting the light pass through her palms. Wrapping my hands around her waist, I waited until she finished with her mother, who gave me a grateful look. I growled, watching her. My anger continued to boil about how her mother was treating her own daughter. Even through my mate's damn pregnancy, she hovered over my mate as she studied stupid manuscripts and history books.

"Thank you, Clara. I think I'm all right." Eden pulled her daughter's hand away from her. Elijah hovered over the two most important women in his life, but damn if he wasn't a pushover. Eden wore the pants in that relationship.

Then again, didn't Clara control me?

"What happened?" My voice came out harsher than I planned, but fuck it. I'm tired of playing nice. With a full-blown war about to implode, being nice to the in-laws was no longer on my list.

"We were traveling back from one of the outlying packs, we had limited warriors to not look suspicious, but that proved to have backfired." Elijah grunted. "We transformed into our half beasts, even Eden, and we fought them off, but damn they were strong. Stronger than we ever could have imagined," he said, exhausted.

"Won't that hurt the baby?" Clara questioned, rubbing her mother's stomach.

"It should be okay." Eden rubbed Clara's hand. "I didn't have much choice. That's why I wanted to get checked, make sure everything was okay." Clara hummed, barely looking her mother in the eye.

"We've heard what's going on, what happened to you both last night. It's getting too dangerous to travel with the rogues. They may not have numbers, but they have dark magic. August mentioned that Cyrene was coming?" Eden asked. Grunting, I confirmed.

"Wesley and Charlotte from the Black Claw pack of Earth are coming as well," I added. "Bringing warriors and more witches from their coven," Elijah swore, his hand running through his dirty hair.

"This isn't good," he pressed. Pulling Clara to me, I had her face pressed against my chest. Her demeanor calming as she felt the fire on our skin.

"Clara, it's time," her mother pressed. "It's time you take over."

I growled loud enough for the room to shake. The nurses outside the room screamed while picture frames, supplies, and knick-knacks fell to the floor. The room shuttered, and the bed buckled beneath Clara's mother, causing it to groan.

"What is the meaning of this?" Elijah shouted at me. Torin's fur sprouted from my neck, fangs growing larger. "You have no right."

"No!" I snapped. "You both have no right! Ever since you both got your hands on your lost daughter, you have been pressuring her, damn it!" Clara kept her mouth shut, her fingers balled into fists leaning against me. "Her entire pregnancy, she was shoved with learning the ways of our land, the ways how a queen should rule. This is getting ridiculous. She feels she must be a perfect luna, princess, future queen, daughter, ambassador, mate, and a fucking mother. She's been with us barely seven months, and now you are going to throw the crown at her!?" I slung my hands at the king. I didn't give a fuck anymore.

Elijah's eyes softened, his claws retracting, sitting with Eden on the bed. Eden's eyes didn't look at Clara while she pulled the sheets up her small stomach. "I know it's a lot to ask," Eden whispered. "It's just, I can't fight." The silent tear that left Clara's cheek almost made me groan. I didn't want Clara guilt-tripped into this.

"And I can't leave my mate to fight, you know this," Elijah added. "Mates pulled apart, especially in pregnancy, is dangerous." Before a word slipped out of my mouth, Clara jumped in.

"I understand." Her head bowed. Growling, I pulled Clara away from her mother.

"No, she isn't ready. She needs stability right now. Shit, the entire land is falling apart. Can you not rule from the palace while we take orders?" I snapped. Elijah came around the bed, standing in front of his mate.

"Eden knows Clara can run the kingdom. Eden is not physically able, and surely Clara can understand that." Clara only nodded to me, her sweet face pleading.

Fuck.

"What do you mean?" I huffed. "From what I can see, you are dumping your problems all on my mate. You both have more experience. You've been through the Shifter War. Can't you delegate this one?"

"We can, from afar." Elijah sighed. "Eden won't be able to fight. The pup growing in her won't allow her to shift as you can, and we all know that. The vampires also know she is with a pup, making it extra tempting to come after her. With the witches and possible sorceresses and sorcerers using this dark magic, they will surely find her. They are hitting it where it hurts, taking out the leaders, and I won't let my mate take the fall." Elijah paced to the window.

"So, you paint the target on your daughter's back!?" I roared. "You will let her die?"

Fucking selfish prick.

"No, that isn't what I'm saying." Elijah spat. "We aren't just dropping this shit in both of your laps. We also have a plan. A plan that is going to help save thousands, but yes, we do need Clara to become queen to control the land here in our realm." Elijah's tall stature only reached the base of my nose, his breath haggard, his wolf showing his true colors. Fire in his eyes told me one thing, but the fear inside his heart for his family told me another.

"As royals, we have an obligation to protect our people. You know this, Kane. And unfortunately, it's going to take my family to make sacrifices." His eyes softened, his hand calmly touching Clara's cheek.

"And by gods, we do have a plan to save as many as we can."

Chapter Twenty-six

Kane

"**M**otherfucking damn, shit, fuck!"

"Any other words you want to add to that, babe?" I had Clara wrapped up in my arms. I couldn't let her walk right now. There was not a damn thing I could do to make all her worries go away, so carrying her around like a damn barbarian was the way to go. She just slumped into my chest, her head resting elegantly across my shoulder. Her finger trailed over the tattoo like it was so damn mesmerizing.

Taking heavy steps up the stairs, hoping to warn the warriors to leave my presence, I was relieved to see they had opened the door without saying a word. They both flinched as I glared at them both to leave.

"Be nice," Clara whispered, not looking up as I set her on the couch. My mother walked out of our bedroom, gently shutting the door. Her modest smile let me know that she understood the mood I was in as she left.

"What are we going to do?" Clara's shoulders sagged while I snatched a glass of whiskey and drank straight from the bottle. Clara didn't look up to scold me, her hands staring at her picked fingers which were becoming raw. Grunting, I set the bottle down and scooped her back up.

"Don't do that, baby." Pulling her head to my shoulder, I let her lay in my arms. She was fucking tired; we all were dealing with shit this land had never dealt with before. The evolution of magic or this newly created magic was far beyond our control.

As much as we thought we were safe after killing a rogue king just months ago, now we faced something stronger, more daunting. Clara's mother had kept her womb empty for the longest time. Being a pregnant royal could be a mess. Mates were to stay close together during pregnancy because the women couldn't shift, at least not in the latter part of the pregnancy. All their strength went to the pup, their womb, to keep it well protected.

Now Clara's mother was helpless, and if her father stayed away from her, it could be dangerous for the baby as well as the mate bond. Many would find that the king and queen running away cowardly if this was any human occurrence, but it wasn't. This was bonding werewolf shit, and no one would think anything of it.

"It's hard to understand." Clara gripped the sofa with her hand. "That they can leave like that." Pulling her closer to me, I leaned in to kiss her forehead.

"As much as I don't like it, it has to be done," I said distantly.

Clara's parents explained a very delicate plan. It would all have to be determined once Cyrene arrived, and she agreed to the dire circumstances we faced.

Clara's parents wanted to take all the children they could from the kingdom and take them to Earth. They would reside just on the other side of the portal in the Ever Green pack. Half the warriors from the palace would go with them, along with omegas that weren't trained to fight. They would take care of the youngest while those who were strong enough would stay put.

"And Evelyn, what will she think?" Clara's hand cupped her mouth. "I won't be able to see her, talk to her."

Cyrene, being a powerful sorceress along with witches that still hailed from the Cerulean Moon Kingdom, would close the portal for good.

There would be no communicating with the other side to know if they were all right. Light magic was how the portal was created. The dark magic laced with dragon's blood wouldn't be able to open it, or at least we hoped it wouldn't.

"She will be safe there. Once we know that the blood magic will not taint Earth, then Evelyn, along with all the other children, can return. Unfortunately, that just means we are locked in here." Clara pulled up her legs to her chest, silently sobbing.

"I know it's the right thing. I want her safe. I just don't want her to forget me." Cupping my hands around her face, her blotchy cheeks, her tear-stained face, and her red eyes held so much sadness it made my heart break.

"Baby." Taking the pad of my thumb, I wiped away a tear. "She will never forget her mother."

"I did." She choked.

"That was different." I growled. "You had a spell cast on you."

"And now my mother and I have a strained relationship. What if the war lasts a long time? What if she starts talking and walking and—" I put my finger over her lips.

"That's not going to happen." I growled. "I won't allow it. We have the numbers. We have a powerful light sorceress on our side coming in with reinforcements. It will be all right." Clara's forehead thumped my chest. If she hadn't been so damn stressed out, I'd have spanked her ass.

One thing I could take away from that kinky-ass-fae-kingdom that looked appealing.

A whimper left our bedroom, and Clara's head popped up to listen more carefully to our daughter's cries. I pulled her back to my chest. "I'll take care of her. I want you to go take a nap." Going to protest, I smacked her thigh. Her eyes widened, and her cheeks blushed.

Well, maybe.

Two weeks had passed. We tried to remain optimistic, and dare I say, Clara was looking more like herself. It wasn't a joke when the luna was considered the sun of the pack. Clara's sunshine was radiating as she helped the little orphaned pups from the massacre pack their things.

She made sure to pack them clothes, a few toys to put in their bags, and gave them all the playtime they wanted. The youngest pups didn't remember their parents' death. We had secretly hoped they wouldn't remember the blood bath, but when night came, they asked when they would be coming back to take them home. That had been difficult the past few days to finally tell them they had gone to meet the gods.

Unfortunately, Roland had seen it all. He eventually opened up to Clara about how they infiltrated their territory. All done by the magic that the witch had surrounded them with. They killed the men while they slept, the women waking to feel the burn in their chest when their mates died, but the children still lived and slept in their arms.

Roland would be joining Kit at the Alabaster Shifter Academy once the war was over. The younger pups would travel to Earth while the eldest, the Juniors and Seniors, would stay and finish their training by actually fighting in the war.

"You are packed and ready to go!" Clara said cheerfully, holding Evelyn on one hip and a hand around Roland. Clara was the only one he would talk to and shied away from me completely, just like the other pups. Evelyn reached for me, giving me some satisfaction a child, albeit my own, would look for me.

"Three days." Eden stood beside Clara. Her womb had significantly grown the past week, all with the help of Clara. Her power had helped grow her mother's pup quickly, which was another talent that my mate looked to have. Once Eden said she gave birth, she would like to come back through the portal to help, but that was deemed impossible.

Cyrene had agreed quickly to the plan once she arrived. Shutting it down was for the best, and she would help reopen when the war was over. Cyrene would also put a stipulation in the spell that if she died, it could still be unlocked, but there would be many clues to finding the right combination of spells that we would have to face.

So, basically, we couldn't let her die.

"Three days, and we get to go on our own little adventure." To Clara's surprise, Roland took Eden's hand as she led him to the playground. Clara let out a shaky breath while the omega decorated with white flowers covered the pack house.

The Cerulean Moon Kingdom palace was compromised, not necessarily captured, but vampires had been seen trying to get in through the magical wards. The warriors that protected the palace had now retreated to help other packs bring children from far and wide to make the trip to Earth.

The people were more important, not things.

A small ceremony was to be held privately in my office to pass off the royal title. We were to keep our identities as king and queen hidden until it was truly necessary. As the title was passed to us by ingesting the blood of the current king and queen, we were given the official royal command of controlling all of the Cerulean Moon Kingdom.

I hope I never had to use that.

Clara's sundress swayed, her fingers reaching for a sandwich on the outside buffet table for the incoming packs of shifters and wolves. The territory now housed hundreds if not thousands of shifters, traveling fae, fairies, and elves that were too worried to travel the country roads.

"Alpha?" the voice echoed clear in my head.

"Jasper?" I questioned. I haven't heard from Jasper since the incident with the death of Sorceress Prinna. With all the drama settled around our own kingdom, I didn't think to ask him about theirs.

What a great king I'll be. I rolled my eyes.

"Yes, am I disturbing you?" The hesitation in his voice made me laugh. Even if he was a prick all those months ago, I'd still be cordial for the sake of my mate.

"No, is there a problem?" I could hear Jasper's wolf grumbling in the background, something about not being mated yet, which I found fucking hilarious.

He deserved it.

"I've come to ask a favor of you and Clara. It's in regard to one of our dukes. He's very loyal to Vermillion, supporting as much as he can financially. Taliyah feels like she should at least entertain the idea of helping him."

I grumbled, tightening my hold on Evelyn. She cooed at me, planting a sloppy wet kiss on my cheek. Licking her cheek back, she squealed in excitement as I laughed at her. Wolves stopped to stare at my interaction with Evelyn, but it wasn't me they were staring at wide-eyed, but my daughter. She let out a growl, her eyes narrowing until they walked away.

That's my fuckin' baby girl.

"What do you need?" I rattled my voice through the link. I didn't feel like helping the twat, but in dark times as these, those with like-minds needed to stay together.

"If there is a chance you are going to the dragon shifter territories, can you look out for a human girl? Odessa is her name. She ran when she found out she was the mate of a vampire. He didn't have time to explain and didn't want to scare her more." I groaned, not wanting to take up his offer just because I would help some bloodsucker. But I had to be reasonable, not all vampires were bad, or so Clara said.

"We are headed that way this afternoon. I'll let you know if I see anything." Jasper sighed through the link. "Have you gotten laid yet?" Torin chuckled, almost howling at him. Seeing Jasper's wolf Xander rolling his eyes was such sweet revenge.

"You know the answer to that," he quietly spoke. "Thanks for rubbing it in."

"Anytime."

Chapter Twenty-seven

Jasper

Groaning, I left the servant hallway. I hated asking for favors from Kane. I owed him enough for not killing me so many months ago. Now the debt was becoming more profound, but what else could I do? Vermillion was a mess, and if Taliyah didn't have Duke Mortus' deep pockets to help run the country, we would be royally screwed. I couldn't help thinking *would it be that bad? Maybe the Cerulean Moon and Golden Light Kingdom could absorb some of the lands.* But I knew then that more people would suffer, stretching both of those kingdoms into failure.

There was no win in this.

Walking back into the small study, the tea growing cold, Duke Mortus sat, his ankle crossed over his knee, eyeing Taliyah. Taliyah looked poised; drinking her tea like the duke didn't scare her, but I knew better. Taliyah was intimidated by the whole idea of being in charge. She wasn't raised to take over a kingdom, just do her bidding for her half brother.

Studying him, I came back into the room, putting my hand over Taliyah's knee, sitting thigh to thigh with her. She gave a grateful smile as I kissed her cheek. "He'll do it," I linked her. The slight smile grew wider as she relayed the message to Duke Mortus.

I didn't trust the fucker. The gleam in his eye, the smile that many of his kind failed to show, was too wide. Maybe he did have a human mate, but I couldn't be sure. His heart did not beat, so Xander couldn't detect the fault. Usually, vampires' hearts began to beat as soon as they found their beloved or mate. Then again, I wasn't that in tune with vampire anatomy. Maybe they had to bite them first for their hearts to beat.

"I sincerely appreciate it. I'll be sure to send more gold over in the morning. I think that will be enough to keep the unmated vampires fed, at least for a few more weeks," Mortus said dryly.

"We thank you again, Duke Mortus. Also for your wonderful recommendations on the Parliament representatives. They have been of great help to the country's different regions. Lord Virion has done an exceptional job with taking care of the rogues." Taliyah smiled, standing up to dismiss the duke. The duke had indeed been helpful in that regard. The new counselors had taken a lot of the burden off Taliyah.

"I'll keep you informed if Clara and Kane hear anything. They are heading to the northern area of their kingdom this afternoon." My mate smiled.

Duke Mortus' decorative rings clinked on the metal handle of his cane, bowing low as he retreated into the hallway. "Thank you so much for your help. I do, surely appreciate it."

Fuck. I wish I could tell if he was lying.

"Could you reach into his mind?" I murmured to Taliyah. Her hand interlaced with my fingers, pulling me out of the study.

"It was strange," she mused, placing her finger on her lip. "It was like, there was a wall. Then again, Mortus is a very old vampire, and I'm still learning to dive deeper into the minds of supernaturals." Pursing my lips, she led me up the stairs.

"Where are we going?" I asked. Taliyah had spent so much time outside, walking around the kingdom and accessing damages from rogues. She had begun planning where plots of land would be great to start crops. It would bring more gold back to the country, such as planting groves of trees, vineyards, and the like. The soil had rested for so long that it had become rich with nutrients, and vegetation had grown wildly where I had trees transplanted for our first date. All of Bergarian would reap the benefits of the fresh produce once she started the project.

"Come with me." Her voice went low. The skip in her step had Xander stir as she led us down the hall. Her body in front of me, her head turning back, beckoning me with those red eyes. My cock stirred, hoping that what was to come would take care of my growing problem.

As we entered our bedroom, it was completely dark, with no fire roaring in the corner of the room. The door shut harshly, Taliyah pushing my back against it. The wooden door groaned under pressure, and my eyes widened as her fangs hung low from her mouth.

Hot damn.

"I'm tired of waiting." She growled. Xander perked his head up inside me, his head cheerfully cocking to the side like a damn puppy. "You've taken care of me for weeks, every night, yet you wait to make me yours," she purred.

Do what?

"I—I—"

"Cat got your tongue?" she cooed, unbuckling my belt with her magic. It was swiftly ripped from the loops of my pants. My breath caught like a virgin being fucked for the first time. My hands were raised by the force of her magic, touching the door, watching as she took control.

Her eyes flashed a bright, glowing red, and back to the subtle red I was used to. "The fuck?" I whispered.

"Don't tell me this is something you don't want?" Her eyes fluttered flirtatiously.

Where in the hell is my mate!?

"Oh, it's still me, Jasper." Taliyah's long red fingernail trailed my jaw. "But we do have a problem." I gulped, she watched my throat bob, and the hint of lust in her eyes had my cock come to life.

"We have been with the bond so long, pulling at it, tugging" —she pulled on the button of my pants until they fell to the floor—"that it has caused me to go into a blood heat." Clearing my throat, I tried not to look at her tantalizing perky breasts trying to burst free from her red corset dress. Her braided updo fell around her as she willed the pins out of her hair.

Crimped, curly hair covered her breasts as the tie of her corset unraveled. Invisible fingers pulled her dress slowly on either side of her arms. The fabric peeled away from her body, each breast exposed but covered all the same as her hair moved to cover her nipples. Going lower, the dress fell away from her wide hips, now pooling to the floor.

Shit, shit, shit.

"If Duke Mortus hadn't shown up, I would have taken you earlier. The tantalizing waiting has me all hot and bothered," Her hair flew behind her.

Dear gods.

"May I ask"—I cleared my throat—"what is a blood heat?" My voice went an octave higher than I wanted to, but fuck, I was completely off guard. There wasn't any warming up to this, not that I minded, but hell, she was still a virgin.

"It's like a shifter's heat." Taliyah stepped forward, her claw ripping off my tunic. My bare chest heaved, her tongue licking straight up my chest and neck.

Don't come.

"I need to feed, but feed from my bonded mate." Her breath tickled my neck.

"Fuck, yes. Fuck her!" Xander howled. My hands grabbed her arms, the pressure intending to leave bruises. Her moans filled the room while I pushed her to the bed. Slamming my mouth on hers, I wasn't going to be gentle. I couldn't, because Xander had enough of waiting.

Her hair rose around her, her body slightly off the bed until my hips pushed her back into the mattress. *Floating sex might be fun.*

Taliyah's breasts pushed up off the fluffy bedding, my fangs nipping, pulling at her nipples. Cries of ecstasy filled my ears as I began to suck. "Jasper!" she moaned. Taliyah's hips pushed upward into my cock. My fingers trailed to her hips, ripping her lace underwear.

Come dripped from my cock, smearing on the inside of her leg. Clawed fingers pulled at my hair, pulling my head to the side. Before my mouth could descend to her puffy pink pussy, her strength tested my own when she pulled me up her body, tilting my head yet again and digging her fangs into my unsuspecting neck. One of my hands gripped her tit, pinching her pale pink nipple. Her mouth widened in a silent cry lifting away from me. Blood ran down my neck, my cock about to explode, and my lips grazed her hips as I licked from bottom to top of her pussy.

"Jasper!" She gurgled on the blood she had drunk from me. Hell, she was glistening with her own arousal as my tongue sunk in deep. My rough tongue rubbed against her clit.

"Just one before I fuck you." I growled. "Come for me, right on my tongue." Taliyah didn't argue, her fingers pulling my hair right into her cunt. "God's, you taste good," I mumbled. Her scream of pleasure had my tongue lap more of her lower lips. Licking everywhere but what she wanted.

"Please, Jasper!" she cried again. This time, blood-red tears welled in her eyes. "I need you!" my mate cried, her come dripping down her passage as I opened my mouth wide, drinking her.

Crawling above her, she flipped me over with her magic. My cock ached, standing attention in front of her pussy while she straddled me. She looked glorious, her pale body contrasting with my tanned hands.

"Go slow, little witch, don't hurt yourself." I strained. Taliyah lifted her body, taking her hand to guide my cock over me. The tip of my dick entered, my hands gripping her thick thighs. Her lips parted, a gentle squeak leaving her mouth.

She slowly entered me and let out a cry of pleasure. The hint of pain on her face lasted but a moment until she pushed back up my shaft. "That's it, little witch," I whispered. Traveling up and down my cock, I growled, gritting my teeth.

Meeting her thrust for thrust, I moved my hips to get impossibly deeper inside her. Incoherent screams left her ruby red lips, hair tossing along with her bouncing breasts. Sitting up, I latched onto one with my mouth, the other with my fingers.

"Mine." I growled. Putting one hand on her ass, one finger came closer to her asshole. The intrusion startled her, but her riding didn't stop, and she bent over slightly, letting me in. "That's it." I looked up at her as she pushed upward, only to fall back down on my cock.

Slipping one finger inside her, she groaned. "That's my good little mate, taking my finger," I mumbled into her neck, my finger pushed in and out of her tight little hole.

"Oh gods," she whispered, her nipples grazing my face. "You like that?" I growled, trying to insert another.

Both of her holes were so damn tight. Her cunt squeezed around my cock as I felt myself inside her, massaging her walls. Every part of her was mine, mine to have.

Taliyah took her claws, reaching my back until she scraped them down my skin. Fuck, it was painful and erotic all at the same time. Her nostrils flared, no doubt smelling my blood. "I want to taste you," she cried. My body stirred with something new, a desire to taste not her arousal, but her blood. *Holy fuck!*

"Then taste me." I growled in her ear. "Bite me again."

"My beloved," she whined as she bounced. With both of us having our fangs descend, we bit into each other simultaneously. It was beautiful timing. We both fell over the edge of bliss, drowning in our own pleasure as our souls wove in and out of the invisible seams. My teeth stayed embedded in her skin. I could feel her venom hit the bone until she gently pulled away just enough to suck my blood.

My body fell limp as I laid us back on the bed. Making sure my cock stayed in her pussy, I cupped one ass cheek with my hand. She was mine, my mate, my beloved was officially mine. Taliyah couldn't leave me, I wouldn't leave her, and we would spend the rest of eternity together.

I had been a selfish prick for so long. I would be sure to please her, take care of her and do whatever my mate wanted of me. I'd spoil her until my sins were washed away.

Taliyah continued to drink. It felt so damn good. I didn't feel weak like I sometimes felt after she fed. The thrumming of her purr left her throat, and the small gulps filling her stomach supplied me with warmth. Xander retracted our fangs, finally sated from the months of restraint. He retreated into the back of my mind, finally quiet.

Thank gods.

Groaning, my hands came up to rub my mate's back. "I love you, my mate," I whispered. Humming, she lulled me into a deep sleep.

Chapter Twenty-eight

Clara

We had to make this quick.

Kane and I ran to the northern area of the Cerulean Moon Kingdom. With us being faster than any warriors with my royal and his alpha blood, it was best we made the journey alone. The more paws in the soil, the more vibrations could sound out signals to rogues. Torin opting to travel on four legs instead of two made it much easier for him to keep us with Giana and me.

It was for the best, even with my father's reluctance to let us go alone. It was still planned that all the children and those deemed too weak to fight would cross the portal in three days' time. It had to be closed; the sooner, the better.

I felt terrible for the Golden Light Kingdom, but Osirus would take care of his own. It was too dangerous for anyone to cross the lands, especially large caravans full of women and children. They would have to find their own haven.

Kane and I raced through the pride lands, the high, golden grasses tickling across our fur and the sparse trees made me uneasy. There wasn't the beautiful coniferous forest to keep us hidden where our wolves like to roam.

My mother had been distant since Kane's outburst, the pregnancy surely wearing on her and the state of the nation. I could understand it. She wanted to protect the unborn pup inside her body and the kingdom, yet I couldn't help but feel jealous.

Was she trading one child for another? Of course, I would hope for her to pick the unborn pup, but it all seemed too easy of a decision. Maybe that was why Kane had been so angry.

My parents never meant for me to be taken away and grow up without them. That was making them even more protective of my much younger sibling. I huffed, seeing the hot, heavy breath as I ran through the thicket. Torin's eyes glanced at me quickly, seeing the rapid change of my heartbeat.

My mother cared; she did, just in her own way. Now all these months of planning, of her pushing had come to a head, and now I could take over.

I just hoped I was good enough.

It was a small ceremony in Kane's office with Cyrene as the officiant. Marcus, who had returned four days after the massacre of the small pack, looked worse for wear. His hair was disheveled, his eyes dull, and there was no spark and zest for life.

This darkness, this Dark War, was ruining everything.

"You are to keep this a secret," Cyrene had instructed. "Your royal command should only be used when it is absolutely necessary. Use this command if, for whatever reason, warriors begin to either disobey or doubt you. There will be dire consequences if you use it beforehand. You will be hunted." Cyrene looked me in the eye. "These dark entities are trying to kill the nations at the core, the royalty, and that now befalls upon you both."

Don't have to tell me twice.

Mother and Father gave me a solemn glance, my mother holding her stomach tightly. I would have given anything to have grown up in this world and understood it better. But this was how it had to be. Father and

Mother were one, one in power and soul, and would not serve justice here if they were separated.

"You've seen a vision," I heard my mother speak as Kane, Marcus, and I left the room. Cyrene mumbled so low that I barely heard it. Hiding behind the door, I let Kane and Marcus whisper among themselves as they trailed down the stairs.

"We must pray for help, for as much help as the gods are willing to give us." The chalice that held my parents' blood before Kane and I drank clinked on the desk table. It ultimately tipped and fell onto the dented floor.

The chalice rolled on the wooden floor. No one dared try to stop it until it clinked against the desk. It pounded the side, causing me to jump. "Three mated pairs of this realm will be the key. One in helping my power grow, one in bringing reinforcements, and the other treading between the veil of death and life as they kill the final chess piece." Her voice had gone low. "Pray that The Fates are on our side."

As we rested, just on the outskirts of the foothills, we took drinks from the small spring. Pixies flew close, examining us, touching the water with their toes. Their tinkling voices came close, almost pleading, only to back away when two elves approached. They were nomadic. These elves held large backpacks, walking sticks in hand, and bows on their back.

The largest one nodded. His long red beard swayed in the wind. He was no ordinary elf. He was much taller and more muscular. The male beside him looked similar in facial features. "We could sense you through the trees," the tallest one said. The trees behind him bowed, yet there wasn't a hint of wind.

"We are heading toward the fight. Are you leaving?" The look of disappointment had me shattered. Shaking my head, my paw stepped forward, only for Kane to transform into his skin. "We are going to warn the elven tribes of the impending war." Kane pulled back his shoulders. The elf rubbed his beard, grunting to his brother.

"We heard about it, but it is only rumored. Many live in bliss, coddling some dragon shifter and his pet human." My ears perked up. "I don't take rumors lightly, so I go to seek the truth for myself," he rumbled.

"There is a fight," Kane's claws racked across his thigh. "And quickly approaching. There is a warrior encampment against the rogues just south of the Crimson Shadows pack. They will take your help gladly. We should be back late evening." Kane's gruff voice held no room for argument or conversation as he shifted back in his wolf.

The trees behind the massive elf leaned forward, touching the elf's cheek. "You will be welcomed. The elven tribes are expecting you. Zaos is the chief." The burly man trotted through the stream, continuing until he looked back. "I'm Folen. I'll see you in battle."

Their backs retreated, and our paws trotted across the stream. "Wow, he's uh, very tall for an elf," I muttered. Kane shook his head, not caring, just wanting to do our duty and get home.

Keeping my maw shut, we continued our run and finally ended at the elven territory. Zaos greeted us with clothing, and the elves took us in gladly with warm welcomes. After greetings, his gaze landed on Kane and me, and our friendly greetings turned serious.

"There's a war," I spoke for Kane. His mind was elsewhere it had been since the outburst with my mother. The overwhelming feeling he radiated was to protect me. Hell, even Torin spoke to Giana about trying to force me to go with my family through the portal.

Then what kind of mate would I be? Both of us would be weakened, and our power was much stronger together.

"Surely you have heard of the rogues?" I questioned. Zaos's lips pursed to a thin line, nodding his head. "They have taken many packs and prides, hunting those who travel to seek refuge in the Cerulean Moon Kingdom. It will only be a matter of time before they penetrate your mountains. We believe they are after—" A boy screamed. His laughter made the trees shake.

"Did you see how big he was? Creed is huge!" Kane growled, pulling me to him. The little boy, not paying attention, ran right into my leg, causing me to laugh.

"Easy there." I laughed. The unkempt boy's eyes looked up in wonder.

"Princess Clara!" Chuckling, I poked his nose.

"Yup, how are you?"

"F-fine!" He brushed himself off.

"What is this I hear about a dragon?" I had completely forgotten about the side mission, to address the human woman that had run away from the duke that was helping Taliyah.

"Creed! He's a huge black dragon! He's got big scary muscles, but his mate is super pretty. She's as tall as you!" Kane's fingers wrapped around my waist, pulling me back into his chest. The poor boy looked hurt as Kane glared at him.

"Don't mind him. He's just jealous I'm giving you all my attention," I whispered, cupping my hand. Kane grunted behind me, putting his nose in my shoulder. "See?"

"Don't cause any more trouble," Zaos ordered. Leaf saluted and dashed off into the thicket.

"That's another reason why we are here." Kane growled louder this time, causing Zaos to back away. "A vampire is missing his human mate, and we are here to retrieve her. We are trying to keep peace with Vermillion as the new royals try to rebuild." Zaos's eyes widened, his heart racing.

"I see you know something," Kane grumbled. Annabelle, his mate, walked closer, the beautiful elven silks from the silken flower plants shining against the sun. Her dark hair hung down by her hips, and she wrapped her arm around Zaos.

"Something wrong?" She noticed Kane's glare.

"At least act kingly," I warned Kane. His eyes softened, giving me a glance. His quick kiss on my forehead had me giddy once more until we both tried to handle this new situation. "I'm taking you know of a human girl then?" I asked.

"Human girl? You mean Odessa?" Annabelle replied. My eyes widened.

"Yes, her. Her mate is looking for her. It was a big misunderstanding and we are trying to get her to go back." Zaos and Annabelle's silent conversation had Kane growl in annoyance.

"We have urgent matters to attend to, and you keep staring at each other," Kane snapped. My hand gripped Kane's, pulling him away.

"No, you are right," Zaos rubbed his chin. "Annabelle? Will you go fetch them?" She sweetly smiled and bowed to both of us.

***

Odessa wore a dress similar to mine, her smile reached her ears as she looked up at the gigantic man beside her. Kane mentioned that this dragon had issues, that he was nothing but the scum of the soil. He tried to take away the alpha position from Adam from the Toboki tribe when they were younger.

Kane had spent a lot of time with Adam before he found Amora, his mate, but once his friend had his mate, there wasn't much point in being close friends. Your mate becomes your best friend, your one and only, your lover.

Kane stiffened, but I swatted his hand away. I had to go into this looking all queenly and understanding. He could have changed all those years ago, but for the sake of my mate, I would be wary.

"Hi! I'm Clara," I jumped in front of Odessa who cowered away. Creed's massive body of scars had me backing away once I saw the large scar running down his face.

"I'm Odessa, and this is Creed," she muttered. Creed pulled her to his side, bracing his arm around her.

"I'm Kane, Alpha to the Crimson Shadows pack. We have come to ask a few questions," he gritted his teeth.

Way to go, Kane, scaring the shit out of her.

"You can come with us, Odessa." I held out my hand. "We are going to go to one of the treehouses and talk there."

"We can talk out here." She pointed down to the grass. Glancing at Kane, he only grumbled.

"Really, it will only take a few minutes and you can come back outside. We will not hurt you. I know you must be scared by all this." I softened my appearance.

"You're human, taken away from your home and now living in a strange place. We only want to clear up a few things that might have happened that you don't understand." Odessa looked like I grew two heads. I just needed to know what was going on, and I couldn't have this big dragon flip out when I told him that Odessa had her real mate waiting for her.

"If Creed comes with me, then I'll go," Odessa challenged.

"If it is all right, Princess," An elf with crazy colored hair and a questionable wardrobe bowed lowly, "may I accompany Odessa? We've become good friends. I'm Daine." He smiled devilishly. Creed growled, his nose grazing Odessa's neck.

Oh, we have a situation.

"Thank you, Daine, but I'd rather have my mate go with me," Odessa spoke louder. The entire elven tribe within hearing distance stopped what they were doing to stare at the poor couple and my eyes just about bugged out of my head.

As Kane would say, we are in some deep shit. Creed stood beside her, standing up straighter, pulling Odessa in his embrace.

Oh, gods, it was so cute.

Daine burst into laughter, breaking the silence, holding his sides until another elfpulled the vine-like rope on this elf's hand. Creed growled, making elves stand back in fear. "Oh, right, sorry." He wiped away a fake tear. "Honey, you are not mates." A witch smacked the elf on the back of his head.

"Shh, you fool!" Glinda hissed.

"She can't hit me, and you can't hit me anymore! I'm a grown damn elf. Only my future mate can hit me." He waved his finger around. "Pull on the damn leash, but don't hit my pretty head! It's why I don't think before I speak!" Daine pointed to a vine wrapped around his wrist, like a safety device to pull a child away from danger.

"But I have a mark here," Odessa weakly spoke.

"Aren't you cute!?" Daine laughed. "That, my dear, is a hickey, not a true mark. He temporarily marked you, that's all that is." Glinda pulled on the leash hard enough that Daine fell backward in the grass with a yelp.

"It's true. He isn't your mate. We have come to talk to you about this in private." Kane growled again. I jumped around, my dress twirling at the shock of how he would be so blunt.

"I'll handle this, Kane. You need to be more tender," I hissed. "You are being an ass, and if you aren't careful we won't have more play time later." Kane's eyes softened, his head bowing to me.

Softy.

"Odessa, you don't bear his mark. So let us figure this out together." I tried to lift the tension.

"We've told them nothing," Annabelle said as Glinda approached. "They don't know."

"Know what?" Odessa cried. "He's my mate and no one can tell me different!" she snapped. "Creed, can we go home, back to the cave? Let's go." As Odessa tried to leave, my foot stepped out trying to touch her shoulder with my hand, but Kane's menacing gaze didn't leave Creed.

"How about we all go, then? Let's all go meet and talk privately." I tried to stay diplomatic. "We really want to help, and I want to listen. This is more of a unique situation than what I was planning on walking into, but I think we can work this out. You just need to be honest with me, and I'll be honest with you." The eyes of the crowd trailed back to us until Kane let out a loud growl.

"*Is she scared?*" I linked Kane.

"*Possibly. I don't trust Creed. Adam said he was a serpent.*" Kane growled, and Odessa pushed further into Creed's body.

"*Are you sure Creed is a bad guy? He seems so tender with her,*" I linked Kane again.

"*Adam's my friend, he wouldn't lie to me like that.*" I wiggled my nose, pouting out my lips as I thought. Turning around, I could see the tenderness in this brutal man's eyes. His fingers clasped around her hand gently, his movements slow and calculated. Her eyes darted everywhere wary of us, but the moment that her eyes met his, seeking his reassurance, love sparked.

There was something there.

Facts, get the facts, ran through my head. Even miles and miles away from mother, she was haunting my mind.

Zaos led us to the large conference room table. The table was so large the building had to be built around it. Drinks and snacks lined one wall, but we all walked past it, ready to give way to the tension.

As we all sat down, with Creed holding Odessa in his lap, I took a large breath, trying to clear my mind of the day's worries, and concentrate on the couple in front of me.

Chapter Twenty-nine

Clara

"*I'm going to screw this up,*" I linked Kane.

Zaos gave a brief history of Creed, which I came to understand more with Zaos' unbiased opinion. Alpha Adam had questioning offenses that Zaos found deemed worthy to bring up to me. Such as dark fairies roaming the dragon's territory. Of course, they could be seen by the elven scouts miles away due to listening to the foliage.

Dark fairies stayed to the south, their skin far too delicate to travel this far with no coverage. They went great lengths to get here, which caused Zaos to worry. Along with Adam allowing them to be there.

What brought more disturbing news was Odessa's claims about how she got here. She ran from the duke purposefully because she felt in danger and had no intention of going back.

Sugar, this was going to be tough.

"*You are not going to screw it up,*" Kane linked me as he rubbed my shoulders, his nose tickled my neck. "*Just use what your mother had taught you.*"

"*So far that hasn't worked.*" I slumped in his arms. "*I automatically believed in higher authority such as Taliyah and didn't hunt deeper as I should have. I assumed Taliyah knew what she was doing."* Straightening my back, my attention went to Odessa.

"Zaos has informed me of the situation about you, and I want to say I'm truly sorry for what you both have been through." Creed's enormous arms shielded the small human. "Odessa's confession of how you saved her as she ran away from the duke has been enlightening." I sighed. Kane still didn't believe that one, I could feel it in Torin, but I was going to listen to myself.

"However, we are here to discuss with you, Odessa, why I am here. Please, hear me out before you become angry. I want us all to talk about this calmly. I really want the full story."

Because something isn't adding up at all.

As I explained to Odessa about the Queen of Vermillion requesting me to bring her back for the duke because he said she was his mate, Odessa shook violently. Her bright eyes grew dark, her face paled, and Creed's worry seeped through his dragon. Smoke filled his nostrils and the ground shook.

"Please, Odessa, tell me what happened. Obviously, you don't think the same and I need to know why." Leaking my calming aura, Creed's anger slowed, and Odessa's eyes softened, I was no longer provoking the fear into her as I once was.

My mother ruled differently than I did, I knew that. The lessons that I had been taught were my mother's ways. I wasn't going to rule as she did, I had to do this on my own, and seeing this shaking human before me reminded me of that. I could see my mother returning to Odessa without a second thought because what would a human know about a mating bond? Paying attention and looking deeper was what I should have done from the beginning.

My hand came across the table, rubbing Odessa's knuckles. "I promise, I won't take you back. I just need to know." An elf woman, one that might have been Odessa's friend, whispered to her. Creed's arms relaxed, watching us both.

Odessa gripped Creed as a lifeline. Words fell from her lips like a gushing waterfall, my shock and horror must have been written on my face. Kane continued to growl behind me at the obscene torture this woman went through.

Humans had been brought to Bergarian forcefully, being used as blood bags by high-ranking nobles such as the duke. My hand covered my mouth, the sickening feeling in my stomach as I realized I could have sent her back there if I did not listen.

Odessa paused, her body shaking, rocking herself back and forth. For six months, she endured more than anyone I knew. To be bitten, to be sucked dry, to become weak. Humans could do nothing, their life hanging by a thread. All those humans still left there had a very short amount of time.

"Fuck," Kane whispered, running his hand through his hair. "Good thing we didn't send her back," he murmured. *"Good job, baby,"* he linked.

"This is terrible." I placed a hand on my chest. "Taliyah is being lied to and manipulated!" I slapped the table with my palm. The table jumped, but I was getting too upset to hold back. "Mind-link Jasper, have Taliyah search the duke's basement," I snapped at Kane. My hands trembled, shaking as Kane linked our friends.

Gods, this keeps getting worse. I pulled my hair, feeling the burn in my scalp. Earth was being dragged into Bergarian. How in the heck were they getting here? The portal? We had to close it.

Jumping up from the table, I rubbed my forehead over and over. My eyes glazed over, instantly linking my father. "Father? I need advice."

"Shouldn't you ask your mother?" He grunted.

"What? Listen, I need advice about the treaty with the Golden Light Kingdom," I countered.

"Oh," he muttered. *"I'm allowed to help with that, then."*

What the fudge nuggets?

"Father, we need to talk about that, but later. Listen, Vermillion's nobles are harboring humans as blood bags. Taliyah and Jasper have no idea." Father paused, his wolf scratching inside his mind. His claws were racking up and down the walls.

"You need proof. Physical proof. Once you get it, then the Golden Light and Cerulean Moon Kingdom can band together without question and take over according to the treaty. I doubt Vermillion has the soldiers to rid of the problem, they're broke."

Cutting my father off the line, I turned back to the table.

"I need proof," I spat out. "My parents need proof that there is probable cause before we demand answers, or we will start a war." Kane shook his head, now rubbing his scruffy chin.

"Taliyah's soldiers were in the area," Kane whispered. "They went to check the basement of the duke's home. There were no humans."

"He moved them then! He had to!" Odessa screamed. "I'm not lying!" Looking at Odessa, I knew she spoke the truth. I continued to pace, rubbing my arms. Kane pulled me from my worry and had me back in his lap.

"I believe you," I reiterated. "I'll never let you go back. Abuse is not to be tolerated, mate bond or not. It's unacceptable. Your emotional scars are clear in how you are trembling."

"Even if Clara believes you, we need proof. We can't start a war over a mate." Kane growled. He leaned back in his chair. "This is a delicate situation. The duke is the tipping point of the rogues going against the crown. The duke deciding to side with them would be disastrous if we go poking our noses in his business," Kane said sternly.

"So, you leave the rest of those humans to suffer?" I growled at Kane. A whimper left his lips, his eyes softening back at me.

Poop, now I feel bad.

"I'm just stating facts, love. I don't like it either. It is just wise that we have concrete evidence. I can't imagine why the duke would be her mate and torture her like that, but some people, like vampires, are evil enough to do it." He rubbed my arm, defeated.

"Not all vampires are bad, like Sebastian... We can't group them all like that," I whispered. Kane rolled his eyes.

"You need physical proof?" Odessa murmured.

"This will cause a war if I pry too deep without evidence. We would need the alliance with the Golden Light Kingdom to help us and, per our agreement, I need evidence of wrongdoing. Vermillion has been sitting on the edge of a new age for a while. Even with a new queen on the throne, it is unsteady. The entire Parliament is corrupt, and I'm afraid Taliyah just isn't prepared to handle it either. Even she, herself, cannot see that many of them are out to get her." I slumped back in her chair. "It will take two kingdoms not to just destroy the rogues, but also rebuild it. I need Osirus's help to succeed."

Odessa pulled away from Creed, setting her arm on the table, palm facing up. The entire room gasped, staring at the many holes in her arms. "Fucking shit," Kane spat out. "The bastard didn't even use his venom to heal her. Did he even numb it beforehand?" A tear fell down Odessa's cheek, landing on one scar. I cradled her delicate hand. It was riddled with scars, deep marks, some indented deeply.

"This... this will be enough." I gently closed the palm of her hand.

My body silently swayed. My mind reeled with new information. Could it be possible that all of this was tied together? The duke was powerful, especially since he was the major source of Vermillion's money right now. Was he supplying blood to the rogues, having them work for him right under Taliyah's nose?

It was the perfect cover, but how did it all connect?

Glinda gently swayed into the room. Her gentle voice had me calmed, seeing her motherly demeanor. She kept her voice soft as she spoke. She was worried for Creed and felt that Creed had black magic embedded into his body. I gripped my hand to Kane as I listened.

Glinda was to test Creed later this evening to see if this magic befell upon him. The way Creed's eyes widened, his emotion as he heard of the possible curse, had him pulling on Odessa. Their hands were woven together, his soft pats on her head, her arms had her melting into him.

How could they not be mates with the way they held each other? Craved each other? Did they fully know what a bond was? The duke must have lied because I saw everything that Kane and I held dear in those two.

"Please send word once you know if he has been cursed," I spoke a little louder. "I would like to know what caused him to be cursed as well as what spell is haunting him." Kane pulled my chin to meet his eyes. "I want to be fully informed. Please send a falcon for communication. We will be leaving back to the Crimson Shadows pack. My poor daughter Evelyn doesn't get much time with her mother." Kane pulled me to his chest.

"You are doing so good," Kane rumbled inside my mind. Sighing heavily, I shut my eyes tight. "Can we just go home?" I wanted to cry. There was no escaping this torture to all these people.

"Thank you," Odessa said. "Thank you for not making me go back."

"Odessa, I'm sorry I jumped to conclusions. I'm still new at all these formalities. I really hope you can forgive us."

Please forgive me for being a terrible queen.

"Nothing to forgive. As long as I can stay with Creed, right?" Odessa asked longingly.

"O-of course! You honestly look like a mated pair, anyway. I would ask you to take good care of her, Creed, but I think you already do that." I smiled at them both.

"Congratulations on your union." Kane stepped aside, crossing his arm over his chest. "I believe you are of excellent character. Not once have you tried to show your power to any of us, even though I know you could wipe us all out of the room in an instant."

Wait, what?!

"He's pretty damn powerful, love."

Kane bowed low to Creed with his arms crossed. "I hope to work with you soon, maybe get some revenge on a bloodsucker." Kane chuckled. Creed's smile, or at least that lip curl had me giggling.

I poked Kane in the stomach. "Baby, that's racist."

Chapter Thirty

Clara

The crackling of fire had me wincing. Heat traveled across my skin while I shook my head into the fluffy pillow. Rubbing my eyes, a large bang hit the floor next to the window, the curtains immediately flaming to life as soon as my lids peered open.

I groaned, coming to my senses. My heart raced in my chest. Feeling the bed beside me for Kane, I was met with cold skin. Kane laid beside me, his body lifeless with claw marks on his chest. My fingers drenched in his blood, my heart felt the jab of loneliness, Giana crying out in pain.

"NO!" I screamed, my body flung to him, trying to use whatever power I could push into my mate, to heal him to bring him back to me. There was no life left in his body; there was nothing to heal. The soul had already departed. "You can't leave me!" Shaking him, my mind cleared even more. The only reason I could be alive was because of my daughter.

Taking what was left of my tattered soul, I turned to the cot beside the bed that held her. She wasn't anywhere to be seen; the fire that engulfed the room had already had the cot turned over. Jumping from the sheets, I looked to the floor, under the bed and blankets. Giana retreated further back into my mind. A wall was erected, casing me to scream in frustration.

Where was she? Standing up in a familiar white night gown that Kane loved so much, it was now tattered, torn, and discolored. One side of the room was entirely engulfed in flames, both my daughter and Kane gone.

"What's going on!?" I screamed out into the darkness. The bedroom doors were wide open, and the burning of the fire stilled. The flames slowed, the heat still forcing its way into my lungs, the smoke trailing upward.

My mate was gone. He still lay in the bed. My reason for living was gone, but here I stayed to look in the empty room. I couldn't even cry as I ran to the window. The panic grew inside me, seeing nothing but ash and the Bergarian soil. Bodies lay broken, blood dripping from the front steps of the pack house.

There was no life left.

Deep chuckles came from the entry to our room. My back didn't turn, too torn by the scene of the land I had called my own. Whoever stood behind me in that far corner was the one who did this, the cause of it all. It was the only reason why he was the only one left in this hell.

Thunder rolled into the distance, lightning scorching the sky with red light. I winced, each crack that lit up the now barren land, the embers glowing further into the distance. "Who are you?" I tightened my fists, hitting the door frame. The curtains fell around me, reducing nothing but ash.

Did it really matter who this was now that everything was gone? Feeling Giana scratching on the other side of the wall, told me yes, that I needed to know. Turning slowly, my face keeping steady with the chair rail around the room, the fire illuminated the far wall. A cloaked figure stood. It was clear of any debris, the matte attire wrapping around him like a second skin. A chest plate of silver body armor glimmered.

The dark cloak that gathered on the floor. His attire wasn't what really caught my attention, but something else entirely one would usually miss. The bright flames gave light to the front of his body and gave shadows behind him. Three distinct personages stood behind the cloaked figure with various-sized horns, moving about unlike how a normal shadow should be. I was not standing in the presence of one, but four.

Three shadows and a sorcerer.

"There are three names you need to remember." The voice was slick, smoother than silk. One would almost find it calming, but if one could listen very closely, you could hear not the one voice but the underlying tone of three more. I shivered.

Before my heart could beat again, a warm hand grabbed my throat. It squeezed as I put my hands up around his wrist. I felt drained, Giana no longer moving inside my mind, and my body fell limp. The hood of his cloak fell back, and the sorcerer's face slit from one side of his mouth to the other. Glowing blue and purple eyes stared back at me. All of his teeth were razor-sharp, pieces of meat still stuck inside his mouth.

I gagged, trying to look away, but the grip grew stronger. Leaning in closer, his lips grazed my cheek. "All hail, Jarrochek, Azrad and Jolgath."

His grip loosened. I dropped to the floor, only the floor was no longer there. A large pit of darkness swallowed me as I screamed.

Continuing my scream, I fell onto something soft. My arms thrashed about, not knowing what could be lurking inside the softness. My cries had alerted someone because now I had my hands pinned above my head and a large body sitting on my hips.

"No!" I screamed again, pushing whatever was on top of me to the side, but they quickly retaliated.

"Open your eyes!" The familiar voice had me shaking my head. I couldn't; it was a trick. I had no one left. Bergarian was lost, and I slept through the entire thing. "Clara, baby, open your eyes!" Taking deep breaths, I finally saw the other half of my soul.

"Kane?" I sobbed, reaching for him to hold me. "Oh my gods, you are alive!" Evelyn screamed in the basinet, her arms reaching toward me. "Evie!" My tears didn't stop flowing. I was so happy to have my little family back. I couldn't let them out of my sight. I could never let anything happen to them.

Kane's arm didn't let go of me, still snug around my waist. Banging on the door caused it to come unhitched, Marcus in his boxers, Cyrene and our visiting alpha and luna, Wesley and Charlotte, ran in.

"I'm so sorry," I cried out again, kissing Evie's cheek. Kane didn't let go, watching everyone. My sobs became hysterical. Something was wrong with me.

Cyrene stepped forward, but Kane gave a warning growl. I couldn't take care of my mate. I could barely take care of myself. "It's all right." Cyrene's hand reached forward, palm outwards. A light glowed from it, giving me some sort of Xanax. I sniffed, Kane reaching me over and placing me in his lap.

"You had a terrible cry," Cyrene observed. "A nightmare?" I nodded. I had never had one this bad before. It felt so real. The lamp on the bedside table was on, setting shadows up on the wall from the growing crowd in our room. "Gods." I closed my eyes. The shadows, those shadows were going to haunt me.

"Can you tell me what happened?" Cyrene stayed away to keep Kane calm. He continued to growl, sometimes purring to help me.

"Can I take Evie for you?" Charlotte stepped in. She had arrived at the same time as Cyrene, and I had been a terrible luna not welcoming them like I should.

My voice grew silent. If I opened my mouth, I was sure I'd start crying again. "Yes," Kane grumbled, surprising me. He took hold of Evie, handing her to Charlotte. Evie looked at Charlotte and at me, questioning the exchange.

"It's all right, little one." Cyrene waved her hand in front of Evie, and she fell asleep on Charlotte's shoulder. Small hiccups came from my body. Gods, this was embarrassing.

"Can you tell me what happened?" Cyrene sat on the end of the bed. Kane gripping me tighter still. I shook my head. I couldn't tell her what I saw.

I saw death, the end of Bergarian, in front of my eyes. What the hell was I going to do? Did the dream mean I would fail? Was it from The Fates? These shadows? Some evil? A spell? My pants grew quicker, my breath shaking.

"Love, it's all right," Kane's voice whispered in my ear. "Everything is okay," he murmured again. "I will protect you with my life." I cried out again, burring my face in his chest. *Dear gods, no, he can't do that. Don't give your life for me.*

"May I see your dream?" Cyrene asked quietly. "All I need is your hand, and then you can go back to sleep."

"I can't go back to sleep now," I whispered. "I need to get up, go plan. We need to get the children through the portal, now." Getting up, Kane pulled me back.

"Let her see your dream," Kane cooed. "We will work on this together, all right?" Biting my lip, I reluctantly let her take my hand. Marcus stood with his arms crossed, his body rigid as he watched Cyrene read my mind.

Her eyes widened; lips parted while she stroked my hand with hers. The room sat still until she removed my hand. "Yes, we should have the children leave tomorrow," she muttered. "And unfortunately, I will have to take my leave as soon as they cross over."

"But why?" Charlotte whispered. "I thought you were to remain here for a while? Or at least until we had a better idea who it is."

"I have an idea," Cyrene said. "But if we want to win this war, I am going to have to train someone very special that will tip the scales."

"Who?"

"A new dragon who has no idea what power she holds."

Chapter Thirty-one

Kane

*M*otherfucking shit.

It had become my favorite phrase because I couldn't come up with another one that was worse. Cyrene waved her hand in front of Clara, causing her to fall limp in my arms. Tightening my grip, keeping her head close, I made sure as much of her body was touching mine.

I couldn't keep her safe from her mind. Physically, I would fight off any fucker that dared try to hurt her, but what I couldn't do was save her from herself. She put too much on her shoulders, part of it being her damn mother.

Clara tried to please her and become the queen that her mother wanted her to be, but she wasn't her mother. Clara was a tender-hearted ruler, and she would lead us all into greatness. I just wished Clara knew how highly we all thought of her, and that she didn't have to worry about failing.

"She saw your deaths," Cyrene's hushed whispers became stern. "As you know, dreams hold snippets of the future. I believe dark entities, demons, have inhabited someone's body and used their powers to infiltrate her dreams. Trying to bring down her confidence, her abilities. Making her feel like she has already failed."

"Fuck," I whispered, standing up from the bed with my mate. "How do we protect her then? Are they doing this?" Cyrene pursed her lips, covering her mouth with her hand, thinking.

"This is strong magic. Like combining several sorcerers together." Wesley shifted to Charlotte. His face grew hard.

"Like I said, three couples will need to work together to bring down this evil. If one couple fails, we all fail. There will be no return to the peaceful land we once had."

"What couples? Who do we need to protect?" Wesley interrupted. Remus's wolf was powerful, but Wesley had complete control over him. He was the negotiator of all alphas, making him extremely strong and powerful in the Earth realm. Most packs were at peace on Earth.

"It isn't about protecting." Cyrene sighed. "It's about them finding themselves to prove their true potential. Clara feels inadequate, and with these demons trying to penetrate her walls to feel less than, it will be difficult. The other couple, I must go and see as soon as possible. She needs to be trained to use her powers and push her confidence."

"Who is that then?" I growled. Clara stirred, shifting her so her head cradled against my chest. She sighed, falling asleep again.

"A new species of a shifter. A griffon and dragon hybrid." Cyrene backed away.

Marcus hung his mouth open, dropping his arms to the side. "A griffin? I thought it was just a story," he interjected.

Cyrene shook her head. "Far from it. In fact, this war has been brewing for a long time, right under everyone's noses. I'm glad that Hecate recently visited me in a dream, giving some insight. I don't know the whole story, but I plan to figure it out. Odessa, though..." Cyrene went to the window, looking out over the courtyard. "She will have trouble. She was brought in as a blood bag, all to end up with the dragon shifter's magic. It's a lot on her, and her mate will not be pleased with her joining the fight. He's certainly possessive."

"And the other couple?" Wesley asked. Cyrene smirked, looking to the east.

"Osirus and Melina. They are both coming into their new powers. They will be fine alone." Her voice grew soft. "But with a price. Time is of the essence, and I don't have time to train them all in their magic."

"Goddess," Charlotte whispered, petting Evelyn's head. "This is so unreal."

Cyrene smiled at Charlotte, walking to her and stroking her arm. "You've beaten one of these demons before, your wolf is strong, and we will need that. You will do just fine." Wesley pulled his new mate in close, his wolf growling. He didn't want her to fight, and I didn't blame him. She has only had her wolf for just a month, just recently made luna.

Clara stirred, her eyes opening. "I fell asleep?" she squeaked, trying to get down, but I held her tighter. "Stay still." I growled in her ear. She obeyed, leaning her head into my chest.

"In the morning, we will prepare, Your Majesty." Cyrene bowed. "I suggest rest and maybe something to help you sleep." Cyrene winked and walked out.

"Let us take Evelyn," Charlotte offered. "There is a crib in our room." Clara shook her head, reaching out for her.

"Thank you, but I need her." Clara sniffed. "It's my last night with her." Charlotte gave a sad smile, sorry for our loss of our daughter for who knew how long. Charlotte handed off Evie.

"Let us know if you need anything." Charlotte turned. "We are here to help, Clara. You aren't alone." Clara gave a grateful smile, silently waving as they left. Taking Evelyn from my mate, I took her across the room and into her nursery.

"What are you doing?" Clara whispered harshly. I didn't stop. I walked into the nursery and set her in the crib. If Clara was going to go back to sleep, it was possible she'd have a nightmare and end up waking up our little warrior. I wouldn't have that, especially with the way I would put my mate back to sleep.

Shutting the door, I turned on the camera monitor to the nursery. She stayed sleeping, with a blanket swaddled around her. Her soft breathing had me relieved as she rested. Clara was a different story. She sat in the middle of the bed on her knees. She wore her beautiful white gown that barely covered her thighs. Shivering, her eyes went to the monitor.

"She can't be alone, Kane." Her eyes watered. "I can't let anything happen to her."

"Baby." I sat on the bed, pulling her to me. "I can't let anything happen to you." The base of her palm wiped away her tears.

"You aren't alone, baby." I rocked her. "There are so many people here to help. Just because you are queen doesn't make you invincible. You can't take everything on yourself. I am here, Marcus, Wesley, Charlotte, our warriors. Your parents and all the omegas and children will be safe." Kissing her forehead, she relaxed.

"We are fighting, baby. As much shit as Cyrene talks in cryptic sorceress shit, I think she knows we have a chance. Otherwise, we would all leave this realm and close the portal." Clara hummed, thinking over my words.

"We are gonna make it." I squeezed her. "We may lose some, but that doesn't mean we give up before we start." Clara took a deep breath, my fingers tipping her chin upward to see my face. "I'll never let anything happen to you, our daughter, our pack. I swear this to you."

"You can't leave me, ever," Clara pleaded. "You can't leave. You can't die," she prayed.

"I will fucking fight the Grim Reapers myself. I will never join the white light of the afterlife until I know you are with me. I'll fucking haunt you." I chuckled. "Maybe do some crazy ghost fucking or something." She laughed, leaning back into me.

"You and your sexcapades, I swear." Her smile brightened, the light returning to her meadow-colored eyes.

"I'd never let you go, even in death, baby." My head lowered, capturing her lips. At first, it was slow and steady. Her tiny breaths turned heavy as I deepened the kiss. My tongue slithered into her mouth, reaching around hers, sucking and pulling her lips. She would only let it go if she didn't think.

Moaning, her fingers trailed up my chest, pulling on my nipple rings. "Shit." I growled into her mouth. Tearing her nightgown over her head, making sure not to rip her favorite clothing, I stared down hungrily at her nipples. They were so pink, her areolas slightly larger from breastfeeding our child.

"Gods, you're beautiful." I licked my lips until I latched onto one. Falling back into the sheets, one hand fisted on her breast while my mouth tasted my mate. Her body shook underneath me, and her legs shook.

"Please, Kane!" Her fingers trailed up into my hair, and I groaned, latching onto her other tit. One hand traveled lower to her mound. She was completely shaven, and her clit was already throbbing as I inserted one finger.

Make her forget her worries.

"You are so wet," I hissed, feeling her pussy react to me. She was always so wet, always ready for me to take her. I wanted to take things slow, worship her, and let her know she was worth everything to me. The days had been long, too long, not being able to love her like a true mate should.

Inserting another, my body lowered, my tongue circling her clit as I finger fucked her. "How's it feel?" I growled into her pussy. Her body shook. Taking one of my hands, I steadied her hips. Her damn body was going to fly off the bed.

"Alpha," she cried out, her hands pushing my face closer.

Fuck yes, I was her alpha.

"More," she cried, her hips moving at the rhythm of my tongue. I would give her everything. I wouldn't play with her today. I wanted her to forget, feel her orgasm, and fall asleep in my arms right where she needed to be.

Licking three more times on her clit, she fell apart, her head threw back, and her breasts reached for the cool air. Saying my name repeatedly, her body shook in the tremors of her pleasure.

"I want you to forget everything," I ordered her. She shivered, feeling my alpha command. She could ignore it, but she loved to obey it in bed. "We work together, do you understand?" The tip of my cock lined with her pussy, and she licked her lips, watching my cock disappear into her body.

"You are worth it, Clara." I pushed inside her. "You are strong." I pulled out, watching her squirm. Slowly, with each thrust, I made her feel the ridges of my cock. "A beautiful queen," I grumbled in her ear. "A wonderful leader." I pushed deeper inside her. Putting one leg over my shoulder, I tilted my pelvis so I hit her g-spot.

"We do this together." I gritted my teeth, trying not to come too quickly. "No more bad thoughts of not being enough." I growled. My mate's eyes met me. I growled again until I slapped her thigh. Pulling back out, I hovered over her pussy.

"Alpha." She reached for me, but I kept the tip of my cock at her entrance. "Do you understand?" She nodded. I pushed back into her forcefully, causing her to cry out. "No more putting yourself down." I moved into her faster.

"I don't want to hear any negative thoughts about yourself." My hips frantically pushed into her, one rough finger rubbing her clit. "Ah!" She moved her hips, meeting my thrusts. My cock ached, and my balls felt heavy as I drew closer.

"You are too damn perfect." Watching her breasts bounce, I released, and she followed suit as I pinched her clit. "Fuck yes, baby, that's it." Her silent scream of pleasure had me grinning. Her come coated my cock thoroughly as I laid on top of her with my forearms on either side of her body.

Kissing her neck, her arms went around me, fingers threading through my hair. "I'm serious. No more thoughts of inadequacy, you hear me?" I snarled. She shifted, moving her pussy around my cock again. *Fuck, I could go again.*

"Promise me," I barked. "I'll know. Giana will tell me." It was her damn mother that did this to her, ever since those damn lessons started.

"I promise, Alpha." Her eyes softened, cupping my face. "I'll try my best."

"You better, or I'll slap your ass." She giggled. It felt so damn good to hear her laugh. My nose traced her neck, kissing her up and down until I reached her mark.

"I'm scared," she muttered.

"We all are, baby, even me. But like hell, we won't give up." She shook her head.

"No, we won't."

Chapter Thirty-two

Kane

Clara was able to go back to sleep, but her body was restless. I wrapped her in a cocoon around me, holding her still so her body didn't thrash. Keeping our daughter in the nursery was wise.

I stayed up for the rest of the night, watching both of my girls sleep. Evelyn was only a month or so old, and she had grown much. Her little knees were already scraped from crawling, her babbles turning into small words.

Who knew how long this war would take? It could take years for it all to end, and we wouldn't watch our child grow. If we didn't fight, there would be no tomorrow, and she would never have a life. I growled, feeling Torin inside me. He was tormented, his hide continually ruffled under my skin.

We had to have patience and ensure our mate was well taken care of. Cyrene's warning ensured that we played key roles in this war.

As dawn approached, I let go of Clara, who immediately left my arms to grab Evelyn. She brought her to the bed as we held each other close. Evie didn't know what was coming, that we would part from her today, but how she gripped hold of my finger gave me more of the drive I needed.

"Will she remember us?" Clara's voice cracked. "What if she ends up like me, not knowing her parents?" I growled at her.

"It won't happen." My hand reached over and laid on Evelyn's stomach. She growled playfully, trying to bite me.

"Oh, she's feisty!" Clara laughed, tickling her. "She's just like her daddy. I hope she doesn't have your temper," Clara mused.

She does when her mother isn't around, but I won't tell her that.

The long trek to the portal was full of chatter. The carriages held luggage, weapons, and supplies for Cyrene and her fellow witches to help her in aiding closing the portal. No somber tones were used as we traveled up the mountain.

Many children grew excited to visit Earth, some to spend time in the Pineville Creek pack, and others to the Black Claws. Our daughter was to travel to Wesley and Charlotte's, along with Clara's parents, giving them more distance in case the portal was reopened.

"Luna, Luna!" A high-pitched squeal came running behind Clara when she jumped from the carriage. Kit, wearing his workout uniform, grabbed her legs and hugged her tightly.

"Kit! I am so glad you are here!" Clara bent down to hug him closely. Evelyn rubbed her hand over Kit's hair, causing his hair to become ruffled. She giggled, playing with it.

"Is little Evie coming too?" Kit's voice grew solemn. Not many of the children knew the true reason for their departure. Many blissfully thought it was a camp or a vacation to the Earth realm to keep their thoughts away from darkness. Many would lose their parents, but we would make room for a new generation with their sacrifice.

"Yes, Evie is going too." Nona, who had worked with my mother watching our daughter, understood all of Evelyn's needs and her fiery temper that Clara had yet to truly see. *Fuck, I feel sorry for Nona. There will be no relief in sight if Evelyn wants a damn cookie.*

"Come here, baby girl." Evelyn reached for me, her head rubbing under my neck. She nuzzled, pulling in my scent. "Fuck, baby, I'm gonna miss you." Her hand patted my shoulder, head popping up.

"Fuck!" she squealed. *That's my damn girl.*

"Kane!" Clara scolded. "Trouble!" she hissed, but she smiled anyway, watching Evelyn lean back into my neck. My scent covered my child's body. No one would touch my little princess. Nuzzling her one more time, I handed her back to Clara, who did the same.

"I love you," she whispered. "We love you very, very much." Hugging both my girls, Kit held out his arms. "Can I walk her across?" Torin rumbled, not wanting a male, even if it was just Kit training to be our family bodyguard. The line is now much shorter, now just waiting on our family.

Clara's eyes softened. Fuck, she was going to let him.

"Of course." She hummed, handing her over. I waited for my scent to hit Kit, waiting for him to hand her back, but he didn't.

Hell.

"I told you, I think he's her mate. Your smell can't deter a mate bond, silly Alpha." I pulled Clara tight, feeling her sadness leak through our bond. Evelyn's questioning gaze watched us as Nona held her hand behind Kit's back, pushing them forward.

"Protect her!" Clara called out to him, her hand reaching. "Stay with her, will you, Kit?" Kit looked back and smiled at us. His grin reached his ears.

"It would be my honor, Luna." Nona pushed them both forward until they faded into the portal.

"Gods." Clara clutched and fisted my shirt. "This is terrible." Eden and Elijah came closer to us, pulling Clara into a hug. Reluctantly letting her go, I stared down at Eden, eyeing her warily.

"You will do great," Eden stroked her hair. "I know you can do this." Clara sobbed, pulling away from both her parents.

"Just don't expect me to do it your way," Clara said. Drying her tears, she backed away back into my arms. "I'll take your lessons into account, but ultimately, I'll do it my way."

Eden paused, staring at her daughter. I swear Elijah stepped back three steps. "I'm sorry?" Eden said calmly. "What do you think I have taught you that wouldn't help you?"

"For one" —Clara held back her shoulders— "you said always listen to the leaders of a pack or territory first and not the people. That they should gather enough information to decide a fate. If I had done that, we would be in a heap of trouble sending a helpless human back to Vermillion to a duke who claimed to be her mate. We wouldn't have magical dragons now to aid us in the war, either!"

"*Fuck, that was hot, babe,*" I purred through the link. "Warrior princess, damn." I could feel her smiling on the inside as Eden shot daggers at Clara.

"You took the word of a human who knows nothing of this world, about bonds, and could very well be bonded to this vampire." Eden growled, her large pregnant belly coming closer to us. She was not as pretty when my mate was pregnant. My mate glowed beautifully, and Eden looked rough.

"Even if she was truly mated to him, which we found out twenty-four hours ago she wasn't, I would have *never* sent her back to the duke! He abused her!" Clara hissed.

"Mate or not—"

"No, mother. Mate or not, my tushie! She had every right to walk away!" Clara yelled.

Clara stomped her foot. "And ask for a new mate if she wanted. One hit to a woman is it, or in this case, a bite without permission!" Clara's fangs grew, and Giana's eyes glowed fiercely.

"I've got a raging boner." I rubbed my dick on her ass. "Feel that?" Clara's seriousness faltered, and she laughed. Elijah grabbed Eden and pulled her closer to the portal.

"I still love you, Mom, and we will take care of everything. We will work on us later. Please keep everyone safe!" she yelled out, waving goodbye.

"We will, darling." Elijah smiled, pushing Eden through the portal. "I wish I had your balls, my princess. I'll be sure to have her calmed down before we come back." Elijah chuckled at his mate's speechlessness and disappeared into the mirror.

Twirling my mate quickly, my lips slammed into her. Sucking her bottom lip until I lifted her around my waist. "Gods, you make me so hungry for you," I whispered. She rubbed against me, tightening her hold around my neck.

"I know what you are doing." Clara seductively licked my ear. "Trying to make me forget, not to worry."

"Is it working?" Kissing her shoulder until one of the dragons that guarded the portal shifted his wings. He sat up higher in the cliffs, his roar now capturing the warriors' attention below.

"They have a strange smell." The graveled voice of the guardian flapped his leathered wings, taking to the sky. A ball of energy pushed into the dragon guardian's underbelly, causing him to fall from the sky. Three dragons came close in the distance, blowing fire and brimstone toward the ground.

"They are coming straight for us!" Clara screamed. She shifted into her wolf as I turned into my half-beast. Hearing static, Clara yipped. Fuck, some black magic was being used to ruin the link.

"Take cover!" I yelled out. Wolves sprinted into the woods behind the portal until one crashed on the side of the cliff. Black claws lengthening by the enemy, scratched up the side of the mountain, pulling themselves up the cliff next to the portal.

"Shut it down!" Bounding toward the dragon, my claws ripped upward as it hung from the cliff side. I was trying to get into its delicate skin underneath the scales. It howled in distress as I reached its eye and scuffed across its tender place. It fell backward, sliding down the cliff.

Clara jumped as I finished my own assault, landing in front of Cyrene and the witches, who were already chanting for protection.

Two more dragons, one holding a warlock, held a ball of fire, throwing it toward the warriors. Wolves pounced at the opposing brown dragon with red markings. My warrior's claws were not as strong as mine. They slid off the dragon, falling to the ground. One gigantic claw stomping two of my warriors.

I boomed forward, scraping up the scales. "Upward!" I thundered, getting the message across to them. Twenty jumped on top of the spiny back, trying to pull at the scales. The dragon breathed its fire, catching fur aflame. Burned hair and skin seeped into the once clean air.

An orange dragon, hovering over us all, spat out its fire over the trees where we once hid. Branches fell to the ground, catching the rest of the wood on fire. Pixies flew from the damage, screaming in their bell-like voices. Some angry, lowering their fangs, and flying toward the orange dragon now landing.

You do not mess with fucking pixies.

Pixies went straight for the eyes, unable to penetrate the scales. Both dragons that remained near the portal shook their heads.

"Almost done!" Cyrene and her accomplices had a tornado of pink and purple lightning pushing it forward toward the portal. The warlock that sat on the orange dragon wheeled her magic ball, forcing it to Cyrene.

Shit.

Cyrene was too far away from me, but my mate wasn't. Clara leaped forward not toward Cyrene, but toward the warlock. Clara's small agile body contorted, having her twist her body mid-air until she fell right into the enemy. The slow, torturous wait for their bodies to hit the ground had Torin racing toward my falling mate.

The dragon reared back from a pixie poking his eye, his wing getting in the way until my sharp claws ran right down the leathered wing.

Screeches and drops of blood decorated the ground as I caught Clara's small form. The warlock fell on her back, the magical ball of lightning falling, disintegrating into broken sparkles.

Cyrene wailed. The clouds grew dark until the tornado of electrical currents was sucked into the portal. Lightning flashed, striking the ground in front of the dragon, having everyone fall back as the bright light blew torrential winds in our furs. Warriors fell to the ground, and dragons fell backward, falling off the cliff. The warlock was knocked off his feet, held by four warriors on top of him.

The clouds dispersed around us. Cyrene and her companions now lay on the ground. Cyrene's weak body lifted one arm, then the other, pushing her face from the dirt. Clara's head came up under my neck, my soft spot, a sign of protection against anyone that dared want to hurt me. Purring in my chest, we watched the smoke depart, seeing the glass-like mirror was now just an empty stone archway.

Chapter Thirty-three

Taliyah

"Your Majesty," Melinard, one of the head butlers, knocked on the door to my study frantically. "The soldiers you sent to Duke Mortus' home have returned. There are no signs of humans, and in fact, the duke is right outside in the foyer quite, well, upset." Melinard shook. He was a tender-hearted man. His mate and children resided in the palace to escape the outside persecution. It was a dangerous world out there, and I felt like most of those who lived here were the only ones left besides the town shelter that were good.

Jasper stepped out from the shadows. His skin was more sensitive to the light sources, not as much as a newborn vampire, but enough for him to want to keep away from the light until he was well acclimated. Xander healed him quickly, but keeping Xander healthy and strong was Jasper's goal.

Jasper's eyes now glowed red from his recent feeding, his fangs now hollowed, allowing him to feed from me. I didn't think it could be possible to see him as dangerous, but Melinard thought differently. "Your Highness," Melinard stuttered. Bowing, he wouldn't look Jasper in the eye. It was true that Jasper looked wild. His wolf, his blood lust, was at an all-time high.

We would have to make sure no humans came close, if we could even find them.

"I'll deal with him." My claws scraped across the desk. I still wasn't sure how to control the wolf side that I had received. It could be weeks before she surfaced, or if she surfaced at all. With my hybrid powers, I wasn't sure if she would appear with such strong genes I already had.

"I'm coming with you." Jasper growled, stepping in front of me. The static danced between my claws as we entered the foyer. The duke's eyes showed the brightest red I had ever seen. He had drunk human blood, which further soured my mood.

"She is my beloved, and you let Princess Clara decide her fate? Then believe the lies she spouted that I had a harem of blood bags hiding in my basement?! I'm gone three days to check on the outskirts of your worthless country, and this is how you repay me?!" Spittle flew from his mouth, landing on the freshly waxed floors. Jasper stood beside me, holding my wrist, ready to pull me back.

"Oh, I see how it is," Mortus drawled. "It's because the former gamma is puppy friends with the princesses' mate. She'd want to make him happy." Mortus' hiss echoed in the foyer, and the few guards we had now gathered at the entrance and servants stopped their jobs to look on.

"I'm pulling my funding if this is how little you think of me." He spat. Taking a large breath, I felt Jasper's bravery fuel my own, causing me to step forward. The growl inside my chest pushed forward. Mortus just smirked.

"She isn't your mate. It was confirmed just a day ago." I growled, showing my fangs.

"Just because you are marked now doesn't mean you can overpower me, you abomination." Hissing at him, my fingers tingled with heat pushing toward Mortus. His quick and agile movements were so fast that none of us saw him move as he sat on top of the banister at the top of the stairs.

"Fuck, he is a traitor." Jasper growled. "He moves like the rogues." Mortus chuckled, swinging his legs.

"The only traitorous thing in this palace is you as its queen." He snarled. "The day of reckoning has been upon you a long while, and a new era is forming for those who are tired of lurking in the dark." Mortus' eyes glowed brightly, and his deep chuckle had me hovering above the ground, leaving Jasper on the floor. My hair flew wildly around my head, and Mortus' eyes widened only to become stone-cold.

"An abomination, you say?" I giggled. "You can't be serious." Mortus frowned, looking me up and down. The crackling of fire, the slow burn of fire, trickled down the ashes of my dead skin. "Not when this supposed abomination witch has graduated to a sorceress."

Mortus jumped from the railing, reaching for my body to latch on to. As much as I had practiced in the dark of my study, I was no match for his swiftness. He ripped out his claw, raking across my chest until I used my body as a giant volt of electricity. Shocking Mortus, he let go as we fell to the ground.

Jasper swooped in, his eyes narrowing as he caught me, pulling me away from the middle of the foyer. We turned only to see that Mortus was long gone. "Shit! Don't ever do that!" Jasper cupped my face. The power I had used against Mortus drained me severely. Something I was not accustomed to since I only practiced in small doses.

"You're pale," Melinard spoke softly, giving Jasper a wet cloth. "Your Majesty, Parliament is to convene in an hour. Guests are arriving. Should I send them away?"

"No!" I choked on the dribbles of water that ran down my lips. "I must speak to them about Mortus." Melinard nodded, his eyes glancing around the room.

"Let it be known that no family of Duke Mortus is allowed in the palace," Melinard said ominously to the rest of the room. "Get back to preparing the meeting room."

Jasper picked me up, carrying me up the stairs. My head winced as I saw the rail where Mortus sat.

Gently laying me on the bed, Jasper cursed, running to our en suite bathroom and grabbing another towel. "I can't believe you did that, Taliyah." His hurried words had me wincing. "We are a team, damn it, and then you go all floating and shit. When were you going to tell me about that?"

Looking away from Jasper, my hands fisted the bedding. "B-because I just did it this morning." Jasper stood back, his mouth gaping. "You did what? Is it like, 'Oh poof, I'm a sorceress now'?" He slapped his hands to his side.

Shaking my head, I sat up straight. My dress had a big tear down the front, the scratch from Mortus healing far quicker than any witch or vampire, Jasper's bite had taken care of that. My wolf was also coming far closer to the surface than anticipated.

"When I was doing my meditation." Jasper sighed, running his hand through his hair. Sitting beside me, he moved me promptly to his lap, kissing my neck. "Then what happened?" He calmed. His scent surrounded me. I didn't realize he had a fragrance before. It smelled of sandal wood and a fresh breeze.

"Hecate came to me, saying it was important that I receive this gift, although early in my training." She sniffed. "She said I wouldn't be able to use it for long, but to use it to help protect the Cerulean Moon Kingdom." Jasper stiffened, his hair rustling on his neck.

"What the hell does that even mean?" I shook my head, covering my mouth. I wasn't sure what Hecate meant, but the only thing that popped up in my mind was death. Death could stop me from using my powers.

"The fuck? You are not going to die, Taliyah!" Jasper wrapped his arms around me, shielding me from the world but what he couldn't protect me from was my thoughts.

"I will fucking shield you from your thoughts too, Taliyah." He spat. "My little witch can't think badly of herself, do you understand?" The growling in his chest had me pushing my thighs together. Angry Jasper was really hot.

Bad Taliyah.

"I can hear you," he whispered dangerously in my ear. "We promised to keep our links open, and I know everything that goes through your head when you are near. Now, you listen here." His angry whisper had me whimpering. Pushing me back on the bed, his claws reached around my neck, the pressure on my chest causing my arousal to fill the room.

It was insane to love it when he was like this. He had been so docile and calm the past few months as he tried to show his tender care, but something stirred inside us as we bit each other. We wanted something much more than the usual romance. We wanted it hot... heavy.

"You are weak, about to meet the Parliament of vampires handpicked by Mortus." My eyes widened. "Shit." I breathed.

"So you are going to fucking bite me to help heal yourself faster." Jasper's erection pushed against my thigh. My fangs lengthened, and my leg pushed harder into his cock. Now that I had a taste of what it was like to be mates, I wanted more.

Even after finding out about the major betrayal of one of our greatest funding nobles. Crazy bond.

"Jasper," I warned. My hair rose from the bed.

"That's it." He growled. His hand pushed up my dress, flipping it over. Vampires were sexual creatures when it came to feeding off each other. It was intimate, full of trust as we prodded arteries, taking their blood essence. Neck feeding wasn't to be taken lightly, and when combined with a sexual experience...

Magic.

Red eyes stared back at me, I'd miss the dark-colored browns that used to look at me, but these eyes were full of the bond. The unbreakable attachment we had toward each other. Jasper's pants were already down, my body reacting to him as my magic pulled down my underwear. His lips hungrily attached to mine, weaving his tongue into my mouth.

Rough fingers prodded my opening, and he groaned, feeling the wetness between my folds. "We don't have much time," he mumbled into my lips.

"Just take me." My voice was strained, leaning his head to the side. My fangs entered his neck as soon as he impaled me with his cock. We both strangled a cry, feeling him move inside my body. My hips adjusted, allowing him to dive deeper as I sucked his neck.

He yelled my name like a prayer, holding me tight until I retracted my fangs, feeling him come inside me. My fingers gripped his shoulders. The fabric that once covered his body was now ripped from my red claws.

Licking his neck, he buried his face into mine. Licking my neck, I urged him to suck, but he shook his head. It was dangerous for him to go too long without drinking, especially now with his blood lust. "Jasper, even if it is just a little." He grunted, his eyes flashing red back to his wolf.

"If I'm going to drink, I'll do it to the bastards sitting in that room." He nodded to the far wall. "I'll fucking destroy them." Electric currents went through Jasper's hair. Part of my magic had not seeped into him yet. It would take more time.

"Excuse me, Your Majesty, Your Highness." Melinard's strangled voice came from the door. "They are waiting patiently for your arrival." Jasper looked down at me once, pushing his lips to me for a searing kiss.

"We do this together," he whispered.

"Together," I agreed.

The room that would be nothing short of a modern conference room stood with dimmed lightning. My seat at the table was a long walk with all the peering eyes that watched us sit in our seats. Glasses of water and snack food sat out on the table. None of it had been touched.

"I heard a disturbance a few days ago," Dorian announced. "Soldiers invaded Duke Mortus' home without warrant or reason why." His eyes wandered to Jasper and back at me. Murmurs filled the chamber with twenty vampires.

"I had reason to believe humans were in immediate danger, so I called to send them in." My voice came out stronger than I realized, giving me the boost of confidence I needed.

"And were they there? These humans?" Dorian chuckled, crossing his arms. "Because I didn't see or smell anything." Jasper slammed his fist on the table.

"You respect your queen." He pointed. "Speaking condescendingly like that can get you in the stocks." Dorian snubbed his nose at Jasper. The entire room found Jasper to be lower than low to try and steal a mate of another, but most of all because he was a werewolf. These vampires were old, older than me, and were stuck in their old ways.

In fact, all of these vampires were from a time when they preyed on human blood when they traveled outside of the realm. The normal dulled red eyes were now lit with fire. Undertones of bright red shifted through. My eyes narrowed, staring at Dorian. Using my magic blessed by Hecate, I reached inside him. He shifted in his seat uncomfortably as I felt the glamour spell on him.

My body pivoted, going down the line. All of the oldest vampires had a sheen of magic on all their faces. Duke Mortus had planned to ruin me from the start. My teeth ground together, the lights in the room dimming as the spark of magic flowed through me. They didn't like me because I was part witch. They didn't know that my mother was a coven leader, much more powerful than a mere witch.

Jasper stood from his seat, reading my thoughts. He knew my power. He felt it in bond now more than ever. His hand went to my back in comfort, but not to pull me back.

"Guards," I boomed. The side of the room that held the traitors pushed their chairs back. "Arrest them for conspiring against the crown with the rogues and feeding forcefully from humans." Protests and yells of curses rang across the table. The few loyal vampires on the right side of the table stood defensively, two jumping in front to protect me.

The room lost its light before it abruptly came to light again. The traitors disappeared. Lord Virion, one who had been recommended by Mortus, still stayed at his end of the table. He had a passive look as he looked down at the now empty table.

"I... had no idea." He faked a shutter and rested his hand on his chair. "I understand if you need to arrest me." He smirked. The vampires that stood in front of me climbed off the table. Lord Virion had no glamour spell on him, and I couldn't detect a lie. My head tilted, reaching further into his mind only to find an empty cave of nothingness.

Jasper snarled. "*I don't like it,*" he linked. "*Usually, you see something.*" It was true, either a thought about what they ate for breakfast, their hidden fears, or their emotion. This was literally nothing.

"*We need to evacuate,*" I linked Jasper. "*And pray to Ares we have him on our side.*" Lord Virion took the pad of his finger and traced the long mahogany table. He rubbed his thumb and finger together in distaste.

"But I do have an idea how to run this country now." Three dark shadows were cast on the wall behind him, moving in ways Virion was not. Horns of various sizes sat on their heads. Virion tutted, standing in front of me. "We all do."

Chapter Thirty-four

Taliyah

Time slowed. Virion's thumb and finger that rubbed together gathered bright blue and black lighted flames. The flames ignited higher, jumping to the table and setting it ablaze. The few vampires left of my Parliament stood back, unable to take the heat. Jasper pulled Melinard out of the line of fire as the tendrils of fire reached out to touch the walls.

The white ball of energy I pulled together with my hands was quickly put out by Virion's flames. Grunting, I pushed another into his body. Backing up only slightly, I shoved a stream of light toward him again, the crackling of electricity slowing him down but not enough to make him stop.

Standing tall, he took in my white light until his own black and blue flame came together as we pushed each other with our own forces. The light versus the dark. As the energy surged from our bodies, they grasped hold of each other, intertwining, pushing, and pulling against each other.

"I'll give you a choice, and you must be quick." Viron gritted his teeth, his disgusting smile ripping his skin further up to his ears. He pulled deeper into his body to force out the ever-growing energy. The shadows on the wall now had flaming blue eyes staring down at me, pushing away from the wall and sitting on either side of Viron's head. "Join me now. With your light and my darkness, I can promise you that Vermillion will be returned to its former glory. All you need to do is pledge your allegiance to me." Viron's forked, snaked tongue licked his lips.

Sweat formed on my brow, my body weakening by the second. Jasper growled, shifting as he jumped through the table of flames only to be pushed away by one of the shadow figures. He hit a decorative portrait on the wall, causing him to black out with a whimper.

I growled, feeling the desperation from my mate. I couldn't do this. This was beyond anything I had ever anticipated.

"Tick tock, little witch," his voice strained. "I only offer this once. Your people will be safe, a nation to flourish, and your people will finally accept you and your mate."

Jasper groaned in the corner, his wolf's head bobbing back and forth as he tried to rise. Feeling a surge of power from my body, a graceful figure of my wolf appeared in my mind. Long flowing white hair, red eyes, and gentle paws scraped across the deep colored grass. "Time to make a choice," she whispered to me. "Choose the dark or choose the light." Her soft words blanketed my heart in warmth, her strength pushing power I never knew I could have.

"And what of the other nations in Bergarian?" I yelled over the tremendous roar of electricity surging in the room. The only light left was the dancing of dark and light powers.

"Who the fuck cares? You save your nation. The rest is for me." Viron's smile cracked, his lips breaking until fangs lit up his face straight to his ears. Three sets of horns sprouted from his head, dark claws lengthening as the blue light streamed faster. He was an abomination, something so dark I had never seen anything like it.

"I fight for the greater good," I whispered, knowing damn well he heard me. Virion chuckled, his demon smile webbing his skin back to that of normal lips.

"Little do you know, there will be no good after I defeat both the realms." Jasper awoke as I screamed in anger. Taking one of my hands, I willed another orb, throwing it toward him to try and get him off his feet. Viron chuckled, knocking it away. Jasper pounced in front of me, pushing me roughly onto his back. Virion's blue stream of electricity fell to the floor, igniting the rugs and the table.

With my stream of light now faded, Jasper bolted to the window as I grasped his hide. He jumped from the third-story conference room. Glass shattered around us, and the small sounds of glass clashing together had me looking in the reflection of those broken pieces. The palace would be no more after this night.

Clinging to Jasper, his muscles rippled when the first set of paws landed on the ground. Jasper gracefully landed on the darkened soil with the rest of the vampires that lived with us all in the palace.

We stared up in disappointment. All the work done to rebuild a kingdom had been lit up in flames with the hottest fire we ever experienced. Bricks crumbled, and metal melted as we stepped further away. The blaze was now so hot that the entirety of the massive palace was engulfed in the dark flames.

As much as I wanted to break down and feel sorry for myself, I couldn't. The soldiers stood by. No one even dared to bring buckets of water. It was all futile. Now those that were left of Vermillion, the ones that were so innocent, were left in my care.

The giant chandelier that hung in the foyer longer than seven generations of my family crashed to the floor. The glass shattered, the wood splintered, and stones collapsed upon themselves. I closed my eyes, taking a large breath, feeling Jasper wrap his arms around me.

Jasper didn't need to say anything. He comforted me as we watched the hope of Vermillion burn.

The innocent families that stayed at the shelter in the center of town now gathered to watch the spectacle. Their red eyes filled with unshed tears as I gripped my tattered dress.

Deep down, I knew this was coming. I ignored the signs as much as I had hoped we could turn Vermillion around. I took the lowest blow trusting someone I thought was there to help the crown, only to have it be the greatest mistake of my life. What would the people around me say now? Would they have me beheaded for what I had done?

I would take the high road and sacrifice our country to do the right thing. Betraying other nations and watching them burn while we rebuilt would have haunted me to no end.

Jasper laced his fingers with my burned ones. They were sore and blistered, but his touch only cooled them as they healed.

"Your Majesty, are you all right?" Melinard stepped up with his mate. They both looked at me in pity as I kept my composure.

"You ask me if I am all right." I paused, looking back at the blaze. "But I should be asking you that. All of you." My gaze went to the crowd. "I must be honest with all of you. Vermillion could have been saved if I had sided with the darkness, with the rogues, to a man that I believe holds so much evil that both realms will be compromised." I bit my lip. A baby cried in the back of the crowd.

"But I did not. We would never be safe from him, and who knows what would happen in the future if he came knocking." Utter silence swept the late afternoon. The trees that had begun to sprout leaves as of recent tickled the bark of branches.

"We will rebuild!" I shouted. "We will become a nation again, but not until we help our neighbors and friends." Jasper pulled me closer. I put my hand on top of his chest, seeking its warmth. "For those left, we will continue on. We will survive. Gather your things. We leave immediately." The crowd stood still, swaying to the breeze that pushed the flames higher.

"Where will we go?" One of the servants asked. Her lashes blinked the crimson tears that touched her cheeks.

"Leave that to me," I put my hand on her shoulder. A loud scoff came from the middle of the crowd. All eyes now gathered where the sound came.

"Right, listen to you? Did you just hear what she said?" The vampire pushed forward, standing before Jasper and me. "This is why we shouldn't trust you, some half breed and your werewolf! You aren't even fighting for the vampires!" Jasper growled, stepping forward. I let him go, he had been too quiet, and maybe this was what we needed. What we both needed to have the skeptical ones fear us.

"Did you just hear what she fucking said?" Jasper pulled the vampire by the decorative collar on his tunic. He was of the upper middle class, not quite a noble, but still prominent in his community. "She isn't here for a quick fix; she's looking at the long term. Did you want Lord Virion to come back later and fuck us up then? Or be rid of him for good, so your children, the next generation, can live in peace?"

"Shut up, O'Neal," a low-class witch stepped up. "You're just pissed because you lost your human blood bank." Anger spread like wildfire, vampires arguing with one another, accusing each other of human feedings. Shoving began, children cried, and claws came out.

"Enough!" I yelled so loudly a bright light came from my body, giving me more attention than I intended. I gulped, watching the crowd go silent once again as it faded. "*You can do it,*" Jasper linked me, still staring down at O'Neal.

"There will be no feedings on unwilling humans! This law has been enacted for years!" Some nodded and others rolled their eyes, but filtering through every vampire would be difficult. Sure, we had the rogue vampires. Those were easy to spot. They had evil entrap them with not just their selfishness, but black magic now gave way to a different smell they acquired.

"If you want safety and security, I will do my best to provide that for you. We will rebuild." I paused again. "If you do not wish to follow, you may go on your way and find shelter on your own. If you end up becoming rogue, following the darkness, you will see me fighting against you because you are no subject of Vermillion."

Turning my back, I sighed, putting my hands to my face. It felt hot, scalding for that of my average body temperature. Breathing heavily, my hand leaned against the tree, trying to catch my breath.

"Your wolf is trying to force a shift." Jasper moved my hair away from my neck, kissing it. "We need to go to the Crimson Shadows pack. Their wolves will help assist you on the shift. We do best in numbers."

"Fuck my life," I muttered. Jasper chuckled, pulling me to his chest. "She isn't coming now, but soon. It will give us time to get everyone to the pack. I've already linked Kane. It has become a central hub full of warriors and refugees seeking shelter." Wrapping my arms around Jasper, he kissed the top of my head.

"You did so well." Jasper rubbed my arms up and down. My rigid walls began to fall. Now I just felt the bond holding us together. "We are going to get through this."

"Are we really?" I questioned him. The surprised look on his face had me close my eyes in shame. "Because right now, things look grim. There is no more Vermillion." I whispered, looking at the burning palace. It once stood tall at the highest point of the country. Now, it sat in ash. Nothing was left.

"I'm trying to give them hope." I looked over Jasper's shoulder, only for him to push me into his chest. "But I don't know if I am strong enough." A tear dripped from my cheek, landing on his chest.

"You came here to rebuild a nation that was barely standing. This place would have fallen far quicker if you weren't here. There would be more starving children, more deaths, more darkness if you didn't do what you did." Jasper rubbed my back, his head leaning on my head. "We aren't the only ones fighting anymore. We all fight against one darkness."

Chapter Thirty-five

Clara

"Where the fuck is everyone!?" Kane's booming voice echoed through the halls of the pack house. He was in a mood, as he should be. We were snuck up on by a warlock and three rogue dragons. At least, we think they were rogue. There wasn't a smell on them at all.

We traveled back to the pack territory with the warlock in tow. He was gagged with vines to keep his mouth shut so he couldn't chant out any spells. His body was strong, and the wounds he sustained from being wrestled to the ground had healed. Even with the magical powers of witches, warlocks, sorcerers, and sorceresses, they all healed like regular humans. Taking the time to use their magic to heal themselves took a different mindset, like meditation.

As he was dragged down the mountain, Kane cursed a storm. The bodies crushed by one of the dragons were carefully placed inside the carriage forcing Kane and me to walk. Not that I minded. Each body was to be respected for its sacrifice to protect the rest of us. I just prayed to the gods they would be well received even in death.

"Marcus!" Kane roared out. His fur ran down his back and covered his arms lightning fast. Even though we do not age, I swear I saw white hairs sprout from the fur.

"You better go to him," I stood at the top of the stairs. Raine cajoling me to join my mate. I had so much work to do by finding rooms for so many elves, shifters, and the stray fae that had come to visit the Cerulean Moon Kingdom territories that I had neglected Kane. A pang of guilt hit me, but it was hard to be in several places at once.

Raine held my shoulders, having me look her in the eye. "Give me orders, Luna." My lip shook. Raine had been nothing but a wonderful sister to me. She was there from the beginning, always drawn to help me even when I swore I didn't need it. Leia came up behind her, her hand resting on my cheek.

"*You're a queen now,*" Leia mind-linked. "*You can't do everything. You have your subjects, your pack. We are here to serve you, Little Fox.*" I chuckled, listening to my old nickname. Nodding my head, I spouted out my running list in my head.

Rooms need to be cleared out, extra cots for the bedrooms. The pack house was becoming a bunker, housing for the sleeping warriors, protection for those who couldn't cross the portal. It was all we had now that the last soldier had arrived from the Cerulean Moon palace, saying it was now boarded up. We couldn't risk anyone staying there. It was the first place the rogues would go to find the nation's rulers.

Now that was Kane and me.

"You want to tell me how those damn dragons snuck up behind us?" A crash of expensive vases fell to the floor. I winced hearing Kane entirely losing his temper.

"I don't think I have ever seen him this upset," I whispered to Raine.

"Oh, he has been this upset, all right," Raine mused as she pulled another cot from the closet. "When you got captured by Darius." Ew, I was gone for a week then. *I bet living with Kane was insufferable.*

Grunting came from downstairs. I hopped down the stairs in the breathable leather pants and tight corset top. Kane was hoovering over Marcus, his arms trying to cover his face from the next blow. Marcus's wounds were already healing, but the snap of his femur bone bending back into place made me shudder.

"My Alpha." I went up behind Kane. He froze, standing up straight instead of hovering over Marcus. "Thank the gods," Marcus uttered, sliding away. My hand wrapped around Kane, and his furry arm returned to his normal skin.

"Everything is going to be all right." I stroked his arm, his eyes boring into me. Pulling me up, he had my legs wrapped around him. He held me tight, sitting on the ground in the middle of the foyer. Torin was stirring inside him, rage building by the second. Torin was a beast. There was no question about that. I don't know where my Kane would be if we never found each other or when it was too late.

"*Thank you, Luna.*" Marcus linked as he shuffled away, not daring to turn his back to Kane.

"We aren't finished." Kane growled. "You are my eyes and ears, and you failed." Marcus's eyes went heavy, shoulders slumping in defeat. "Three of my warriors are dead, Marcus." I duck my head low, Kane feeling my sorrow for those warriors. But it wasn't Marcus's fault. Kane wanted someone to blame.

"It was my fault. I am at your mercy, Alpha." Marcus's haunted look made me question that there was much more than the disappointment he gave Kane, but I let it lie. I didn't have the energy, time, or right to reach into Marcus's life right now. Too many lives were at stake.

"Marcus, you are doing a wonderful job," I spoke louder. Kane stiffened, his mouth opening to argue, but I put my finger to his lips. "They were under the dark magic. We didn't know they were coming. They were silent, odorless. Even the dragons guarding the portal didn't see them until it was too late. You are not at fault." My glare at Kane had him purse his lips.

"Go, get some rest." I tenderly stared at Marcus. His bright personality had considerably darkened. He strode out of the foyer. Warriors and omegas that begged to stay to help with food and accommodations took the long way around to keep out of their alpha's way.

Stroking Kane's cheek, he shivered in my hold. "It's okay, Alpha." I ran my hands through his hair. Torin calmed, his constant growls ceasing while I rocked him back and forth as his head lay on my chest. "We will get through this, right?" I hummed into his messy hair.

"We have to speak with Adam," Kane grumbled. "He will be able to tell me if any of his dragons were responsible, and we need to order him to have his tribe look out for others."

The entire pack house was tracked with mud and debris from the outside. No time to clean, no time to tidy up. We were running on adrenaline making physical barriers to slow down any rogues that dared to climb the walls. Petting Kane's hair continuously, August strode up, kneeling to the floor, placing a fist on the now dirtied marbled floor.

"Better be good news," Kane grumbled. August was now the bearer of all things evil. Each message he gave us was nothing but a wrench in our plans. August held a parchment of paper with Osirus' seal stamped on the front. "Why is Osirus not using the mirror?" I asked, taking the letter.

"Mirrors are compromised. Like the mind-links when we get too close to the dark magic, there is nothing but static."

"Fudge." I ripped the seal open, Kane still holding onto me for dear life, trying to calm his beast. "Double fudge." I rubbed my hands over my eyes. August glanced over my shoulder, swearing a few curse words as he paced the room. Kane paid no mind, his face breathing into my chest all while rubbing his hand up and down my back.

Kane was worse off than I thought. The heaviness of being a king, an alpha, and his worry for me put so much pressure on a wolf who was ready for just fighting. Now, the news I was about to break to him would put him over the edge, and no doubt lead to a steamy session here in a minute.

Not that I minded...

"Kane," I whispered in his ear. He hummed, still rubbing his scruffy beard on my breasts. "There is no easy way to say this, Alpha, but—" Kane came out from my breasts, his haunted soul bore into mine.

Goddess, this was hard.

"Alpha Adam, your friend, who claimed Amora all those years ago, is not his true mate." Kane stiffened, his breathing stopping all together. "He has been using dust, a white magic powder, to erase her memories, making her think they were mates. The same powder that made us all forget our fight at Osirus' palace." Torin's eyes flickered their bright amber. "Alpha, Adam has been working with the enemy," I muttered.

"Who wrote this?" Kane ripped the parchment from my hand, Osirus' signature at the bottom, along with Amora's. He had come to know Amora after the mating ceremony he was invited to. Amora was a kind fae raised with the dragons after her family was killed by rogue vampires so long ago. She was everything a good female alpha dragon should be, even if she did have trouble shifting into her animal. It now made sense how she couldn't shift well. Adam wasn't her mate, making her dragon weak.

"I'm going to fucking kill him." Kane crumbled the paper, throwing it to the ground. The details of that letter were so vivid, so harsh, we dared not read the rest. Amora was subjected to years of rape and didn't even know it. *Goddess, how is she feeling right now? Does that mean those dragons that came to us today were sent by Adam? An alpha we trusted?*

I wanted to believe that Osirus made a mistake, but Osirus would never lie about something like this. This was a major offense with a penalty of death that would be carried out by Kane, no doubt.

August picked up the parchment that Kane and I couldn't finish. He peeked over the rest as Kane stood to his feet, keeping me firmly planted to his body. "There's more," August muttered. August tightened his fist, then ran it through his own messy hair. "Creed is not who we think he is." He trailed off.

Which is what I initially thought.

"Creed is innocent in all this too. He was cast out by Adam after this memory powder erased everyone's memories. Adam is responsible for his parents' deaths." August's eyes narrowed at the parchment. "Fuck," he whispered.

"Oh my gods." I gasped, holding onto Kane. Torin's anger sprouted forth. His radiation of power consumed the room. August fell to the floor, his neck bared. More thuds around the pack house had whimpers invading the mind-link. Peeking outside, many more wolves lay on the ground.

Unknowingly, Kane was using his royal command. My hand traced his cheek, having him stay with me. "Let's go upstairs and calm down," I cooed. "Please, just take me upstairs." It sated him as wolves began to slowly stand.

"Raine and Leia have a list of chores," I spoke to August. "See to it that it is completed. We aren't to be disturbed." August graciously nodded. His hands shook while running out the door. I couldn't let Kane show his royal command out too soon. The results would be disastrous. Rogues would find us far too quickly, and if we were a key in this war, then we needed to stay hidden as much as we could.

Kane ran up the stairs four at a time until we found our room. He kicked the door open and slammed it shut with the same foot. He growled out, gently dropping me to the bed.

"Fucking hell." He paced the floor. I crisscrossed my legs, waiting for what he wanted to do. Concentrating on calming him, letting my power flow through me and the room around us, his pacing stopped.

"He was my damn friend," he finally let out. "I trusted him with keeping the area of the north safe." I listened as he pulled off his shirt. The sprouts of dark hair covered his chest, and parts of his tattoos were gleaming with sweat. The dark circles under his eyes had me reach out, drawing him toward me.

We lost three warriors today in death. Our daughter, our family, along with the weakest shifters, had gone through the portal. That in itself was hard, but they were safe. That was what mattered. Cyrene had left soon after the attack, worried that the power she had radiated led the rogue dragons here.

"It's been a day." I pulled Kane to the bed. He pushed my body to lay back, his body hovering over me. Kane's massive body relaxed against me. His strong arms held his torso to hover over me as he gently kissed my lips. "We need to relieve some tension." My soft smile had Torin purring in his chest.

"I can't be soft, and I don't want to hurt you." He growled into my lips.

"Then don't be, Alpha." Kane's eyes hooded, filled with the desire I had hoped to stir from him. He was like a child who needed to be sated every few hours to keep his beast at bay. We both needed this, to feel each other's bodies, to forget, even if it was just for an hour, to revive ourselves.

My fingers trailed up his muscular arms, his forehead touching mine as I whispered softly. "I love you, Kane. Take what you need."

Chapter Thirty-six

Clara

K ane needed this. Goddess, I needed this.

My mate was one for control, to dominate on and off the battle-field. Right now, he was feeling less than, unable to control the happenings around him. There was too much happening. He was lost in the constant stirrings of troubles.

Kane had lost two warriors. The twitching of pain as the pack link broke from them had him snarling in frustration. As much as a beast Kane was, his brutality both on a battlefield and in training, he hated to lose a warrior. In the short time I'd known him, I knew he had a heart even when he scolded his pack.

Kane wanted to protect them, to face the dangers that lurked in the dark and even in the light. Conditioning them so they would expect the unexpected. Now, with the claws of dragons two of Kane's warriors faced, he felt he didn't prepare them enough. His warriors were taken from this world, which broke him.

The elven territories that sat on the Cerulean Moon Kingdom borders near the dragon tribes, closest to Adam, needed to be warned. Word had been sent by falcon of Adam's treachery. We just hope they received it in time. Maybe they already knew, but nothing was for certain.

My ability to try and organize, to determine, to make decisions was becoming too much for me. I wanted to let go, while Kane wanted to seek control.

This moment was perfect for us because we could both get the relief we wanted. His dominance and my submissiveness.

"I'm serious, love. I can't hold back." Kane hovered over me like a dark cloud. The sparks of lightning invaded his eyes while his cock pushed into my core. I whimpered, feeling the heaviness below his waist. It wasn't a whimper of worry or being scared. It was longing. To let go, to let someone take care of me instead of me taking care of everyone else.

"I don't want you to hold back, Alpha." My eyes half opened as I stared at his muscular torso. "I need this as much as you." Kane's eyes rolled in the back of his head as he pushed his dick into me. I moaned out, putting my arms around his neck.

"Safe word." It wasn't a question, but a command that had me pushing the apex between my thighs harder into him. We hadn't had time to explore this side of ourselves since Evelyn was born, but we both knew we wanted to do more with our time together. Him dominating, me letting go.

"Rose," I muttered. Kane pulled himself from the bed, walking to a chest of drawers. As he walked, he tugged at the ties of his black leather pants, slowly pushing them to the floor. His glorious, muscular ass hitched my breath as he tugged at his cock.

I rasped, wanting to watch him touch himself, something I found so erotic. He grunted as he pulled it harshly, almost punishing himself. He turned, holding a black nylon rope with his fingers, his hand still around his cock.

"You like this?" He tugged it again, the precum glistening, dripping as he strode to the bed. Licking my lips, he smirked. "Words, baby, or do I need to remind you?" Kane's voice grew dark, my legs pressing together as I continued to lay on the bed.

"Sorry, Alpha." Kane hummed, his knee sitting on the mattress.

"Arms up." He grunted. Kane delicately took my wrists, laying them flat against each other behind my head, wrapping each one intricately and ultimately tied together. Once secured, he gave it enough slack so he could position my body the way he wanted.

Kane's fangs grew from his mouth, hungrily gazing at me. I arched my back, begging for him to touch me. One hand trailed down my side while one of his claws slowly untied my corset top, and my breasts fell free.

"This skin," he mumbled. Taking his tongue, he licked around my nipple. It hardened as he blew cool air across its peaks. "I want to mark it." He growled lowly in his chest.

His mouth suckled my nipple, humming into it, his cock rubbing my leg absentmindedly. I moaned, causing a loud smack to my thigh. "Owie!" I yelled, which had Kane grinning ear to ear.

"I want you silent, or I'll gag you." My head perked up.

We haven't done that before.

"Fuck, love, I love seeing you tied up." Kane's hand trailed to my leather pants. He untied the tightly tied strings of my pants and pulled them down slowly. The underwear I wore, already soaked, had Kane growl in approval. "I like what I see." His finger trailed the outside of my underwear.

"All this for me?" My mouth parted, watching his cock bob as he sat back on the bed.

"Yes, Alpha. All for you." My arms pulled on the rope, making the bed creak. He tutted, shaking his head.

"No moving," he warned. His large hand covered my thigh, ripping the last bit of my panties. He licked his lips, his mouth moving closer to my thighs. I tried to be so still as he pushed my legs further apart. "What a pretty sight." Kane wasn't much for words for others, but damn, the way he was talking to me right now had me dripping in the sheets.

He pushed my legs up. I was bare to him. All of me was exposed. I resisted the urge to push my legs down away from my torso because I didn't think

I could handle another slap of disapproval. He hummed, listening to my thoughts. "That's my baby, trying to please her Alpha."

Biting my lip until it bled, he lowered his head. One long, slow, tantalizing lick from the base of my pussy to my clit had me cry out. A slap on my thigh had me pull on the ropes again.

It was a pleasurable sting while his rough tongue assaulted my clit. "No coming," he mumbled into my body. My fingers interlaced with one another, rubbing my knuckles together to concentrate on something else.

The tingles from his touch and the roughness of his tongue had my clit throbbing, begging me to let it go. Kane pushed my legs further up my torso. Gods, he could see everything.

He lifted his head, my desire covering his face. The evil glint in his eye had me wanting to come over his face. Panting, he leaned forward, kissing me hard, needy. Tasting myself, I hummed into the kiss. His hand squeezed my butt while his torso rubbed up and down my pussy.

"What do you want, baby?"

Doodles, he was going to make me say it.

"What does my helpless little luna want?" Oh, I loved the thick velvet growl that left his throat as he teased me. He was prolonging the pleasure because I swear the dam would break as soon as he allowed me to come.

"Please, Alpha?" Breathless, I wiggled the lower half of my body, my arms pulling on the rope. Kane sat back, keeping my legs pushed to my torso.

"I don't know," he taunted. "I'm not sure if you are wet enough."

"Alpha!" I screamed out as his fingers pinched my clit. His cock rubbed against my leg. His other hand tightened around my ankle. He threw one leg over his shoulder, his face buried deep into my pussy.

Continuing to hold back my orgasm, sweat beaded on my forehead. "You can come now." He broke away, licking his lips. "But eyes on me," his voice lowered and sucked. My back arched, my neck straining to keep my eyes trained on Kane; his eyes grew golden while my body released. Crying out, my mouth opened, feeling his tongue lick me dry.

"My turn." He growled, climbing up my body. "You're going to suck my enormous cock in your mouth." He fisted it as his legs straddled my chest.

"Do you want your alpha's cock?" Nodding frantically and spitting out a desperate, "Yes, Alpha," he lowered himself.

"Link me if it's too much." His voice softened just as he coated my lips with his come.

"Fuck, you look so beautiful with my come on your lips." Licking the tip, he shuddered. "Open," he huskily whispered as I let him in. He sunk his cock low into my mouth with my wrists still tied to the bed. I hummed, tasting the salty taste. His balls tickled my chin.

"I'm going to move." His voice strained, sounding like he was in pain. Slowly, his cock came in and out of my mouth, feeling the ridges of the head down to the smooth shaft. His eyes stayed on me, watching himself getting lost in my mouth.

He jerked, groaned, and gripped the iron railing of the headboard, causing it to groan. My wrists tightened again, wanting nothing more than to hold his ass cheeks to the rhythm of his thrusts. Rubbing my thighs together, he pushed harder.

"Fuck, baby, yes." His movements went sporadic until, without warning, he came down my throat. I moaned. "Swallow." He growled. As much as he wanted it to be a command, an order of dominance, he knew I would swallow regardless.

With a pop, he groaned, pulling his shaft from my mouth and stroking it again. "I need more of you." He made staggered movements, falling beside me. Rolling me over, my face now facing the headboard, he pushed my knees up on the bed. "Push your ass up," he barked. Torin's voice came through, his claws raking the brand-new duvet as I tried to comply.

I liked not thinking. I loved the orders he gave me as I spread my legs, my elbows on the mattress. He walked around the bed, his cock slapping his thigh, looking at my ass hungrily. "Fucking beautiful sight." He licked his lips. The bed dipped, his knees crawling up to me.

"All tied up and nowhere to go," he cooed. The palm of his hand hit harshly on my ass. He rubbed it with his calloused palm. The waiting, the anticipating, had me begging in the mind-link.

"Love my marks on you." He hummed. "Be patient." His hand now dipped to my lower back, feeling the curve of my spine. His cock rubbed up against my inner thigh. "Safe word?"

"Rose," I whispered as Kane hissed. The tip of his cock pushed tantalizingly slow into my folds. "So tight." He inched his way in. My ass pushed backward until he slapped my thigh again. "Who the fuck is in charge?" I wailed.

"Y-you, Alpha." I stilled, pulling on the rope again.

"That's right." Hearing the smile in his voice, my pussy tightened. "I'm in fucking charge. Of your pleasure." He pulled out. "Of your orgasms." He pushed back in. My claws raked down the ropes, strands of the nylon ripping. "Of your body." He slammed back into me.

Kane himself forced into me, my pussy clamped, feeling the walls of my body quake. Deep, long, powerful thrusts had my spinal cord compressing. He pushed so hard that my body had to sit up, my arms now leaning on the bed frame while still being tied.

He sensed me being uncomfortable. Kane thrust forward with one flick of his claw. The ropes broke so both my hands could grip the bars. "Fuck, baby." My hair dripped with sweat.

"Can I come, Alpha?" My nipples pushed up against the cold bars. Kane leaned closer, pinching my nipple. "Come on my cock." I fell over until the blue moon of Bergarian was seen in my eyes. Eyes glazing over, my wolf howled in the back of my mind.

"Fuck yes," Kane continued. If he had already come once, he could go longer if he wanted. "Do it again," Alpha commanded me. Letting my walls down earlier, giving him complete submission, my body racked again with another orgasm.

"Fuck, you are drenching the sheets." His fangs came close to my ear. Rolling me over, not letting his cock leave my body, I gaped at him with excitement. "I like looking into your eyes as I come in you." He panted.

His thigh muscles flexed above me, his arms going under my back and his hands pulling my shoulders to dive deeper. Goddess, he was so big, I still didn't understand how he could fit.

"One more baby, one more." I shook my head. If I came again, I swear I would sleep for a week.

"I can't." I breathed. He slapped my thigh, and the thrill of the sting had me push my breasts into his face.

"You will, for me, to please me." He gritted his teeth. Biting down on my nipple and one hard thrust later, his load spilled into me, my body soaking up his desire.

Small kisses on my breast led to my face, and his once stern, immovable face softened, kissing my lips gently, he became my gentle giant once more. "Are you okay?" he murmured, kissing me, so I was unable to speak.

"Of course I am. I was made for you." I chuckled. Hands running through his wet hair, he rolled over, pulling me to his chest. Laying my head on his chest, I listened to his heart slow. Kane ran his rough fingers over my back.

Wow, I didn't realize how much I needed this. To give up the worry, give up the planning and what move we did next. Kane did it all for me and took control of our time together, so I didn't have to think. It was refreshing and beautiful, and Kane got his fill.

"You have no idea how much that helps." He sighed. "I'm sorry you have to put up with my ass." Smiling, kissing his chest, I shook my head.

"It helps me too, Alpha," I tickled his side. "It helps me let go. Take things slowly. It helps you feel in control when everything around us is... just not."

Kane gently laid me on my side. He checked my wrists, kissing each one as I lay. He stood up to go to the bathroom, coming back with a warm cloth to clean my mouth and then between my thighs. I sighed happily. His scent surrounded me. The beautiful comfort of his nature smell had me humming in satisfaction as he crawled back onto the bed with a water bottle.

Pulling me up so I was half lying on his body, he made me drink half of the water before setting it on the nightstand. We didn't cover up in blankets. We lay naked, feeling the fan above us cooling our hot bodies.

What I wouldn't give for everything to return to the way things were. To have everyone live in happiness. No longer have the nightmares, the worries, the stress. Have our families come home and just be.

"Love, soon," Kane mumbled. "I will fix things—"

"We," I interrupted. "We will fix things." With a kiss on my forehead, he laid my head next to his neck as I breathed him in.

Chapter Thirty-seven

Clara

We slept through the night. No one dared to bother us. Everyone understood Kane's mood wasn't to be messed with, which had been a blessing for both of us.

August had more bad news for us this morning, which he refused to deliver. Raine pulled me aside, knowing that Kane was already thinking about the day's preparations to travel and his worries about traveling in such a large group that was sure to gain attention.

However, the news would upset Kane either way because Vermillion was no longer. The palace, that was thousands of years old, had been reduced to rubble and ashes in hours. Taliyah and Jasper had nothing left except for the few thousand loyal subjects.

Jasper's mind-link had been spotty when he talked to Raine. Various sentences were blocked, but she understood what he needed. Vermillion's subjects needed help immediately. Marcus, who took over Kane's duties for the night, allowed them to come to our territory.

Our pack territory now housed so many that we were bursting at the seams. I wasn't sure how many more people we could hold. Sure, many were all hidden in the darkness of our thick forests, some even finding caves and underground burrows that were centuries old. Luckily, we were mostly comprised of animals and enjoyed spending time in nature.

Taliyah's power had grown, and she could now cast large spells such as wards. Her promise to cast one so large to help protect our territory gave me hope that we would be all right. That was all I had right now, hope.

My body had taken a hit. I wasn't sure if it was leftover black magic from the memory powder or if I was worrying myself sick. I had thrown up three times, my face was flushed, and my body was not healing as quickly. Giana had been mostly quiet, mumbling to herself.

Kane prepared the warriors, doubling up on patrols around the territory and taking up the help of Folen and his brother to help manage the large masses of people. Folen could whisper into the trees, able to discover if any rogues planned to come closer to our territory.

Taking a group of warriors with us, we began traveling to the Dragon Tribes in the Northeast. It would be at least a half day's run with us all sprinting together. I was not up to leading the pack today like I usually did on these long runs, my body still weak from being sick.

Kane eyed me cautiously as we ran, noticing that I stuck close to his body. *"Are you all right, love?"* he linked. His four paws crushed the fallen leaves. I panted, feeling winded.

"As good as I can be," I purred into the link. Kane didn't believe me, but he knew not to ask. We were both caught up in our own minds about what we needed to do for everyone else. We were neglecting each other again.

Autumn had faded from the mountains, and snow gently fell as we traveled north. Kane's anxiousness grew as he came closer to his former friend. Torin was after blood today. He was ready to settle the score. He snarled, shifting from his four-legged wolf to his half-beast as we approached.

Fortunately, we weren't the only ones already on the scene. Kane held out his arm, pausing us all as we waited in evergreen foliage. Looking at the open area of Adam's tribe, we saw the elders backing away from a heated argument. They were dressed in deep purple garbs around their waists. They were the oldest in the tribe. Supposedly the wisest.

Looks like they were in some deep poo.

Creed stood with another man, who looked like his father, scolding Adam. His tattered robes and cloak held dried blood with dirt and debris. Adam sneered at Creed's father, yelling that Creed was the one at fault for the death of the alpha, his stepfather, and mother.

Goddess, what drama was this?

Kane motioned for the wolves to surround the tribe, linking them to get the women and children away from the upcoming fight.

"All lies!" Amora screamed, walking up to Adam. Her claws lengthened, running toward Adam, scratching his chest. The brutality of his now ex-mate made Adam falter, falling to the ground. Dragon warriors pushed her back. "You want proof!" Amora yelled. "Look at my mark!" Pulling her tunic to the side, the once light mark was now dark. Nicholas, Amora's bodyguard, wrapped his arm around her.

Holy crap. Mates.

"This is the mark of a true mating! The dragon is dark, solidifying the bond. My dragon is stronger now! Can you feel it!? Feel how she burns in anger at the one we used to call our mate and Alpha!" Amora's dragon radiated, growling until she shifted again. Her muscles rippled across her light green scales.

Yup, poo has hit the fan now.

I snarled, listening to the outrageous lies Adam spouted. It was obvious Adam was lying, yet members of his tribe looked dumbfounded. How could Kane not have known any of this for so many years that he was lying?

"Look." Marcus nodded his nose to the satchels that hung from the elder's waists. Bits of white powder hung around the outside.

"Memory powder!" Kane boomed. The ripple of betrayal gripped his heart as he watched his former friend. All hell broke loose as we heard the name Apollo shouted across the snow. Kane's claws raked across a nearby tree. Adam and Apollo attacked each other, the elders trying to fade into the crowd.

Nope, not happening.

Warriors pulled the innocent back while Kane, Marcus, and I wrestled the five elders that tried to pull away. Kane quickly gripped hold of two, ripping arms out of sockets. They wailed in pain as I grabbed another by the ankle.

My more diminutive form was a challenge as I pulled the large dragon shifter away. I pulled him further from the innocent dragons who were being herded away. I felt weak, but I was able to roll the elder to his back. His eyes reddened with anger, pulling at the pouch attached to his waist and throwing the white dust into my eyes.

Giana sneezed, roaring, pulling the healing agent inside us to bypass the memory powder. "Got this," she murmured. Shaking our head, the memory powder flew off our maw. I blinked, still remembering the task at hand.

"Figured out how to heal us," Giana answered my question before I asked, and she forced us forward. Landing on top of the elder, his eyes widened as he realized it wouldn't work on us.

My teeth pulled at his shoulder, and he wailed, dropping the powder beside him. The blood on my maw dripped as I pulled away, ready to go for his neck, until I felt a sharp pain impale my stomach. His claws pulled out, full of my blood. I paused, feeling the warm glow of my healing taking over.

Rolling off, I whimpered. The outside of my body healed faster than the inside. Giana wailed, howling, not just in pain but loss. My vision doubled, and my body staggered to get away. This was just a flesh wound. I should have healed far faster than I was.

The elder propped up on his good elbow, grinning wickedly as the blood from my stomach healed. Gods, the pain I felt inside my body was worse than I expected. I retched, throwing up blood from my stomach.

The elder crawled toward me, his claws pulling at the bloody snow.

Chuckling, he pointed to my stomach until he spitefully threw his head back. I whimpered again, slowly steading myself on all four paws, trying to ignore the searing pain. "Your wolf can't heal that." He snorted.

Pouncing forward, I sunk my teeth into the hand that dared to impale me, twisting it until I heard it crack. Holding back a scream, the elder continued to chuckle until I pushed him to his stomach, standing on his back. "Kane will be distraught once he finds out," he said. Growling, my teeth went around his neck, snapping it before another word could be heard from him. Once his body grew lifeless, I fell to the ground, panting.

"Are you all right?" Marcus nudged me with his cold nose. He had the memory powder satchel beside him. Whimpering, still feeling the searing pain in my stomach, I hummed, gritting my teeth. Kane ran toward me, blood dripping down his torso's front and scooping me up.

"Clara." He whimpered, holding me. "What happened?" I grunted, shifting back in his arms as he held me. Marcus pulled a dried piece of leather from a nearby clothesline for Kane to wrap me.

"Your stomach—" Kane's half-beast body looked down at me with the most concerned facial expression. I didn't think it was possible with the hair, the teeth, and the blazing red eyes he had. His claw ran over the lower part of my stomach. Claw marks from the elder ran across it. It wasn't healing. The pain subsided, feeling the warmth of his padded paws.

Yells of mercy echoed the clearing. Adam lay on the ground, half-charred as Creed hovered over him. "He's gone," Kane murmured, holding me close, shifting back into his human form.

"Take the powder back," Kane commanded Marcus. His teeth wrapped around the satchel, bursting through the crowd. "We will have Taliyah look at it and see what she can make of it." I nodded, holding my hand to my stomach.

Something was terribly wrong, but I wasn't sure what. I moved awkwardly, shifting in Kane's hold to feel the beating of his heart. Not caring about the blood covering our bodies, I wrapped my arms around his neck, needing to feel his warmth. My body tensed again, feeling the rolling of pain in my stomach again.

"Clara," Giana whined.

"What's wrong with us?" I bit my lip as I asked her. I wasn't sure if I wanted to know. Were we dying?

"No, we aren't dying." Giana whimpered softly. "Just the pup."

The pup? What pup? My lips parted, my arms stiffening around Kane. He held me tighter to his body, grumbling, begging me to tell him what was wrong.

"What?" I asked her. Giana only whined. "I've been concentrating on becoming immune to the memory powder and worrying about you. I didn't realize..." Giana howled.

"Giana, you can't blame yourself. I've been feeling off for days... I didn't pay attention either." I bit my cheek, squeezing my eyes tight. I could not break now, not now.

"You're blocking me." Kane growled. Shit, I was blocking him, more like Giana was. Giana didn't want Torin to know, not yet either. He would flip out in front of all these people. Kane already felt like he couldn't protect his warriors, and now he would be doubly upset he couldn't protect me.

"Look." I nodded my head to Odessa and Creed. Creed had forgotten. He had been doused in memory powder. "Oh, gods," I gripped Kane. The scene unfolded, Odessa brimming with tears until that searing kiss was planted on the dragon's lips. Slowly, Creed's arms wrapped around Odessa, and my heart lightened to see that something went better than planned.

Odessa opened her eyes, seeing Creed shining enough love down for the entirety of Bergarian.

"It's just so sweet." We walked closer to them. "It's like a fairy tale!" I sniffed. I stood beside Kane, who was completely naked and had Odessa blushing. He had no clue about my pain. Concealing it from him was taking everything I had, but I didn't want to ruin this moment for this wonderful love that was before us.

"I'll give you a fairy tale when we get home, baby." Kane slapped my butt, pulling me in tight. "I'll be your prince charming too." I tried to keep my facial expressions light, despite the rolling cramps inside my stomach.

Osirus had landed shortly after. His concern over the rogues had grown, asking for updates from Kane. "We took the memory powder. We sent it back to our witches to see if we can come up with a counter-spell," I said absentmindedly. I continued to stare out over the bloody snow, letting the pain sink into my stomach. My head turned, seeing Apollo limp into the woods. He wasn't healing. He had claw marks running down his back, his tunic torn.

Goddess, we needed to go home. But there was one last thing I had to do.

Kane picked me up, already shifted back into his beast. "You are tired. Let me carry you home."

"I need to heal someone, and then you can carry me." I whimpered. Kane pursed his lips, nodding. "If you must."

Kane tightened his grip. He was frustrated with me, but he knew I wouldn't rest until everyone was cared for. His fangs closed tightly together, hearing the grinding against the enamel.

"I'll tell you as soon as I heal him, okay?" My voice shook. Kane pressed his cheek next to my forehead. Without another word, I shakily ran to the forest, finding Apollo lying by a nearby stump.

"Gul," he muttered. Feathers lay on his cloak, some still in his hair. I had missed when he fought, but the size of the feathers had me realize he was something I had never seen. "Ya need yer mate." He was old, his smell crisp like the mountain air.

Not speaking, afraid a cry would leave my lips, I kneeled, touching his forehead with my hand. Giana took a breath in and pushed the remaining power we had to heal his wounds. There was no use in using the leftover power to heal my womb because my dear pup was already sleeping.

Pulling my hand away, his eyes opened, grabbing my hand. "I smell blood." Looking between my legs, the worn leather was stained with drops of red blood that ran down my legs.

"It's all right." A tear left me. "You are going to be all right." I turned, half running, half falling, until I reached the clearing. Kane was waiting for me, his arms opened, running toward me and pulling me into his arms.

"You're bleeding." He growled.

"I'm sorry," I whispered, beginning to cry. "I'm so sorry I failed."

Chapter Thirty-eight

Kane

Clara fell limp into my arms, her last words piercing my heart as to why she would utter such a thing. We just took care of a large problem, getting rid of the source of draons's blood being given to the rogues.

As much anger I radiated over Adam's betrayal and lies, Clara overshadowed that. I cradled her to my arms, Osirus clearing his throat as I watched him land gracefully into the snow. His face frowned, tilting his head to dismiss me.

Pulling her close once more, my nostrils flared. She smelled of blood that wouldn't come from any sort of wound on her body, but from within. Another mixture surrounded it, it was barely there, and Torin roared inside me with fury.

She was pregnant.

I ran into the woods, and warriors followed, hearing my whimpers. Fuck, how the hell did this happen? How was she pregnant? Did we not know? Surely, she didn't.

"They didn't know!" Torin howled inside me. "Giana has been working tirelessly against the black magic memory powder. They are now immune, but with the cost of our pup."

Carrying Clara, whose heart beat lightly in her chest, I stood over the cliff of the mountains, watching our pack return home. Clara continued to bleed, but not enough for it to be life-threatening. It was disposing of our pup, our child, our baby as she liked to call it. I could feel the remnants running down my arm as I howled into the mountains.

The echo returned with such force it had me step back. Clara would never return from this. Hell, what mother would? To lose a child that was nestled into the womb, supposedly cared for by their bodies. Clara's body didn't fail, though—far from it—but it was her fortress to protect our child.

I howled again, our beast crying for the first time. I didn't know if I felt more sadness or anger. I shouldn't have let her come with me. All this time she had wanted to be there for every battle, every tiff that was fought with our warriors.

She was a damn queen—my queen. She should have been nestled and protected behind the castle walls. But my Clara, my luna, my moon, was not like that.

I ran with swiftness down the mountain, feeling every scrape of rock, stick, and thorned bush, ordering Torin not to heal us. I wanted to bleed, feel the pain in my body as Clara felt in hers. Her body was weak. Giana could not heal her after healing Apollo.

Why the fuck would she go heal him? Why take that extra strength she had and bestow it upon someone she didn't know? I howled again, animals jumping from the thickets, trees brushing by my head. Clara sat bundled in my arms, tightly against my chest in her own world.

The pack was silent as we entered, night had fallen, and the usual blue moon no longer held its gentle hue. Red surrounded the moon in a harsh halo. My eyes squinted through the darkness. Torin pushed our bond to Clara now that we had returned, and now my vision lacked.

"Kane." Marcus's gentle tone had me stiffen. He was the friend I needed, not the beta who took my orders. My usual snap fleeted, listening to him. Marcus's eyes softened in pity, his shoulders slumping as he saw me hunched over Clara's still sleeping body.

"Dr. Talbert will have you stay in your quarters. He's got nurses to tend to her tonight. Borders are secure, and Folen is taking care of the whispering rumors of the roots. Take your time with her." Marcus glanced at Clara, his hand reaching, but I pulled her away.

My hanging head pulled up from my sleeping mate, seeing our pack members. Warriors took a knee, putting their arms over their chests as they watched. Warriors that still sat in their wolf forms whimpered, the women coming with small white and gold flowers, putting them at the base of the pack house steps.

Losing a pup in the womb was rare for werewolves. So rare that my mother never heard of such a thing as I mind-linked her during our journey home. Our doctors would have time on their hands trying to understand Clara's body.

Fuck, they couldn't touch her. I would take care of her.

I snarled, Marcus stepping away. Torin surfaced. I could see the reflection of his red eyes in the fear of the pack. My maw opened to snap orders until August howled. Other wolves followed, filling the air of the forest of our home with sad whimpers.

The howls didn't stop, my eyes brimming with unshed tears as I stepped on Clara's favorite flowers leading us to the pack house. The double doors were opened, candles sweeping the stairs as we ascended.

Doctors stood on either side of the door while we entered. Laying her on the bed, her head fell to the side on the pillow. *"We can clean her, Alpha,"* one nurse mind-linked. I grunted, shifting in front of everyone in the room.

"Leave us." My hand came to my mate's cheek, wiping away the dried blood. The nurse pursed her lips, backing away slowly. The shuffling of feet and the harsh whispers of whether they should stay or go were ignored. I pulled the soapy water bin and began to wash my mate's body.

The door shut, and piece by piece, I washed each section of her.

My mate now lay clean; the soft smell of vanilla candles sat by her night-stand. She hadn't stirred. She sighed softly, her brows forming a worried arch. Kissing each cheek, I pulled the cover's over her body.

Feeling the heat of a body behind me, my worried sister placed a hand on my naked back. "Clara would want you to take care of yourself too." The gentle sternness in her voice almost made me smile. "I feel her healing. Giana is doing her job." Raine coddled me, putting a sheet over my body. "To be sure, we should let the doctors examine her."

"No," I spat out. I couldn't let any male touch her, even if it was to help her. I was a fucking selfish bastard, and it was my job as her mate to help her. If I couldn't help her now, I would be running rampant throughout the pack, ripping warriors to pieces for not doing their fucking job better.

"Can I check her then?" Raine had so kindly delivered our daughter. Torin trusted her, loved her, and would almost do anything for her besides our mate.

"I stay." I grunted. Lifting up from the bed, wrapping the now dirty sheet around my hips, Raine sat on the bed. She kept her link open, letting me hear the words she spoke to the doctor on the outside of the door.

Raine hummed, taking a clean cloth and examining her new scar. "It looks like that powder was on her fur when he scratched her." Raine touched the jagged scar. "It's what caused her to scar and ruin her womb."

A knot formed in my throat. The possibility of only having one child strongly hung in my mind. We had Evelyn, but I knew that Clara wanted another. She wanted as many as we could.

"I—" I choked back, rubbing my hands up and down my face.

"Her womb is all right, brother." Raine pulled the sheet back over Clara's naked body. "The powder only touched the outside of her body." Relief filled me. I sat back in the chair beside Clara's bed, burying my face in my hands.

I couldn't protect my mate, couldn't protect the warriors. *Fuck, how the hell are we supposed to win this!?* "Kane?" Raine came to my side, awkwardly pulling me into a hug while I leaned into her.

"Fucking shit, I'm losing it, Raine." Raine hummed, stroking my hair as Clara liked to do. I don't fucking cry, I don't let anyone break me, but gods damn it I was so fucking over it.

"No one said you had it to begin with," she innocently joked. "Big brother, no one said you had to have it all together. No one said that you were to protect everyone, just that you would, in your power, do your best." I sobbed, holding onto her.

"Clara thinks she failed. I'm the one that is supposed to take care of her." I growled. Torin sat in the back of my mind, staring back at me. He had no emotion, just a blank look in his eyes.

"I know Clara, and she would not think that at all," she said sternly. "Now, what do you think she would want you to do right now instead of whining over what you should or shouldn't have done? Would she want you sitting here upset? Or go kick some fucking ass?"

I sat up. My sister's eyes held such anger. This wasn't her. This was someone new I was seeing for the first time. "It's all right to be upset, we all are, but that doesn't mean we give up now, does it?" she snapped. "That is what *they* want! They want us to feel helpless, to give up, give them the upper hand." She growled. "I'm going to tell you what to do until you process this shit. Do you understand me?"

Fuck, Raine's alpha blood shone through, Torin now tilting his head in amusement.

"You get cleaned up, shower, and you stay here with Clara until she's better. The pack and I will do the rest. Dad, Mom, and me will hold down the fort until then. You both seem to think you have the world on your shoulders. We are here, and we are not gonna leave you."

I sighed, hugging my sister. "Thank you," I whispered. As much as I didn't want to admit it, I needed this.

"I'll listen." I grunted. "But…" I held my hand out, touching her nose. "When she's better, all fucking hell is going to break loose."

Nothing would bring our pup back, not even blaming her fucking parents who left keeping theirs.

Chapter Thirty-nine

Taliyah

"Everyone is settled." Jasper shut the door to the royal cabin. We had members of Parliament staying in other bedrooms as well as our closest servants. We even had those with small children or babies staying in the living room quarters, dining room, and a family staying in the overly large bathroom. Three young children slept in the bathtub filled with blankets and pillows. I would say it was adorable if we weren't in such danger.

Letting out a sigh, I plopped myself on the oversized bed. Maybe we should give this room to a family that really needed it. Jasper and I could use a tent outside and cuddle up under the stars.

"I'm going to stop you right here," Jasper got on his knees in front of me. His hands rubbed the outside of my thighs as I hunched over from exhaustion. "You are a queen. You have opened up this cabin to people that really need it. Being a little selfish for a room to yourself so you can work on your magic is perfectly fine. Clara and Kane are doing the same thing with the pack house."

My heart was pained. Rubbing my hand over my forehead, I could not imagine what Clara was going through. She was the sweetest person, saved me from a terrible fate, and helped me understand Jasper, even forgive him. She didn't deserve any of that.

"How are they?" I closed my eyes, feeling the sorrow of the entire pack. Since my powers had strengthened to sorceress, I could feel things I never wanted. I could feel emotions, read the room or the large plot of land we now inhabited. It hung so heavy my shoulders wanted to slump to the ground.

This pack loved their alpha and luna, even with the terrifying ways Kane ran the pack with an iron fist. He was brutal in their training. Punishments were harsh, but they all gave him respect because he wanted to see them strong and protected.

"Kane's at his breaking point." Jasper stood up, making me lay down on the bed. He rolled me over and pulled my back against his body. Nose in my neck, he breathed heavily as he sighed. "Raine is acting Alpha for the next few days while her parents help manage the hordes of people." We sat in silence, Jasper rubbing his thumb over our intertwined fingers.

"I need to cast the ward," I whispered. Jasper's body tightened around me.

"As much as I don't want you to, I know it must be done. You're so tired," he said. I hummed, turning my body so I faced him. Kissing his lips, he wrapped his arms around me once again.

We would all be so much safer once it was cast. It would give us some protection, let me know if someone or something was coming that was considered an enemy. We even toyed with the idea of putting a glamour spell on the entire pack, but that would pull too much power with the three witches that resided here.

Genesis, Gemma, and Gloria were powerful, but even more so when their fourth sister joined them. She was stuck in the elven tribes, unable to travel.

"What do I need to do to help?" Jasper's thoughts of incompetence ran rampant. Xander was pacing back and forth impatiently.

"Just hold me." My fingers trailed his bare chest. "I can do it right here in bed." Having looked at the territory borders for well over an hour, I had a good idea of how far to cast out the ward. The crystals sat on the table next to the map not far from me. Incense had already filled the room. Now, I just needed my mate to calm me to help prepare.

"That seems so little, to just hold you," he muttered.

"But it's not," I whispered. My eyes began to shine, filling the space between us with glowing red. His eyes glimmered in return as I pulled the power that grew inside him. Crystals on the table clinked together, hovering over the map.

My people and the pack fell into a deep sleep; the entire area was surrounded by an invisible ward. I wasn't sure how much it would help against the dark magic, but any sort of padding was better than nothing. The crystals gently laid back on the table, and our eyes were no longer illuminated. Jasper's half-hooded eyes of exhaustion made my heart ache. He still had not eaten.

Pulling my hair away from my neck, my artery pumped the blood quickly through my body. With my racing heart and my pale neck, Jasper licked his lips, staring at my skin longingly. "Jasper, you need to." Part of him hated it. It was the wolf in him. The more he fought, the worse he would become. "Please, it feels good to me too."

Jasper slowly went to my neck, licking the skin and finally piercing it with his fangs. My body relaxed, feeling the blood flow out of my body and into my mate. His grip around my body tightened, making me feel secure as he continued eating as I fell asleep.

"Taliyah." Raine ran toward me, embracing me in an enormous hug. "Sorry I didn't welcome you yesterday." Her voice trailed off. "I had to—" I shook my head, rubbing her arm.

"You were busy." Raine's eyes softened, her face frowning.

"And you have dealt with a lot too. I'm hoping the pack helped you and your people settle in."

"They did," I said quickly, not wanting to linger on the subject. "The ward has been created, so no one will be able to leave unless you tell me. Same thing for anyone wanting to come in." Raine closed her eyes, her palms coming into a praying position.

"Thank you, that is so helpful." A vampire child and pup ran by, screaming in laughter. My worry about two different species housing so closely together was fleeting. Maybe we all would be able to get along even with our differences.

"Your Majesty." Three women approached, bowing lowly. "We would love your input on what we have extracted from a dragon. We aren't sure what to make of it or what to do with it." My head tilted in confusion until one woman held out a black satchel. One dark red orb lay in the fabric that surrounded them. "We pulled this from The Black Dragon. It is remnants of black magic that had encompassed his soul."

All my history books, spells, and magic enchantments had burned in the fire. Trying to understand this orb in front of me was going to be difficult. My hand reached underneath the fabric to keep my bare skin from touching. Looking over it, the three witches leaned in, watching me study it.

"Sorry," one of them said. "We are just eager to have you here to help." She smiled. "I'm Gemma. These are my sisters, Gloria and Genesis." They all bowed again. "We can tell you exactly how we did it, if you like."

Their eagerness made me laugh. I should have known these were the three sisters that resided here. I put the two orbs back in the bag. "Meet me at the royal cabin. We will study it together. Maybe find a way to understand this magic." Nodding enthusiastically, they ran to their destination.

"You've got some fans," Raine said. "They are good witches. Wish their sister was here, but she has her duty at the elven tribes." We all had to do what we could to protect each other.

Raine led me to Marcus, who was holding a large bag. His eyes were dim. No life was left inside him as he stoically stood with Jasper. My mate was frowning, his concern radiating. "*What's wrong?*" I asked through the link. Jasper only shook his head, giving a small smile.

"*We will talk later.*"

"*Or I can dig in your head,*" I joked. Jasper's small smile had him pull me closer, kissing my forehead. Marcus's facial expressions didn't change. He handed the bag over to Jasper and walked away.

That wasn't the Marcus I was used to seeing at all. This war had torn us all to pieces, but the defeated soul he had now had me guessing what it might be. The knowing look Jasper just gave me confirmed my suspicions.

"Oh gods," I muttered, Jasper pulling me into his chest. "This is so awful. This has to stop." I sniffed. Jasper rubbed a hand up and down my back, kissing my forehead. Raine, who was talking to another wolf, turned to give her attention back to us.

"This is memory powder," Jasper muttered. Raine growled, folding her arms.

"That shit has caused trouble," she snapped. "Please be careful with it, it can erase your memory, and only a bond or those witches expelling it out of your body can cure it. It isn't to be messed with." Feeling defeated, I grabbed the bag. It was time to get to work.

We worked all day. The three sisters now lay scattered on the floor of my bedroom. The table Jasper erected was now filled with endless notes, papers, and small spell books from the sisters, and I was in no way any closer to knowing what these orbs were.

The powder was still sitting in its bag, untouched. I had an overwhelming feeling that these orbs were so much more important. They had remained untouched, too fearful of whatever magic it held to penetrate me, but we were running out of time.

Looking behind me, making sure all those in the room were asleep, I took my finger and touched the ball like it was iron hot, but it wasn't. It was insanely cold. Feeling it again, I left it for longer, and it was so cold that it burned.

Sticking my finger into my mouth, the healing properties of my wolf healed it instantly. Taking the water on the table, I dripped several drops of water, all for them to freeze in an instant and shatter around the orb to dust. As the dust settled, they melted.

The hell is this?

My eyes blinked at the pools of water around the orb. The tint of blue coloring the water had changed into made me groan. I had more questions than answers.

Pulling the memory dust closer, I opened the satchel, grabbed a spoon, and dropped the dust on the orb. The dust went up into flames as a red fire until it burned away, turning into a final blue flame until it vanished.

"It's crazy, isn't it?" a low feminine voice came from the corner of the room. My hair hit me in the face as I whipped around. It was Hecate, the goddess who had granted me my upgrade in power. "It's even more powerful than I imagined." She frowned, walking to the table. Her fingers brushed the parchments of notes.

"You won't find anything in your history books, notes, or magic spells with this one, darling. This is something completely new, different, lethal, and since it involves demons, I'm taking it upon myself to step in."

The gods didn't step in, never. It was against the laws of the Celestial Kingdom. So why she was helping now had me stepping away from her. If Zeus knew what she was doing, he could destroy us all.

"You worry too much. He won't do anything," she muttered. "He's got his head too far up Hera's ass right now." I gasped, hearing her talk about the High God like he was incompetent.

"Oh, he is incompetent," she snipped.

Great, she is reading my mind.

"You said demons are at work here?" I asked, changing the topic. Racing back through my memories, Virion flashed in my mind.

"Yes, three to be exact, and they have inhabited your ex-Parliament member who had disguised himself as a vampire. He's a sorcerer, a powerful one that has been practicing necromancing. Virion has allowed three rogue demons to inhabit his body to gain power in both the Bergarian and Earth realms. With his deep education in black magic and necromancy, he summoned three powerful demons. They will be unstoppable if we don't destroy them soon."

My mouth hung open, feeling the darkness invade the room. "Virion's power grows by the day, and none of you will be able to stop him," Hecate leaned forward as my back hit the wall. Her mouth set into a grim line, and she stepped away from me. "That is why I am here, because if Bergarian doesn't destroy him, the gods are next, and it will be too late."

"Why can't the gods intervene then?" I argued. "Why can't you all come down here and do something?" I hissed. Hecate chuckled, rubbing her hands down her face.

"Zeus is bullheaded and can't look to the future. Hades will have nothing to do with any of this right now. He's too pissed off about Persephone leaving him for her mate. That is a story for another time," she snapped. "The point is, we can't intervene, Zeus is law, and he won't budge. Now, I can help in small ways." She smirked. "And I have a weapon that will help you."

Hecate waved her hand. An enormous man with a beard, leather apron, and heavy boots walked toward us. He held a sword. It looked so ordinary I wanted to laugh if this was to take down Virion. "This is Vulcan. This is the last piece of magical weaponry he said he would create. This sword needs to be impaled through Virion's heart. It will dispel the demons, kill his body, and return the demons to the deepest parts of the Underworld." Vulcan put the sword on the table. He nodded until he vanished into thin air.

"I've given you the tools, Taliyah," Hecate warned. "And unfortunately, your time using your powers is almost up. I needed you to cast the ward over this territory to keep the sword safe until it was time."

"What?" I whispered.

Good gods, was I going to die?

"Silly little witch," Hecate whispered. "You will not die. All will be well if my warnings are heeded and the sword impales Virion."

"Then why will my powers be gone?" My fists tightened. "Did I do something wrong for you to take them away? I have to help, I have to do what I can, I have to—" Hecate placed a finger on my lips, and for the first time, she smiled at me.

"You and Jasper concentrate on your people. I have other chess pieces that will come into play."

Chapter Forty

Kane

Charlotte gracefully walked into the room. Her band t-shirt and black leggings made me chuckle as Wesley held his arms crossed over his chest. It certainly wasn't something my Clara would wear, but it suited Charlotte. She had her black-rimmed glasses, the ones with that reflective blue glare. Not sure why she was wearing them when her eyesight was just fine.

"Tea, Alpha?" Charlotte smiled, pouring a cup. I frowned as she offered it. It only made me remember the happier times when Clara offered tea so playfully to me.

"No, thank you, and call me Kane." Charlotte blushed, bringing the cup and saucer beside the bed for Clara.

"Sorry, I'm still learning." Wesley chuckled, pushing against the wall and coming to put his arms around her.

"You are doing fine. You worry too much." Wesley kissed her cheek. "Being thrown into a luna position isn't anything to worry about. Especially now." he frowned. "Sorry our honeymoon was cut short," he told her as his knuckles traced her cheeks.

Charlotte had a shitty upbringing, along with battling a demon a few months ago. We felt guilty requesting them to come, but Wesley was a hell of an alpha, and both he and his mate would help us win.

"I just hoped I helped as much as I could. I didn't have a set way to kill her. I just knew that the demon had invaded a body. Kill the body, and the demon returns to hell, or that was what Hades said." I let out a breath, my head hitting the headboard. Clara's head rested peacefully in my lap as she slept.

Our bond had healed her nicely, but she was tired. Maybe she was growing tired of my inability to take care of her. Of course, she would put that to rest damn quickly. She woke up crying, saying how sorry she was. She didn't know she was pregnant and didn't even pay attention. We both didn't listen to her body, too busy worrying about everyone else.

I rocked her gently. Gods, it was so fucking hard. We both cried together well into the morning. It was then we decided it was neither of our faults, that we would continue and have more children if the gods granted it.

Hell, they fucking better after all this shit we are going through.

"So, this Virion has three demons instead of the one that Charlotte dealt with." Wesley pulled Charlotte into his hold. Plus, he was a sorcerer, so that meant what? He was unstoppable? Did we know what kind of demons we were dealing with?

I shook my head. We had talked this to death with Marcus, Jasper, and Taliyah. We just didn't have answers. Just vague statements from Goddess Hecate that only seem to speak with sorceresses.

"And we need to do it with this sword." Wesley rubbed his chin. Charlotte noticed the tension in the room as Clara groaned in her sleep.

"I do have some good news, Kane," Charlotte chirped. She pulled a phone out of her side pocket and tapped on the screen. You couldn't call people in the Bergarian realm, only internet and emails, but those didn't work anymore because the portal was closed. "I've made contact with our pack back home." She smiled, showing me the screen.

"H-how did you do that?" My back leaned up from the headboard, causing Clara to move. Stroking her hair, she went back to sleep.

"Magic, science, and technology all working together. Cyrene was helping me with it before we got called here, and I finished my side of the tech part. I had to fiddle with some wires and use some of Cyrene's enchantments, but it worked. It was meant to only work while the portal is open, so it was an awesome surprise to find it working." Wesley beamed at Charlotte. "Videos are too large to send or receive, but I did get an email back after requesting how Evelyn is doing."

Reading further into the email, Evelyn was doing fine. A picture of her riding around in a stretch limo with her head hanging out had me smile. She was going to be a crazy child, just like her dad.

Along with the email, notes of how the packs were adjusting. Ever Green and Black Claws were at full capacity, no different than here. The children laughed and played, and they continued praying to the gods that things would work out.

Fuck, I hoped they would too.

"Clara's parents sent another email if you want to read it. I didn't open it," she hastily said. I shook my head. Hell, there was no privacy.

Clara and Kane,

We hope all is well with you both. Clara, your mother has calmed down considerably and realized her mistake in trying to make you become something you are not. Especially since you did not grow up in this realm. You will make a fine queen, and Bergarian is all that much greater for you to see things through different eyes.

Seeing you stand up to your mother had done something to me. It may have been your powers leaking through, but I feel like I have found my voice again, and I thank you for that. You healed me, my little princess. I believe that I felt like I lost you, and for so long, I believed it was my fault for not protecting you.

Parents often feel like they should be the ultimate protectors of their children. We cannot watch and protect them at each second of the day because fate has its own way of wiggling into their lives.

I let your mother help me for too long and let her take charge. Now I'm back, all thanks to you. Always know that being a parent is difficult. You will make decisions one day regarding your own children that you will feel is the right thing until they surprise you and decide to take their fate into their own hands. Just as you.

Your mother is due any day now with your new sibling. Once the portal is opened, we plan to be there to help pick up the pieces.

We love you, little princess. Know that.

Love, Dad

If I was holding a piece of paper in my hand, I would have crushed it with my fist. They were still on the other side protected, awaiting a child while my mate had to suffer. I couldn't help but partially blame them.

"Thank you, Charlotte. This was the greatest gift," I muttered. "I would like Clara to read it when she wakes."

"Of course." She smiled. "Would you like me to watch over her so you can attend the meeting?"

I nodded, gently moving Clara's head back to the pillow. She slept so soundly that she didn't stir as I pulled up the covers. "Please come get me as soon as she wakes." I grunted as Wesley followed me out the door.

The room already held loud chatter of head warriors and trainers. Folen, Jasper, and Taliyah all sat waiting at the long conference table. I took the head, rubbing my hand down my tired face. I had not slept, I was mentally and physically exhausted, but we couldn't stop now.

"What's first?" I slapped my hand on the table. The iron sword wobbled in its place in the middle. It didn't look anything magnificent. No jewels or decorative gold and silver. It was just an iron sword with an anvil in the middle where the handles sat.

"Falcons are no longer good communication between territories and kingdoms," August spoke. "We even tried emailing, using some sort of tech, but it bounces back."

"Emailing inside Bergarian won't work. We've known this," a warrior spoke. "That's why we sent the falcons." August rolled his eyes, turning and glaring at the warrior.

"I was just reiterating, so we are on the same page." August crossed his arms. "When Taliyah let the falcons out of the ward, the falcons turn back and try to get back in."

"They must notice something in the air, in nature, that something is wrong," Taliyah murmured to me. Even though she was queen, she was still soft-spoken.

"Then how do we communicate to King Osirus?" I barked. "We need some sort of communication to plan."

"What about the roots?" Marcus said behind me. "Have Folen speak through the trees to see if we can get a message out there to someone." Folen rubbed his beard.

"I can try." He looked to me for permission.

"Do that, then."

"What do we do until then?" Jasper stood behind Taliyah, his hands on her shoulders. She looked tired, hell we all did, but Taliyah looked like a different tired. Her eyes were soft, her cheeks flushed.

Taliyah's wolf was rising, I could smell the undertones of Jasper's wolf around her, but another smell caught me off guard as I studied her. It was a smell I should have noticed with my mate, but was too busy to take the time.

Shit.

"Right now, we sit tight." I lay back in my seat, trying not to draw attention. "Hecate said we were all chess pieces, and with no communication, no rogues trying to get in, we wait until we hear about Folen's phone tree." Folen rolled his eyes.

"Hey." One of the warriors that stood in the back pushed through the crowd. "How is Luna?" His voice softened. The room fell dark, my beasts' hair rippling down my arms. Torin hated talking about Clara's health. It reminded us all over again how she wasn't safe with us.

We didn't protect her.

Grinding my teeth, we tried to concentrate on her words. "What happened is unfortunate, but we still have each other, a future. We can't stop now. It's what that evil wants us to do."

"She's doing better." I growled. "A few more days' rest, her body will be good as new." I scraped my claws into the wood, the warriors backing away. Wesley put a heavy hand on my shoulder, clearing his throat.

"All right, we will set up another meeting for tomorrow after we hear about Folen and the trees. Please take the time for the warriors to train and see Raine, Naomi, or Liam regarding housing for any refugees." My claws sunk into my body, my back resting on the chair.

Chapter Forty-one

Clara

There was a small humming coming from my bedside table, along with the typing of a computer. I raised my brows, still keeping my eyes closed. I wasn't ready to feel the room's light, but Giana forced me to get up.

It was time to get up and face reality again.

Torin was in a mood, which meant that I needed to ensure he and Kane were okay. As much as I thought Kane would go on a rampage, he did the complete opposite when I finally woke up the first time.

Goddess, seeing your mate so miserable had to be the worst thing to ever witness. He has always been my cuddly little wolf, and he was so broken now. Our pack didn't realize what a big softy he really was.

He babied me like I was a little pup. He helped me change in the bathroom, bathed me, and treated me like a little doll by even daring to brush my teeth. That was rather embarrassing, but it made him feel like he was in control of my healing.

The bleeding slowed, Giana rested for a few days, and my strength was slowly returning. My body was almost back to the pre-pregnancy state. I rubbed my stomach, still listening to the little tapping on the side of the bed.

It abruptly stopped, and a warm compress was laid on my stomach. Opening my eyes, I see sweet Charlotte trying to take care of me. "Hi," I mumbled. Her eyes grew wide, and she snorted in shock.

"I'm so sorry. I thought you were sleeping." She giggled, taking the compress away.

"I was, but I feel like I need to get up and see Kane." Charlotte hummed, pulling the sheets back up my body.

"I can get him for you. You need to be resting. He would get mad at me, and I don't know if my heart could take the famous Alpha Kane yelling at me," she chided. Shaking my head, she brought food from a tray and set it up so I could eat.

"He's in a meeting. Wesley said they should be out soon. There isn't much to report since the last time you woke up. They are just waiting on Folen speaking with the roots to see if they can work some communication through that since the falcons aren't working."

I slumped back on the bed. If it wasn't one thing, it was another.

Charlotte picked her computer back up and had me read an email from my father. Charlotte had become incredibly handy when it came to electronics. Her ideas regarding technology and magic were astounding, and she hoped to implement a security system for wolf packs on Earth.

Bergarian would stay as close to nature as possible, still having wolves scouting the territory, but these security systems for small packs on Earth would be great since they lived all around technology with the humans.

"It is just so beautiful here. I came here to visit Wesley's parents in the Blue Waters pack, but I didn't realize just how remote everything is. It's so peaceful." Her forlorn face went to the window. "And now—"

"It won't be for long." I stroked her hand. "I would really like you to come back and visit. I'd love to see about getting a more stable internet here." Even when the portal was open, it would be spotty. "It would be great to communicate with packs with a steady stream once this war is over."

"I can most definitely do that." She beamed. "I'm still happy to be here with you and your mate. It's a real honor. Never in my life would I have thought I would be here among royalty, let alone all the fun fantasy stuff." Charlotte began to braid her hair nervously.

"I can say the same, I used to work in a diner and make cinnamon rolls, and then one day I make some friends and get chased up a tree by my mate." Charlotte laughed as I continued to tell her how I met Kane. She intently listened and loved how I was so accepting because it didn't come so easy for her in the beginning. Nothing was easy for Charlotte.

Her life was a struggle from the start. As an orphan, she bounced around from place to place. She also had trouble with an obsessed vampire that worked with the demon inhabiting the witch's body.

"Is it hard?" I grabbed her hand. My power seeped through, calming the tension in her shoulders. Charlotte sniffed, rubbing her thumbs over my hands. "Is it a bit hard coming here, knowing we are helping vampires?" She nodded.

"Wesley had to really persuade me to come. I can't lie to you. Being in the same area as those... others..." Her voice trailed until I pulled her into a hug. "But I know there are good ones out there. Your sister is mated to a very nice one, so is your friend Leia, but... it is hard to separate that sometimes. Humans can be bad too. It's just been harder regarding supernaturals and their grouping." Charlotte pulled away and pushed her strawberry blonde hair away from her face.

"Want me to let you in on a secret?" Her eyes were glassy as she hung onto my every word. The poor woman had been raised and abused by one, much longer than I ever had to endure from my vampire encounter. "I feel the same. Deep inside, I feel exactly the same. I guess that shows how 'human' we really are."

Charlotte giggled, sitting up from our hugging position. "I'm glad, I'm really glad. I'll always treat them nicely, though, but I can't help but still have nightmares. Just don't tell Wesley," she whispered.

"It will be our secret," I playfully whispered back.

Charlotte helped clean up the room and even helped pull my hair back into a French braid and change into one of my favorite dresses. She continued complimenting how beautiful I looked and how sexy Kane would find me. I couldn't help but chuckle at how excited she was. She was looking for the light in this darkness, keeping my mind away from dark thoughts.

I was grateful for that. It was what I needed. Just girl time with someone who has experienced pain in their life. I didn't feel pitied while she was here, just the love she had for the now, the current moment she was living in.

"Oh, let's do make-up!" She pointed to the vanity seat. "Come on, hurry! Wesley says they will be done any minute!" I quickly sat down as Charlotte began. "Now, I don't have much experience, but my friend Amanda back home taught me a lot."

Charlotte began with my foundation and then eyes. She pulled stray hairs from the braid to frame my face. She smiled giddily as she held up a mirror. "I think he's going to pounce on you." I threw my head back and laughed because I knew she was right.

Kane was always in the mood for a good pouncing or tea.

Just then, the door creaked open, and Wesley stood there smiling. It was strange seeing an alpha smile as often as Wesley does. This giant man with the neatly trimmed face and man bun radiated nothing but love and affection for Charlotte when his eyes sought hers.

Charlotte jumped up from the vanity bench and ran toward him. "Hi, puppy!" Wesley groaned, rolling his eyes. I started laughing until he whispered something private in her ear.

Ha-ha! Puppy!

"Did you hear that, kitten?" She blushed, turning around, covering her face. It was a good thing I didn't hear what was said because it was obviously scandalous. "What did you two young ladies talk about while we were gone?" Wesley smirked, pulling Charlotte on his lap in the decorative chair.

"Just girl stuff." I smiled. "Got a great makeover too. What'd you think?" I stood up and gave a twirl in the pale blue dress, and Wesley let out a whistle in agreement.

"Looks stunning on you, Luna." Kane growled outside the door, strutting in with his hand over his crotch. "But you always look stunning." Kane's soft eyes looked me up and down. Skipping over toward him, I put my arms around his waist.

"Easy," Kane mumbled. "I'm still healing."

Huh?

"What do you mean still healing? Did you go out and fight some warriors? They can't take your aggressiveness right now," I chided. Kane gave a fanged smile, kissing my lips.

"No, I did something else," he murmured. "I'll show you later." I raised an eyebrow and glanced at Wesley, who was snickering in the corner.

"What did you do?" I asked both of them.

"Oh, Wesley, you got a new tattoo!" Charlotte squealed. "Aw, it's my name!" The dark tattoo on his arm had swirls of roses around it with claw marks on the side. "It's so rugged and feminine simultaneously." She looked it over.

It already looked healed. It was dark black with hints of deep reds and greens. Kane stood there smirking like he did something naughty. Did he get another tattoo? He was running out of room unless he started doing his face, which was a big no-no. That was my big rule.

Unless...

Cheeses.

"Don't you worry your pretty little head." Kane kissed my forehead. His big smile had me relaxing in his arms. "We are going to get our mind off some things. I hope Charlotte has kept you away from the windows like I have asked."

"Uh..." I tapped my finger to my lips.

What were they up to?

Charlotte sheepishly hid her face into Wesley.

"Good, let's go then." Kane put his hand behind my back and led me down the lighted stairs, Wesley and Charlotte following close behind.

The last light source touched the trees, and the forest surrounding us would be in darkness by the hour. We would all take turns sleeping, waiting, and watching for any signs of evil to come, but this night we would not fight the darkness at least.

Mason jar lamps, fairy lights, and patio bulbs hung in the trees. Pixies that had sought refuge on the territory lit up the sky as they flew from tree to tree. Soft music played in the far corner of the courtyard. Small fiddles and harps from traveling elves seeped through the air, and dare I say, I thought I saw a smirk raise on Kane's lips.

Food was presented in a buffet style on the far side of the house, the warriors already taking heaps of food on their plates and bowls. They even had the chocolate fountain going, and without the typical hordes of children that usually sat near it, the adults enjoyed it much more.

"What is this?" I whispered. "Everyone looks so happy." I rubbed my chest, feeling the warmth in my heart. Everyone looked optimistic, no longer weary of the impending battles that may come in the next few days.

"It was agreed we needed a break." Kane sighed. "Wesley mentioned the numerous parties they like to have, and I thought, why not? We should have our wolves remember what we are fighting for during this dark time."

Goddess, Kane is getting all sentimental on me.

"What about the lights? Won't it lead people here?" Kane pulled me to his chest, placing a finger on my lips. "Taliyah's ward causes a darkness in the night so no one will see."

Magic could be so incredible if it wasn't used for evil.

Charlotte and Wesley led us to a table with a large spread of food. Taliyah, Jasper, Marcus, Raine, Dean, Leia, and Kyler already sat waiting for us. The number of chocolate sponge cakes, honey-drizzled honeysuck-les, exotic fruits, and plates upon plates of steaks had my mouth watering.

"Come on, Clara. Let's forget our worries tonight." Taliyah stood up and led me to the table, and had me sit beside her. Naomi and Liam walked behind Kane, placing a hand on each shoulder. Feeling my bottom lip tremble, Kane put his large hand over my thigh.

This was my family, not those at this table, but the entire world that fought against the darkness. They all wanted the same thing: to live in peace and harmony, and with this joyous night of celebrating each other, we would all remember what we were fighting for.

Our happiness.

Chapter Forty-two

Clara

Our table sat in silence as our gaze went over the crowd. There were squeals of laughter from two tables over. A wolf trying to drink alcohol from their mate's naval had everyone cheering. For once, everyone looked relaxed and at peace, daring to have some fun we all longed to have.

The courtyard corner was flooded with wolves, shifters, and fae dancing along to the sway of the music. Drums and fiddles rang victoriously over the yard, and food was plentiful. It eased the built-up tension of walls that had surrounded me for so long. I had Giana reach outward at our table and bring peace to the ones carrying the physical and mental burden we all had.

"This is nice," Giana purred.

It really was.

We had done our best to keep as many as we could safe. This was our final stronghold, the last line of defense we had. With so many shifter colonies, prides, and packs with their alphas living all in one land area had been difficult but had gone over well, surprisingly.

Having too many alphas could cause fights, wanting to protect their people. However, there was a common goal here: to protect everyone.

Marcus stayed reserved for most of the meal. In fact, he barely touched his steak, and his eyes didn't wander to the few single she-wolves that had eyed him seductively. Marcus would typically be all over that, and here he was, staring at a half-eaten steak.

I go to open my mouth to speak with him, but he stands up abruptly, putting his napkin on his plate. "Where are you going?" I blurted out, not meaning to startle the table, but it was too late. All eyes were on him.

"What I do best, Luna." He winked, but it was the most somber wink I had ever seen. He held his shoulders back, and a she-wolf he had spent many nights before wrapped her arm around his, squeezing it longingly.

I wanted to yell at him, but I had no words to say. He was defeated, and the war had gotten to him in ways I didn't understand.

"Leave him," Kane muttered in my ear. "It's been hard for him too. He's just handling it in a different way." I hummed, leaning my head on Kane's shoulder. I still wished that Marcus would stop his ways of trying to get in women's pants and just wait.

Then again, I guess we all had ways of hiding our feelings.

Our table went to idle chatter, Taliyah smiling at Jasper's words until I heard a faint thumping. It was so soft I had to really listen and realized it was coming straight from Taliyah. *"Kane?"* I linked him. He took a drink of the ale Folen had told him to try and raised his brows for me to continue.

"The faint thumping..." I glanced at Taliyah, who was now sitting in Jasper's lap.

"I think she's pregnant. I thought I smelled it earlier."

"And you didn't think to tell me? This is so wonderful!" Gods, why hadn't they said anything? Was it because of the miscarriage? I didn't want them to hold back on my account. It was something to be celebrated. I was too excited to think of any consequences until the next statement blurted out of my mouth.

"Taliyah! Why didn't you tell me you were pregnant?" I chirped excitedly.

Jasper spat out his drink and began coughing. Taliyah's eyes widened, and her hands gripped Jasper's chest, but her vision never left me. Lips parted, her tongue wetting them.

"Oh shit." Kane rubbed his forehead. "Love, they may not know, we have alpha and royal hearing, remember?"

"Uh-oh." I slumped in my seat.

"Holy hell *what*?" Jasper regained his composure, slapping his chest repeatedly. Then, turning Taliyah so she was straddling him, he cupped her face. "Are you?" Taliyah's mouth opened and closed repeatedly until her breath caught.

"Hecate said I wouldn't be able to use my power much longer. I thought I was going to die!" Jasper growled, pulling her to his chest.

"I said that wouldn't fucking happen now, didn't I?" He soothed her with his hand running up and down her back until he pulled her away. "Now, are you pregnant?"

"I-I—" Her pleading look had me nodding frantically.

"Sorry, I thought you knew. Kane said it was because of my alpha hearing," I babbled. "Come to think of it, you have a different smell too." Kane pulled me back into his chest.

"It's all right. They needed to know, love." Kane kissed my neck as I nuzzled closer to him.

Jasper sat Taliyah unceremoniously on the table. The table glasses clinked until his ear went right to her stomach. His arms encompassed her waist as he listened. His smile widened, pulling her into a hug.

"I'm going to be a dad!" He squeezed her tight, twirling her around the table. "You hear that, everyone?! I'm going to be a father!" Howls from the Crimson Shadows pack joined in on Jasper's celebration.

Jasper's old warrior friends gathered around him, hosting him up on their shoulders like he was the one that was carrying the pup. They handed him beer mug after mug, forcing him to chug it down. They were all so happy, except there was part of the crowd that was not.

Vermillion's citizens all looked on not in hate, but in confusion. Their fears of what their country's new heir would be swirled in their minds. Would it be a werewolf pup? A vampire? A witch or warlock? Would they be willing to give up the idea of being ruled by a vampire when the time came? Vermillion had been led by a vampire, no other species, for centuries.

My gut churned. The thought of more problems even after the Dark War for Vermillion had begun more worries. Members of her Parliament were already whispering to each other. Their worried faces stared at Taliyah as the scene unfolded.

Not paying attention to heated stares, Taliyah laughed and began crying as the overwhelming emotion engulfed her. Kane nodded to me to take care of Taliyah as he stood up with Wesley and Charlotte to join in on their taunting fun of Jasper. He was now hung upside down as everyone tried to get him to throw up the alcohol he had ingested, trying to simulate morning sickness.

These wolves were crazy.

I stood up, taking her in my arms. "This is so wonderful," I whispered in her ear. "You're going to be a great mom." She sobbed into my shoulder.

"But now I can't protect anyone for much longer. Soon I'll feel too weak to keep up the ward." She sniffed. "I've failed already." I shook my head, petting her hair.

"No, no, you didn't fail anyone, Taliyah. A baby is much more precious, and paying attention to your body is important." Pulling her back, my hands on her shoulders, I wiped away one of her tears. "And take my advice, pay attention to your body. If the ward comes down, it comes down. We will manage. We have each other, right?"

Taliyah smiled, her hand going to her stomach. "I'm sorry," she murmured. I knew what that sorry was for, and I wasn't going to have her feeling guilty.

"There is nothing to be sorry for." I lifted her chin, my eyes boring into hers. "I am so happy for you, and no, I am not jealous. I have a beautiful daughter already, and fate has other plans for me. I still plan on getting knocked up again, and with any luck, maybe our kids could be paired together," I joked. "And!" I added. "You won't have to shift until after your pregnancy. Your wolf is going to be too busy keeping your little one healthy." Taliyah sniffed.

Pulling her into my arms again, the lights flickered in the trees. The music stopped as a horrible rumble of thunder swept through the yard. The wind blew, knocking over trays of food, tables, and chairs. The entire area went dark, and a crack of lightning raked across the sky, lighting the area once more until it faded to black.

Kane pulled me into his arms, Torin's hair slowly appearing on his body. The ground shook again. The loud cracking of lighting had us all ducking to the ground. "What's happening?" I screamed over the noise. Wolves didn't howl. No one dared make a noise as we waited for the tremors to stop.

To feel the soil beneath your feet shake so violently frightened all of us. Kane planted his feet into the ground, his body being the steady foundation to keep me above the danger. His eyes grew fierce, looking at me the entire time the soil trembled.

"I'm not letting you go," he said with promise. "Not ever. You will not be in danger any longer." I stroked his cheek, knowing he couldn't keep that promise as much as he wanted. We both had a job, and if he went, I went with him.

Even with the tremors of the soil, our love for each other will never waver. The pack house continued shaking until shingles, shutters, and cracks of the foundation broke into our home.

Wesley held Charlotte close, her eyes widening and not just the ground shaking, but her body too. She was petrified, and we all should be. The world was breaking around us, and we had no way to stop it.

As quick as the disturbances came, they ended. The strings of light that once hung in the trees now lay on the ground, fluttering back to light. The breath we all held as a group was let go, and our shoulders slumped.

What exactly happened?

Folen, who stood by one of our most giant trees, a willow that once had bright yellow flowers dripping down its vines, put his ear to the soil. Folen murmured into the dirt, his head cocked to the side as he listened.

Whispering profanities, he jumped up, not daring to wipe the soil from his clothing. "Bergarian has been cut open." His brother, whom we had now come to know as Tolith, came running from out of the woods.

"Shit, Folen!" he cried. The pack stood in shock, watching him grab his brother. "Beyond the ward, the trees." His eyes narrowed. "We have to do something!"

Folen turned to us, his brows wrinkled with worry. "The trees," he muttered to our group. Even with his low murmuring, the entire pack could hear his voice. "They are gone."

"Gone?" Marcus charged behind Kane and put his hand on his shoulder. Kane put his hand on Marcus's to comfort his friend.

"Gone, there are no more past the barrier. Before I heard the last whispers, they said..." Folen shut his eyes, his fists tightening. Everyone waited as he prolonged the information he was about to give. Kane gripped me tight, unable to be patient.

"Spit it out, right now!" he barked.

"There is a split in the soil, a break." Folen now looked at all of us. "It's so wide none of us would be able to cross and so deep... it may touch the Underworld because laying inside is nothing but fire."

I shivered in Kane's hold. This was much worse than I ever could have imagined. We had no way to get to talk to Osirus, let alone bring our forces together.

"Does Osirus know? Can we get a message to him?" I panicked. We would only win if we worked together; now, that plan has withered.

"It will take twice as long for the roots to reach around the canyon," Folen mentioned, "but we can try."

Chapter Forty-three

Under the Moon

"That's it, darling," hold still. Osirus meticulously bound Melina. The slickness of the nylon-type binding and the tiny broken, scratchy fibers from the material scratched her skin delicately. She moaned out, feeling how tight the bindings were.

And yet so freeing at the same time.

Osirus had perfectly bound Melina's wrists behind her back, tied at the wrist, and laid delicately on the curve of her back. Taking her legs, he had used the rope to gently tickle her skin, seductively bending her knees until they were fully bent. He bound them ankle to thigh and just behind the knee, making her spread her legs ideally. Her already played-with puffy pink lips dripped their essence, making it perfect for viewing as he pushed her thighs away to look at her with lusting eyes.

Melina looked powerless like this, tied up in his bed where she should always remain. Melina was too strong-headed for that, constantly pushing his buttons, but secretly he loved that about her. As much as he tried to keep her safe from harm, she was her own wild and crazy half-siren that would dare push the envelope for Osirus and dare to punish her further.

But this was far from punishment for the both of them.

Melina had enjoyed their rope play the past several days. The heat of the war was upon them. They had no control over anything, it seemed. Dragons, fae, pixies, shifters, and even the sirens had begun filling the palace. The grounds had their ward from a series of several witches, but only that would hold them for so long.

Apollo, the new alpha dragon to the Toboki tribe, had circled the mountains for signs of Virion while Creed watched the south intently. From dusk until dawn, everyone was to remain on the palace grounds for protection. The night was too dangerous for anyone to fight due to the darkness looming over the middle of the land.

When Apollo and Creed did their rounds, they noticed the foliage was being eaten by blackness. It crawled out of the soil, slowly reaching all things that streamed with life. Osirus's nervousness was well hidden from the rest of the world besides his mate.

Osirus had never dealt with anything like this before, and with Vermillion coming down a fortnight ago, things were looking grim.

Right now, he wanted to forget. Get lost in the moment with his mate because he wasn't sure how long it would be before he could touch her pale skin again, riddled with his red handprints on her body. When his deepest part was released, the dark fae hidden inside him surfaced. He wouldn't touch her.

Melina deserved all the light in her life after dealing with the lonely childhood life of being alone. He wouldn't show her the darkness inside him. Right now, it was about her and him, alone and lost in each other's bodies.

Now his mate sat in her frog tie position, legs spread just as he commanded. He licked his lips, observing as she sat up straight, fluttering her eyes flirtatiously toward him. She was enjoying this too much, and he would slow down that over-enthusiastic pussy he saw gleaming in the candlelight.

"Daddy," she cooed. His smirk grew wider until it reached his ears. She was so perfect like this, so innocent looking with those cute twin French braids he did on her head. Crawling up on the bed, his tight undergarment barely holding his raging erection rubbed against the fabric. Groaning, he palmed himself right in front of her.

Melina frowned, struggling with her wrists tied tight behind her in a reverse prayer position. "Can you untie me?" That was what she said she wanted, but Osirus knew better. She wanted to be taken care of, his little darling that wanted his cock in her mouth, her pussy, and maybe his seed spread out over her breasts.

Osirus tutted, his body inches from hers, but he dared not touch her. Melina wasn't allowed to move, not one bit of her body was allowed to touch him, or she would be denied the ultimate pleasure to come.

His arm grazed hers, and he noticed the little moan that hummed in her throat. His balls tightened to his body, listening to each sound that escaped her. Being a siren, being bonded together, her powers grew each day. Melina didn't fully realize what kind of effect she had on him.

Gentle humming could put hundreds of mateless men to their knees, commanding them all the same. Osirus was no different. In actuality, the power hit him more so. He loved to receive such a gentle vibration from her vocal cords.

The thought of gagging her crossed his mind, but she truly was his good girl. She would never dare use her powers on him unless he beckoned her to, which he decided to do tonight.

Pulling the leather crop from the nightstand table, he grazed her lower back with the leather. Her body tensed, and her skin tightened at the feel. Osirus took the time to appreciate her backside. Her knees on the bed, her ass pushed out behind her, giving him the perfect view of her plump peach. Melina's breasts stuck out, and her mouth hung open in a way that made him want to fill it.

He bit his lip, his fangs lengthening as he traced the skin beside the rope connected to the ropes holding her legs in a spread wide frog position. He liked every bit of this newfound bondage, and it looked like his mate did too.

"Oh darling, what will I do with you?" His purr rattled Melina's ear with want and need. She was ready to come at just a flick of her clit, but she knew better than that. Osirus would tease her, taunt her until she was begging. Melina knew Osirus's obsession with her begging for his cock to enter her body, and she was all too happy to give it because she wanted to please.

The frayed leather from too many floggings danced across her collar bones, her breath clamped, waiting for a gentle slap on her skin, but it never came.

Osirus noticed the anticipation growing, her heart pounding in her chest. "Why, darling, do you want to be smacked?" Osirus knew she knew better than to answer that question. He didn't want her to answer. Rhetorical questions would not be tolerated.

He trained her so well.

The crop slid down her luscious side, now running over the ropes that bound her. Pulling it back faster than his mate realized, he slapped her thigh. Her body bounced, and her naked breasts jiggled in the air. Pink, tight tits pebbling before him.

Osirus's will was faltering. He leaned closer, gently suckling her nipple. Her hips wiggled, desperately wanting friction in her lower region. "Stop," he warned, causing his large hand to slap her thigh in a warning. "Let me finish."

Melina held back the sharp pains of pleasure as he bit down on her nipple. Her eyes rolled in the back of her head, her body swaying at the erotic pleasure she felt down to her clit. "My darling tastes so sweet. Does anything else taste sweeter than this?" Melina bit her lip, wanting to snap at the absurd question.

Her pussy tasted better.

Osirus let go of the crop, his sharp nail trailing down the front part of her chest and down to her sweet shaved pussy. Her legs quivered as he circled her inner thighs. "I think it might taste better here," he cooed. "Should I taste the sweet nectar inside this flower?"

Melina tried her best not to whine, trying her best to be the perfect little submissive Osirus liked to see. The complete trust she had in him was unfathomable. She trusted him not just with her life, but with the absolute pleasure he could give her.

Her eyes stared at the ceiling, daring not to look into her dominant's eyes. "You may speak, little one. Tell me what you want."

"Please." She gritted her teeth, trying not to whine too badly, not yet. She had to draw out the pleasure that he wanted since he was doing it so well to her.

Hold off begging just a little longer.

"I think you can do better than that." His husky voice went to her ear. Sharp fangs nibbled at her earlobe. A small grunt left her throat.

A little longer.

"Do you want me to tongue fuck your pussy?" Those words had her reeling, her back arched, pushing her breasts toward him. He sat back, furthering his body away from her. It was the hardest thing for him, yet he wanted something more than the immediate satisfaction from touching her.

His stubborn little darling.

Osirus leaned in, nipping at her ear. "Or do you want me to ravage you sensuously as you take my cock with no foreplay? Denying you the pleasure of coming around me?" She whined.

There it was, the helpless whine he loved to hear. He smirked, kissing her neck. "What a good little darling you are," he cooed.

"Please." She leaned forward only for him to pull away, and her body fell forward. Not the sexiest moment on her part, but it made Osirus chuckle.

Her ass now laid firmly planted above the mattress, her belly soaking in the softness of the duvet. Fuck him. She was tied with her arms around her back and her legs tied in such a way her glorious puckered hole sat in wanting. Her pussy now was slick.

His words turned her on more than the touching. He went behind her ass, staring at it longingly. Melina muffled into the mattress until her face turned to give him her opinion. "Please," her voice ground out.

"Please what, darling?"

"Please, make me come." She breathed.

"I know you want to come, but how?" Osirus tapped his lips, his claw tickling his bottom lip. His face lowered, licking her clit, to her hole and just before her puckered rosette.

"Oh, gods!" Melina screamed. One more lick, and she was sure to fall over. Osirus laid on his back, lowering Melina's pussy to his face. He licked excitedly. "I am not the gods, Melina." He sucked.

"Please, let me come, Daddy!" Melina was crying, trying to hold back from coming. She didn't need to be edged the next time they were in bed together. She needed this.

Osirus, realizing his time was short, hummed into her pussy. Taking one long suck to her clit she cried actual tears. "Please!"

"Come," he mumbled into her petals. Osirus's finger that had gathered juices from her pussy now tickled her back hole as he pushed in a finger.

Between the teasing, the licking, and now prodding of her backside, she cried out in endless shame as she came. She came so hard that she saw the beating of her own heart in her eyelids.

Osirus rose from his comfortable spot between her pussy, rubbing his erection against her ass cheek. He was painfully hard and could see the ruddy color of his cock shining through the paleness of his undergarments. He pulled himself free, rubbing the tantalizing ass in front of him.

"Do you need your safe word?" Osirus groaned, grasping his cock and rubbing the pearled cum from the tip of his cock with his thumb. His heavy breathing turned to a growl, waiting for his mate to reply.

The large smack of his hand and the jiggle of her curves sent him to pump his shaft. Balls heavy with seed, ready to provide for her pussy. "Melina, I have no patience," he hissed. "No more games." Melina bit her lip. The teasing had ended, she had already angered Osirus, and now she knew he would take her fast and hard, just the way she liked it.

"No safe word. Fuck me, Daddy." Osirus rolled his eyes in the back of his head. He wasn't sure how long he would last, but he would do his best.

Tickling her opening of the lips, he pushed forward. Tantalizingly slow at first to watch his cock disappear. "The gods have blessed me," he groaned to himself. Melina's lips parted, feeling so full.

"Move," she ordered. Another smack to her thigh had her moan.

"Don't get bossy," he ordered. "Who's in charge?" Melina wiggled her ass, and another slap on her ass had her yip in surprise as the jiggle tickled her clit.

"You are, Daddy." She halted her movements.

"Excellent. Now I want you to do something." Osirus kept himself steady before he began the new rhythm of movements that would drive his mate insane. "I want you to sing for me." Melina threw a glance back at Osirus. She wasn't allowed to sing, to try and control her mate. It was ethically wrong, and she didn't like the idea of controlling him.

"Easy," he cooed, rubbing her back and ass. "I want to forget our problems, enjoy you." Melina's eyes dipped in understanding. Osirus had been nothing but attending to those who now stayed on the palace grounds. The worries, the burden, it was too much. Even getting lost in this scene, he thought of what else he could do to help end this war.

Melina cleared her throat, humming a tune that had Osirus entranced by the third note. It was soft, calming, and one that had him drive his wide eyes of alertness down to the gentle haze of foggy tunnel vision.

His hips moved and gyrated as he watched his cock disappear and reappear from her pussy. In and out, his cock coated with her slick wetness. The movements caused Melina's nipples to tighten underneath the sheets. Her gentle humming continued as she got lost in his constant pounding.

The bed shook, and the pictures around the room fell to the ground, but Melina and Osirus were now in their own haze of pleasure. Osirus rocked, his hair falling around him as he put his chest to Melina's back. Her face took a glimpse at Osirus's hooded eyes falling on hers.

His hands wrapped around each globe of her breast, and he pulled her nipples tight. Pushing her further into the sheets, her legs still bent from being tied, her knees fell lower until only her ass sat up in attention so Osirus could push her deeper into the mattress.

Melina's spine was being compressed at the thrusting movements. Her body could no longer hold back the orgasm as Osirus plummeted into her g-spot. "Osirus!" she screamed as she fell over the edge. Osirus was too dazed to care if his mate came without asking. He was lost in his own world thanks to his mate.

The bed shook again, and the sheer canopy that surrounded them fell as Osirus let out a shout of pleasure, feeling Melina's pussy contracting on his cock. Spurts of seed coated her, his feeling to impregnate her more robust than ever.

He wanted that, a family with her.

Not until this war was over, not until the danger was gone.

And just as Melina stopped her humming, he was again back into defensive mode. He untied her under the sheer fabric from the canopy of the bed, letting it lay on their bodies as they came down from their high. Osirus rubbed her wrists and her ankles as she lay there panting.

"That was wild." She turned around and snuggled into his body. The wind from the cracked window blew the sheet, causing Osirus to lift his head in confusion. Melina followed suit, her post-orgasm faze fading fast and the coldness seeping in.

"We... didn't do that, did we?" Osirus pulled her close, daring not to let go of the post-scene. Osirus looked out over the land. The high tower which held their private chambers looked over the land to find a crack in the Bergarian soil miles from there. His naked body strode to the window as the distant yells fell into their ears.

It was far off, but Osirus could see the magnificence of how large the canyon was. His lips pursed together in distaste, Melina still holding onto him, not looking outside. "What happened?" Her body shook, going into a sub-drop from the high pleasure endorphins that capsulated her body.

Osirus ground his fangs, watching fae and dragons below fixing over-turned statues. An aftershock from the quake held fire inside the split of the canyon. Osirus put his hand through Melina's hair.

There was nothing they could do at night. It was too dangerous for fae to fight without sunlight, and the vampires were too fast for them to catch them. Dragons would have to oversee the night while his soldiers scouted during the day.

Alaneo fluttered up to the now broken window of his chambers, his chest heavy with the breath, watching Osirus. "Send the dragon to scout?" Alaneo worded it like a question, but it was a statement. Osirus only nodded.

Alaneo looked down at a now sleeping Melina. He smirked at his king before flying off to the dragon's resting spot.

Tomorrow would bring the beginning of the end.

Chapter Forty-four

Kane

The once joyous gathering fell into damped silence. There was no more singing, the quake that shook the soil now bringing nothing but desolate stillness. The wind blew, shaking the tablecloths that were once so meticulously placed on the head table to bring a smile back to their luna's face.

No one dared to move. They all now stared at my mate and me with uncertainty and dread. There was no more joy to be had. The more miniature packs and prides now joined ours. This was to be our last night together as a pack. We were one against the enemy.

"We will leave at first light—" screams from the witch sisters that had resided in the Cerulean Moon Kingdom's palace for years had them falling to the ground. They clawed at their plain brown and black dresses, huddling together while Taliyah ran to them. They clutched their hearts, their bright eyes dimming into a flat blackness.

No one dared to proceed, unsure if the witches had been taken over by a demon or dark magic that could reach out and clutch them too. Taliyah's hand reached out, putting it on one of their shoulders, her eyes closed, muttering to herself.

Her hands trembled, breaking away from their shuddering sobs. "Their sister," Taliyah diverted to Clara and me. "She has gone to meet the stars." Folen growled out, taking the walking stick that he held with him at all times and crushing the ground.

"What do you mean? She is in the strongest area of the elven territories! They are protected! They are—" Taliyah shook her head, her head bowed.

"It seems that the elven lands have been taken over then." She cringed. Folen stood back, his brother catching him with his arms.

"All those innocent children," he rasped. "All of them?" Taliyah shook her head.

"I only know that their sister and her mate are gone. Their sisterly bond is broken, shattered."

"Glinda!" Genesis cried.

"Enough!" I growled out among the crowd that began to murmur. Gently using the power given to me by Clara's parents to be rulers of this territory, I felt their fear trickle to defeat.

They didn't think that we could win.

"You all act as if you have lost." I gritted my teeth, lacing my fingers with my mate's hand. She squeezed it tight, begging me to continue. Her heart still wept for our lost pup, but the hope we would try again shined through in her eyes.

My mate was strong for us, and with this impending battle, we would end it all and finally have our peace. She would no longer have to worry about tomorrow, no longer felt the pressure of being queen. She would rule with a grace that this kingdom had never seen, and I would stand there beside her when she did.

The crowds' emotions did not falter. Their feet shuffled in the dirt, their eyes averted from my gaze. "You dare give up before we started." Clara had our bond warm, the royal blood we shared now pushing through to the surface to encompass the entire territory of on-lookers. There was a time we would use our power to drive the minds and hearts of our people. This was that time.

Clara put her forehead next to my arm, nuzzling into it. Her hand stroked my forearm as I gazed upon the darkening crowd.

"How dare you all! I'm disappointed." I smirked. Marcus's brow raised in confusion, soon followed by Jasper, who skimmed back at the crowd.

I did not smile. The only smile I had was for my mate. She alone could make me feel joy and happiness, but this smile was anything but happy. It was essential to the next words I would say.

"The strongest warriors of Bergarian, the Crimson Shadows pack, who have been known to take down hordes of the fastest rogues to date without losing a soul?" I smiled again, my fangs scraping my lips. The swaying bodies and the lack of eye contact from the warriors had Torin grinning ear to ear.

"And these same warriors who have trained the outlying packs and prides to live up to our battle standards, giving them the tools to be our equals... are afraid?" Taking deep pained breaths, they rubbed their foreheads with their dirty palms.

"Disappointed." I jostled my head. "After everything your luna, your queen, has sacrificed for you? She has yet to give up, and you hear of one area that may or may not have succumbed to the fall of a sorcerer?" Clara gripped me tighter, but her gaze did not leave the crowd.

"Disappointed," I said again. The heavy hearts of guilt showered down on Clara and me. "Do you want to live in peace again? Do you want your wolves, your people, the children... to live with the guilt that you gave up before it started?" I choked back a howl. Clara wrapped her arms around my torso, her back to the crowd and her head buried in my chest.

Murmurs floated in the sea of people. More had gathered from the other areas of the territory, listening as I broadcasted it through the link.

"Disappointed." I shook my head again as the silence continued. The seconds felt like hours as they muttered to each other.

"I fight for you," Marcus finally called out among the crowd. His heartache was heavy, his soul empty, but the small flame of hope grew brighter.

"I will fight for my mate, my child." Jasper pulled Taliyah to his chest, his hand going to her stomach. She rubbed her hand longingly over his as she sniffed.

"For Vermillion." Taliyah smiled at the servants beside her.

"For our future," Wesley joined in. Charlotte was in his arms. Her rational fear for the vampires that stood feet away had her lips twisted.

"For new friends." Charlotte held her hand to one of Taliyah's servants. She took it gladly, putting her other hand over hers.

More and more people said their reasons why they would fight. Their voices slipped against each other until we could no longer hear the individuals' reasons why they fought, just the constant wave of white noise. Once it died, Clara, who had yet to say anything, stepped away from me, her gaze rising to the moon overhead.

"For Bergarian, for all of us." The fear of the crowd had officially diminished, and the rustling of the mind-link being overpowered by families, friends, and neighbors filled our minds. It was the busiest roar of voices we had ever heard.

"We can hear all of them now." Clara's eyes brightened. "I guess we fully accepted the calling, huh?" My hand went around her waist, my nose brushing her neck. "That was a great speech, Alpha. Maybe you should do it all the time," she chided.

"Only during acts of war," I grumbled. "And this won't happen again for a very long time." Clara hummed, reaching her arms around my neck and eventually her legs. I chuckled, carrying her to the pack house.

Once I reached the top, the people had stopped moving, the mess already cleaned. "We leave at first light. Osirus's soldiers will need the light sources."

Torin was restless, his body craving our mate's touch. Clara nipped at my neck as we walked up the stairs. It had been days, her recovery, her sadness that had poured into me, wrecked everything I was.

I only wanted to see the bright light in her eyes, those same eyes that made me fall to my knees to worship her. My mate didn't deserve any of this. Sometimes I thought the gods were punishing her for choosing to still be with me.

"Alpha," she teased. "Are you needy?"

"Always for you, love." My hands rubbed up and down her back, holding her close. I had done as much as possible to take care of her and do the things she needed to heal. Held her close and rubbed her empty womb with my hand, but all of that was nothing for the pain she felt.

I don't know why I didn't feel it before, the pain she had when those claws ripped across her abdomen, spilling innocent blood of our child. I realized she hid it from me so I didn't kill everyone and everything in my sight.

She still looked after me, even when she was in pain. Clara wanted me to be okay and not have me worry. I was going to remedy this problem, but now was not the time to chastise. It was the time to show her how much I loved her.

I was going to taste her again. Have her body squirm because of what my tongue would do to her. I'd lock my dick away for the night.

"Are you—" I wanted to ask if she was all right, to ensure that anything I did wouldn't hurt her. I didn't know how a woman's body worked, what pain they felt, especially since she shielded me. Which I didn't fucking like.

"I'm not made of glass, Kane," she joked. "Giana healed me just fine." Her finger brushed back my hair, and the tenderness in her touch had me purring into her chest that I laid on.

"I'm not worried about you physically," I murmured. "Other ways too." My mate cupped my cheeks, pulling me closer to her pouty lips. She kissed me softly, her mouth parting, letting my needy tongue rub against hers.

My body took over, my hands squeezing her torso impossibly closer. My cock was angry, but I wanted it to be about her tonight. Not fuck her into oblivion, not rut her until we both couldn't see straight. I wanted to love and worship her body before tomorrow.

Show her the love she deserved all along.

My lips left her with a gentle pop. I gently pulled the soft dress from her body, right over her head. She was left bare underneath. No bra or underwear to be seen.

"Clara." I growled in warning. "What were you doing?" She bit her lip, her hands running through my hair.

"Just a surprise for you." She licked her lips. Again, always about me.

"Tonight is just about you, love. Tonight is just about how much I love you," I whispered. Her body reacted to mine as my hand came down on one of her breasts, sucking her nipple until her body moved against me.

Her body rubbing against my leathered pants made my erection extremely painful. My dumb ass wouldn't be able to take them off, not now. Not when I had a surprise for her when the war was all over.

I couldn't stand it when my mate was in so much pain for the few days of her healing. My body had to feel something, and sparing was out of the question. Fucking killing one of my own warriors wouldn't do.

So I fucking got my dick pierced, and it hurt like a motherfucking bitch. I got the best piercing that would fit my mate's needs. A deep shaft reverse Prince Albert. It would be perfect when I fucked her and had the ball rub against her clit each time I pulled out and forced it back in her wet pussy.

I bet Torin was pissed he didn't heal me faster now with our mate wanting our cock.

"Kane." She tugged at my pants.

"No." I panted. "Just you." My nose nestled into her pussy, as I breathed deep. "Tonight is all about you."

Chapter Forty-five

Clara

Before the light sources breached the eastern horizon, we had all begun our journey to the edge of the ward. Taliyah had stayed back while Jasper fought for her and their child. Taliyah cried in his arms, begging him to come back to her.

The worst part of it all was that there were no guarantees. There were no promises that could be made that would ensure that anyone would return. For all we know, we could be marching to our deaths because the magic instilled around Bergarian was far more potent than any of us could have imagined.

The somber undertone as our footsteps reached the boundaries stopped as we stared through the ward. Taliyah's power had already weakened from her pregnancy, and the tar-like substance embedded into the soil before the ward was now reaching for the plants still living on our protected side.

Jasper linked his mate, his face hard as he concentrated. That was another problem we faced. All of our links would be broken, the static would fill our minds, and we were all truly alone with our animals. We wouldn't be a pack, but all single entities fighting against one prominent being.

The ward broke, the liquid glass poured to the ground, and the black tar seeped beneath our feet. It did not grab us to pull us under; rather, it went around and took on anything growing in the soil. Folen and his brother gritted their teeth, their hands touching the ground as they felt the life force of Bergarian fade.

Kane led us forward. Carriages carried tents, weapons, and a new powder concoction that Taliyah and the three sisters had given us. It was to be the antidote to the memory powder. Each day we were to touch our forehead with a single finger of dust to protect at least our minds from being erased.

Giana prowled in my head, the static pushing against our minds. The further we stepped into the now dead land of nothing but black and gray, the stronger the dark magic became. Unfortunately, the power our wolves carried with us to get rid of fatigue was weakening. Along with that, more pain in a shift and healing significantly slowed.

"Let's shift!" Kane yelled across the group. With no mind-link, Kane's voice echoed through the crowd as the hordes of warriors passed along his command. The horses were manned by the several that would remain in human form, their clomping of feet bringing up ash from the burned grasses.

The trees burned by the tar-like substance, they had all lost their leaves, and the branches hardly covered our bodies for protection. There would be no hiding for our bodies to recover from the constant state of alertness that would have to remain until this war was over.

We traveled onward, still slow enough for the magnificent horses to keep up. The horses were stronger and sturdier than Earth, and it amazed me how each animal I had come across in Bergarian could live up to the expectations of their masters.

The light sources should have been high in the sky, but it wasn't for certain anymore. The black clouds thickened as we reached the supposed area where the soil had cracked. Folen continued to touch the ground, shaking his head as we continued. There would be no help from nature, and the three sisters who were still trying to overcome the death of their sisters still remained weak.

They might have been the only witches besides Osirus that would be able to help us. They were the very few that wanted to stay on the side with peace. The sisters had worked with my family for over a century. When word broke that witches and warlocks were going rogue against their kingdoms, my mother was very harsh on them.

After severe interrogations and promises of death and pain, my mother released them. As much as I wanted to be angry with my mother for jumping to conclusions, she was trying to save us all from pain if they supposedly turned on us.

So much was to change, so many things I wanted to do. First, we had to get through this hurdle. A hurdle that was, in fact, the journey across the enormous canyon that now stood.

Dark clouds rose in the distance from the canyon. They ascended into the sky. The light sources were now permanently blocked, and darkness fell upon us all.

Torin halted us with the raise of his arm. I had given him complete control of the royal power we shared. I knew nothing of war. I barely knew enough about fighting, so it seemed best for him to take the lead.

The horses stayed gathered into a grove of trees and escorted downward to protect them. They would be hidden for now, and those that had remained in the human forms found it necessary to join in on the fight. They would at least have the horses and their speed.

Kane and I stood watching the crater in the once flat plains of land. The crooked dark branches gave it an ominous and deadly appearance. We continued to skim over the crater for any signs of life when luckily, we saw Osirus mounted on his horse across the way.

"Thank the gods," Giana muttered. "At least they came."

"Yes, but how much use will they be when the sky is filled with clouds? They won't be able to use the light to strengthen them," I replied. My hair stiffened on my back. Kane's claw came down to pet my back in reassurance.

"There are ways around that," Giana purred. "The dragons, look." Giana had our heads look to the sky. Large wings of more than twenty dragons began to fan the sky. Our maw lifted as the clouds departed, only to hear a screeching roar as blue lightning showered down on the flying dragons. Their scales blackened, and their movements ceased as they began to fall from the sky.

Fae watched in horror, screaming for someone to help until their dragon brothers of their tribes raced to catch each one. A dragon for a dragon, they pulled them safely to the ground, only for the clouds to cover the holes of light that had been initially opened.

Fudge.

"Glad you all could make it," a voice replaced the static in our mind-links. There didn't need to be a loud announcement. This sorcerer was in our heads, in our minds, a sacred place only meant for packs and mates. "We were tired of all the chasing, taking things out one by one. I believe this will suffice and rid most of you so we can take our place on Earth. For those that don't know me, I'm Lord Virion, soon-to-be emperor." The crowd went silent.

Instead of rising from the canyon of fire and brimstone, he descended from the clouds like a god. Clouds parted, letting him slowly descend to the nearby cliff that overlooked the split battle ground below. My friends and family stood behind us, trying not to show their apprehension, but who was I kidding? We were all fearful of what was about to come.

Osirus pulled his sword from his sheath. We could hear the sheen clear across the canyon. Virion snickered, his eyes turning a bright blue, and the sickening smile that ripped his face horizontally looked on either side of the canyon. He was not as terrifying in my dream as I remembered. He was worse. I didn't think my nightmares could be brought to life so easily.

A shudder racked through me, Kane standing by my side, holding my head close to his thigh. "I'm feeling generous today/" Virion pulled back.

The dark cave behind him was a stark contrast to the pale face and red suit. He gripped hold of the lapels of his Italian suit jacket, straightening them.

The fire from the canyon grew hotter, blue and purple flames rising, casting the shadow of three personages on the back of the rocks. "Give up now, and I'll make your deaths quick." His tongue went from ear to ear as the snake-like tongue wetted his lips.

Kane turned his body, looking over the warriors. Wolves, vampires, fae, and elves were ready to fight. Their postures stiffened, smelling the burning sulfur. The look of determination as Kane radiated the royal command from the previous night's speech had our warriors growl in agreement.

Osirus stood on the other side, his head nodding to me that he was planning on doing the same. We would fight until the demon was struck down. If only he knew of the weapon we wielded, he would be in better spirits also.

The sword from Vulcan, which we now named The Reckoning, hung behind Wesley's back. He had opted to stay in his human form to hold it tight to his body and hopefully have a chance to use it.

"We won't give up that easy." Kane growled out. "We stay to fight." His stance widened, claws extending, ready to pounce him like he was standing in front of him.

Virion clasped his hands together, giving a condescending look. The shadows behind him flew straight toward us at a frightening speed until we heard choking inside the crowd. Screams from a familiar voice had me jolt backward, running toward the gasps and cries.

Leia was next to Kyler in her human form, holding onto him as the shadows wrapped their bodies around him. He was being suffocated, slowly. My maw went to reach for the shadows, but all I bit into was air. The three shadows were working together, choking Kyler's throat.

Leia's tears fell, her body trembling to hold on to Kyler as his breath left him. The tears in his eyes as he tried to pull the shadows away were all for naught. His fingers couldn't hold onto the shadows.

"Love." Kyler's eyes closed. Leia's tears ran down her cheeks as her body began to shut down. The shadows released him, having him fall into Leia's arms. She petted his hair, at least she tried, until the shadows covered his body as fire engulfed him.

Warriors looked on in astonishment, the wolves howling, the vampires screaming while Leia gripped the ashes of her burning mate. My fur enveloped her, my power falling around her trying to heal her from what was coming. Ashes ran through Leia's fingers as she stared at them longingly.

"You can't heal a bond, Clara," Giana whimpered in my head. "She needs to be with her mate in the stars." I howled sadly. Other wolves followed. Leia was my first friend. She introduced me to Raine. She was the comedic relief of our trio, the one that had my back when I needed to smile.

Visions of our spa days, the pampering, the laughing, the beautiful memories of helping her find her mate in the pack house prison. Oh gods, what the hell was happening? *This can't happen, not now, not ever!*

Leia's hands were covered in her mate's ashes, and she bowed to me. She gently smiled, petting my fur. The tears came pouring down my furred cheek. "He's there." Leia's tear matched my own. Leia stared off into the distance, her arm outreached. "We are going to be okay." Her heart was slowing, her breath beginning to cease. She laid down into his ashes, her hand buried in the remains. "Don't give up, Little Fox."

Chapter Forty-six

Under the Moon

L eia laid down in her mate's ashes, her eyes fluttered closed, and her heart stopped. The surrounding crowd was still in shock at one of the royal's most trusted couples in their inner circle was gone. None of them could help the dying pair. No amount of physical strength could have pried the empty embodiments of the ghost-like shadows.

Clara's maw tightened, and Giana reamed in her head. Clara was not one for violence, she never was, but something broke her at this moment. She had lost her pup, which she never knew she had until it was too late. Her daughter had been sent to Earth along with her family. Children, weaker shifters, all waiting for the Cerulean Moon and Golden Light kingdoms to fight for their home.

The action presented before her, watching her close friend die with no way to aid her even with her healing powers, engulfed her heart with fire. Revenge fueled her, and the longing to rip something or someone to shreds increased.

The crowd stepped back. Wolves whimpering, the vampires watching in awe while Clara stepped back. The constant growl in her chest, her lips rising above her teeth in warning, and the hair on her back made the crowd afraid.

Clara was the light. She was the one that brought the light sources so close to the Bergarian surface. She had brought new hope when she arrived in her home world. Now she radiated violence, a new side of her they had never seen. She was now a warrior. Her trying to defeat a rogue king months ago was nothing compared to this. Clara, their queen, was no longer frightened. Her revenge radiated to take back what was rightfully theirs, Bergarian, their homes.

Clara snarled, foam beginning to drip from her maw. Raine, ready in her wolf form, approached her, her head rubbing against her fur. The links were broken. There was no way for them to communicate, but even her sister-in-law's soft, gentle nudges as she whimpered beside her did not deter her.

Kane approached his mate, his clawed hand going to calm her, but to no avail. Her stance did not waver. She growled, barking, foaming coming from her maw.

Virion looked over the soon-to-be battleground with a smug look. Crossing his arms, the shadows dance gleefully around him. "Changed your mind yet? It will be less painful if you go willingly." Clara snarled, shaking her head, foam spraying the warriors.

Clara's anger fueled their own. This day would go down in history when they officially saw their queen ready to defend the entire land. Virion frowned. He parted his legs to better grip the cliff he stood on. The cave behind him slowly revealed his rogues. Vampires, witches, warlocks, shifters of every kind that had refused to side with either kingdom descended the cliff, half falling to the left and the other to the right.

"I'm a bit disappointed my right-hand couldn't be with me today," Virion said casually, tugging at his red suit jacket. "A bloody shame, but in the end, there was less blood to spill for my hands." Virion had no care for Duke Mortus anyway. He was used to getting on the inside of Vermillion. Having one kingdom fall before the other two was much easier than planned.

Osirus's horse reared back, screaming a boisterous neigh, his sword swinging around in a perfect vertical circle. "Oh, you are quite welcome." Osirus smirked. His horse pounded the ash of dead grass, trotting forward. "In fact, we can get rid of you and solve all of our problems." Virion glared, his black fingernail tracing his jaw line.

"All right then. Let's get this started."

Along with the cave behind Virion, more rogues came to the scene. The dark canyon rose with fire. Each kingdom fought for its own part in this war. As the fire grew, more rogues that had hidden inside poured out, immediately attacking the wolves and fae that stood too close. Clara rushed forward, along with her mate, running straight for the cliff. Their job was to climb the cliff and get rid of the source.

Wesley and Charlotte, not far behind, began running with them. In her wolf form, Charlotte ripped into the neck of one witch who dared to pull out a red orb of fire. Charlotte, already trained, killed a witch with a demon inside. She dodged the blow and aimed for the back of the neck. The witch, caught by surprise, dropped the orb that fell to pieces. Charlotte gripped the back of the spine, cracking it instantly. A dark shadow left the body, being sucked back into the fire.

The demon had escaped the witch's body. It would not be able to return to another unless summoned by another rogue witch. The sword dangled from Wesley's back as he ran, but as soon as he came close to three wolves, he pulled it from his back. The rotting sulfur from the canyon was nothing compared to the bodies of these three rogues. They held a different smell.

Death, burning hair, and flesh. All oozed from old wounds. The spell cast over the land not only hurt the Cerulean Moon Kingdom's wolves, but also the rogues. Wesley gritted his teeth, wondering why they weren't healing as they should when a bright light ascended above the canyon.

Cyrene hovered over the canyon, and a bright shield encompassed her body. Her thumb and middle finger touching in a circle as she looked over the carnage. Wesley smirked, his fangs showing through, not as painful as he thought it might be. The rogues circled him, thinking that they had the upper hand.

The sword swung in a violent circle, slicing the necks of the two. The last wolf jumped on Wesley's back, scratching it down with his claws and a jaw on his shoulder. Wesley roared, feeling the pain engulf his skin. Charlotte, who had already dealt with the witch, charged with hunger. Her mouth opened, her teeth cracking the neck of the assailant on her mate. Wesley groaned, stumbling forward, his wounds being deep.

The healing process was there, but it was too slow. Wesley wasn't sure how he was to carry the sword to its destination until he felt another furred body hovering over them. The fire in the eyes of their queen had dimmed, her eyes softened, her snout touching the head of Wesley, who laid on his stomach.

Charlotte continued to fight the rogues surrounding them as he was healed instantly. His fist hit the ground, grunting thanks to Clara, who turned the fire back in her eyes. Her lips lifted over her teeth as she stared down the surrounding rogues. Five witches, three wolves, and two bears.

Kane had not left Clara's side, his claws dripping with the blood from the bodies he had already disposed of. The rogue death numbers were growing far greater than he had expected. It was welcomed, but they still had a long way to go.

The rogues before them circled until they all pounced at the same time. Wesley took the sword, impaling one of the bears, while Charlotte took down the witches who had turned their bodies into their demon forms. Some with long black hair, horns protruding from their heads, the hooved feet clomped into the dust as she attacked. Claws raked down Charlotte when she jumped low from the ground. The underside of her belly had been unfortunate, but gave her the perfect advantage of attacking from behind.

More of the Warrior pack wolves swarmed, trying to ease the burden of the attacks of two alphas and lunas, but it proved futile. They had their strength, although not as strong as they used to be because of the dark powers raining on them, but they prevailed.

As Kane pulled out the heart of the last bear that lay on the ground, he bit into the heart that lay in his hand. Blood spurted from the muscle until he threw it into the Underworld's flames.

Virion looked over the Cerulean Moon Kingdom's side of the canyon. He chuckled, seeing them all fall one by one. The shadows behind him stalked into the cave, leaving Virion to his own devices, and called for one weapon that would not be taken lightly.

Virion had summoned a dragon from the bowels of hell. It had been resting in the deepest parts of Tartarus, one to supposedly be dead for thousands of years, but he found it. With the help of his demons, they brought him out of his slumber.

The strong tremors inside the cave caused the rock to shake from the cliff. The battlefield that ensued with war halted. Even the rogues raised their heads in question.

In slow, calculating steps, a deep red dragon with erratic patterns of black and blue emerged from the darkness. It was horned with two on the forehead and four on each side. It was much larger than any shifter dragon had ever seen. The claws were easily three meters in length, the four matching pairs of fangs long enough to pierce the sturdiest trees.

Each step, each rumble had both enemy and kingdoms rattle with fear. It licked its lips with its long, forked tongue, and drool that would keep the flames ignited once it left its stomach poured from the lips. "Fuck!" Kane yelled. He was never one to admit fear, but this beast was something he had never seen.

"Take cover!" Kane grabbed Clara as she was healing dozens on the field. There weren't many places for anyone to hide due to the charred trees, but they could try. The dragon let out a thunderous growl, its wings unfolding to the length of two football fields.

"Shit, shit, shit." Wesley nodded for Charlotte to take cover, but she wouldn't leave his side. "Now you choose to be stubborn?" he yelled as the roar overpowered the entire land. Wesley shifted into his wolf, the power that Cyrene was radiating now powerful enough to keep the pain of the shifts at bay. He grabbed the sword in his teeth and had them run underneath the cliff.

The dragon pushed the air beneath its wings, firing a constant flow as he blew it into the sky. The fire fell from its mouth. Heat of reds and oranges dusted the ground, burning not just those of the kingdoms, but rogues as well. Virion chuckled, wielding a rock that rose up from the ground into a glorified throne. He tapped his fingers on the arm rest, watching the scene unfold.

"This is the best entertainment yet." He willed a glass of red blood in his hand. Sipping it eagerly, the shadows loomed over him, dipping their shadowy fingers in his drink.

Virion's dragon blew flames again, screams of innocent lives being burned to a crisp. The fire was so hot that many did not feel their demise, but the mates certainly did as their souls burned for their mates.

A loud horn blew in the distance on the other side of the canyon. Virion lifted his head up in curiosity until he heard a roar comparable to that of his deviled dragon.

A white, gleaming dragon came to view. Its scales were white as pearl. It could reflect the light source rays if the light sources dared to poke through his darkened sky. The golden claws and the stark white teeth had Virion tightening his fists. This was to be a quick, easy win, but with a dragon of this caliber, he knew he might be in trouble.

Horus, Osirus's pet dragon, had ascended to the sky, its mighty wings comparable to that of the deviled dragon. Horus had never formed to his full length and height, always keeping himself relatively small to fit in his small dwelling.

Horus's jaw snapped, flying upward into the deviled dragon. It grabbed hold of the scales, his teeth so sharp it punctured through the armored scales. The deviled dragon wailed in pain, but the claws came forth to grip hold of Horus. It scraped down Horus' belly, not able to penetrate.

"What?" Virion ground out. His fists tightened, and for once, the shadows behind him cowered. "What is the meaning of this?" His hand pushed out, palm upward. "Why can he not be punctured!?" One of the shadows lowered its head, whispering in his ear. Virion's eyes widened and then scoffed.

"Let's have the devil dragon eat a sorceress then?" Virion eyes Cyrene who still hovered over the canyon. He hadn't paid much attention to the little sorcerer because who could match him? He was hoping for a show, and now he was on pins and needles, hoping to finish this war by twilight.

Virion lifted his fingers to his lips, whistling at the dragon for its attention. It whipped its head to him, despite Horus' bite into its shoulder. Virion pointed to Cyrene, who was oblivious to the attention. Her power radiated stronger and more potent than before with each passing second.

She continued to meditate, siphoning powers from deep within. She knew she had a purpose, and that purpose was for this moment. The hours of training, studying, meditating, and only focusing on the goddess, she was blessed.

The deviled dragon rolled its body in the air, causing Horus to fall, and pushed his mighty wings toward the radiating power of Cyrene. As the deviled dragon came closer, it was attacked from above by a powerful bird-like claw. The screech came from the highest part of the battlefield, echoing to the side of the cliff.

"What the hell is that?" Virion hissed. "Those things are extinct!" Apollo cawed, his claw dipping into one of the tear ducts of the dragon. Horus, who had recovered from his fall, sprinted forward, its fangs crushing the devil dragon's neck.

Their wings entangled with one another, the two dragons fighting for flight. Crying out in pain and wrestling with Horus, blood dripped from the devil dragon's neck and into the flames. The heat of the fire cooked their scales, and the pressure from gravity had them spiraling down into the canyon. The fire dimmed. Apollo had to let go of the devil dragon's eyes unless he wanted to be swallowed whole. He screeched, calling the attention to Osirus, who had his mouth set into a grim line.

Chapter Forty-seven

Under the Moon

O sirus clutched his sword, swinging it again as he plummeted through another rogue that dared get too close to his horse. His eyes continued to gaze back to the canyon, waiting for Horus to reappear again. His jaw tightened, and his wings fluttered until he saw Melina flutter over to the canyon. She was wearing light armor made of mithril from the gnomes of the south. He had her covered from head to toe and wasn't about to take any chances of her being hurt.

As much as he wanted her to stay back, stay deep in the palace walls, his mate was something else. She even said she would take her 'punishment' after the war was over.

Melina peered over the canyon, everyone too busy to pay attention to her brightly covered wings fluttering with curiosity. With a dagger wrapped around her thigh, she held onto it for a false sense of protection. As she leaned over, fire hovered deep into the pit, and the shining reflected scales began to wink at her. "Horus?" she whispered inside. The roaring of wind and fire should have been too much for anyone to hear, but Horus heard it all too well. His head tilted up. He was perched on a cliff inside, well above the smoldering flames.

Beside him was the dead devil dragon, its head detached from its body and claw marks on its chest. Horus began to eat the heart of the beast, and Melina shuttered. Horus was known to absorb the magic held inside beings. This was what happened to Sorceress Prinna just a month ago. Osirus, who had been too worried that his mate was hovering over the Underworld, wrapped an arm around her waist. She screamed, feeling the sudden touch, but the gentle whisper in her heart had her settle. "Just me, darling. Now stay with me, or you won't sit on that ass for a week." Melina giggled, despite the war before them. It was her coping mechanism to deal with her surroundings for the carnage.

Grunts from behind them had them stiffened. They turned to see a group of vampires, one holding a sword that caught Osirus's eye. It was different from what he had seen across the field. Osirus snarled, lifting his lip in warning, but the vampires chuckled as they approached. "Get ready, darling, like I told you?" Melina tilted her head in defiance, ready to join her lover in their hand-to-hand combat.

She began to sing, which usually could reach a radius of thirty feet, but with the black magic dulling all of their senses, she could only reach five. One came close and was immediately captivated by the spell and threw himself over the canyon. The other four smirked, pulling a root-like substance from their pockets. The same substance that Carlos used to stuff his ears to not be affected by her hypnotic song.

Melina growled in frustration. The sword on the other side of her hip was drawn, and she hovered above the ground as she swung at them. Osirus kept his eyes on three, his dark fae genes coming to the surface. His skin darkened, and his wings of delicate dark swirls of patterns darkened deeper.

With Osirus's skills, he rid the head of two in a matter of seconds. The last vampire came at him from behind, a small dagger empaled his back, and his hand went to his wing. It pulled, trying to dislocate it. With the pain surging through his body, he flapped his wings twice until he heard that unbearable tear.

Half his wing tore, his fangs lengthening as he ripped his body from the vampire's clutches. Black tar dripped from the rogue's mouth. Osirus smirked, pulling the vampire's head back, sinking its fangs in its trachea, and then ripped. The vampire went limp. He spat out the black sludge and threw the vampire over into the canyon.

A blood-curdling scream came closer to the canyon. The vampire, holding the sword that was now burning red hot, had slashed straight through the armor. It was his mate, his one and only that he had found after eight hundred years of searching. His ears pinned back, and his good wing fluttered until he saw her clutching her stomach.

Osirus roared, lunged forth, and pulled the vampire away from her, his dagger pulled from his thigh and plunged into his heart. Virion, who was sitting on his stone throne, laughed sinisterly as he watched Melina tumble.

"That had to hurt." He chuckled.

Melina had initially killed one vampire that had come at her with the same sword. She took the vampire by surprise, but Virion had another ready in its stead when she was too busy trying to dispose of the body. When she turned away from the canyon, it pierced the sword's tip into her body. The Death Sword punctured her armor like butter on toast, ripping through her wound.

The scream she let out was obviously painful, so loud that the surrounding fae heard it all too well. They rushed to her simultaneously as Osirus gritted his teeth in agony. He felt their bond inside them, the unbearable pain she felt. Once the vampire was disposed of, The Death Sword dropped to the ground, only to vanish into the soil.

It reappeared in Virion's hand, waving it around his throne like a plaything. "Have to say, she got close," he spoke to himself. "Guess I'll have to hang onto this."

Osirus gripped Melina, she was bleeding out, and her healing was too slow. His eyes diverted to Cyrene, who couldn't break her meditation, and then he looked to his sister in spirit. She was already staring at him, her claws gripping the ground, ready to jump the enormous canyon, but was swept up by another dark figure.

Kane, growling in annoyance his mate would attempt such a jump, held her tight and backed away. He grunted, putting his nose into her fur, smelling the sweet scent of his mate. "Hang on." He growled. The run became a steady gallop with his large, thunderous legs. The claws gripped the ledge, jumping into the air.

The canyon was far too large for him to land. He held Clara with one arm while the other claw extended, gripping the side of the canyon. The rocks fell around them, and Clara whimpered until Kane used the strength in his powerful arms and slung her above him. Clara caught the ledge with her front paws while her hind legs kicked bits of dirt and debris down on top of Kane.

It didn't hinder Kane's powerful strength as he climbed quickly up the canyon side, just in time before the bowels of the Underworld's fire rose up against his backside. Kane stumbled on top of Clara, covering her from the heat. She wiggled beneath him, trying to get free and see to it that Melina could be saved.

Once freed, she bolted to Osirus, who gave her pleading eyes. "Please," he begged. Not once had he begged in his life unless it was for his darling mate. He begged her not to fight, but her stubbornness and eagerness to help aid in her new home world had won him over.

Her family, the Atlanteans, and the king of the kingdom could only help in protecting the palace. They couldn't travel far away from the ocean, and the journey alone would have weakened them without the aid of the salt water.

She was their representation, Princess of Atlantis, and he could not deny her.

Melina gasped, the light leaving her eyes. "Gods, please help her," Osirus sobbed. His grip tightened around her, his hand filling with his mate's blood while he applied pressure. Never in his life had he felt so helpless. Clara's snout went right to Melina's forehead. Her forehead glowed brighter until Clara whimpered and Kane pulled away.

"It's too much." Kane growled. "If Clara gives much more, it will hurt her." Clara wiggled through Kane's arms, attempting to try again until the static that ran through Clara's mind broke. "I can heal her more!" Clara growled to her mate. "I can get it to slow down! I see dark sludge around her wound. I can slow down the bleeding enough to get her out of here!" Kane opened his maw in shock, repeating the words that Clara had just said to Osirus.

Cyrene grimaced, trying to break down the mind-link barriers. It was just taking time with new incantations to unlock the complicated black magic. Apollo had graciously given her a vial of his blood that she hung around her neck to aide her with his magic.

Osirus gripped his hold around Melina, wondering how they would take the black magic from her wound. Clara tried again. The bright light became brighter than any light on the field. Fae had circled the royal warriors in an attempt to save the Golden Light Kingdom's queen.

Clara paused, her snout now baking away. "I've slowed it down, but I can't work the black magic out of her." Osirus watched Kane relay the news and nodded his head solemnly.

"Take care of her," Kane ground out. "We've got your soldiers covered."

Osirus glanced around his soldiers, they all looked on in determination. They wouldn't stop. They would continue to fight. Their armor was gleaming, taking in whatever reflective light they could from the break in the clouds.

Dragons still hovered overhead, dodging the blue lighting with the greatest of speed. They worked together, bringing breaks in the clouds, enough for the light sources to shine briefly to have the fae recharge.

"Go," Kane ordered Osirus. Osirus didn't smirk or have some witty comment to say. Clara touched her snout to Osirus's forehead that healed his wing enough to fly his mate to safety.

Kane roared in the background while Osirus flew to the outskirts of the battlefield. The tents set up for medical purposes were streaming with people. The finest physicians of the fae kind were on stand-by, healing wounds that would otherwise fester and not heal from the black magic.

Everyone stopped when King Osirus landed. Physicians and aids rushed to the king and ushered them into the royal medical tent. They worked for hours on the queen. Her heart remained at a high steady beat, the black sludge covering the wound and now weeping outside of her body. "Fix this! I'll kill you all myself if I have to!" Melina whimpered, her body slipping into a coma and no longer responding to his mate's touches.

A full twenty-four hours later, he finally saw a dark figure come in the doorway. The dragons on the outside had thoroughly brushed away the dark clouds in the sky. Creed walked toward one physician, nodded his head, and grabbed a scalpel from the table.

Creed's alpha blood thumped through his veins. The physician eagerly grabbed the drops of blood before his wound healed again. "This will help. Thank you, Alpha Dragon." Creed only grunted, his eyes meeting that of Osirus. "Next time, call for me," he whispered enough for only Osirus to hear, before Creed stepped out of the tent.

Odessa hovered in the sky, her wings flapping valiantly as she radiated power that accompanied Cyrene. It had taken Odessa hours to feel confident enough to brave the skies to help the entire land of Bergarian. Her fear of unworthiness and inability to wield the dragon's power enough was frightening to her.

What if she messed up? What if she failed?

Once Creed laid down the law, pinning her to a nearby tree, he promised he would never leave her side and that she was the key to this war. He felt it in his bones. He felt Hecate urging him to help his mate. As much as he wanted Odessa to hide among the burned forests, he knew he had to let her go.

Creed had held her back. He was being selfish, never wanting to see his mate in pain. It was almost too late until Hecate invaded his mind demanding him to give her the strength she needed through the bond. Odessa's heart ached in her scales as she transformed. The purple tendrils of electricity encompassed her body. Vampires and witches all dared to try and approach, but the electric shocks that reached out to the rogues killed them instantly.

Odessa stood in shock, her electricity thrumming through her. Cyrene reached out her hand as she hovered over the entire battlefield needing the help of Odessa. With newfound confidence, Creed stood at her side, and nudged her side for her to take flight. Odessa hovered over the entirety of the field, along with Cyrene, as the black clouds began to break and the setting light sources came to light just next to twilight.

As the light sources set at the end of the day, the blue moon came overhead. Watching her mated pairs slowly dying, the goddess brightened the moon herself, going against everything the gods had promised each other. Helping the supernaturals and mortals.

She argued that if she didn't heighten the light of the moon, there would be no more gods. This dark magic was far more powerful than even the gods had imagined. Hecate grabbed her hand through their shared sacred bond, giving thanks to her sisters' willingness. It seemed only the female gods were looking out for the stubborn males.

Folen's brother was at his back. They fought with each other as the vampires surrounded them. The fae had come to find a newfound energy with the blue moon rising in the sky, and more fae continued to fly over the canyon to help the shifter kingdom.

Folen was caught off guard by a witch who knocked his sword from his hand. His brother turned to feel the lack of movement from Folen, only for three vampires to take advantage of his lack of attention. Folen growled, lurching at the witch who was not prepared for his sudden bravery. He cracked her neck, only to feel a rush of pain. Turning, he saw his brother being held down by three vampires.

"No!" He growled out, trying to jump forward, but a bear caught him, pulling Folen up off the ground in a giant hug. "No! No!" The vampire holding his brother's head smirked until it was ripped clean off his body. Folen felt his brother's bond break inside him. He howled in pain. It pained him so much to lose the only sibling he had left, and he began to cry red tears.

Kane roared from behind him, gripping the bear that held Folen and cracking its neck effortlessly. Kane, being in a blind rage to kill any rogue in sight, left Folen to his devices. Folen kneeled to the ground, picking up his sword. He swung it around his body, charging at the leftover vampires that had killed his brother. With the swipe of his blade, one vampire fell to the ground while the others ran in fear.

Folen knelt to the ground, picking up his brother's body, his head barely attached, but he cradled him anyway. From that day forth, he would never trust a single vampire, may they be for good or evil. Because this image of this brother being taken from this life before he had found a mate had devastated him too greatly.

Charlotte caught the two vampires that dared to run away from Folen. She snarled, snapping her teeth harshly. She followed Wesley, who was trying to climb the cliff, but when she saw that Folen and his brother were in trouble, she abandoned the climbing and raced toward him.

But it was too late. Folen's family was dead, but that didn't mean she couldn't help in another way. Revenge.

Chills ran up her spine. She hated the evil vampires. Her vision tainted from her days living with one for so many years. Charlotte didn't want to touch the dirty things, but she would do it for the elf that had been friendly to her. She leaped forward from the underbrush, surprising one with a quick snap of the neck. They were much easier to kill than the witches that had been possessed by demons.

The other vampire stood with his back to the cliff, his hand reaching trying to find a magical hidden door or cave he could duck into. Charlotte licked her lips, the black sludge causing her to gag.

"For Folen," she whispered to herself as her wolf pounced on the vampire, pinned to the rock wall, and ripped into his chest with her claws.

Chapter Forty-eight

Under the Moon

O sirus looked to the south. The constant haze that accompanied the morning light made him lose hope. The three orcs, Sugha, Valpar, and Thorn, had left just a day after Mortus' brutal killing. They said they would be back for the war. They would do everything they could to bring more of their kind to finally find the mates that were promised to them. What troubled Osirus the most was that the reinforcements may not come.

The war started far sooner than Osirus had anticipated. Apollo had barely taken the reins of becoming the Alpha of the Toboki tribe, and Odessa was still trying to prepare and gain confidence in her new powers.

Melina stirred in the corner, her hand reaching for her stomach. Osirus rushed forward, forgetting about the orcs, and took to his mate. The physicians gathered, fanning incense, and began to rub essential oils on her neck and face.

"Darling?" Osirus lightened his voice and gripped her hands. He would forever be indebted to Creed for saving his mate. Melina groaned, trying to sit up. The black tar had hardened, crusting over and falling to dust around the table. Her body was still pale, her eyes still dulled in a fog. "How are you feeling?"

"Like I was hit by a truck." She chuckled. Osirus shook his head. He still did not understand the meaning of Earth. "We need to get back out there." Osirus put his hand between her naked breasts and pushed her back down on the bed.

"Can't do that. You need to stay still. I will go fight in your stead. You are in such deep shit, though. You just don't understand." He chuckled, trying to lighten the mood. "Twenty spankings for you." Melina gave a small smile, then felt the bumps between her fingertips on her stomach. Her small smile faded as she lifted the sheets.

"Wait," Osirus begged, but her hand was already rubbing the raised scars above her womb. They were red and irritated, but the wound was closed. Physicians remained worried her uterus may not recover, that she would not be able to give Osirus an heir they wanted. Sensing Melina's distress, he put a hand over her stomach.

"You will be fine," he soothed. Melina shook her head, and a ruddy tear fell from her eye. The black magic was still being pulled from her body in any way possible. "And you will have children," Osirus said, determined. Melina glanced at the physician standing. He pursed his lips and would disagree with his king.

"Do you understand me, Melina?" Osirus said sternly. "You will. I promise you. Have I ever broken a promise?" She shook her head, deep, dark tears trailing down her face. "I must go," Osirus said reluctantly. He had stayed too long. He was needed back on the field with the rest of his men, with the rest of Bergarian fighting.

Melina nodded, giving an apologetic smile. Kissing her long and hard, Melina traced her fingers over his jaw. "I love you." Her hand never left her stomach. "And I love you, darling," he replied softly.

Osirus stepped out of the tent, the flap opened by the wind. Horus had just taken to the sky, his wings causing the ash and dust of the ground to be swept up and into the eyes of all who fought. It hindered them all from trying to battle, but at least Horus was back in a fighting stance after absorbing the devil dragon's power.

A horn in the distance sounded. The soldiers around the physician's tents stilled as the sea of deep greens settled upon the horizon. Hordes of orcs, all being led by the infamous three that wanted mates, raised their swords, axes and clubs, all screaming with a mighty fury of longing.

Osirus smiled, bowing to Thorn as he flew to the cliff to find the one sorcerer to stop the madness.

Sugha stood at Thorn's side, his large club with spikes of iron swung, and the fire instantly captured two vampires as they fell into the canyon. Valpar stood in front of a warlock. The warlock had electricity weave in and out of his fingers until it formed into the signature balled orb. The warlock pushed forth, Valpar was unable to move his large muscular arms in time to block the electricity. Once it hit its chest, instead of the magic absorbing into his body, it fell down with a plunk.

The warlock raised a brow, not understanding. Little did he know that orcs repelled magic. Valpar snickered, his large, bare feet stomping the ground, leaving imprints into the soft ash, and swung his sword until the warlock was cut clear in half with one fatal swoop.

Sugha leaped over the canyon, seeing a warrior she-wolf cornered into the underbrush of thorns. His fire blazed with fury. Taking his club, he charged forward as he saw the she-wolf shift from her wolf to the soft skin that reminded him of Odessa. His eyes widened all but a moment until he came barreling in like a battering ram knocking rogue wolves and shifters.

Sugha noted the foul smell of the enemy and committed it to memory. His wide feet easily stomped the rogues that lay on the ground, and his club was thrown over his shoulder. Looking down at the helpless she-wolf, her fear reeked from her body. She shook uncontrollably, her wounds slowly closing. "W-what are you?" She took in a large breath. "You aren't a rogue." Sugha leaned over, his hand reaching for hers until she came out of the thorns.

"An orc," he replied. "I'm Sugha," he said, puffing out his chest. "And you are a werewolf, correct?" The she-wolf was swimming with questions, but the bright light over the canyon grew white, encompassing the battlefield, had her ignoring her curiosity. "Nala," she yelled over the blinding light.

"We can fight together as friends? No?" Nala smiled, taking his hand. Sugha's heart filled with warmth, making a new friend, even if she wasn't his mate.

Cyrene had broken through the thirteenth level of black magic. Odessa continued to fuel her power until the bright light burst from both of their chests like the rings of Saturn. It pulsated through the air like the sickening beat of the clubs of Earth until the last blast caused them both to faint.

The canyon grew closer to absorb their bodies until an ivory colored dragon flew and pulled Cyrene into her scaled arms, flying her to the nearest medical tent. Creed, who had been fighting off the witches and warlocks below, trying to break the concentration of two critical beings of the war, stiffened seeing his mate falling from the sky.

Creed had mercilessly killed hundreds to protect his mate, along with Horus, who was impressed by Creed's strength. Horus bowed his head when he saw that Creed had captured his mate in his arms, Creed bowed the same, having the honor to fight with a full-blooded dragon.

Meanwhile, Clara, Kane, Wesley, and Charlotte had climbed the cliff. Along the way, they dealt with numerous witches and warlocks trying to conjure their magic and throw it at them as they climbed. Still, the Sword of Reckoning could quickly avert the blasts.

As Kane stood on the cliff, Virion was the only thing between them and ending this war. Virion had taken the Death Sword that had ripped through Melina's abdomen and clanged it against the arm of the throne. "You idiots!" he screamed at the shadows on the wall. "How did those blasted orcs get in here?" The shadow's bright blue eyes scowled down at Virion in irritation, flying toward Virion, one whispering in his ear.

"Yes, I know it will change the war's outcome. Along with that sorceress and dragon. Why the fuck couldn't we penetrate it?" Virion growled. Wesley slung Charlotte's wolf on the cliff, her nails accidentally making too much noise. "Ah, well, well," Virion purred. "Just the supernaturals we wanted to see. We will end you, and then the entire world of Bergarian will be lost anyway. Strike at the spirit of Bergarian, yes?" Osirus fluttered downward, standing next to Kane's gigantic form. He nodded his head, pulling out his own sword of steel.

Kane growled, Torin baring his teeth. "There is only one outcome of this war, Virion, and that is you being pushed back into the bowels of the Underworld where you belong. Along with your cowardly demons that have yet to show their faces." He growled.

"Oh, I'm sorry, you wanted to see them? Better than this mug I have right here?" His wicked grin that went ear to ear lengthened again, the forked tongue flicking rows of fangs. "That can be arranged. Which demon would you like to see first?"

Kane, a wolf with very few words, lunged forward trying to get a grip on the enemy so Wesley could force the sword into Virion's chest. Virion stepped out of the way in time to sling the Death Sword upward, catching Kane on the side of his face. Blood trickled from the cut. Kane put a claw to his face feeling the black sludge forming inside.

Clara whimpered, feeling the blade through the bond. The three shadows slinked forward, going straight toward Wesley, who held the sword in a battle stance. He had no armor to protect him, only the leather pants he donned the entire battle as he carried the sword. Osirus stayed back, the blade was made of iron, and now with the powers of Vulcan, he could burn to a crisp within seconds.

The shadows swept around him, the sword swinging and cutting through one of the demons. A blood-curdling scream came from the three-horned demon shadow and fell to the ground. It crawled toward him, trying to reach the others, but Wesley swung again at his next attacker.

Kane shook his head. His vision went blurry from the black magic inside the Death Sword Virion carried. Clara pounced behind Virion so quickly, that he barely saw her until her teeth planted into his neck. Taking the sword he tried to hide behind him, but she let go quickly, now slinking toward Kane to cover him.

Osirus took this as his chance to join the fight, his sword fighting skills being far superior from years of practice. Virion smirked, shaking away the blood that now dried and flaked away from his red suit. "Got to love this healing thing," he casually mentioned. "I can sort of see why being a shifter is slightly appealing." Osirus slung his sword down, the light metal scratching up the Death Sword. Virion pushed onwards, both blades touching.

Their faces were so close, Osirus could smell death escaping Virion's breath. Osirus snarled, his fangs lengthening, dripping a silver venom from his mouth. "My, my, angry little pixie," Virion taunted. It was just enough for Osirus to push his sword harder against the demon blade and break his own blade down to the handle. Osirus cursed, throwing the handle, and backed away.

The three shadows that tried to get close to Wesley returned to Virion's body. He inhaled deeply, feeling even more power return.

Three distinct voices expelled from Virion's mouth. "Here, puppy, puppy." Wesley gripped the handle of The Reckoning until he threw it at Kane, who caught it with his claws. Torin had enough and he would be sure to end it now.

Clara tried to heal Kane's wound on his head, but all she could do was slow the bleeding and the dark magic enough to where it didn't affect him as much. She whimpered, knowing the magic would seep into Kane the more he fought, with every beating of his heart.

She stumbled, getting closer to Osirus. Shifting, she lay naked in front of Osirus, who pulled off his cape and wrapped it around her. "He's been hit already." She breathed shakily. "How is Melina?" Osirus looked to Kane, who was now in a full-blown battle against Virion.

Wesley, now back into his wolf form, heard the scraping of nails of company they did not need. They peered over, growling and snapping at the vampires, trying to join in on the fun.

"Better, Creed gave us his blood." Clara's eyes brightened, hope filling her face. "Can we get more? Are Odessa and Creed all right?" Clara tried to scoot closer to the cliff, only for Osirus to pull her away.

"They are fine," he said sternly. "Odessa was taken to a medical tent along with Cyrene. The links appear to be working, and we are beginning to win on the ground. We just need to take Virion." The two blades had heated to bright red, Kane continuing to take more small scrapes and blows to his body. He groaned, and Clara tried to stand up.

"You can't get near him," Osirus pulled her back. "Your mate will have my head, and you will be nothing but a distraction to him."

"But you can't fight either," Clara sighed. "Vulcan's iron is far too powerful." Osirus gritted his teeth. He hated feeling helpless. All during this war, he had felt nothing but weak, and here he was, watching the scene unfold like a faeling.

Kane dodged another attack. The scrapes on his forearms and chest now oozing with blood and black sludge. He wouldn't give up, not now. The black magic across the land was slowly dying. With the combination of Cyrene and Odessa's dragon powers, they could overcome the darkness.

Unfortunately, he had to get rid of the source, and that was Virion.

Virion rolled on the ground, springing up at lightning speed, scraping the back of Kane's knee. He roared, swinging the sword and unfortunately the flat of the blade only knocked Virion to the ground. The shadows gathered around Kane while Virion stabilized himself. Virion wasn't the most skilled warrior, but with his demons' constant healings and power surges, he was doing better than he expected.

The shadows wrapped around Kane's neck. Clara screamed, pushing Osirus away from him. She shifted, after her third step, ripping into Virion's neck again.

Clara concentrated on her healing abilities. Every bit of healing she did on the battlefield soaked up everyone's pain and misery. It had built up in her body, weighing her down, but she had her own idea of how to expel it. Giana howled, forcing the pain of her warriors into Virion's shoulder.

All the warriors she had healed came down tenfold. Virion clawed into Clara's eyes, and she whimpered, falling back onto her fur. The pain Virion felt had the shadows release Kane, his breath heaving as they had tried to choke him.

Osirus yelled for Kane to move. His wings flapped rapidly to push Kane out of the way, but once the shadows touched Virion, he used his velocity to take the Death Sword and shove it straight into Kane's chest.

Virion let go, letting the dark magic seep into Kane's chest cavity. Kane's eyes glowed red, his fur darkening as his body pulled in more magic. Clara screamed, gripping her chest, feeling her mate slowly fall to the ground. Kane's body was turning back into his human form, patches of hair falling from his body.

With the momentum of Kane being pushed by Osirus, Kane's body moved forward. Kane held The Reckoning in front of him, the blunt of the handle moved into his abdomen to hold it steady. Virion leaned forward, ensuring the demon blade stayed firmly in Kane's chest. "Long live Emperor Virion." Virion smiled, black sludge dripping from his lips. The shadow's blue eyes winced, laughing to themselves. They had won. Once the beast of Bergarian died, then all hope would be lost.

Clara dug her claws into the rock cliff, the scraping not deterring the evil being in front of her. She was going to make sure Virion would never breathe again. Clara jumped with the full weight of her body forcefully into Virion's back. His body leaned forward, impaling himself with The Reckoning that Kane held with his stomach.

Kane, who had wholly changed back into his human form, stumbled, along with Osirus, backward as Virion's body fell over them.

The shadows that once only spoke to Virion in their ghost-like forms screamed in agony as they permanently detached from him. They spiraled around each other, the translucent blackness now becoming one dark orb floating into the air until it tipped over the cliff's edge and fell into the flames that had roared to life.

Clara took Virion by the neck with her maw, his skin tearing from his throat, the sinews of muscle embedding into her teeth. He groaned, trying to pull away, but Clara successfully pulled him from the blade that Kane had let go.

In the corner of Clara's eye, she sees her mate still with the Death Sword embedded in his chest. She whimpered, but the mission had to be completed. To rid the sorcerer that dared get rid of them all. Tears welled in her eyes, and her breathing ragged until she reached the edge.

The flames grew hotter, the once orange flames burned blue and black, and a gigantic growl came from within. "The fuck is going on?!" It sounded almost human, but a mighty voice that echoed throughout the land could only mean one thing. A god.

Clara pushed Virion in, his body lifeless, and the flames wrapped around him, pulling him faster into the canyon.

"*Hades!*" Charlotte shouted through the link. "*He's closing the canyon!*" The cliff quaked as the soil moved and closed the canyon until it was only three feet across. The last of the fire flew upward toward the sky until finally, the fire stopped, and the ground heat began to cool.

Clara shifted right at the edge of the cliff. Her body was naked, covered in dirt and soot. Her hair was tangled, her face covered in tears. As the tears fell, they left clean skin in their wake. She didn't have time to wipe it away. Her mate was dying. She could feel it.

Clara reached her mate, a sword still in his chest. "Osirus?" she pleaded with him. Charlotte and Wesley stood over them, waiting, watching.

Wesley had scars across his chest from the vampires that held black magic inside, but they began to heal more quickly as time went on.

"Clara, I-I'm sorry," Osirus choked. "There isn't anything I can do." Kane's head lay in Osirus' lap. Clara pushed him away and began to scream. "No! No, he is fine!" The only reason Clara would be alive was because of their daughter. Their daughter needed her, but Clara really needed her mate, Kane.

Clara pushed her forehead to Kane's. He looked terrible. His skin was ashen, and his lips blue. The black tar continued to leak out of his body. Blood dripped onto the cold rock under her legs that were pushed underneath him. "He can't be. He isn't!"

Kane's breaths were shallow. His body weight of nearly two hundred and eight pounds of muscle laid heavily on her skin. "Kane!" Clara cried as she pushed her forehead to Kane's. The bond they shared was breaking. Clara could feel Kane leaving her. She cried out again, her tears landing on Kane's eyelids.

She could heal him. She could try. Even with his heart no longer beating, she wouldn't give up.

This was her mate, her love. She wouldn't give up on him now.

Chapter Forty-nine

Clara

My head tilted back, staring at the black clouds that continued to fade away. The darkness, the fog, and ash began to dwindle, and the light sources dared to bring light. Osirus had stood, stepping away from Kane's body. It was like he had already given up, no more hope for the lifeless body that now lay in my lap.

Wesley and Charlotte stood behind me. They clutched to each other, fearing one would disappear. Funny that they were both holding each other. I was the one losing half of my soul. Is this what Maria felt all those years ago? When her mate had died at the hands of a vampire, only compelled to live to take care of me? Would I live life as an empty shell just as she did? Going through the motions of life until my daughter was old enough to fend for herself?

I couldn't stomach it. I couldn't bear to think I was going to go on alone. My sibling growing in my mother's belly would have to continue the royal line. I would never be whole enough to take care of a kingdom so vast while my heart remained empty.

My daughter, what would Evelyn think? Her father would rock her to sleep, bathe, clean, and settle her in the night so I could have a few more moments of peace. She wouldn't have a male figure in her life to call a father.

Heart twisting, my tears threatening to fall, I refused to believe that my mate was gone. He had promised so much that I couldn't let him off that easily. We still needed our time. It had been far too short. Just a mere eight months of being together, we had been through much, with much more to come.

"No." I growled out, my fingers pulling his head upward. There was once a time when he held me in his arms when he finally rescued me from Darius. I held his body to my chest, telling him it would be all right.

His heart had long since stopped, but the thrumming of his spirit was still there. He had yet to go into the glow of the afterlife. He said he wouldn't leave me. He would fight tooth and nail with any Grim Reapers that tried to pull him under. My mate wouldn't give up, he wouldn't leave this word, and in return, I would pull him back and save him.

"Princess," Osirus cooed, putting his hand palm up for me to take.

"No," I snapped, pushing him away. "He isn't gone, not yet."

Osirus and Wesley shared a knowing look, both shaking their heads. Charlotte sniffed, burying her face into her mate's chest. *Not today. I will not gain any pity.*

Heavy, slow torturous breathing came from behind me. Osirus had meticulously stepped away from me, whispering to Wesley. The heavy breathing halted, now covering me over with a shadow. Two giant beings, clad in black robes with the traditional scythe of a curved blade and wooden handle in the skeletal hand.

Their free hands held out for Kane, but I gripped my mate tighter. "No, you will not take him!" I screamed. "You cannot! Look what he has done to sacrifice! What we sacrificed! I will not let you take his spirit!" The Grims stood back, turning their heads to each other as if having a silent conversation. My gentle touches to my mate's chest, the sword that had impaled him I pulled from his chest. A gaping hole was what was left, along with the black tar around the wound.

Kane's sticky blood hung onto The Reckoning. I threw it until it landed on the edge of the cliff. One Grim walked over to retrieve it, putting it in his robes.

"You won't leave. You hear me?" I whispered. My tear dripped down my heated cheek, landing in his eyes. "Giana and I won't have it," I sniffed. "We won't." I choked back a sob.

He looked peaceful, his brows no longer furrowed, his face not in a hardened scowl. He looked like he was sleeping, a cold sleep that I couldn't wake him from. "I'm giving you all I have," I whispered. "Every part of me, even if it kills me too."

As much as I loved my daughter and wanted her to run into my arms and cradle her every night, I knew I wouldn't be the same person again. Part of me would be gone, my spirit broken. I straddled his body, gently laying Kane's head down on the rock. The Grims watched intently, their hands at their sides, waiting to see what I would do.

I scowled at them, their expressionless faces making me angrier by the second. Both my hands cupped Kane's face, my forehead touching his.

"Everything, Alpha. I will give you my everything." Giana slowly planted her paws in the soft grasses of my mind. Walking straight toward me. Her eyes glowed so brightly that they drowned out the world around her. Her eyes entrapped me, pushing the bright light through my eyes.

My own world faded. The only one I saw was Kane. I lifted his eyelids, peering into those dull, lifeless eyes, but I saw his spirit stir. It moved beneath the blinding light I sent forth into his mind. Giana urged me forward, my hand reaching out until I fell into Kane's unconscious. He lay unmoving, groaning.

"Kane," I whispered his name, running toward him. His mind was unsettling, the darkness slowly swallowing him whole. Black sludge that coated the floor pulled at my feet, trying to pull me into the night. The tar substance continued pulling until I landed on my knees in front of my mate.

His spirit was dying, the last bit of him almost unrecognizable. The graying skin, the black tar creeping up his face. Giana nudged me, my spirit wanting to repeat the same position as my physical one on the other side. "Heal his soul," Giana purred. "Heal him from the inside."

I took a staggering breath, placing my lips over his. The warmth engulfed us, bringing a bright light to the darkness. My body glowed warmth as I tried to chase away the tar that dared try to cover him. The tar cracked until it began to fall away from his body like clumps of dirt. Small blades of grass began to grow, covering up the blackness. It was the same grass that Torin would play through in Kane's mind.

Torin's fur stroked the side of my arm, but my body was too focused on Kane. Giana wasn't far, her wolf nudging Torin to a calmer part of the grass. Torin was here. I just needed Kane.

Deepening the kiss, longing for him to wake up and yell at me for risking my life, I poured deeper. I set off all the emotions that filled me. Every bit of love I had for him, the love of our daughter, the reminders of why he should be here with me.

Warm hands pushed upward on my back. I sighed, feeling the tingles that began to flow in my body again. The bond mending, the world coming into a clearer space. His claws gently nicked my mark as his hands cupped my face.

"My mate." I let out a sob, pushing my bare breasts into his chest. "You're alive!" It was true, unbelievable, but true. His spirit had not left him. I found him before he had been completely consumed. There was no doubt I would never be able to do this to anyone else because Kane was my connection. He had my heart. My soul wrapped around his so tight that it could not become unwoven.

"Baby, don't cry," his voice came out utterly smooth. My face came up from the mark I placed my lips upon and met his lips again. It was salty, filled with nothing but tears of joy.

A voice clearing had us pause at our glorious moment. "Excuse me," a small voice, meek and mild, came from the grasses now growing taller in the sunlight. She was small, like my height, with white robes and platinum blonde hair. Her eyes held a bright green with hints of gold flecks inside.

"I just came to tell you that this was just one time." She held up her index finger. "One blessing of the gods, you will never be able to attempt such a thing again." Her eyes softened, her hands clasping together.

"Ch-Charis?" I gasped. "Goddess Charis?" The goddess that had blessed me at birth stood right before me. She nodded meekly with a small smile. "Yes," she said before she faded into the meadow. "Thank you," I muttered, only to have Kane roll me on my back.

"I was scared, baby. Scared that I lost you. That I wouldn't be able to come back to you like I promised." His nose went into my neck. "You shouldn't have come for me. You could have died too." I shook my head, cupping his face.

"I'd do it again," I chided. "I'd do it all over again." Kane chuckled, his eyes darkening. His lips twitched, and his mouth smashed into me. His hands roamed my body, cupping my ass as I put my dirtied leg over his.

He hummed in satisfaction, his hand cupping my breasts. My mate was a wolf of so few words. He was a wolf of actions, his love language obviously that of touch. His cock rested on top of my pussy, rubbing it erotically over my lips. I moaned, feeling his length so close to my entrance.

"I want to take you now, but I fear what our bodies are doing." I paused, my lips still puckered, glancing everywhere but him.

"Skittles, you don't think we are doing it in front of people, do you?" I fluttered my lashes, but Kane pushed the tip of his cock closer to my entrance. Something cold prodded there that had my eyebrows reaching my hairline. "Did the little alpha get hurt?" I squeaked.

Kane scoffed. "Little alpha?" he questioned. I giggled.

"Don't change the subject," I playfully hit his shoulder. Kane leaned on his elbow, his finger tracing down my chest.

"Baby, it's over. The war is over." Suddenly my body felt tired, my arms going slack. Kane's hungry eyes turned to concern, pulling me closer. "What's wrong?" he mumbled. "We need to get back."

"I think my adrenaline is wearing off. You're here. That's all that matters. You didn't leave me. I saw the Grims. They were going to take you."

"But you saved me, baby. You did." He brushed my dirty, matted hair away from my face. "You saved me. I am forever in your debt. I can be your sex slave if you wish." I chuckled softly, my eyes shutting slowly.

"Sleep, love. I'm taking care of you now." His arms engulfed me, and the warmth he radiated had my eyes shut until I finally received the most perfect sleep in ages.

Chapter Fifty

Kane

I groaned, feeling the radiating heat from my chest. My skin cracked, breaking away the dirt and grime that tried to engulf my body. Clara lay on top of me, her lengthy hair spread over my bare chest. Her legs wrapped around my torso, and her slow breathing was steady.

Osirus's cloak had covered Clara's bare body that was attached to mine. "Holy shit!" Wesley, Charlotte, and Osirus came over, kneeling at each of my sides. Their soiled hands tried to lift Clara away from me. I growled. "Mine!" I pushed them away, sitting up straight and holding my mate to my chest.

"Oh, he's fine then." Osirus smirked, standing from his kneeling position. His eyes softened, and he put his hands on his hips. "You both gave us a scare. Clara stopped breathing. I was afraid she took her power too far to save you." I frowned, knowing Clara had done something so foolish to save my life, but I couldn't help but feel proud that she did.

To be in the afterlife—without my mate for at least eighteen years—would have been terrible. The separation of souls, even if the living mate was alive to take care of a child, would be brutal. Clara was mine, and I was hers. There was no way she would let me go. I would crawl through the bowels of the Underworld to hunt for her soul, to take her back from the grasps of the Reapers.

"You all right, man?" Wesley was still kneeling, daring not to touch me. My fangs had lengthened, my body shaking as I held my limp mate in my arms.

"Fine," I snapped, coming to a standing position. Nodding to Osirus for covering my mate, I wrapped her tightly into a cocoon and rested her head on my chest. "She will be weak," I muttered. Charlotte approached, her hand grazing my mate's cheek with the back of her knuckles.

Charlotte had been a good friend to Clara. She reminded me a lot of my mate. Both were wolfless before this all started, and now they both better understood saving those lesser than themselves. Charlotte gave a small smile, her hand dropping as Wesley pulled her away.

Wesley and I discussed making him King of the Shifters in the Earth realm, but his modesty was well too attuned for that. He said he didn't need a title. He and his family would serve the crown that ultimately ruled them all. There would be no 'King of Earth', just the ultimate loyalty of his family in the Black Claws pack and making sure the rules of Bergarian were upheld.

'Earth's Head of Security,' Wesley called it. He would continue to form alliances with all the packs and ensure there would be an eye and ear around each pack to abide by the rules. An enormous task he and Charlotte were ready to take on along with the technology craving she had.

"Your scars haven't healed well," Charlotte pointed out. Clara's head rested right above where I was stabbed in the chest. It was once a large gaping hole, now healed with raised scar tissue that would ultimately be covered by some tattoo. I didn't mind the new skin. It was easy to cover with ink.

"Where is the The Reckoning?" I grunted. They all looked around where my body lay, but no sword could be seen.

"Clara was talking into the nothing before she ultimately healed you. I feel the gods played a role in disposing of those weapons," Osirus muttered. "It's for the best. Having god-like weapons in this realm isn't safe." Shuffling Clara in my arms, I began to walk away to head down the mountain. I was through talking, ready to get my mate to a medical tent, when Osirus cleared his throat.

"Um, Alpha Kane?" He snickered. Turning, he looked down at my dick, and I scowled. "When did you do that?" Now Wesley was staring and had his large hand covering Charlotte's eyes.

"It's a piercing." I smirked at him. His eyes grew wide at my show of fangs. "For her pleasure. Only a real man can take that kinda hit." Turning my back to him, I shifted into my half-beast form, scaling down the mountain faster before anyone could make a comment.

The large canyon that once sprouted out the fires of the Underworld had mostly closed. Only three meters of the soil remained apart, and new bridges would have to be constructed for carriages. It would be a constant reminder of the war that took place here.

The world was brighter than it once was. The light sources that curved to the west were bringing nightfall. Shifters were finishing off their killings of the leftover rogues. The black magic ruined them because their heightened smell, fast speed, and quick healing had now faded. I smiled, watching Marcus ripping one bastard to pieces. His eyes concentrated on the warlock who begged for his life.

His own wolf was rabid with determination, but something was missing. The war has done something to him, something I'm not sure he would ever speak of. Marcus had his secrets and his way of dealing with loneliness, similar to what I did for a few years. He just continued, trying to fill the void inside him.

Osirus's medical tents were closer. I wanted my mate to be resting before I had to attend to our kingdom's mess. Opening the flap to the royal tent, I saw Melina sitting in bed, unable to move her legs. "When will I be able to use them again?" she countered the physician. The fae doctor shook his head, running his hand over a vile of medicine.

"I'm not sure. We've never countered black magic like this, Your Majesty. It could be days, weeks, months, or—" Osirus stepped into the tent, his wings flapping uncontrollably.

"She will walk again," he said sternly. "You will, Melina. It will take time." His voice softened, and he cupped her cheek. "What is the update on her health?"

Osirus's voice faded as I led my mate to the back of the tent, away from prying eyes. Dr. Talbert from our pack had already stepped in, seeing me carrying my mate.

"She used her power?" he questioned, pulling out instruments. I would have thought by now he would have realized he wasn't allowed to touch her. "Yes." I growled. "Where is my sister?"

"She's on her way. I know you won't let me touch my luna—"

"Queen," I interrupted. Dr. Talbert's eyes widened, looking down at my mate. "Yes, we were both crowned and kept it a secret until it was absolutely necessary. You will address her as a queen now." Dr. Talbert got on his knees, bowing his head.

"I'm terribly sorry. I had no idea." Grunting, my sister and her mate came into the tent. Raine had areas of dried blood on her neck, forehead, and cheek. Her tattered shirt was covered in dirt and grime. Dean didn't look any different. His pale torso was covered in scratches, scrapes, and blood.

"I'm here." She let out a sigh. "Oh, Clara." she put her hand over her head. "What happened?" Explaining to my sister what my mate had done for me, saving my life, and risking her own, she chuckled, grabbing the wet cloth to clean Clara's face. "Of course she did," Raine cooed, kissing Clara's cheek. "I wouldn't expect anything less of a queen."

My chin wobbled, feeling the sob almost wrecking through me. My mate had given me much, all I did was take from her, and she selflessly continued to provide. "Go, big bro, I got her. Dean will keep watch, and I'll do whatever Dr. Talbert says so he doesn't touch her." My shoulders sagged, not wanting to leave my mate, but it would be unfair of me to stay while our people needed leading.

It is what Clara would want.

"Marcus, Wesley, and Charlotte are outside," Raine said offhandedly as she peeled away Osirus's cloak. "They are ready for orders if you are willing to let some of your responsibilities go." She side-eyed me.

"Just because you are my sister doesn't mean you get to talk so casually," I mumbled. Raine went back to work as I held onto Clara's foot. Squeezing it a few more times, Raine muttered, "I'll talk however I want," wobbling her head back and forth.

I rolled my eyes, walking out and seeing not just the small group that Raine mentioned but my parents as well. Mother came running up to me, wrapping her arms around my neck. "Oh baby, I thought you were gone. I saw him stab you. I couldn't get up there!" She wept in my arms. My hands went to her back, rubbing them up and down.

"You scared the shit out of us all. The gods blessed you," Dad whispered, consuming me in a hug. "We're lucky to have your mate as the queen." I smiled sadly, keeping them both tight to my body. As we released, a blood-curdling scream echoed through the vicinity.

Turning, we see Odessa stepping out of her private tent, and one lone vampire rouge jumped from the other side. His claws were extended, his body oozing with infected wounds. Fangs lengthening, he moved slower than expected, but Odessa trembled as she fell to the ground.

A large wallow that had been fighting in battle jumped from the tent. The muscular, catlike body and the maw of a wolf sped forth and pushed Odessa out of the way. The vampire, taking his chance to strike, punctured his claws inside the wallow's chest, pulling out its heart. It thumped erratically in his hand but wallows ran off pure adrenaline. The vampire, thinking he won, stepped aside and leered at Odessa, only to be pinned to the ground by an enormous paw. The wallow stretched his jaws over the vampire's neck and twisted as we heard a sickening crack.

Odessa shook, her arms wrapped around her frail body. Creed's massive wings covered her in a shadow until he shifted into his human form. He grabbed her, pulling her away from the vampire as the wallow fell onto the body.

"Fluffy!" she screamed, reaching for him, but Creed pulled her away. She wailed in his arms, her arm still calling for her pet.

"Gods." Charlotte shuddered. "I would have frozen too. I know they aren't all bad, but... when you have bad experiences..."

"Then you group them together." Dean stood by Charlotte. "It's understandable. Vermillion has dealt with the wrong rulers for a long time. It will take time for everyone to trust our species once again." He smiled down at her.

"It will take time to trust everyone," I said. "We are all starting over. New land, new rulers, but one thing is for certain"—I looked at the small crowd that gathered—"we all deserve—"

"A second chance," Jasper completed my sentence as he stood behind me. His hand went out for me to shake. I smiled, putting my hand in his and pulling him into a hug.

Chapter Fifty-one

Clara

"A re you sure there isn't anything else I can do?" My mother pulled the quilted blanket over my legs. She said it had magical healing properties. Her mother was a witch and wove it with the webs of extinct spider species in northern mountain caves. I shook my head at her. She bowed her head slightly, sitting back in her chair in defeat. Evelyn was curled up in my arms, her body resembling that of a young toddler.

I'm sure this quilt wouldn't work on me anyway if it had magical powers. I had been fine after day three of my deep healing sleep Giana kept me in. The only time I woke was when Kane came to check on me after inspecting the shifters and fae that needed extra assistance in healing.

It had been two weeks since the day that Virion had met his demise, and each day was filled with more things to do than the last. Kane had taken care of it all. His near-death experience had changed him, for the good or the bad, I wasn't sure, but he was doing it all. Thoughts of inadequacies had passed, and his mind was clearly open for me to see his guilt from being stabbed.

He didn't purposefully get stabbed. I wasn't sure why he was taking it upon himself to 'make it up' to me, but here he was, curled up in bed around his daughter and me. Kane had run himself into the ground. He has barely slept since he woke up from a sleep I never thought he would wake from.

Kane carried me around the battlefield on day three of Virion's demise. The grass, the trees, and the foliage were already breaking through the dark muck of the previously dark magic. Before I could ask why the land was healing so quickly, Folen, along with Zaos and his mate Annabelle, placed their hands on the ground in unison, bringing a blinding light where all their hands intersected. Slowly, out of the burned trees of the north, more elves jogged to the scorched land, all their hands grazing trees, bushes, and naked branches.

After days of healing the soil below, more greens, purples, and blues covered the land, but it was only sparse. That was when Horus, Osirus's mighty dragon, descended from the sky after days of recovering. His head lowered to Folen, confused yet astonished he was receiving such a gift to touch the white gold dragon placed his hand on Horus' forehead.

Blinding light from Horus' forehead radiated while Folen held his palm to him. Horus' claws raked the soil before him, bringing up the dark ash soil as it evaporated. For hours, they stayed like this, Folen holding his hand to touch the dragon. This proved fruitful because now the land looked like the black magic had not tainted it.

Shifters, the fae kind, vampires, witches, and warlocks stared at the world in awe. It looked even more beautiful, lush, and exotic than before the war. Trees sprouted the plains, covering the thick grasses. Significant bouts of shade brought out strange animals from the forest. Animals that I had yet to learn about scurried up trees and buried burrows into the ground.

If a unicorn popped out, it would be freaking cool.

As Folen let go, his face brightened, looking at the sight. Unfortunately, his voice saddened when he looked to his right, where his brother usually stood. His back turned, not speaking a word, and he strode away with a heavy heart. No one dared to follow when he looked back to see us all staring. He nodded his head, taking his walking stick and disappearing into the thickness of the forest.

The elven territories took a hit, about half of their colonies were gone, but they would rebuild. They were once a prosperous nation thousands of years ago, holding a piece of the land as their own. Once the shifter wars were completed, they were only left with a quarter of their people. Their numbers were hurt again, but being absorbed into the Cerulean Moon Kingdom, they would receive significant aid. The three witches who had lost their sisters were already en route to complete undoing spells, restoring at least the homes they had once constructed. It was to honor their sister Glinda.

The bodies of the rogues were burned in a pile of fire. Cyrene had woken two days after falling into a deep sleep. Ondi had tended to her, and she healed faster than expected. Hecate must have had a hand in her healing, knowing Cyrene's jobs were far from over. With Cyrene's help, she created a flame that engulfed all the bodies in seconds. The fire was so hot that it reminded me of the fire that leaked from the canyon. It left no teeth or bones. Their bodies and the memories of their past would now be long forgotten.

Odessa, who had helped Cyrene with her boost of power of the dragon, was swept away by Creed to the sky. His possessiveness pushed tenfold when they both woke up on the third day of repairing the land, finding that Odessa was pregnant with his fledgling. The roars from his fellow dragons echoed through the once ashen plains and swirled with excitement, but that brought Creed to a new fury when he realized all the attention was on Odessa.

Dragons swarmed the tent. Creed's feral growl went off in warning and shifted on the spot, covering his mate. The sweetest thing was watching the scary dragon wrap his tail possessively around Odessa. She rubbed her face into his scaled chest as she rubbed her belly.

I didn't feel jealousy but joy as I watched them. The dragons' problem of not having enough female dragons seemed to be looking up. Especially how Osirus whispered to us that Hecate said their purpose was to help repopulate with a new dragon hybrid. I giggled, thinking how poor Odessa would be a mother of young children for a long time.

Osirus had Melina carried in the same position as me. She had yet been able to use her legs after three days, and the anxiety on her face had her clutch Osirus's tunic. He pressed his lips against her forehead, telling her they were going home. All of us were going home after a week of helping the land return anew. If this was Earth, it would have taken decades to accomplish the regrowth that Bergarian had just experienced.

The aftermath of the war was a pile of ashes from rogues that were being picked up by the wind and carried away, the three-meter crack in the soil, and the new monument that was slowly being erected that would still take weeks to create.

The bodies of those we had lost were brought to the start of the divide in the land nearest to the south. Each body was carefully wrapped in silken threads and adorned with the finest jewels from both kingdoms. Mates were bound together, always to have their skin touching, even in the afterlife. Even in death, they would feel the hot fire-like touches as they reached for the stars of the goddess.

The eulogy was short, but the most meaningful. Osirus and I gave our words of thanks and gratefulness for how they risked their lives not just for the kingdoms they hailed, but for the future of the entire land. All of our hearts warmed once our speeches concluded. I had briefly spoken to Jasper beforehand, asking if he wanted to speak on behalf of Vermillion. Still, the elders of the kingdom had already told him he was not worthy to speak.

My fists tightened, and my brow furrowed as Kane held me against his chest. Jasper shook his head, giving his usual play-boy smile. "It doesn't matter. Taliyah is who is in charge. I do not wish to start a fight." Jasper was a new wolf since he had mated to Taliyah, finally thinking of others than himself. I was happy that I could be a part of that. I was upset that his past, along with Taliyah's mixed genes of witch and vampire, may ruin their ability to rule.

Wesley and Charlotte bid farewell as soon as we arrived back at the Warrior pack. Wesley wanted to get back to his pack, which I'm sure was a mess from the hordes of people from our realm that took it over. They had to rent an entire commercial plane to get them all back at the same time.

Charlotte was more than ready to leave too, as much as I wanted her to stay. Getting to know her more, we found we had a lot in common. Being around vampires had taught her that many could be good, but she was ready for normalcy. Well, as much normal as she could for being just four months of being just turned into a wolf.

I petted Evelyn's hair. Kane was curled up against her, one hand around my waist and another protectively over our daughter. Those two were going to be trouble in the upcoming months. She immediately screamed "Daddy!" when she saw us, and almost didn't give me a second glance. Of course, Kane pulled us both into a hug when we were only a few feet away from the newly erected portal Cyrene had created.

Mom had my baby brother during their stay at the Black Claws pack. Baby Mikel was the cutest little thing. Bright green eyes, full head of hair, and sweet little pink cheeks. He was growing quite quickly with two strong alpha lines, and his chunky little arms and legs made me want to pinch the round rings around his arms.

"Are you sure you are comfortable?" Mother gave a side eye to Kane, who continued to sleep soundly. He hadn't stirred in well over an hour, and I wasn't about to wake him.

I hummed quietly, still running my fingers through his hair. The light scar over his eyebrow reminded me how close I was to losing him.

I was getting restless, laying in bed all day, not allowed to walk or even go to the bathroom by myself, but it gave Kane the dominance of being in control. He wanted it, so I allowed it. Everly enjoyed it too. She got carried around like the little princess she is and was overly spoiled by her daddy.

"Mother, you should go spend time with Mikel. He's still young. Go enjoy the baby time." I bit my cheek in response to my words. I felt like I missed so much with Evelyn. I didn't want my mom to miss her time either. This would be the first child she would raise to adulthood along with Father.

"I have to attend to my firstborn first." Mother pushed a lock of hair away. "I can't believe you almost died, Clara. I felt my heart ripping in my chest, the tears so strong I thought you were gone." She let a stray tear fall. Not something that I could see my mother doing in front of anyone else except her mate and me. "I got you back just to lose you again."

"Mother, I'm fine now." I took her hand away and placed it on my lap. "And things between us will be fine too." Mom's sheepish look had her covering her mouth.

"I honestly didn't think I would hand it off to you this fast, Clara. I thought I would at least be around before I left you to this life. We just got you back, but..." She heaved in a staggered breath.

"You got pregnant," I stated. "It isn't your fault. Bad timing on your body, but look what you have now." My father stood in the doorway, holding Mikel's grabby hand. "And now Evelyn will have a great friend to play with growing up."

The age gaps between the kids was weird by human standards, but this was normal here. Raine and Kane were well over a hundred years apart.

Ew, still gross.

Mikel reached for mother, she pulled her to his chest, and his hand reached out for me to hold. "Hi, baby brother," I cooed, rubbing his chubby hand. "Are you going to give Mama trouble?" He blew a raspberry and shook my hand.

"Good luck then." I smiled at my father, who pulled up a chair beside the bed.

"Taliyah and Jasper have some news," Dad said solemnly. Mother and Father had taken duties that Kane and I would typically have as the new royals to give us a well-deserved break. Thank the goddess, because I didn't want to be in charge again for a while.

I leaned forward to listen to my dad's whispering words, but Kane wrapped his arm around my waist tighter. "That can't be comfortable," Mother mumbled, speaking for Father. I giggled, rubbing the thick forearm around my waist.

I liked the possessiveness. I liked how he kept me safe. Unfortunately, Kane was too worried about my health to give me other things I needed. Even taking off my top while Evelyn slept soundly in the nursery didn't deter him. I felt slightly rejected when he only looked me straight in the eye instead of my breasts. I even tried to use my vision to see if there was an outline of cock in his loose gray sweatpants but to no avail.

"Jasper and Taliyah have decided to resign the throne." I gasped, covering my mouth with my hand.

"They... they can't do that!" Father shook his head, his arms crossed over his chest.

"It's actually a smart decision." He nodded. "They do not trust the elders or Parliament. They may have some control over the people, but if they want money from the leftover nobles to help rebuild, it would be wise for the country as a whole."

"Then what happens? Who takes the throne?" I implored. Father rubbed his chin, something he liked to do when he was in deep thought. The scratching of his fingertips against his beard gave me solace. Something about him being my father and the tiny white hairs that protruded from them helped me realize he was an old wolf with much experience as a king. Not many wolves had white hair, but he certainly did.

"Their child will. If"—he held up his finger—"it's a vampire." I scoffed, folding my arms.

"That's so racist, though. So old-fashioned. Times have changed. The war has changed everything. People have to learn to trust again and still hanging onto old ways—"

"My sweet daughter." He put his hand on my thigh. "You must understand. What they are doing will help the kingdom grow. It will bring it back to its rightful place. Maybe their child will be a vampire, and all will be fine, but until then, they will find an interim king and queen to take over. Once their child is old enough, then the interim king and queen will be their advisers."

"Guess we don't have much of a say of another kingdom, do we?" Father shook his head.

"We do not. Taliyah and Jasper have asked for a favor from you and Kane, however." Father's eyes twinkled. "They want you to find them two vampires that you find worthy enough to stand in their stead. Taliyah will give orders to this newly mated couple from afar. Parliament will remain clueless that the orders are coming from Taliyah."

I tapped my lips with my finger. Raine and Dean couldn't do it because Raine was part wolf, and I wasn't friends with many vampires other than Dean.

Unless...

Chapter Fifty-two

Clara

"They're green." Kane bent over, holding Evelyn in his arms, whispering in my ear.

The Cerulean Moon Kingdom palace wasn't completely destroyed, but a lot of it was reduced to rubble. Our time in the Crimson Shadows pack had been extended while revisions were completed. This meant the pack house had been converted into a small palace itself.

I refused to force the unmated wolves out, there were plenty of rooms, and we weren't going to uproot them to stay with another family. Mother, Father, and little Mikel stayed in the extensive guest cabin, trying to keep their lives quiet for once since we had officially taken over.

We were planning a small coronation party this evening. I was not planning on having anything of the sort, but my poor mother was in the corner in today's briefing meeting, prancing around like a child trying to keep quiet. If it meant that much to her, then I would be sure to let her have her fun.

The traditional fairy lights I loved were already strewn across the courtyard. Hundreds of white chairs littered the now green lawn, the beautiful vines sprouting with exotic flowers of whites, yellows, and golds. The pixies got in on the fun and began throwing sparkle dust around the tables on the north side of the pack house.

You couldn't even tell this place was almost reduced to nothing but black ash once the ward was taken down by Taliyah. In fact, it looked better.

"Kane, you can't just point out someone's skin color," I chastised, patting his arm. "It's a lovely shade." I smiled at the three orcs, Sugha, Thorn, and Valpar. They had arrived an hour ago, just after spending all day traveling. They were the official representatives of the orcs, finally getting permission to bring down the walls of the Forbidden Forest. It was built far before my parents' time, and who was to say we should continue to punish what their ancestors did or didn't do?

"It's an honor to meet you." Thorn bowed so low that he almost reached the top of my head. "We've brought you the treaty, Queen Clara, here!" Sugha, who seemed to be the trio's youngest, was excited to put it in my hand. We had set ourselves outside around a large circular table big enough to hold the three orcs. Kane was close to the same height in his half-beast form, but these orcs had a different kind of power.

Their bodies could absorb magic, and their physical strength was vast. It was the running ability they were lacking. Each species has a downfall in some way or another.

"And with this treaty, it is said you would help us with the ogres that wish to do anyone harm. Are you all still willing to participate in that?" They all three nodded. Their tusks that jutted from the bottom of their jaws had their lips brushed over them.

"Of course, and then the Moon Fairy will give us our mates!" Thorn banged his fist on the wooden table. The cups overturned, and they all slapped each other on the back. Evelyn glared at them, growled, and began to bang her fist on the table as Kane held her on their lap.

Oh, she's going to be tough.

"Yes, little princess!" Thorn hammered his fist on the table again. "I also have a gift." My eyebrow raised, watching a small club being pulled from his pocket. It was twelve inches long with small spikes at the end of it. Evelyn squealed. "Mine!" She growled, pulling it in her hands.

"Take that away from her." I nudged Kane, but he shook his head.

"She's my pup. She's going to be a warrior with some tough skin." Kane grinned proudly, giving her rocks for her to hit. I shook my head, laughing as she continued to bang the table.

"Thank you, that was an interesting gift."

I am so going to throw that out later.

"I just want you to know," I said softly. The severe tone of my voice caused the orcs to stop their playful banter and turn serious. "Just because we bring down the walls doesn't mean you automatically get a mate." They looked at each other and back to me.

"We thought as much." Thorn grunted. "But how long? How long do we wait?"

I bit my lip, knowing they wouldn't like the answer. It wasn't a matter of a specific age. Of course, you had to be over eighteen, but when you came across your mate, you were never sure. Kane waited well over a hundred years for me. Raine and... Leia... were in their early twenties.

"When the Moon *Goddess* deems it to be so," I muttered, rubbing Kane's forearm. "But it is best to never lose hope and always be prepared." I smiled, feeling awful for having to burst their bubble. Suddenly screams from Raine trickled to our table. Sugha shot up from his seat, his heart pounding.

Raine panted, and it had Evelyn scream in laughter as her aunt playfully fell to the ground.

"No, she is not my mate." Sugha shook his head. "She smells of a wet animal."

"Gee, thanks!" Raine said, finally rising. "I came to tell you that Sebastian and his mate are here!" I screamed, jumping from the table when I saw the heat of my mother's gaze fall on me.

Right, got to conclude the meeting.

"Raine, have them meet us in the foyer." Turning, I signed my signature on the new treaty to break down the walls of the Forbidden Forest I was sure many would want to explore it once the time came. Pushing the parchment to Kane, he also signed his name and put our seal on top. Beside it, Osirus and Melina's names were shown brightly in gold ink.

"I'll put this in the archives, and we will send the dragons to push it down. Your people are welcome to all kingdoms."

⁂

I grabbed Evelyn and put her on my hip. Kane had his arm around us as I tried to speed walk to the pack house, which really was Kane's normal walking pace. I squealed again, holding Evelyn. She copied me, burying her little claws in my hair.

"Don't see why you are so excited to see him." Kane grunted. "He was nothing but trouble trying to get you to take him as a mate." I stopped my footsteps and pulled on his hand.

"Please don't say anything. I'm not sure if he has told his mate yet." Kane's eyes softened, pecking my lips.

"I would never disobey my queen."

I had heard incredible news months ago that Sebastian ended up landing in the Back Raven Coven on Earth. Rowan, the elder over the coven, contacted us before the war even started letting me know that Sebastian had found his mate and was currently trying to convince her mates were real.

I wanted to be there, help him out. He was so desperate to find someone, and he found her far more quickly than I ever anticipated. Elder Rowan said that my Jeep died a valiant death, leading Sebastian to his final destination.

Opening the pack doors, Sebastian and his mate stood with their backs to me, taking in the overly decorated foyer for the coronation tonight. Flowers hung from the cabin-like rafters, and strings of lights decorated the walls.

"Sebastian!" I yelled. He turned around in surprise, with his arm wrapped around his mate. She had beautiful blonde hair, and gorgeous red eyes with hints of violet-blue. She waved shyly before gripping onto Sebastian, who kissed her forehead gently.

They were the sweetest, and I was so happy Sebastian found her so quickly. Taliyah and Jasper also joined us, bringing them into the downstairs conference room to discuss how to hand over the kingdom. Sebastian and his mate would be crowned as soon as the new palace was built. With the combined powers of the witches and warlocks, along with the help of both kingdoms, it would take only a few months, right before Taliyah was to give birth to the new heir.

"We really thank you," Taliyah spoke softly. She had tried so hard to be the ruler that the people wanted. She sacrificed a lot of time with Jasper while he begged for redemption. Parliament, which now consisted of new members who fought in the war against the rogues, was completely filled. Their demands for only a vampire to rule made her concede. Was it something she really wanted anyway? Or just fill the empty line of the father she never knew?

"Where will we go?" Taliyah muttered to Jasper. Along with conceding the throne until a full-blooded heir came to power, they also lost any money to take with them.

"Start from scratch." Jasper put his arms around her. "I can be an omega in one of the outlining packs or become a warrior trainer for the pups. We have many places to go in the Cerulean Moon Kingdom," he kissed her cheek.

"That's right." Kane crossed his chest. "In fact, you should just stay here, in the Warrior pack. Marcus will be taking over once the palace is renovated. I'm sure he can find you a spot to stay." Jasper smiled, appreciative of the offer.

"As much as I want that," Jasper replied. "I think Taliyah and I would like the quiet life. Maybe take a cabin north of the Crimson Shadows pack territory. I don't need a rank. Just my girl and my pup." Taliyah laughed, rubbing her still small belly.

"You can still be a warrior, Jasper. You are good at it, and you should use your skill to protect others." Jasper continued to stare into Taliyah's eyes, shaking his head. "You are my only concern, little witch, and our baby."

"We'll think about it." Taliyah winked at me. "I'm sure Jasper can't handle being idle too long."

⁂

Kane and I had returned to our room to prepare for the upcoming 'for show' coronation. I had just finished my hair. My gown was a deep blue with tiny white pearls strung about the bodice. The intricate designs of silver and gold outlined the see-through sleeves that would cap at my shoulders.

It continued to stay there on the bust brought in to mimic my form. I was too small for the regular fitting, so now special seamstresses had to make dresses for me. I blew out through my nose harshly, not understanding the big deal of being small. I mean, I wasn't that much smaller.

I crossed my arms, staring at it. My hair was done in loose curls, and the beautiful flower crown was created by the little pups of the pack for me to wear as I walked down the aisle. Of course, it would be replaced with the Cerulean Moon Kingdom crown once it was all said and done.

Kane strolled out of the shower. His typically naked body was covered with a towel around his waist. The droplets of water dripped down his newly tattooed torso, and the scar over his eyebrow gave him an even more dangerous look.

And he was mine.

Kane stopped in his tracks once he reached the bed. His back expanded, taking large breaths. "Mate." He growled, pulling the towel tighter on his waist. "You are torturing me."

Okay, got a little turned on.

I growled at him, stomping over. I pointed my finger in his face and said, "*You* have been torturing me!" Putting my hands on my hips, I stomped my foot like a child. "You haven't touched me intimately in so long. Do you not find me attractive?" My voice cracked at the end, and his playful smirk dropped.

"Baby, no." He picked me up and sat him on his lap, which was still covered. "We've both been through a lot. I almost lost you and Evelyn, our family and friends. I just wanted you to know I love you more than just sex." My lip pouted out, and I crossed my arms.

"But you do your best by expressing yourself." I poked his chest, rubbing over his new scar. "I like it when you do that." Kane's hand reached up and grabbed mine, stroking it with his thumb.

"You mean that, baby? I feel you do so much for me, and here I am, taking advantage of you any chance I get. Torin has had raging blue balls for weeks." I laughed, pulling his face into a kiss. "I wanted to make sure you were better."

Shaking my head, I pulled off the oversized shirt that I was wearing. His eyes widened, gulping while his hands shook. His cock twitched under the towel, and my butt rubbed it harder into his crotch. It was like our first time all over again.

"I want you to take advantage of me. I like it," I whispered. "So, Alpha, can you show me how much you love me?"

Finally going to get a release.

Kane's eyes darkened into two large pools of desire. He had me on my back faster than you could say biscuits and gravy, and palmed my breasts. "Gods, I missed these." He sucked my nipple harshly. My fingers grabbed his hair, pushing him impossibly closer.

Moaning, he grabbed the other, pinching it until I screamed for more. While he sucked, his finger dipped lower, trailing my hip bone and sliding to my inner thigh. Hot trails of fire-like touches went down to my core, feeling my heart aflutter between my legs.

Kane's giant finger parted my lips, sinking inside my impossibly wet pussy. His nostrils flared, his eyes boring into mine. "Fuck, Clara, you are so damn wet." He growled into my neck. Sucking hard, he nibbled my neck, surly leaving his mark.

"I need to fuck you." He growled. "I want to make you so sore you can't walk straight." He bit my ear. "I'll have to carry you down the aisle." My legs tightened, trying to get the friction on my clit that I so desperately needed.

He huffed in annoyance, grabbing my other breast with good measure before landing a harsh smack on the other. "Don't hide that pretty pussy." I moaned, pulling my own hair with the satisfaction of a bit of pain.

Kane pushed my legs wide open, then pushed them up until my knees touched either side of my body. My pussy was so open that I could feel the gentle breeze of the fan and the heat of his breath near my thighs. "I'm going to put a baby in you." He grunted, lining up his cock. My eyes hazed, and my hand landed right on one hand that still had my right leg pinned to my body.

"And then you will not leave my sight. You will not lift one finger until our pup is in our arms for me to protect, is that clear?" I nodded frantically, trying to not think of the last pup I didn't protect, didn't even know.

"Baby." Kane leaned forward, his hot torso landing on my clit. "We didn't know. It was so early," he cooed. "I'm here now, and I'm going to give you as many pups as you want if you want them." Kane pleaded with his eyes. I laughed, covering my face until he planted kisses on my cheeks.

"Okay," I whispered. Clearing his throat, he sat back up into position. "Back to the business of breeding you." He growled playfully. He placed his cock near my pussy, his cock gleaming with precum, but it looked more than usual. "Kane?" I examined, worried something was wrong, but he palmed his cock as he stroked it. I watched as his hand engulfed the precum, but a small silver ball lay on the head.

"What is tha—"

"Shh." He grunted, slowly lining it up and pushing his cock into me. "It's for your pleasure." He winced as my pussy ate him whole. "That's my good luna, taking my cock, fuck." He was fully engulfed in me, his torso lying against mine, his arms around my back, and his hands on my shoulders, giving him perfect leverage.

He pulled out slightly, only to push in again. "Ohhhh." I squeezed my thighs and locked my feet behind his back. "It feels good." My voice trembled.

"Mmm," he agreed, picking up the pace. "Going to fuck you until your pussy begs for me always. Fill that pretty little hole with my cum." The ball that sat on his cock hit my g-spot. It had me rolling my hips, meeting Kane's thrusts.

After not having sex in so long, my body cried to let go until it finally did. Stars exploded behind my eyes, my back arching giving Kane more room to dig deeper into my womb. Roaring loud enough to shake the pack house, he came until I swore I felt it in my throat. His poundings didn't stop. The slapping of skin and the heavy smell of arousal and sex filled our bedroom.

"Kane!" I screamed, feeling another orgasm building. He continued to thrust, our bodies still making more and more liquid to sustain us. He changed our position, having me lay on my side, one leg over his shoulder. Kane was scissor fucking me, and it hit on a whole new level.

"This pussy is mine." Kane's eyes flashed to Torin. "Going to make it remember me, always fit like a glove." My back arched again, and Kane's hand came down harshly on my butt.

"Ahh!" I groaned at the sting. He palmed it while pushing more of his cum inside me. We both fell to pieces, his large arms engulfing me as he played the big spoon. Both of us were wet with desire, sweat, and the love we had for each other.

"What did you do?" I panted. "To make it like... that?" I couldn't form words, my sentences running together, still coming down from heaven.

"I got my dick pierced, remember?" he smiled in my ear. His nose nuzzled into his mark, squeezing me tightly. "I did it for pleasure, but also because..." He fluttered his eyelashes on my warm cheeks. "To feel pain. To feel something physically instead of the terrible mental anguish of losing our pup."

I rubbed Kane's hand, his breath evening out and my face softening. "Alpha," I whispered. "You didn't need to do that." He shook his head, kissing me on the cheek.

"It was worth it." He winked. "I think I've run out of body parts to pierce, though."

Chapter Fifty-three

Kane

Clara intertwined my fingers with hers. Her warm hands calmed my anxiousness. We stood at the beginning of the aisle overlooking the droves of people in front of us. They smiled at my sweet mate, who waved slightly to the small pups who sat near her. White sheets covered the walkway. The wind gently blew royal blue and deep red petals through the sheets and grasses.

Pixies dropped silver glitter as they strode up the aisle waiting for Clara and me to walk to them. Harps played low exotic music, and soft sounds of wooden flutes and stringed instruments followed the beat of the wind as the wisps gathered around.

Sorceress Cyrene, who had remained for the momentous occasion of tradition, beamed and waved her hand for us to follow. Making sure to take small strides, my arm gripped Clara's tighter. Once filled with rage to protect our land, her precious, soft eyes had me thaw in her embrace. My mate had turned a stone-cold beast into a puppy in her presence. Evelyn was being held by Clara's mother, a matching gown, to be exact. Evelyn continued pulling at the ruffled sleeves and the ornate pearls wrapped around her neck.

Osirus and Melina were unable to attend due to Melina's sickness. Still, many of our friends from afar were able to join. Sean, Carson, and Rex, our best trackers and mischievous three, came from the Golden Light Kingdom, along with their new mates to brag to their friends and family. It was even more exciting to show that Sean was mated to a siren, and his parents couldn't be more thrilled as much as Sean worried for their approval.

Alaneo and his new vampire mate arrived as well. Juliet had been one of many tortured when Sorceress Prinna had control of her Blood Coven. She was meek compared to Alaneo's sense of humor, but the more he rubbed his mate's belly let me know things were getting serious fast for the two.

Whisps continued to follow us until we reached the altar, where Cyrene stood with a small book of spells in her hand. The entire gathering would now witness what we had done just two months ago, away from prying eyes to protect not only us, but the pack.

Both previous King Eden and Queen Elijah bowed to us, taking Evelyn along with them, who pouted. Her arms crossed, much like a toddler would do, and she sat quietly with her grandmother.

Cyrene resumed speaking in tongues, her lips traveling from ancient Greek and Latin until we pretended to drink blood from the cup. It would have been a slap to the gods if we took her parents' blood again.

Cyrene concluded with a prayer to Zeus, but my eyes could not close because they were fixated on my mate. My mate had been through much, and she continued to amaze me with her ability to love, to show compassion and mercy.

Once the prayer was concluded, her eyes met mine, and she smiled, pecking me on the lips. My hungry body pulled her close, wrapping my large hand around her tiny waist. Her arms laid on my biceps as I kissed her fervently. The crowd began to clap, the warriors howling in the background.

Former Queen Eden was none too happy, giving me the death glare behind Clara's shoulder. I winked at her and grabbed my mate's ass while she squealed.

She's mine.

Cyrene led us to two thrones, made of two large oak trees with hollows on the inside big enough for us both to sit. Small carvings of wolves shaped into the armrests. It was simple, made quickly, but its ruggedness only reminded me we were building this kingdom from the ground up.

We held each other's hand while Cyrene replaced the beautiful flowered crown on my mate's head with that of a light metal. The crown had intricate designs of leaves, wolves, and a blue crescent moon in the middle.

My crown, being slightly smaller since I was, in fact, not of royal blood, hung like a plain band over my head. Small engravings of wolves, panthers, bears, and shifters of the like run across the steel-like metal.

Clara grabbed my hand and squeezed it. Her gaze landed upon the crowd of elves, wolves, fae, and pixies in attendance. The wisps that continued to bless my mate with beautiful curls and braids twirled above our heads until they came out into a small explosion out of the tornado-like wind.

The light sources, now officially set, brought forth exceedingly bright light from the flame torches that lit the area. "I now present to you, the King and Queen of the Cerulean Moon Kingdom." The crowd stood, admiring my mate, and I couldn't help but do the same. She was full of grace and beauty and was all mine to the very end of time.

We rose from our seats, my arm wrapping around her waist, in awe of her, not just her beauty but selflessness. "Now you are officially my queen," I muttered in her ear. The crowd continued their cries, raining white and gold petals into the air that continued to rain down like snow.

"Does that mean you will take advantage of your queen?" she quipped, still waving into the crowd. I smirked, putting my hand on her ass in front of everyone.

"Absolutely." I growled, nipping her ear.

"Come on!" Clara pulled me, her blue dress dragging on the grass. The sparkles from the pixies that had rained down on all of us began to brush away at our clothing. I was breathing in so much sparkle I began to cough like a human with asthma.

Clara laughed, pulling my arm again. "Come on, you fuddy-duddy!" She continued to pull me through the crowd of dancing people, saying, "Excuse me," along the way. I grumbled, having to stumble through the crowd, but Clara was adamant about taking me somewhere.

Evelyn had fallen asleep in Alaneo's arms. Juliet stroked Evelyn's forehead as she watched our daughter sleep. She had already eaten twice her fill of meat, cheeses, and cakes to last a few days. Her food coma was the perfect time for my mate and me to slip away.

If only I knew where we were going. Because the people here needed to hurry up and leave.

Clara stepped onto the patio that led straight to the kitchen. Omegas continued to bring out food for the ever-growing number of people that began to show up. It had become a mating frenzy, and all the guest rooms were taken. Many times Marcus had to break up newly found mates from having sex on the dance floor. Eden and Elijah would only stand for so much. The orgasm I gave their daughter underneath her dress during our mating ceremony was their limit.

But it was fucking epic.

Clara giggled, pushing through the kitchen until we reached the downstairs storage closet. She pulled the door open and locked it promptly with a small table. Clara began stripping, pushing down her dress with both hands, but who was I to question? I started stripping too, and her arms were wrapped around me so fast that my cock was standing at attention before she got her fingers in my hair.

"Fuck, Clara, what are we doing?" My mouth reached her neck, sucking on it harshly. My mouth went to the original hickey, and I licked it dry, my breath panting while she stroked my cock. Eden had already made her cover up my hickey right before the ceremony, and that damn well pissed me off.

"Pretty sure it's obvious." Clara rolled her eyes. "With Evelyn getting older, we need to have secret spots." She breathed, moving her thumb over the tip of my cock. "We can hide in closets and have a quicky whenever you want." I growled, liking the idea. "You have to have sex every four hours to keep you sane, remember?" I smiled into her neck.

"Is that so?" I bit down on her mark, causing her to instantly orgasm. My hand went to her mouth, keeping her cries silent. My cock was already probing her deliciously wet pussy. Letting my hand go from her ass, I tightened my hand on her neck. "Arms around me," I ordered.

She wrapped them tightly like the perfect queen she was, my pierced cock sliding in her deliciously wet cunt. "Fuck, baby, you feel so good." My lips grazed her ear, pinning her to the wall. Her hand went around my wrist, squeezing it tightly.

"Do you like it when I squeeze your neck? Letting you know I'm in charge?" She groaned. Her fingers tightened, and her hard tits pushed into my bare skin. Her pussy spasmed, clamping down on my engorged cock.

"You do like it." I pushed in deeper and pulled out again. Thrusting into my mate, I let her feel my rhythm, and she became closer. My cock slid deliciously easy between her folds. As she got close to her orgasm, I pulled out before she fell into oblivion.

"No," she whined until I gave her a sharp slap on the thigh. "Turn around, let me see that pretty little ass, then maybe you can come."

Finding a stool, I set her tiny feet on top of it, having her lean over with her breasts to the wall. "What a beautiful ass you have, My Queen. It would look better with my hand prints all over it." She wiggled her ass, her tantalizing, beautiful, white ass until I smacked it again.

"Fuck yes, beautiful." My cock slid into her pussy, my torso laying on her back and my hand gripping the front of her throat. The delightful moan falling from vocal cords vibrated in my hand.

My thrusts grew frantic, my ball sack tightening, slapping her skin until we both came with a sickening roar. We panted, pulling ourselves up until I pushed her back to the wall.

"Don't clean up." I tickled her throat with my rough fingertips, admiring the pretty marks I left with my mouth. "You can put on your dress, but you leave that cum inside you until it falls down your leg," I ordered. Clara smirked, fluttering her eyelashes.

"Really?" Her eyes widened. "Why do you want me to do that?" she asked innocently.

"So every wolf here knows my scent is not just on your body, but inside," I purred, lifting her back in my arms.

"You are so dirty, Alpha." She kissed my lips. "I like it," she whispered.

Clara was more put together than I was when we emerged from the closet. Her dress was completely on and not a hair out of place. I, on the other hand, had half my tunic untucked and my pants untied.

A foot tapping from Eden greeted us on the other side of the door. "What have you been do—" She paused. "Oh, goddess, Clara." Eden waved her hand to get the smell away.

"You just did it before the ceremony. Could you not wait?"

"Nope!" Clara chirped, holding onto my arm. "We plan on staying in the honeymoon phase for a long time." She looked up at me longingly. I kissed her lips again, only for Eden's face to soften.

"That's good then." She smiled. "Your father and I have plenty of hiding spots in the palace. I'm sure you both will find your own too," she joked.

"Now get back out there and tend to your guests." Clara did a mock salute and dragged me back into the crowd.

❧❀✿❁☙

The blue moon had reached well into the sky, some dispersing into their homes for the night. The few left were the orcs who continued to be taught by unmated wolves and elves how to dance. They all laughed with too much ambrosia in their bellies, and their excitement continued to float into the distance as they went to the local watering hole.

"I hope they don't hurt themselves," Clara murmured as we slow-danced. "Maybe I should go check on them." She dropped her hands to leave, but I pulled her back in my arms. Touching my forehead to hers, I shook my head. "You can't babysit the entire kingdom, love."

She wrapped her arms around me and continued to dance until my mother came to give us Evelyn. Her body was curled like a small pup in her arms. "I'm going to put her to bed," she whispered, but I quietly took her from my mother.

"We've got her, thanks," I mumbled, holding Evelyn with one arm, her head in the crook of my neck, and my mate in the other. I had my tiny little family right where I wanted them, in my sight. My mom smiled, waving us off until we were the last couple dancing.

Clara yawned, laying her head on my chest. "I'm so happy it's over." She sniffed, her hand rubbing the now opened white tunic and rolled sleeves.

"Now things can get quiet around here."

I chuckled, feeling Evelyn stir at the voice of her mother. "For a little while, anyway," I mentioned. "This one is going to keep us on our toes." Evelyn yawned, only to curl back into my neck.

"Hmm, yeah, but I think it will be easier to handle her rather than a whole war," she mumbled.

"All I know is, when she hits puberty, she's yours." I scoffed. Clara playfully slapped my arm, giggling.

"At least we know our story isn't over yet." She nuzzled into me. My arm gripped her tighter as the last harp music played.

"Far from it, baby, because you and our family are forever."

Epilogue

Under the Moon

The desk of the king was littered with reports and papers. Each parchment was more critical than the last. Each 't' crossed and 'i' dotted to perfection. The small quill in his hand barely let his fingers grip it tight enough so he could sign his name due to his massive size.

He sighed, rubbing his hands down his face. The look of dejection was clearly written. This wasn't what he was meant to do: sit behind a desk and continue to sign transfers of warriors to different packs of the kingdom. Each shifter in Bergarian had to send not only a request for a pack transfer to their alpha, but also to their king. Every shifter was to be accounted for, no shifter left behind. His mate wouldn't have it any other way. Each soul was equally important to himself and his queen.

Kane continued, hunched over the desk. He barely heard the sound of slight knocking at the overly ornate door filled with gold leaves and exotic painted flowers.

"Come in." He grunted, not looking up from the parchment in front of him. Kane said he would finish this for his mate, make sure she had nothing to do for at least a week after their newest daughter, Melody's birth.

Clara had two heats before she fell pregnant again. Evelyn was now two and fiercely protective of her younger sister.

The small form inched into the office, wearing a maid's uniform. Her steps were light, carrying a tray of tea and tiny finger sandwiches to the overly large desk that engulfed the back of the room. Kane rubbed his temples with his fingers in annoyance.

The maid wiggled her nose, watching her king until she gently laid the tray down. "Thanks." Kane grunted, writing down more notes on the parchment. The maid pulled a duster behind her back and began to dust the room while Kane continued to ignore the working servant.

He shifted in his seat, trying to concentrate. He hated reading. He hated doing all things stuck in an office. He should be out training the warriors, but he would do his duty and let his mate rest while she heals.

A warm body was felt on his back. The heat caused him to pause his quill and drop it entirely. The feather duster swayed in front of him, dusting the parchments to the side of the desk.

"What are you?—" Kane tried to speak out until the maid dropped the duster. Her hands paused mid-air, and Kane turned to see the maid had bent over in her ridiculously short black and white maid's uniform. She had fishnets on her legs with no crotch and an obscene amount of white ruffles that parted to give a perfect view of a glorious white ass.

Kane shifted in his seat, palming his cock. It was so damn delicious. The stockings she wore with the insanely high black heels had him salivating. Her body began to rise, the perfect view of her ass disappearing between the glorious folds of the ruffled dress.

Kane growled, his hand palming one cheek of the fishnet. The maid stilled like a deer caught by the hunter, waiting to see what he would do next.

"You are tempting me." Kane growled lowly. "Are you trying to rile your king?" The maid whimpered, her body pushed to the desk with a bang. Her low-cut maid uniform had her breasts spilling out of the top. Kane stood behind her, pushing her legs apart and slapping the glorious peach before him.

"Because you shouldn't try and seduce me while I'm working." The maid mewled, pushing her ass back into Kane's cock. "I'm trying to take care of my country, and you dare try your seduction techniques on me?" Pushing his engorged cock into the back of her, she moaned loudly.

"Sorry, Your Majesty. How can I make it up to you?" Kane continued to grip the maid's hips, grinding his cock into her almost bare ass.

"On your knees, face me," he ordered. The maid turned around, gleaming those bright green eyes back at him. Bright red lipstick stained those luscious lips. She bit her lip, kneeing onto the cold stone floor. "Pull it out," he instructed. "Slowly."

Kane watched every movement of her small hands. She pulled out the leather belt from the confines of the metal buckle. It clanked as the leather whipped out of the loops. Her pussy tightened, hearing his pants fall to the ground. "Pull it out." Kane ground his teeth, his hand going into the top of her hair. He gently pulled the hair on her scalp, having her feel the slight sting.

Kane waited to see what his little maid would do. If she would wait to be instructed what to do or take him fully into his mouth. Part of him wanted her to consume him in her mouth so he could discipline her further. Strap her to the desk and make sure she never came. The other part wanted her to be this submissive little maid he had in his grasp.

She waited, staring at the glistening drop of come on his cock. Her big eyes looked up at him, his cock wiping come across her cheek. "Fuck." He breathed, pulling her head closer.

"Now, put it in your mouth." Trembles ran down the maid's spine, her mouth opening, but Kane jerked away. "I want you to look at me while you take me in." He could barely speak. The anticipation alone was going to have him explode.

She lowered her red lips, letting the ball of his piercing clink with her teeth. Her hand reached the base of his cock while the other held his balls.

Kane hissed, but his eyes never left her. They could never leave those dark green meadows of his mate.

Fuck, she had outdone herself. Strutting in that cute little maid uniform. It was all he could do to keep his cock firmly planted in his pants and not rip them off when her intoxicating scent hit outside the door.

"That's it, suck your king's cock." She hummed delightfully, the vibration causing his balls to tighten. "Yes, just like that, baby, just like that." Clara's hand that cupped his balls reached around his ass, using her claws to scratch his muscular body.

"Oh, fuuuuck." Kane's knees bent, having to catch himself on the desk. Clara took the sudden fall like a champ, keeping her mouth firmly planted around his cock. Red smudges of lipstick staining it red.

"Let go. I need to bury myself inside my little slutty maid." Clara giggled, pulling her mouth off him with a pop. Grabbing her waist, he set her up on the desk, spreading her legs. The fish net stretched, leaving beautiful marks on Clara's skin. Kane pulled down the front of her maid's uniform, her breasts bouncing free. He sucked each one leaving excellent red marks along her chest.

Clara entangled her fingers in his hair, lulling her head back to feel the sweet sensation of his teeth grazing her skin. Her legs wrapped around him, wanting to get her pussy closer.

Kane reached down as he bit her nipple, his finger checking how wet his mate was. "Perfect." He growled, finally flipping her over, so her ass was in the air. "Fucking you over this desk with this uniform has been my fantasy." He palmed her ass, feeling the ripple of skin that dared to push free over the wide tights covering her.

Clara giggled, shaking her ass in his face. "I've got more in store for you, My King." Clara's face began to turn red as he stared at her weeping pussy. No matter how often they were intimate with each other, she would always be shy with her overly endowed mate.

He thrust into her, his claws piercing into her skin. Between the tightness of the fish nets on Clara's body, the pure white ruffles, and the feather duster she gripped on the desk, he wasn't sure how long he was going to make it.

"Yes," he hissed, sinking deeper into her pussy. The warmth engulfed him, and he felt the tip of the piercing hitting his mate's cervix. She cried out, now having to grip a hold of the desk.

"C-can I come?" Clara asked. Kane's chest puffed with satisfaction as his mate asked permission. She never had to ask permission for anything, but her giving that part of herself to him made it so hot. "Not yet." He growled, pushing so hard the desk began to scrape across the stone floor.

He concentrated, feeling the pull of his mate's pussy trying to suck him in. The fluttering of her walls and the slick of her come coating his dick slowly dripping to his balls had him gritting his teeth.

Sweat beaded on his brow, and Clara whimpered for release. "Please," she cried out until Kane let out an enormous roar that shook the room. They both fell over, Kane pushing his torso into her back, his cock still spurting his seed.

"Fuck baby, that was incredible," he kissed the shell of her ear. He pulled Clara's chest up from the desk to get a fist full of her breast. He squeezed, humming while he continued to stay inside her.

"I got a bunch of outfits. We can do different scenes." She snickered. "I always wanted to do acting, and I'm so happy we can do this together. I was too nervous to say anything fun, though." She frowned.

Kane had enjoyed the roles Clara loved to play, but having her dress up in the maid uniform, an actual costume, was new. "You can do it any time for practice." He kissed her cheek, gently pulling her off the desk. Her neat French braid was half down, her thick eyeliner smudged, and the red lipstick she wore was all over her face.

"What a beautiful sight." He rubbed the red lipstick from the lower corner of her mouth.

"Marcus just signed the paperwork," Kane said at dinner. The palace had been returned to its former glory a year and a half ago. Still, Kane and Clara felt it was essential to stay connected to the Crimson Shadows pack until Marcus healed from his mental anguish over the war.

Marcus never divulged why he was so upset, but Kane knew he could not leave the pack with anyone else but him. "We can all head out tomorrow so I can hand him the Alpha title." The entire family moved into the palace just a week and a half ago, so Clara could have complete silence while she gave birth to their new daughter.

Melody was cradled against Clara's chest. At only a week old, she had begun to grow, just like her sister. Clara hadn't missed anything with this child. Her time was mostly spent with both her daughters.

"Daddy, tea?" Evelyn held up a fake glass of tea in a toy teacup. Kane leaned over and took the tiny teacup, almost swallowed by his fingertips.

"Mmm, delicious, baby girl." Kane handed it back. Evelyn poured another pretend cup and proceeded to hand it back. This was done ten times until Clara just about had enough.

"Evie, you are going to make daddy have to go pee." Evie gasped and put down the cup. "Go play?" Evie pointed to the toy house they set up in the dining room. The whole castle had some sort of toy in each of the rooms. They were constantly surrounded by guards, diplomats, and representatives of other territories. Evelyn had to learn to play with herself in the same room so Clara could keep a close eye on the troublemaker.

Evelyn's new favorite thing was sneaking away to watch her daddy spar. She would pretend her claws would emerge and fight against evil make-believe characters while Kane trained. Many times, Eveyln tried to get into the ring, but luckily, Clara's mother stepped in.

Marcus trekked into the dining room, sitting across the table from Clara and Kane. Kane nodded, and Marcus did the same before piling on his plate full of food. "How are you, Marcus?" Clara smiled, hoping he would talk at least a little about himself.

Clara only saw Marcus with hordes of girls pining for him. He put on a happy face, but Clara knew better. Just like she knew better what King Osirus was doing just two years ago. "I'm fantastic when in your presence, Clara."

Marcus glanced at the little baby in Clara's arms. He paused, putting his food on his plate, and tilted his head. "What's her name?" he muttered. Marcus had just arrived today to sign the papers and missed the entirety of Melody's birth. Clara's heart raced, Giana scratching her head, and the insane amount of déjà vu rattled her just like Evelyn.

"This is Melody." Clara remained calm. "Would you like to hold her?" Clara stood up to round the table, but Marcus stood up.

"No, no." He cleared his throat, putting his napkin down. "I'm afraid I need to go to the Crimson Shadows pack to help prepare for tomorrow." Kane eyed Clara and Marcus, unsure of what was happening. "I'm not very hungry, and I think my nerves are getting to me."

Kane stood, his arm going around his friend. "Here, I'll walk you out." Kane eyed Clara once more before leading his friend back out the door. Clara kept her face stoic until their backs were far away, and a small smile graced her lips.

Kane walked Marcus to the front gates. The fifteen-minute shifted run back to the Crimson Shadows pack would help clear Marcus's head. Marcus stripped in seconds, not wanting to speak to his best friend.

"Hey." He pulled his arm. "You are going to be a great alpha." He patted his back. Kane could have chosen one of the alphas from Alabaster Shifter Academy, but he didn't. He chose a full-blooded beta with no alpha training. Kane trusted his friend and no one else. Marcus knew how to run the Crimson Shadows pack until it was time for Melody to take the position.

"I hope you're right." He ran his fingers through his hair. "I don't have a luna." Kane shook his head.

"Raine and my parents are still there, remember? Use them until you find your mate. And let me know as soon as possible when you find her." Kane winked. Kane walked away, a skip in his step. He had everything he ever wanted. His mate and his girls. Things were going just incredible for him.

As for Marcus, he turned, staring back at the palace. It gave him a feeling he wasn't sure of. Overwhelming power to help protect what was inside. If he could not save his own mate, he would spend his time protecting the pack he was given to watch over and his best friend's family.

It was the least he could do after his king and queen risked their lives to save all of theirs.

The End

Subscribe to stay up-to-date on new releases! Click Here

Thanks for reading. The stories continue! Please check the next page for upcoming stories.

Books by Vera

Under the Moon Series

Under the Moon

Clara and Kane's Story

The Alpha's Kitten
Charlotte and Wesley's Story

Finding Love with the Fae King
Osirus and Melina's Story

The Exiled Dragon
Creed and Odessa's Story

Under the Moon: The Dark War
Clara, Kane, Jasper and Taliyah's story

His True Beloved: A Vampire's Second Chance
Sebastian and Christine's Story

Alpha of her Dreams
Evelyn and Kit's Story

The Broken Alpha's Princess
Melody and Marcus' Story

Twinning and Sinning From Mutts to Mates
Dax, Dimitri, and Seraphina's Story

Under the Moon: God Series

Seeking Hades' Ember
Hades and Ember's Story

Lucifer's Redemption
Lucifer and Uriel's Story

Poseidon's Island Flower
Poseidon and Lani's Story

Thanatos' Craving
Thanatos and Juniper's Story
Coming soon!

More to Come

Under the Moon: The Promised Mates of Monktona Wood Orcs

Thorn

Thorn and Ellie's Story

Valpar

Coming Soon

Sugha

Coming Soon

Iron Fang MC Series

Grim

Hawke

Bear

More to Come

Visit authorverafoxx.com

for updates and future books!

www.ingramcontent.com/pod-product-compliance
Lightning Source LLC
Chambersburg PA
CBHW070834260626
47170CB00007B/2362